THE LEAK

FOR THE LOVE OF TRUTH

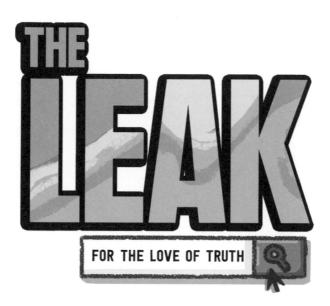

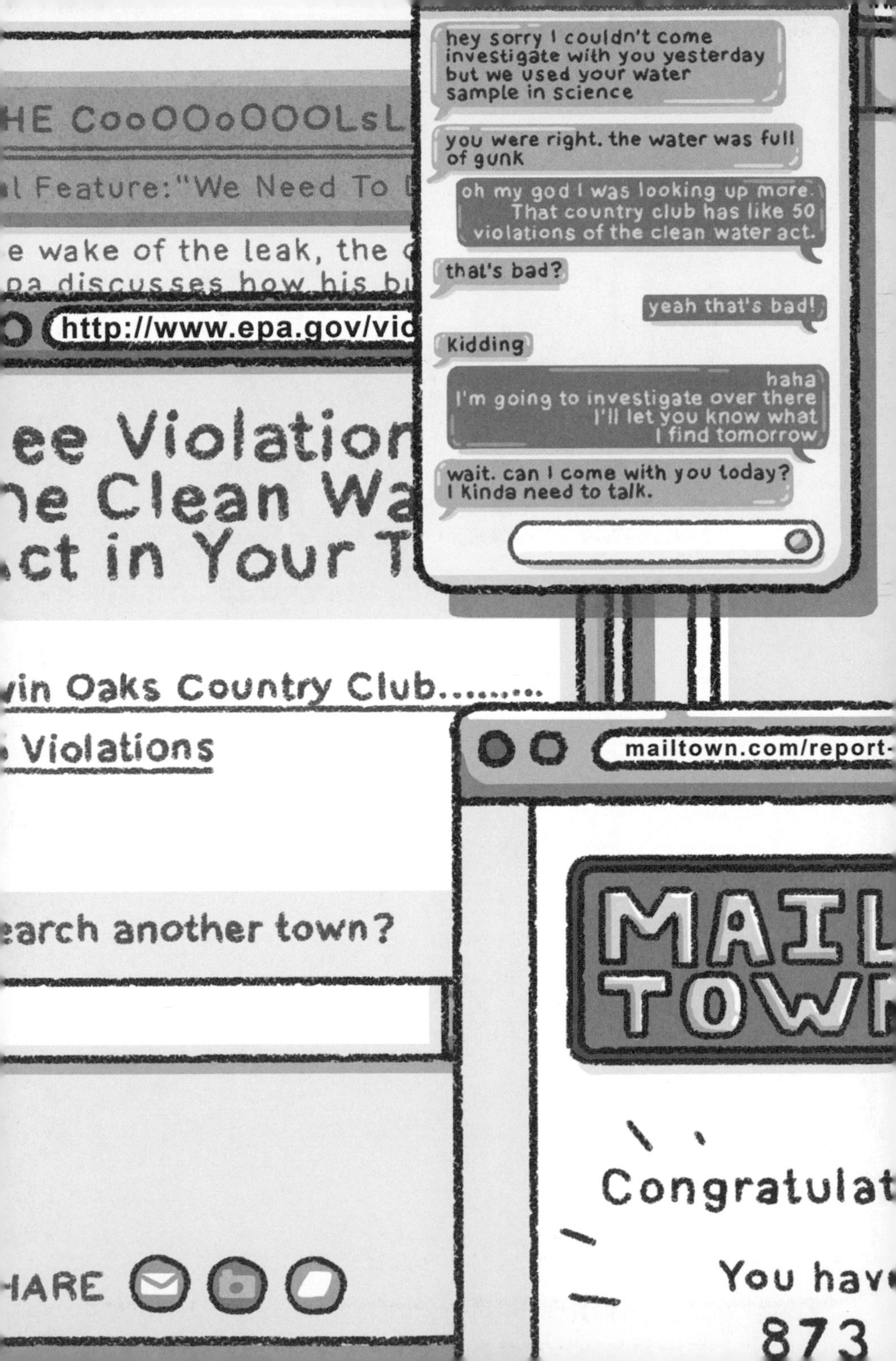

HE CooOOoOOOLsL
l Feature: "We Need To
e wake of the leak, the
http://www.epa.gov/vi
ee Violation
e Clean Wa
ct in Your T
vin Oaks Country Club........
Violations
earch another town?
HARE
hey sorry I couldn't come investigate with you yesterday but we used your water sample in science
you were right. the water was full of gunk
oh my god I was looking up more. That country club has like 50 violations of the clean water act.
that's bad?
yeah that's bad!
kidding
haha I'm going to investigate over there I'll let you know what I find tomorrow
wait. can I come with you today? I kinda need to talk.
mailtown.com/report-
MAIL
TOW
Congratulat
You hav
873

THE LEAK

FOR THE LOVE OF TRUTH

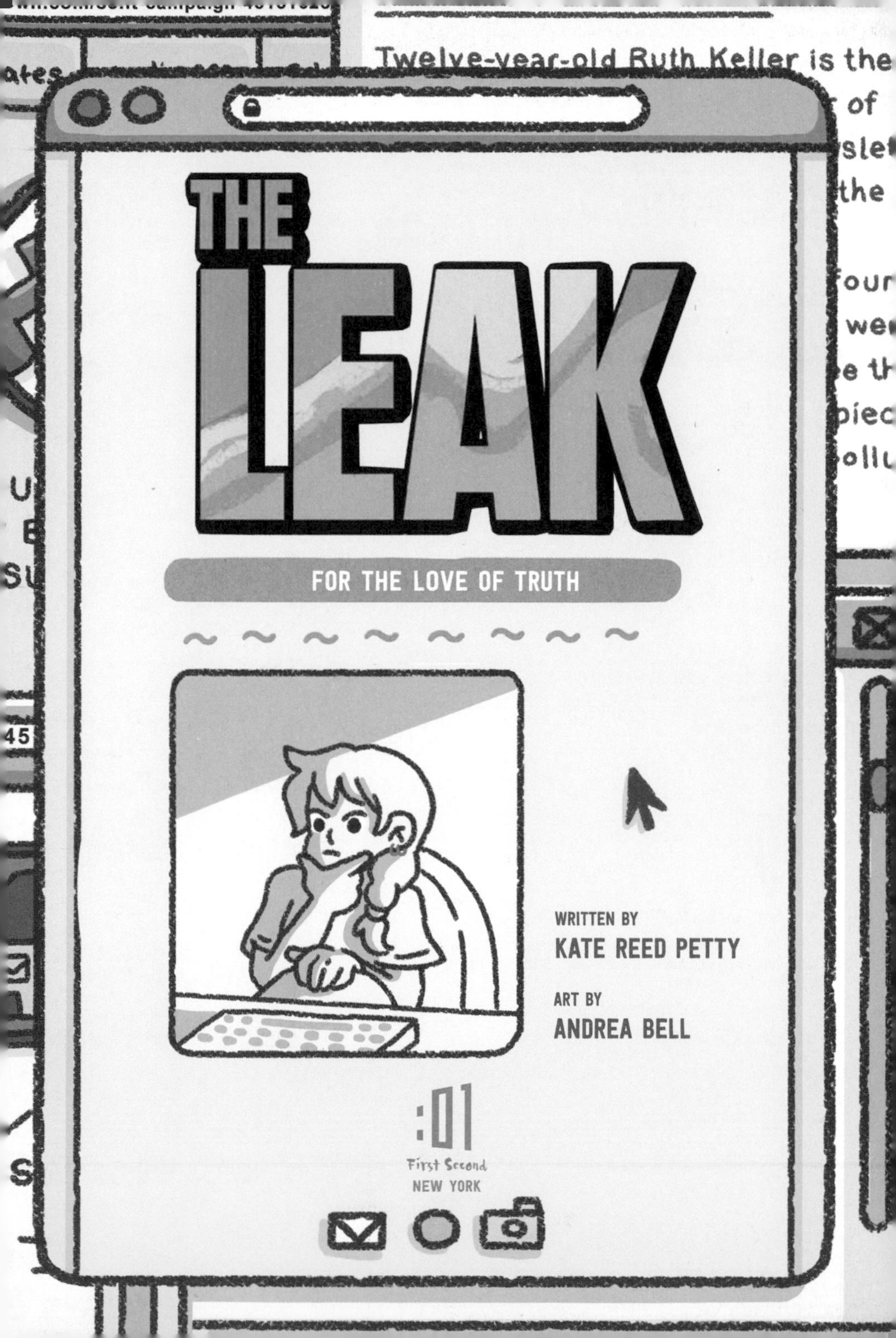

WRITTEN BY
KATE REED PETTY

ART BY
ANDREA BELL

:01 First Second
NEW YORK

This book is for the people of Flint, Michigan

and for Susan Bell Knisely —Kate
and for Liz Bell —Andrea

:01

First Second

Text Copyright © 2021 by Kathryn Petty

Illustration Copyright © 2021 by Andrea Bell

Published by First Second

First Second is an imprint of Roaring Brook Press, a division of Holtzbrinck Publishing Holdings Limited Partnership

120 Broadway, New York, NY 10271

Don't miss your next favorite book from First Second! For the latest updates go to firstsecondnewsletter.com and sign up for our enewsletter.

Library of Congress Control Number: 2020911196

Hardback ISBN: 978-1-250-21795-0
Paperback ISBN: 978-1-250-21796-7

Our books may be purchased in bulk for promotional, educational, or business use. Please contact your local bookseller or the Macmillan Corporate and Premium Sales Department at (800) 221-7945 ext. 5442 or by email at MacmillanSpecialMarkets@macmillan.com.

First edition, 2021

Edited by Mark Siegel and Samia Fakih
Cover design by Kirk Benshoff
Interior design by Sunny Lee
Printed in China by RR Donnelley Asia Printing Solutions Ltd., Dongguan City, Guangdong Province

Digitally inked with a soft 8B lead-type of pencil-brush and thoughtfully colored in Photoshop.

Paperback: 10 9 8 7 6 5 4 3 2 1
Hardcover: 10 9 8 7 6 5 4 3 2 1

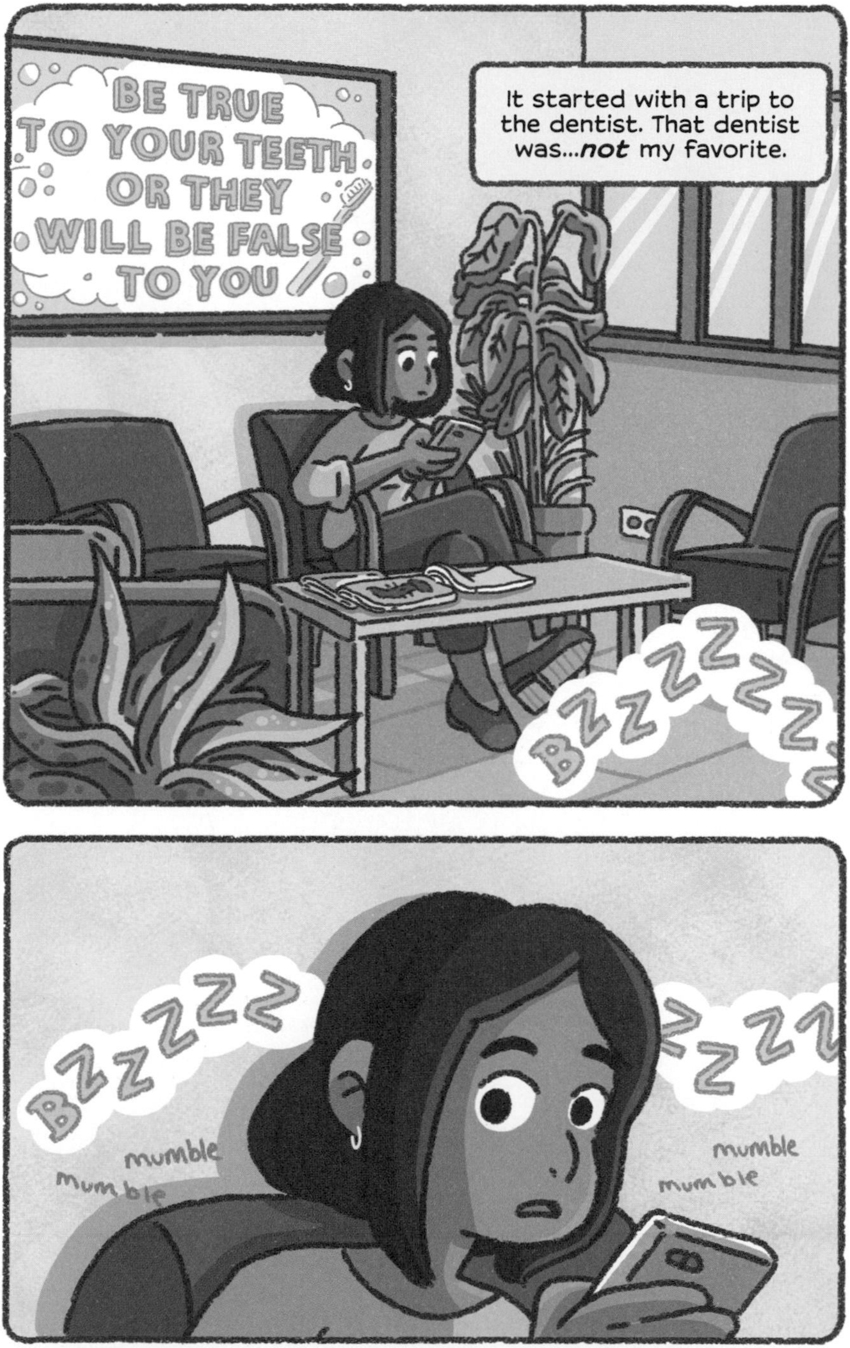
BE TRUE TO YOUR TEETH OR THEY WILL BE FALSE TO YOU
It started with a trip to the dentist. That dentist was...*not* my favorite.
BZZZZZZ
BZZZZZ
ZZZZ
mumble
mumble
mumble
mumble

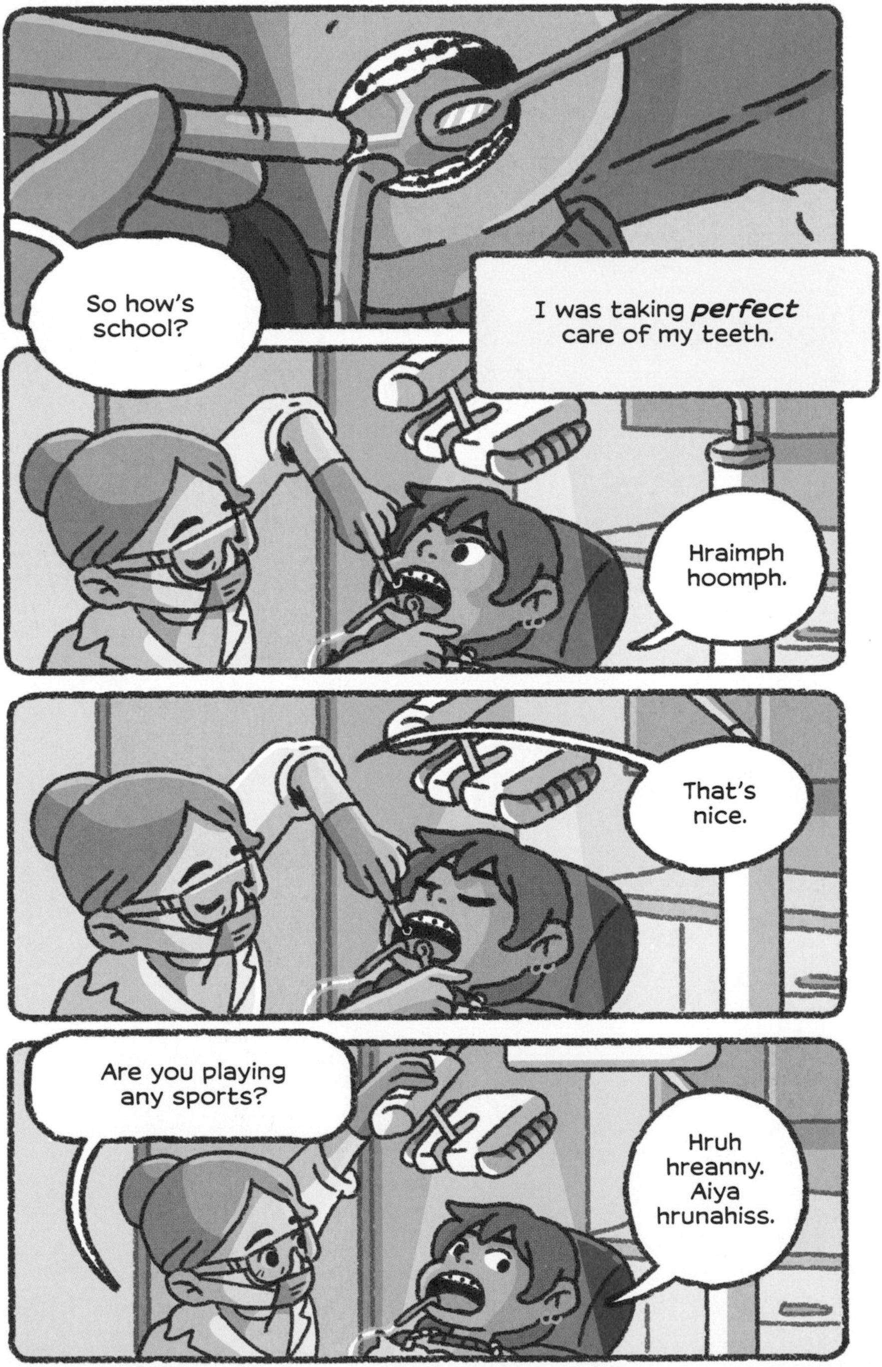
So how's school?
I was taking *perfect* care of my teeth.
Hraimph hoomph.
That's nice.
Are you playing any sports?
Hruh hreanny. Aiya hrunahiss.

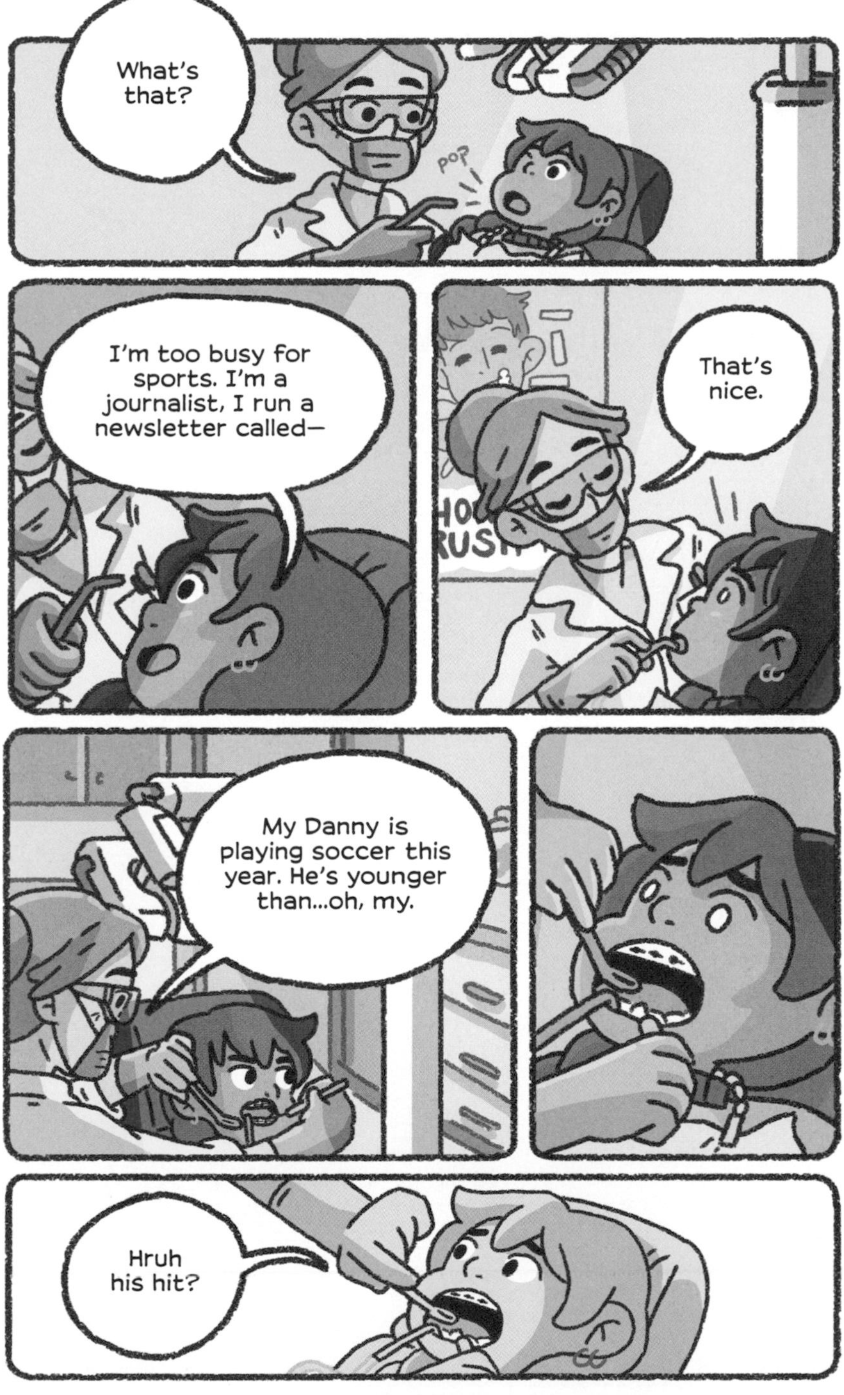
What's that?
POP
I'm too busy for sports. I'm a journalist, I run a newsletter called—
That's nice.
My Danny is playing soccer this year. He's younger than...oh, my.
Hruh his hit?

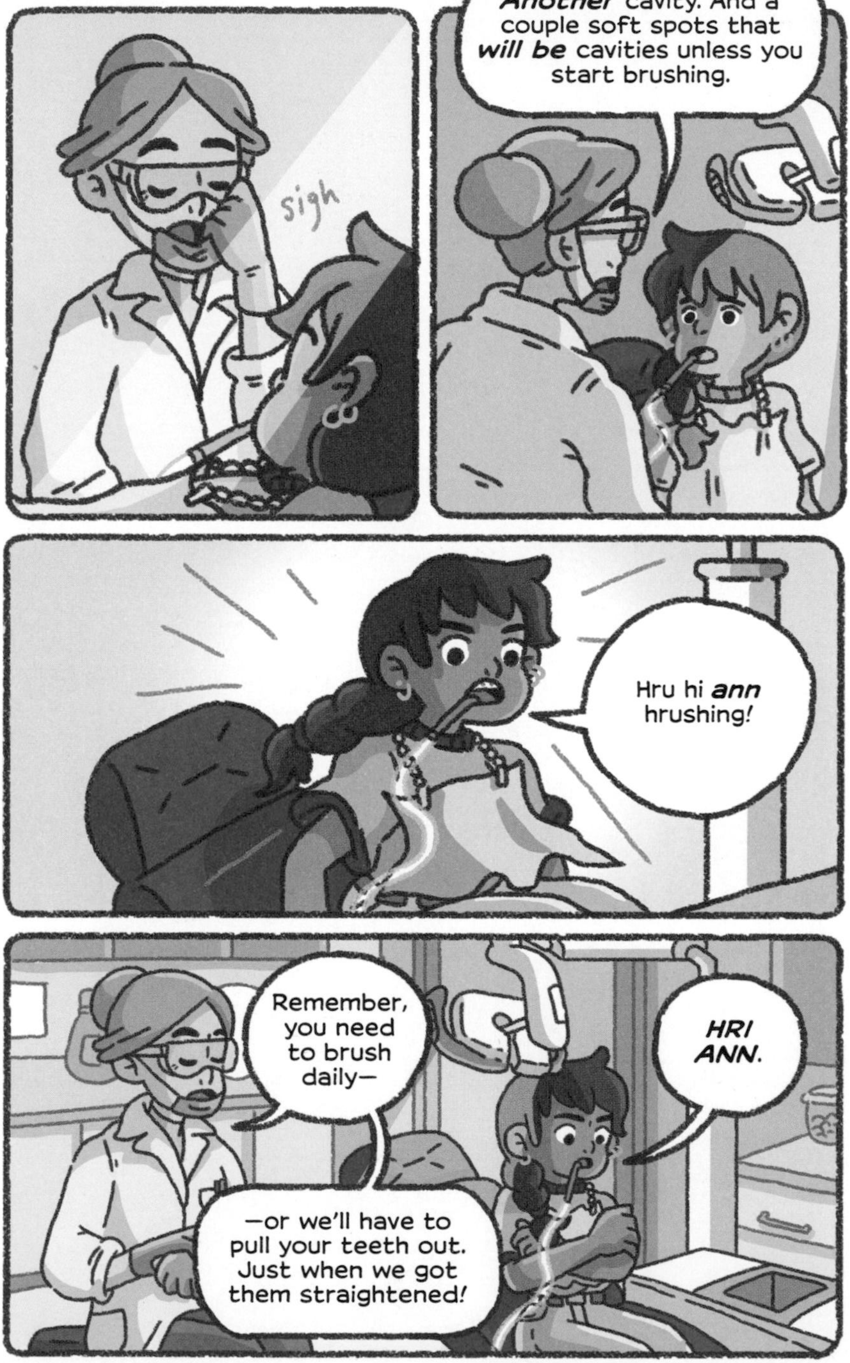
sigh
Another cavity. And a couple soft spots that *will be* cavities unless you start brushing.
Hru hi *ann* hrushing!
Remember, you need to brush daily—
—or we'll have to pull your teeth out. Just when we got them straightened!
HRI ANN.

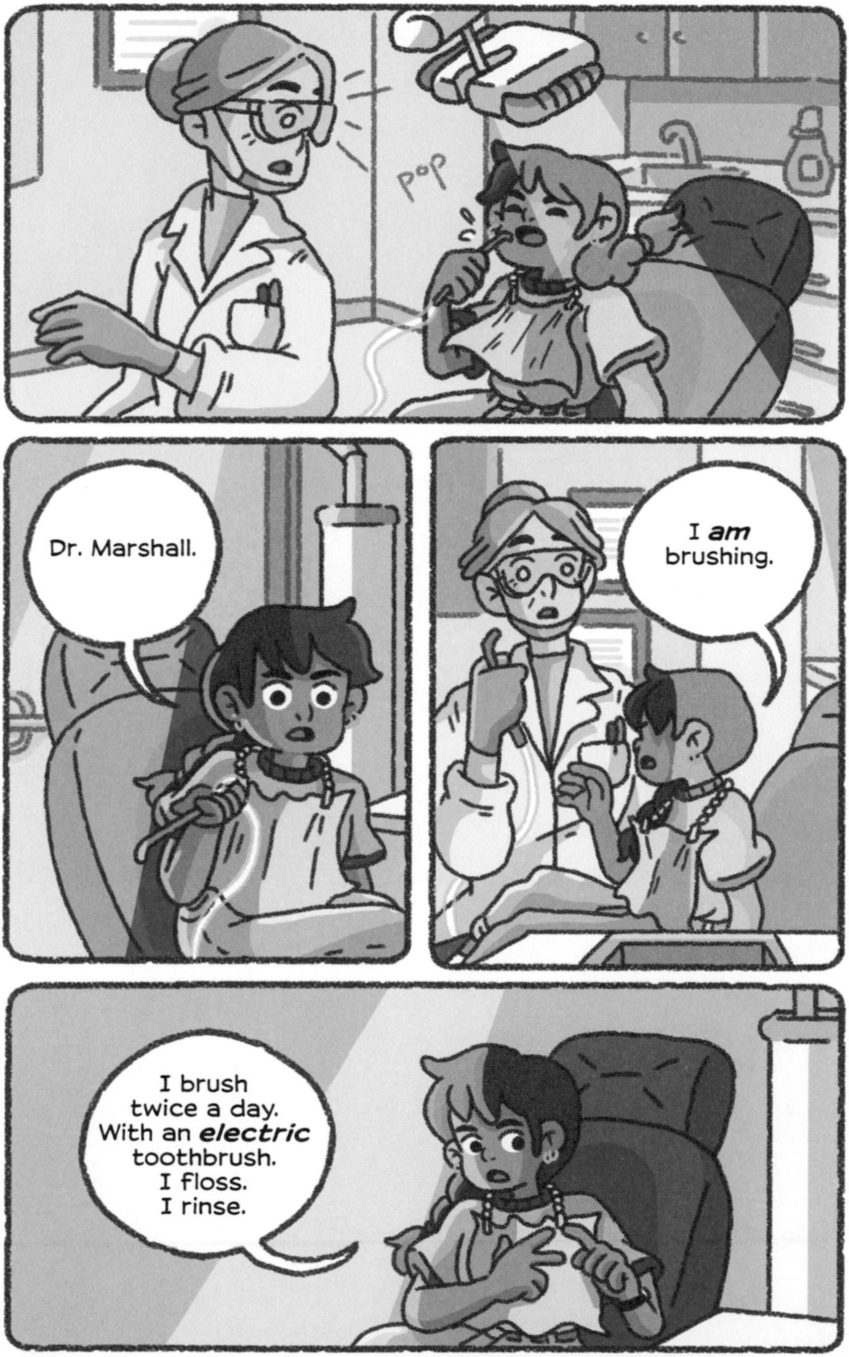
pop
Dr. Marshall.
I *am* brushing.
I brush twice a day. With an *electric* toothbrush. I floss. I rinse.

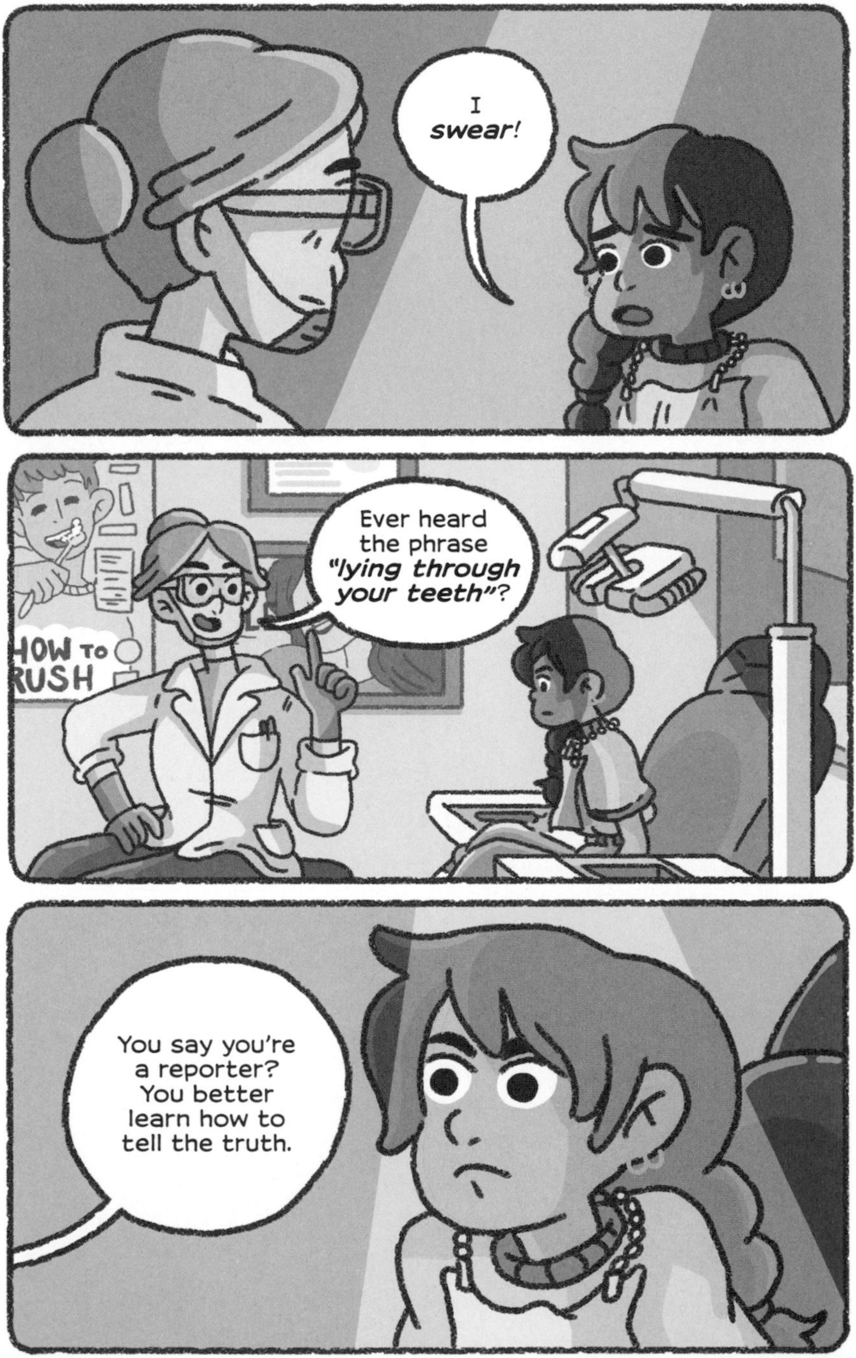
I *swear*!
Ever heard the phrase ***"lying through your teeth"***?
HOW TO
RUSH
You say you're a reporter? You better learn how to tell the truth.

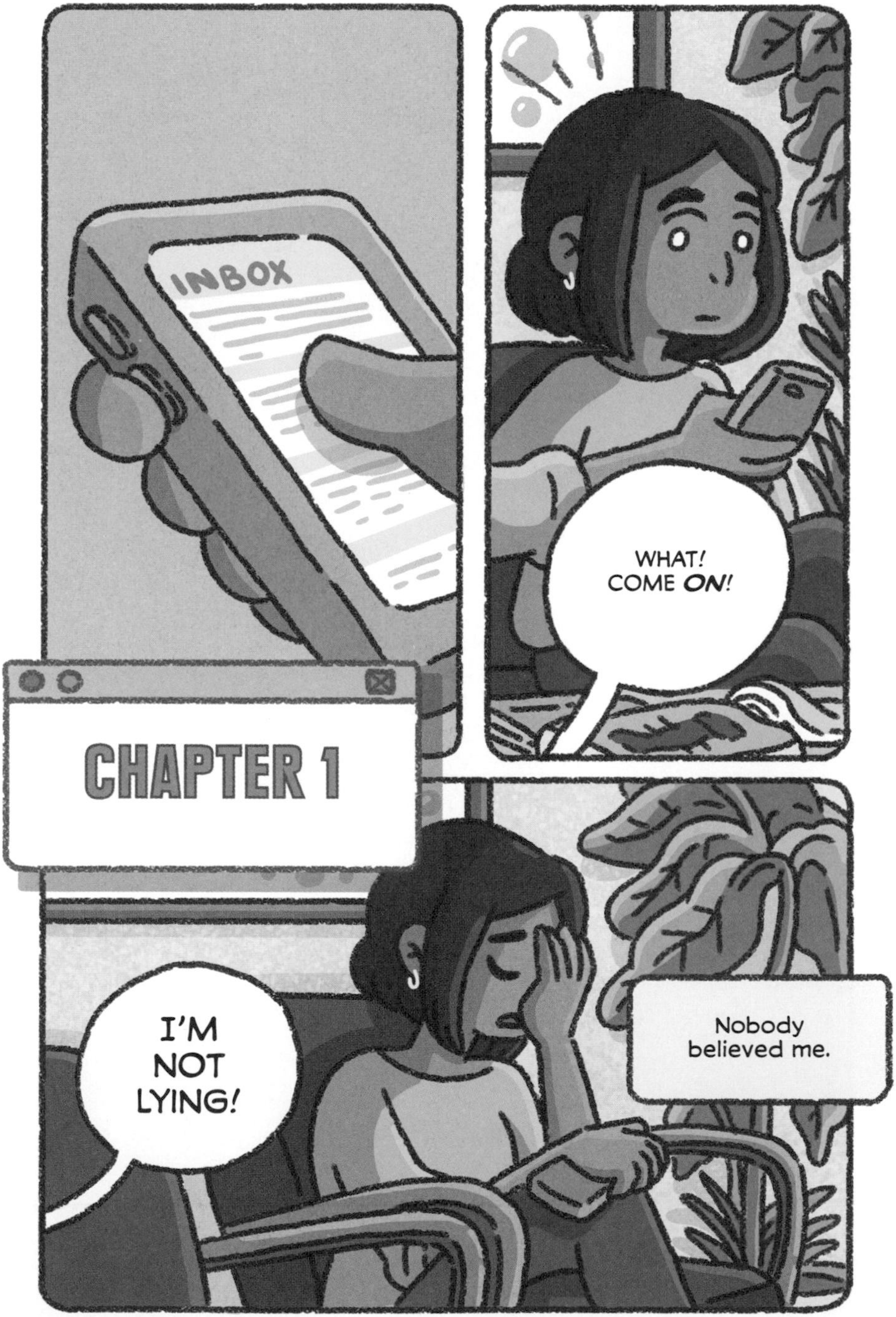

INBOX
CHAPTER 1
WHAT! COME ON!
I'M NOT LYING!
Nobody believed me.

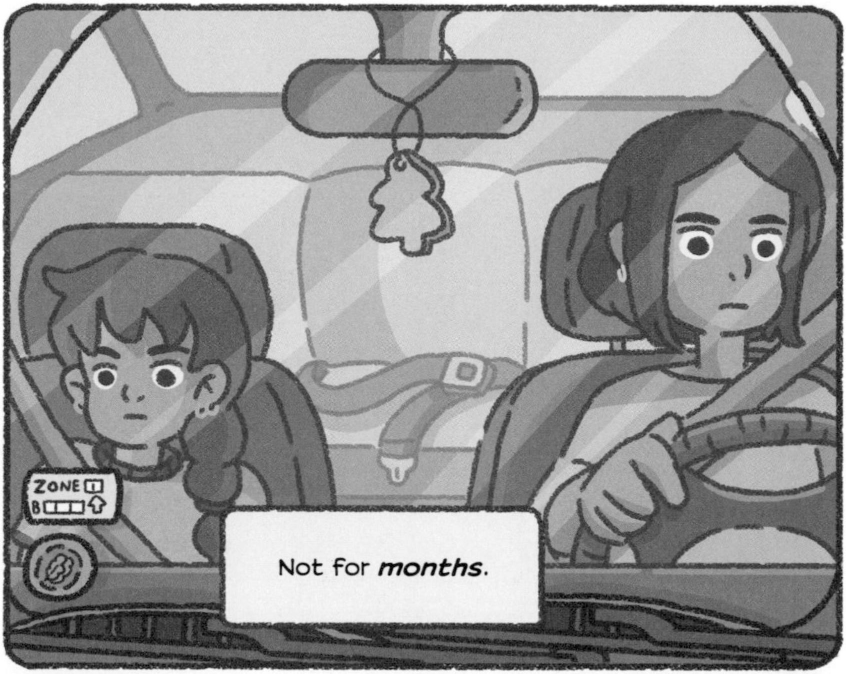
Not for *months*.

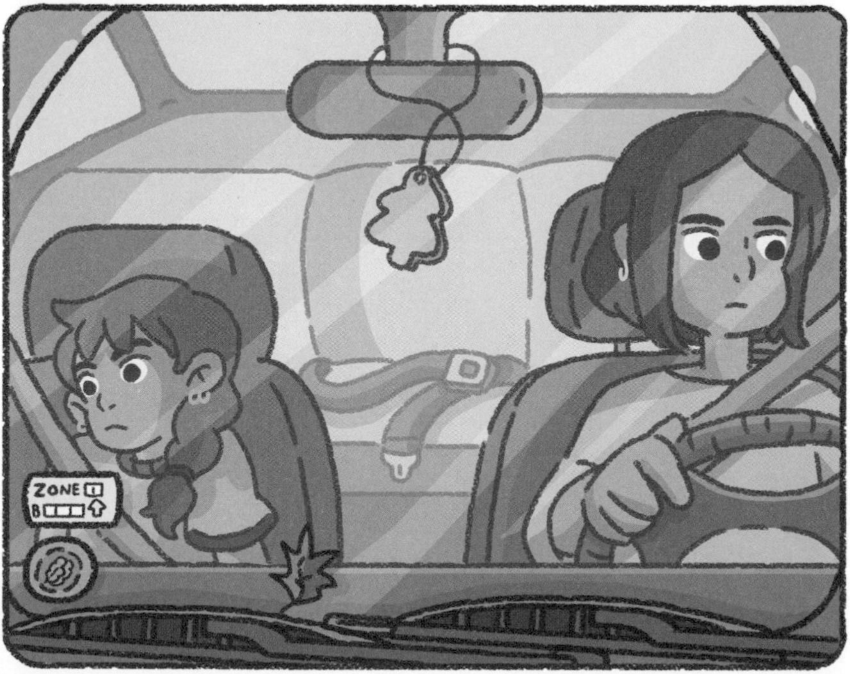

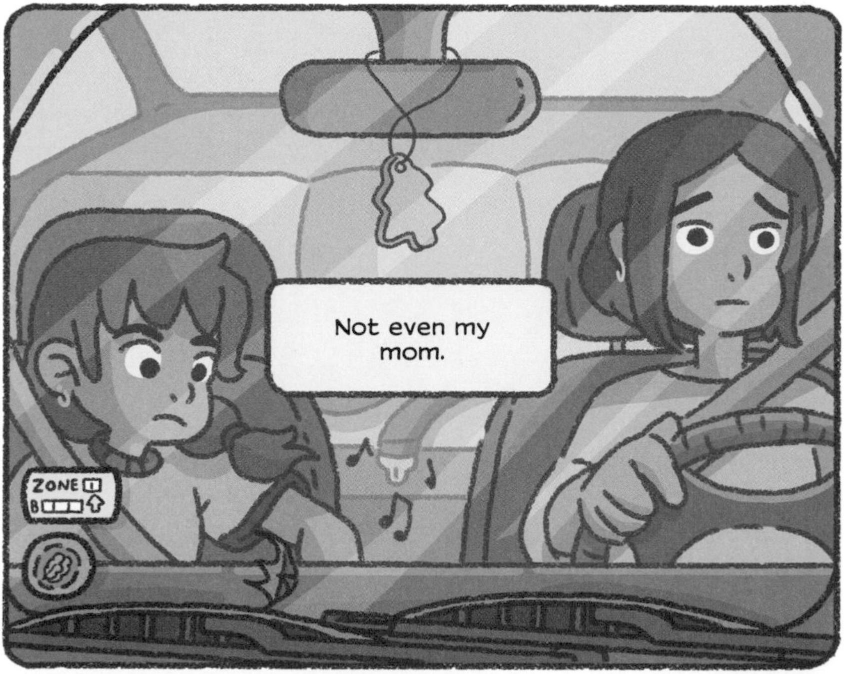
Not even my mom.
ZONE 1
B

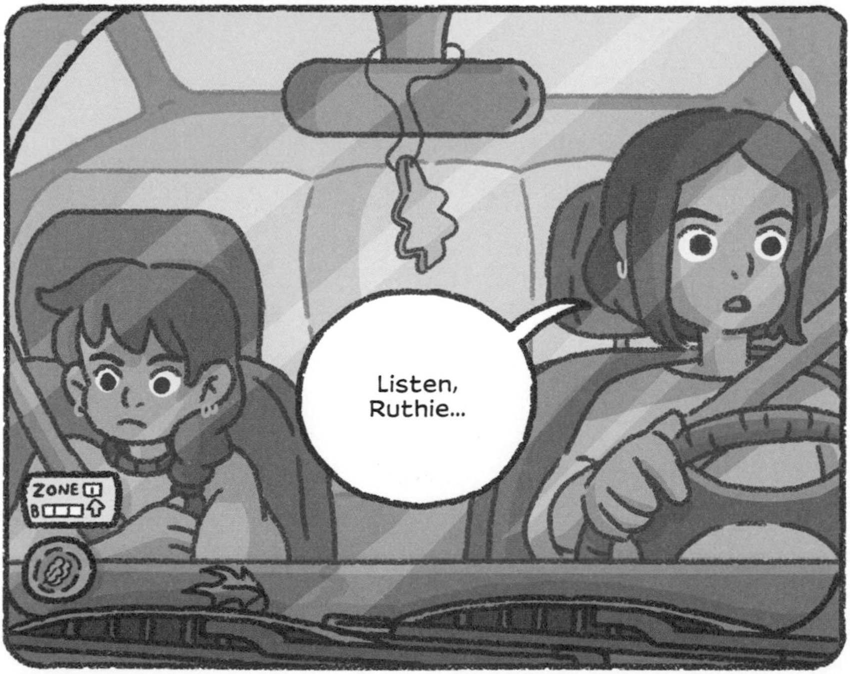
Listen, Ruthie...
ZONE 1
B

—Dr. Marshall doesn't know—
—*another* cavity. Those are *expensive*, you know!
—why you *never* back me up?—
—can't go through life *yelling* at people—
Why won't you *believe* me! I'm telling the *truth*!

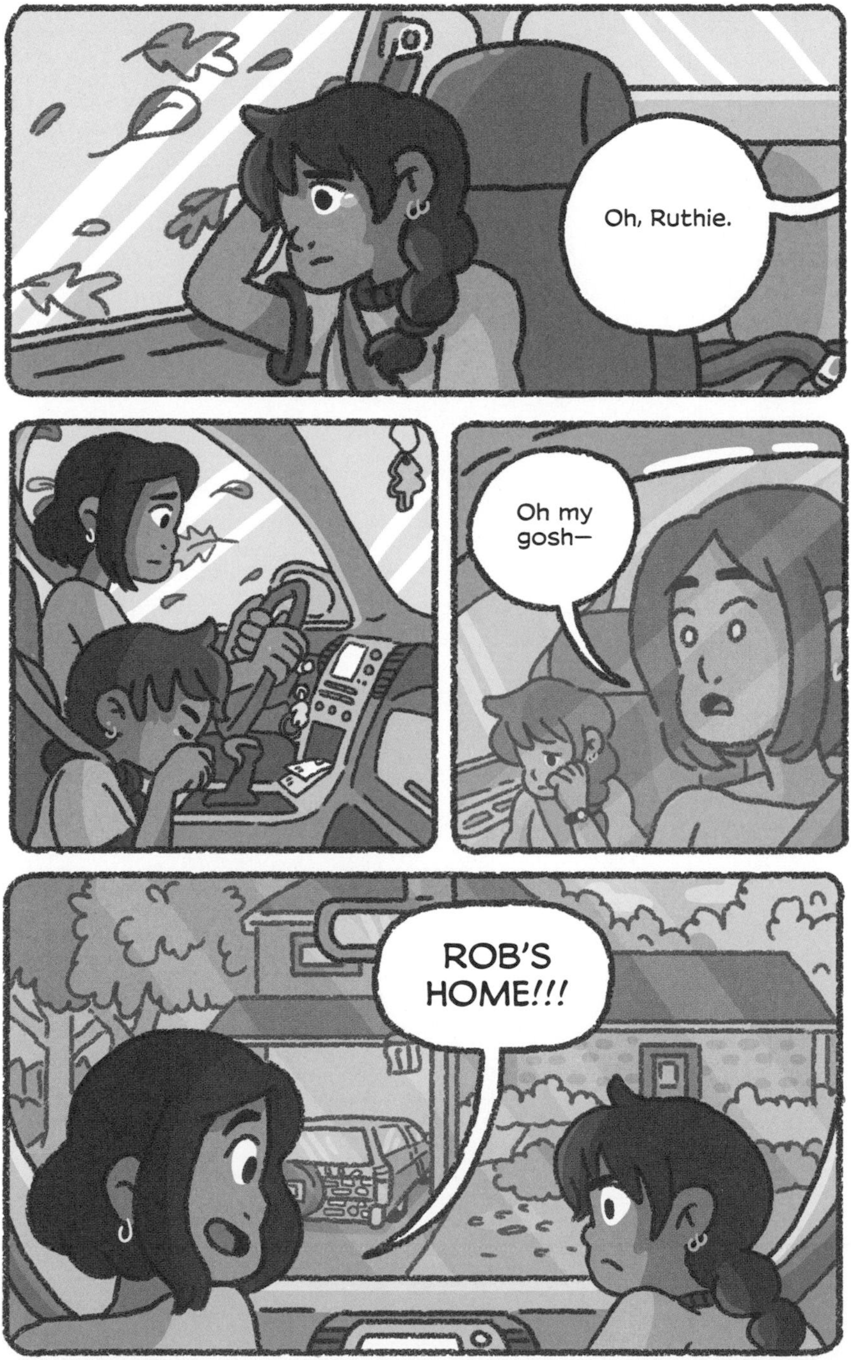
Oh, Ruthie.
Oh my gosh—
ROB'S HOME!!!

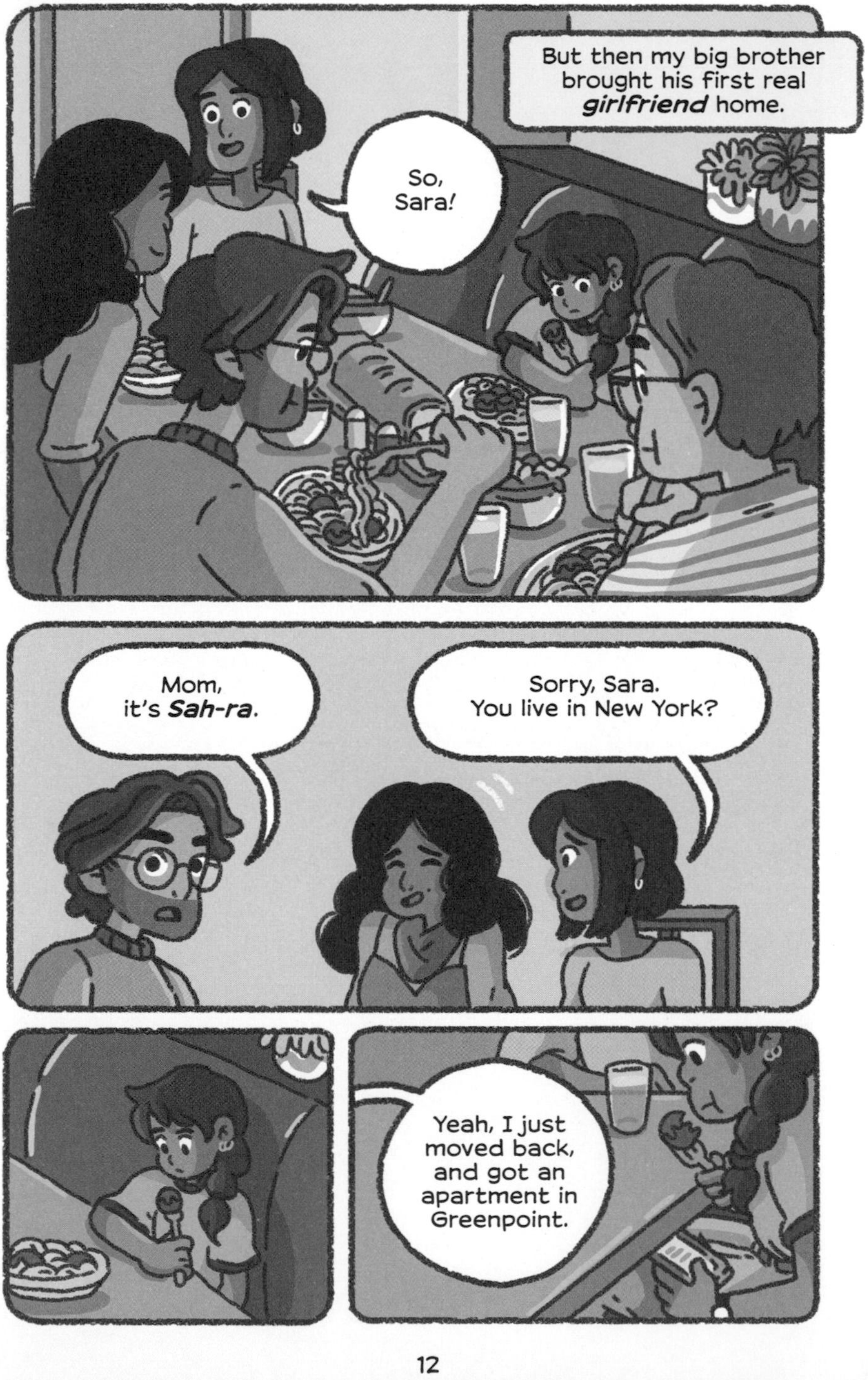
But then my big brother brought his first real ***girlfriend*** home.
So, Sara!
Mom, it's ***Sah-ra***.
Sorry, Sara. You live in New York?
Yeah, I just moved back, and got an apartment in Greenpoint.

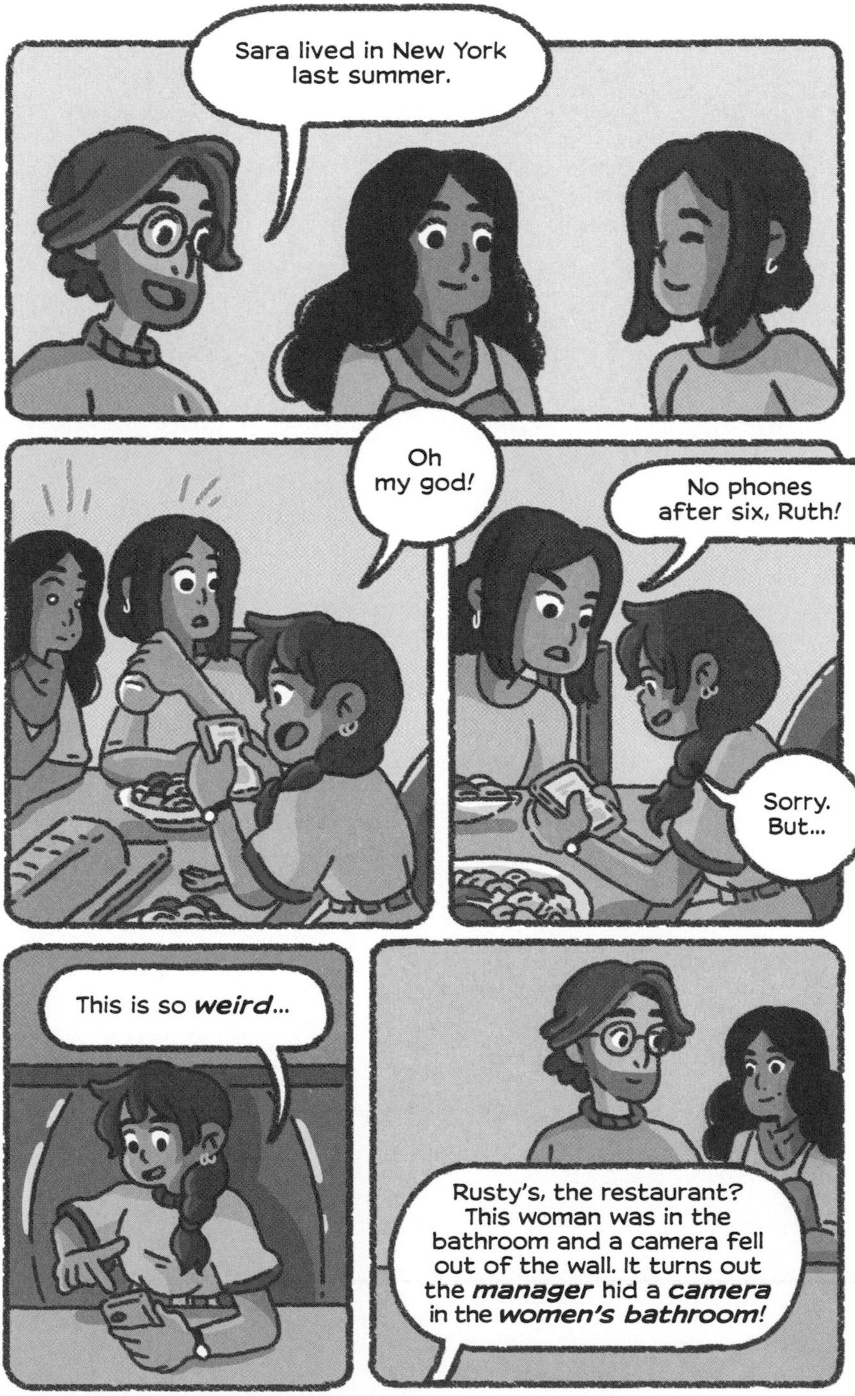
Sara lived in New York last summer.
Oh my god!
No phones after six, Ruth!
Sorry. But...
This is so ***weird***...
Rusty's, the restaurant? This woman was in the bathroom and a camera fell out of the wall. It turns out the ***manager*** hid a ***camera*** in the ***women's bathroom***!

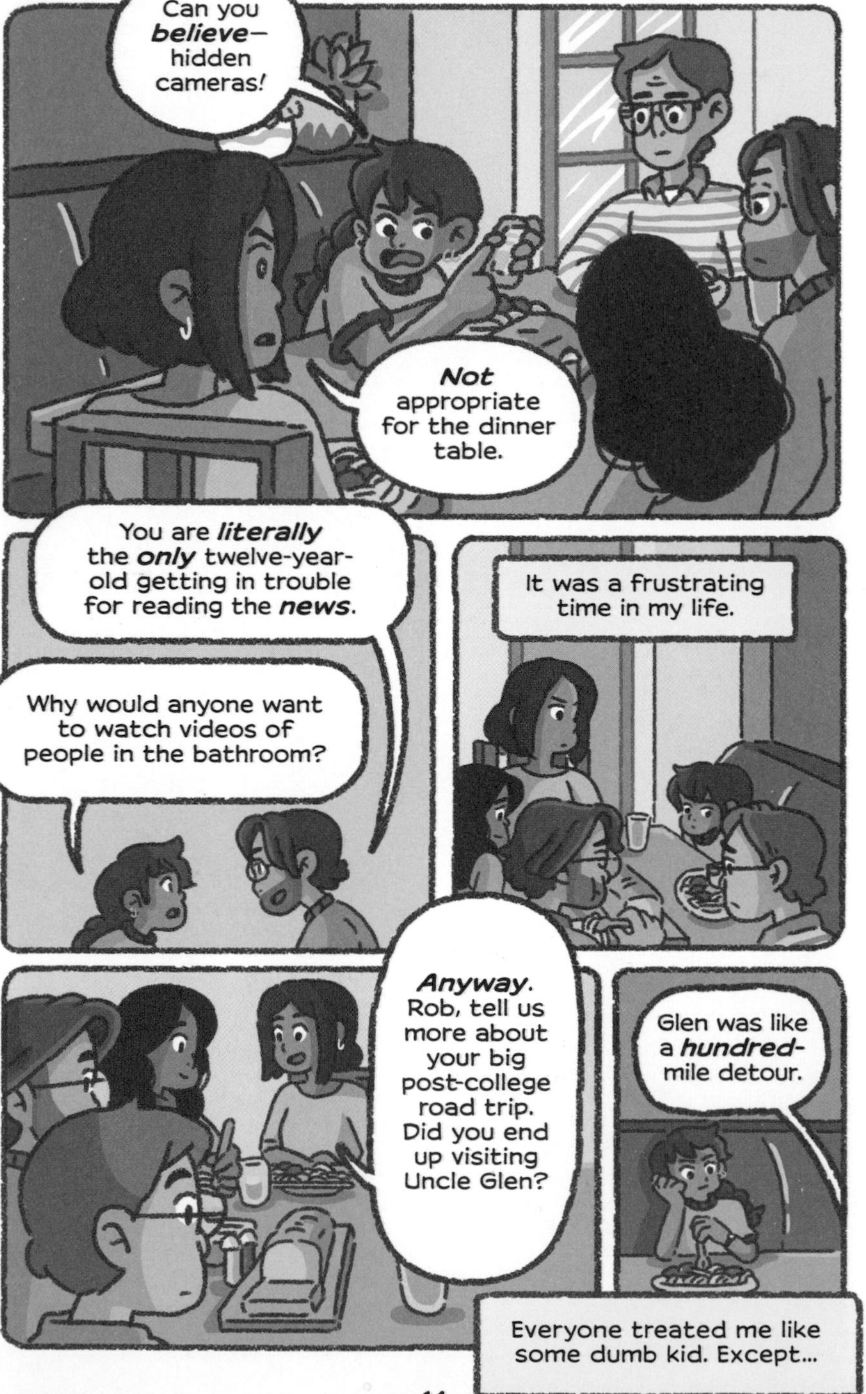

Can you *believe*— hidden cameras!
Not appropriate for the dinner table.
You are *literally* the *only* twelve-year-old getting in trouble for reading the *news*.
Why would anyone want to watch videos of people in the bathroom?
It was a frustrating time in my life.
Anyway. Rob, tell us more about your big post-college road trip. Did you end up visiting Uncle Glen?
Glen was like a *hundred*-mile detour.
Everyone treated me like some dumb kid. Except...

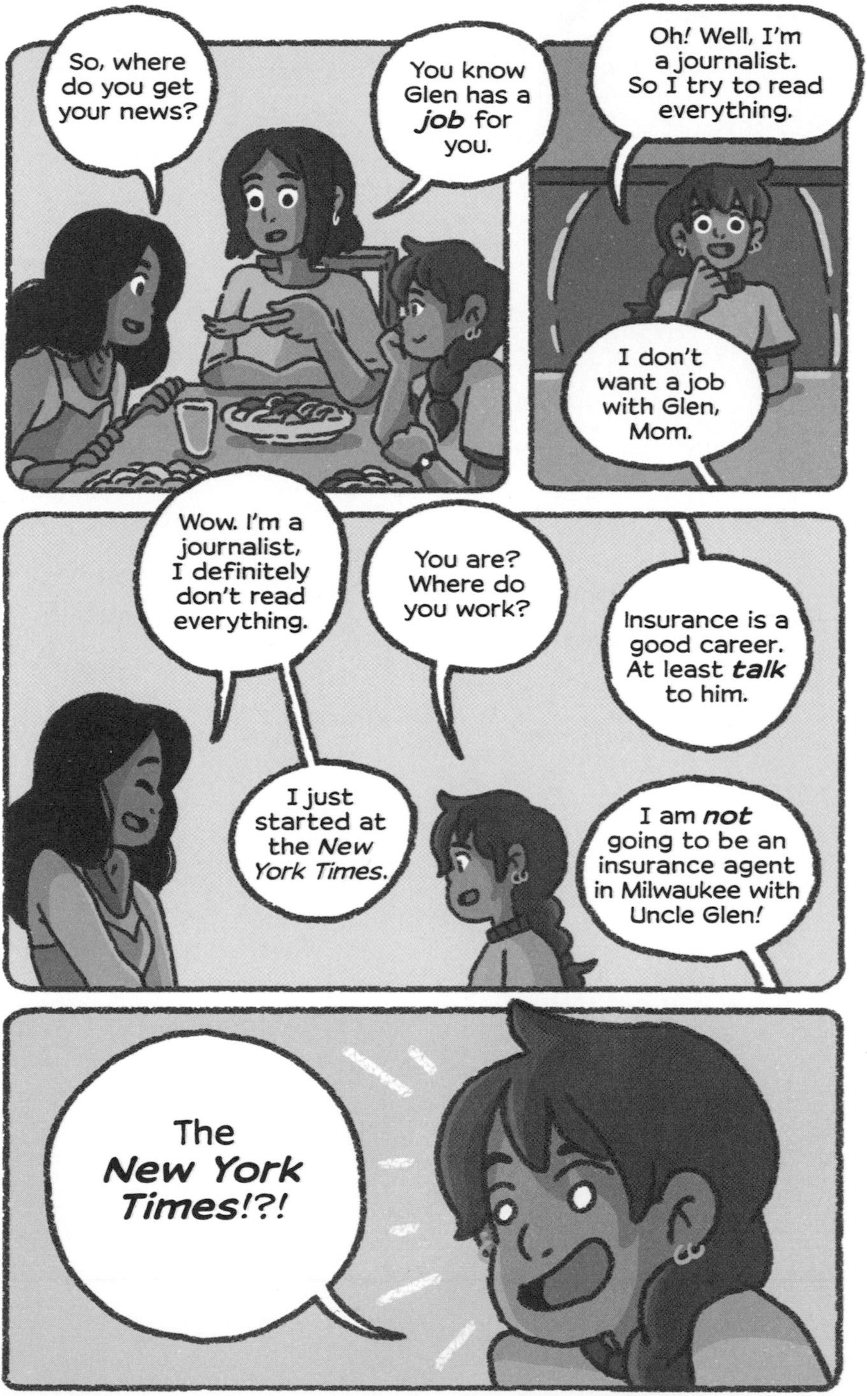
So, where do you get your news?
You know Glen has a *job* for you.
Oh! Well, I'm a journalist. So I try to read everything.
I don't want a job with Glen, Mom.
Wow. I'm a journalist, I definitely don't read everything.
You are? Where do you work?
Insurance is a good career. At least *talk* to him.
I just started at the *New York Times*.
I am ***not*** going to be an insurance agent in Milwaukee with Uncle Glen!
The ***New York Times***!?!

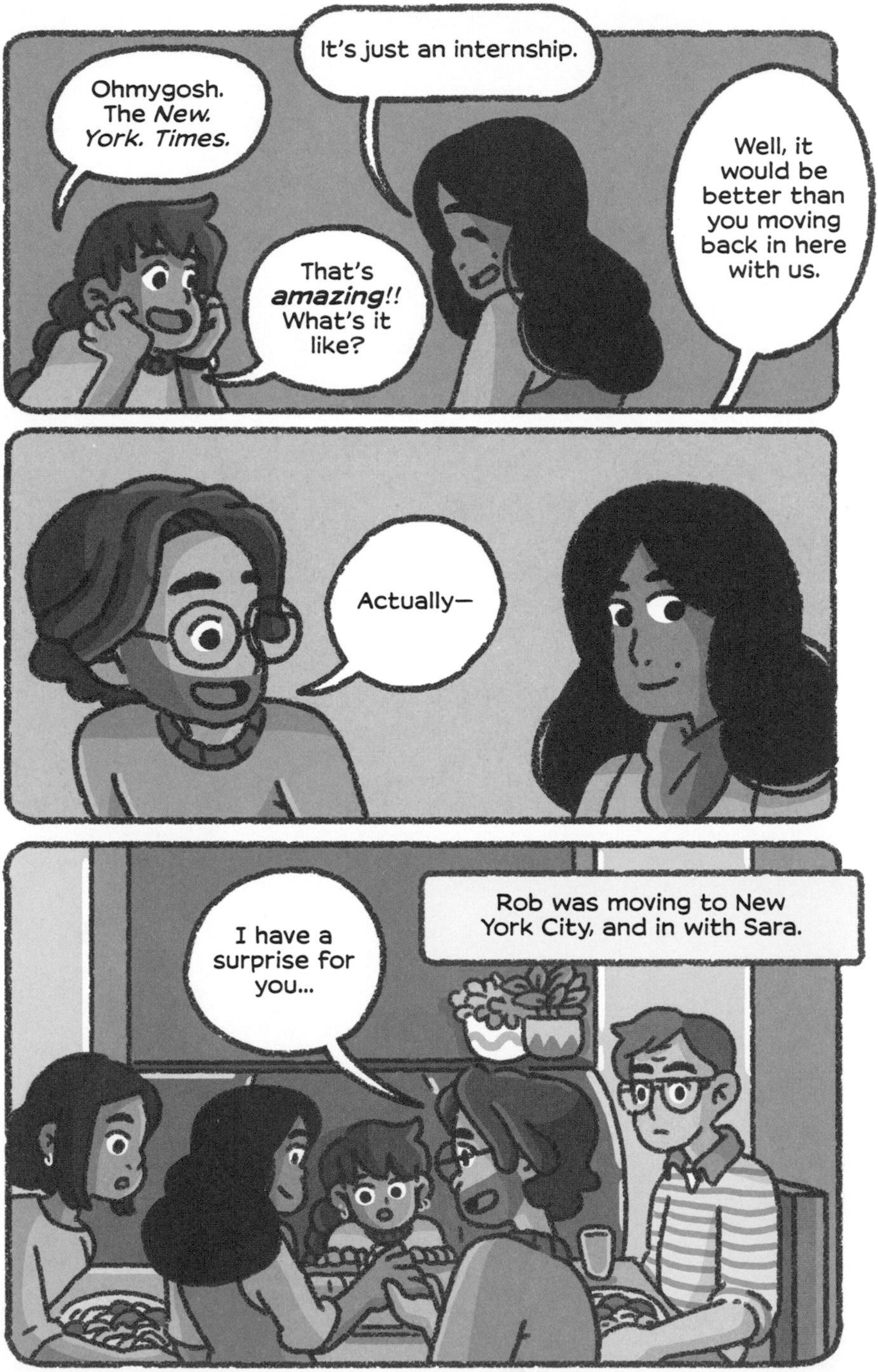
Ohmygosh. The *New. York. Times.*
It's just an internship.
Well, it would be better than you moving back in here with us.
That's ***amazing!!*** What's it like?
Actually—
I have a surprise for you...
Rob was moving to New York City, and in with Sara.

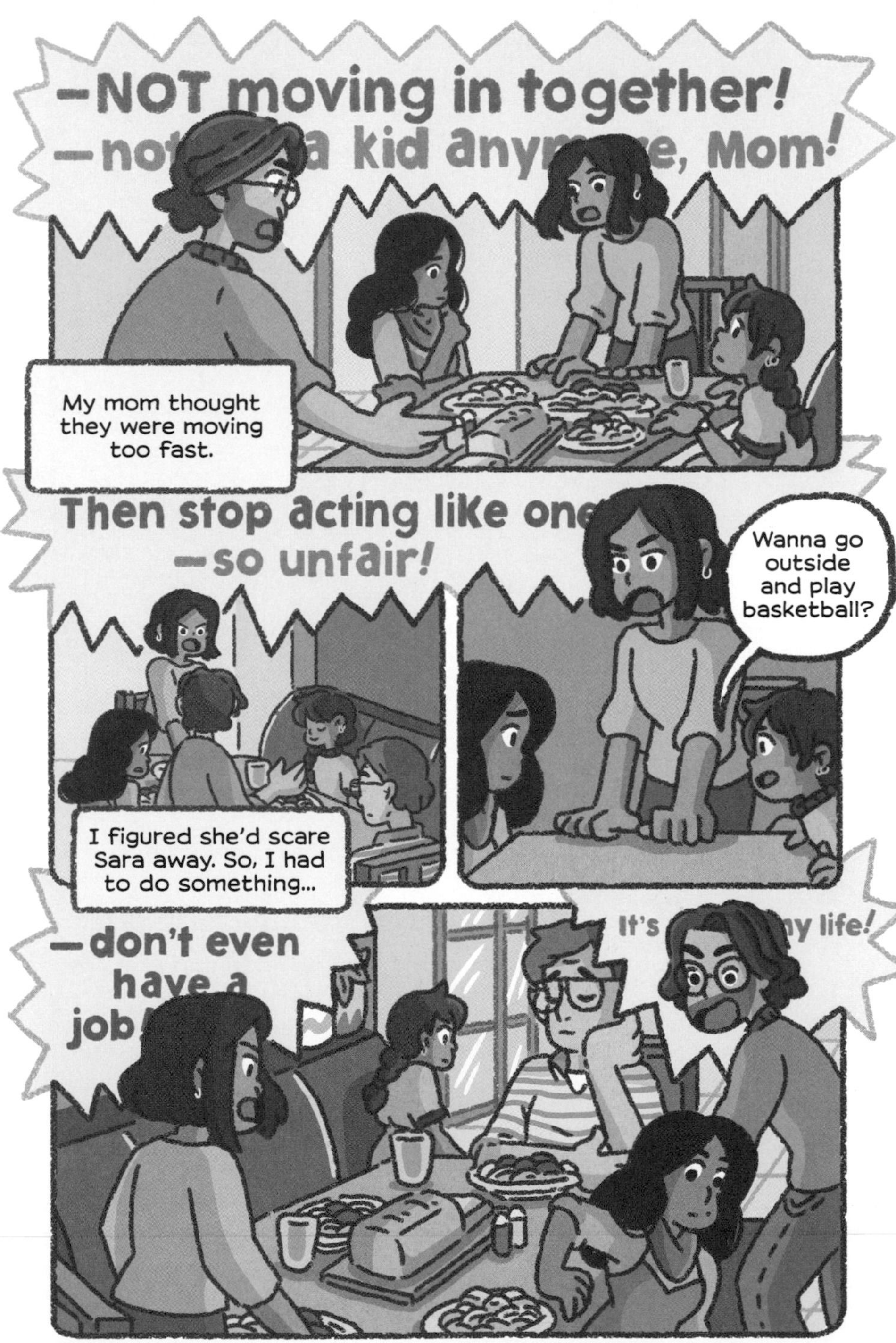

-NOT moving in together!
-not a kid anym e, Mom!
My mom thought they were moving too fast.
Then stop acting like one
-so unfair!
Wanna go outside and play basketball?
I figured she'd scare Sara away. So, I had to do something...
-don't even have a job
It's ny life!

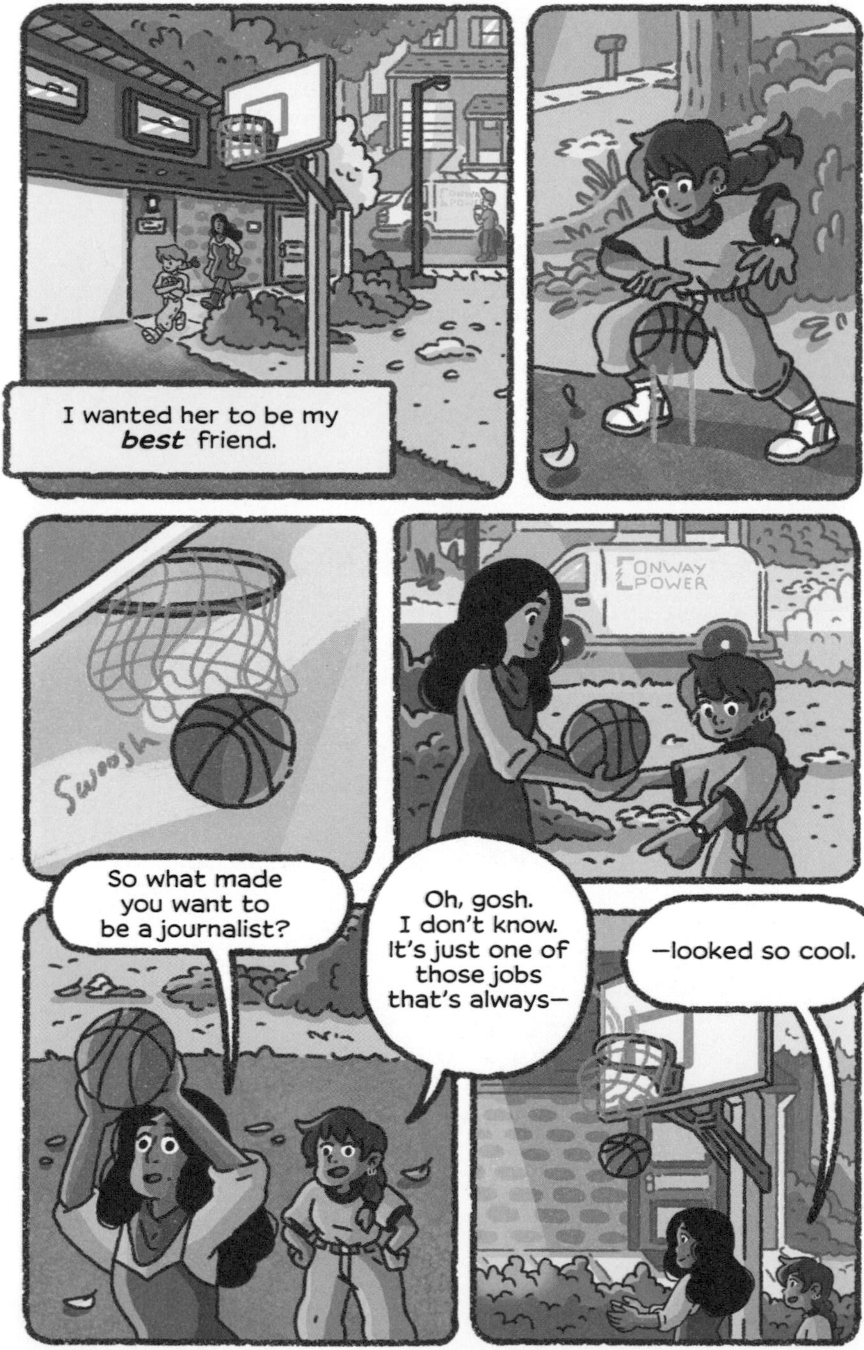
I wanted her to be my ***best*** friend.
Swoosh
ONWAY POWER
So what made you want to be a journalist?
Oh, gosh. I don't know. It's just one of those jobs that's always—
—looked so cool.

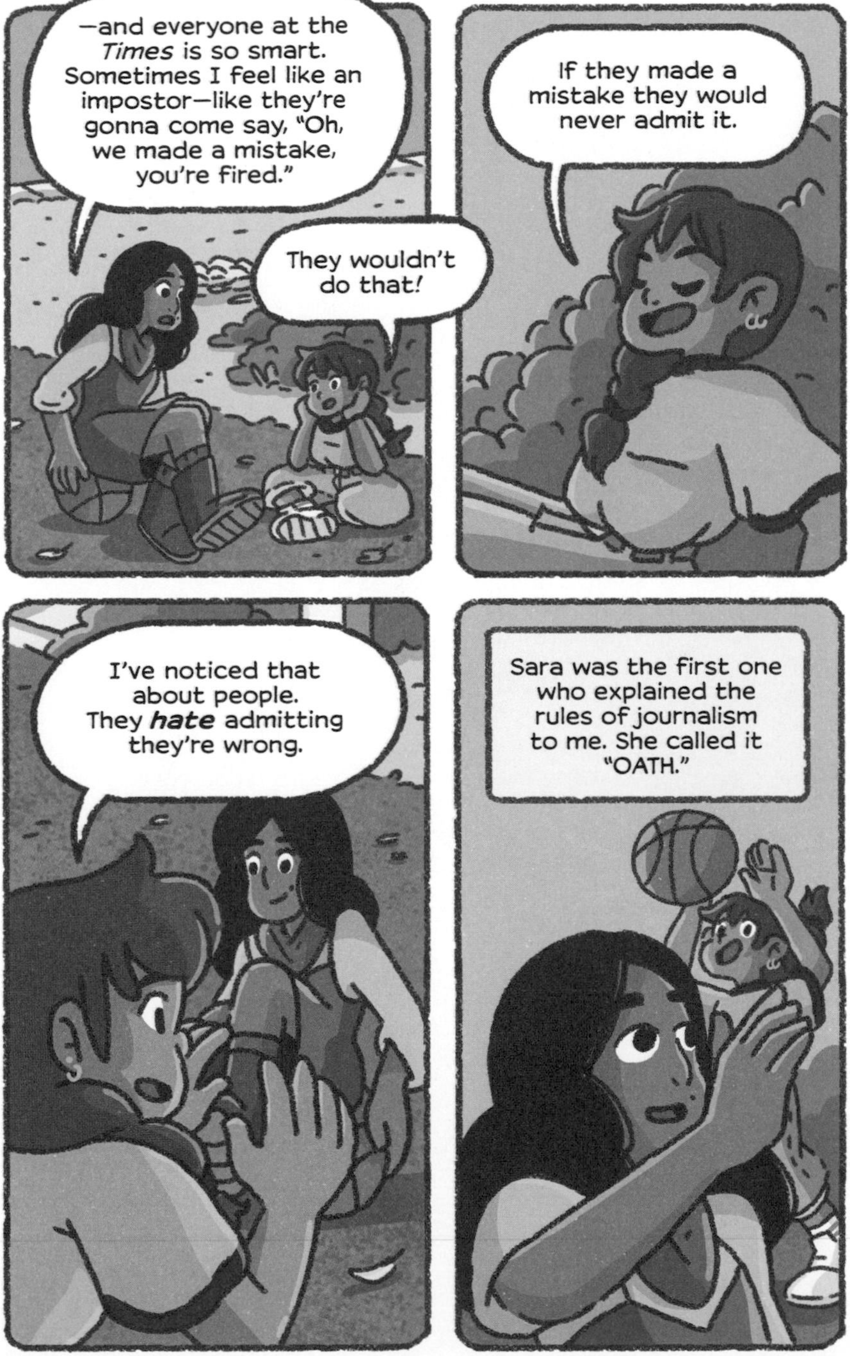
—and everyone at the *Times* is so smart. Sometimes I feel like an impostor—like they're gonna come say, "Oh, we made a mistake, you're fired."
They wouldn't do that!
If they made a mistake they would never admit it.
I've noticed that about people. They ***hate*** admitting they're wrong.
Sara was the first one who explained the rules of journalism to me. She called it "OATH."

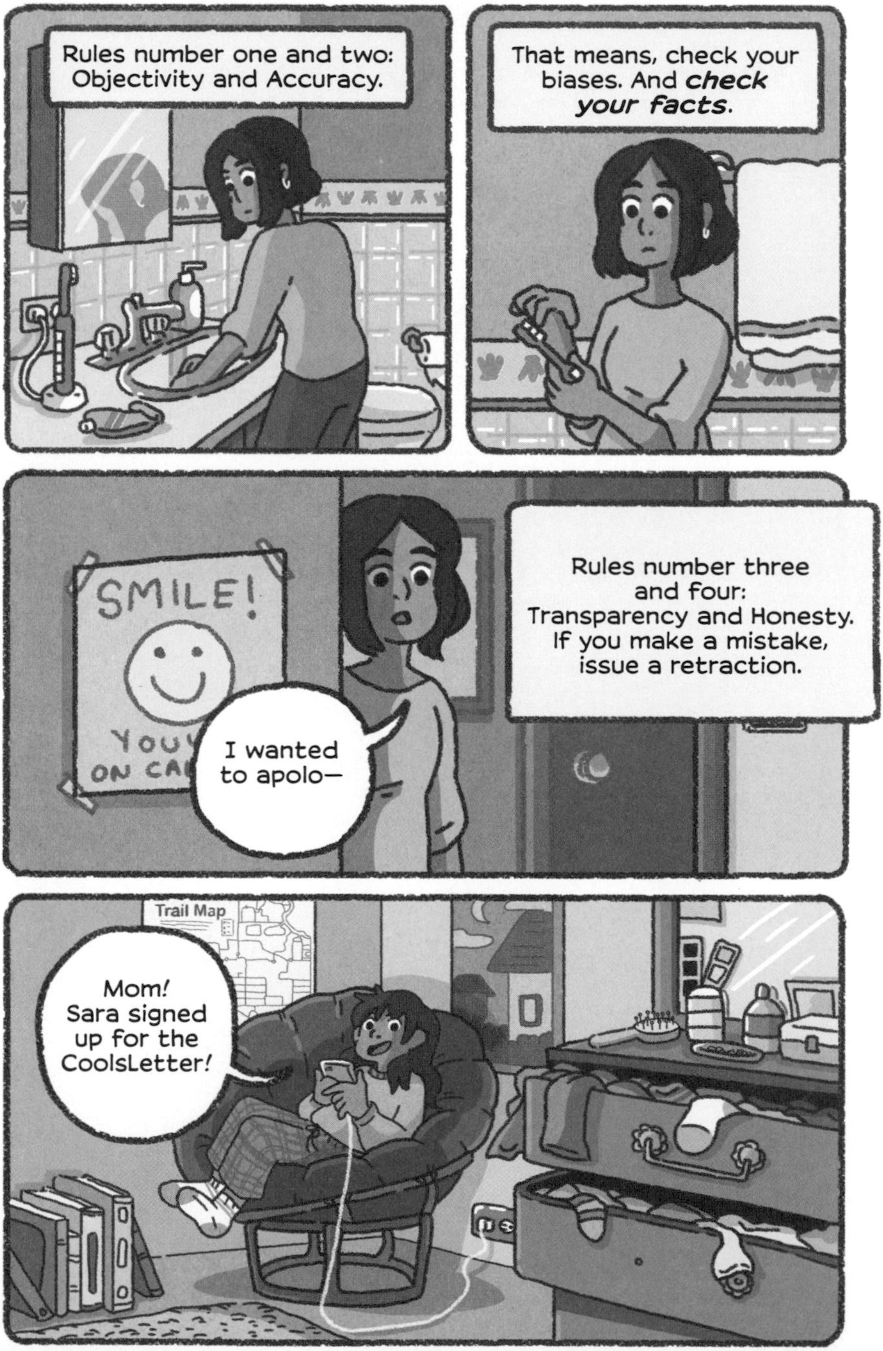
Rules number one and two: Objectivity and Accuracy.
That means, check your biases. And ***check your facts***.
SMILE!
YOU
ON CA
Rules number three and four: Transparency and Honesty. If you make a mistake, issue a retraction.
I wanted to apolo—
Trail Map
Mom! Sara signed up for the CoolsLetter!

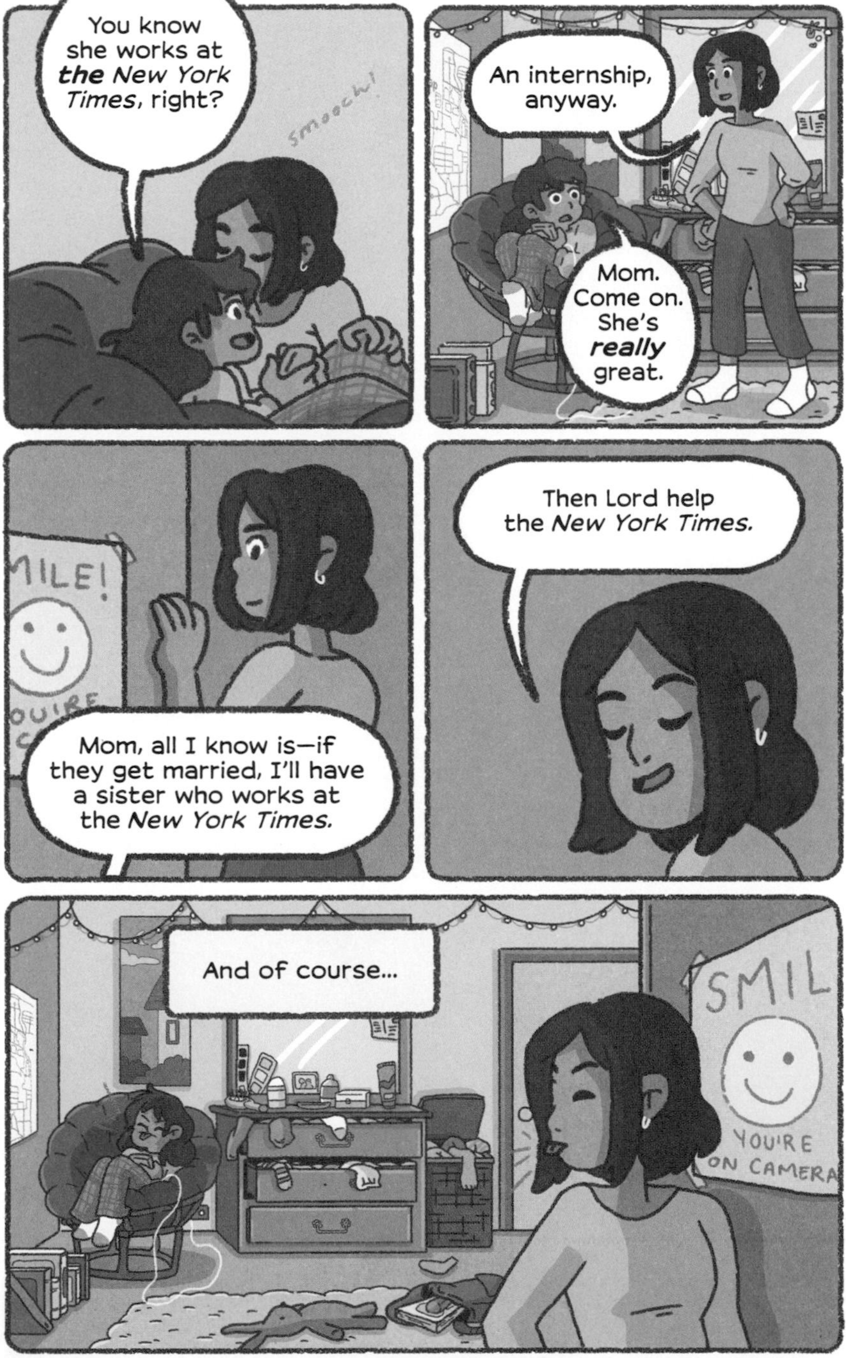
You know she works at ***the*** *New York Times*, right?
Smooch!
An internship, anyway.
Mom. Come on. She's ***really*** great.
MILE!
Mom, all I know is—if they get married, I'll have a sister who works at the *New York Times.*
Then Lord help the *New York Times.*
And of course...
SMIL
YOU'RE ON CAMERA

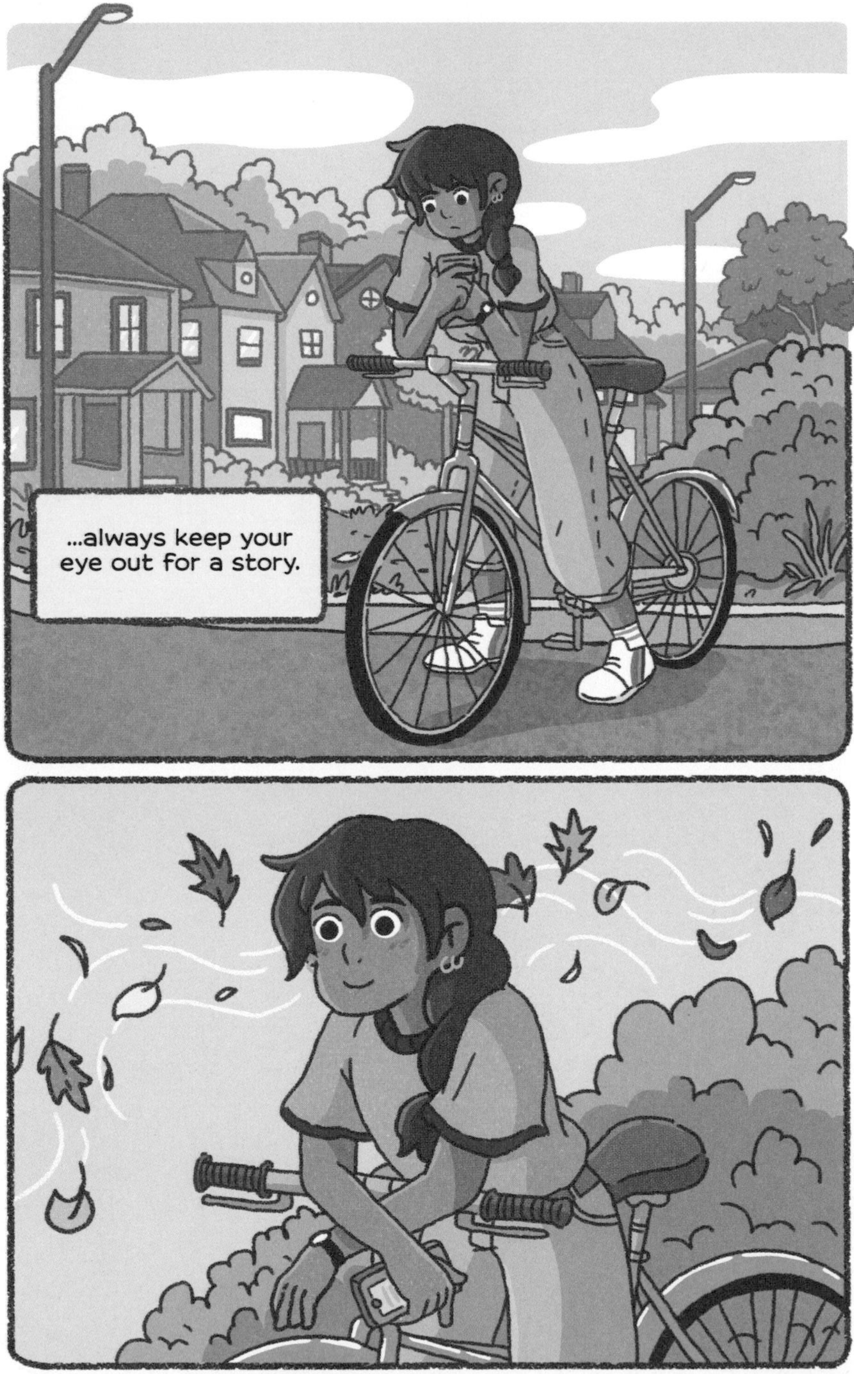
...always keep your eye out for a story.

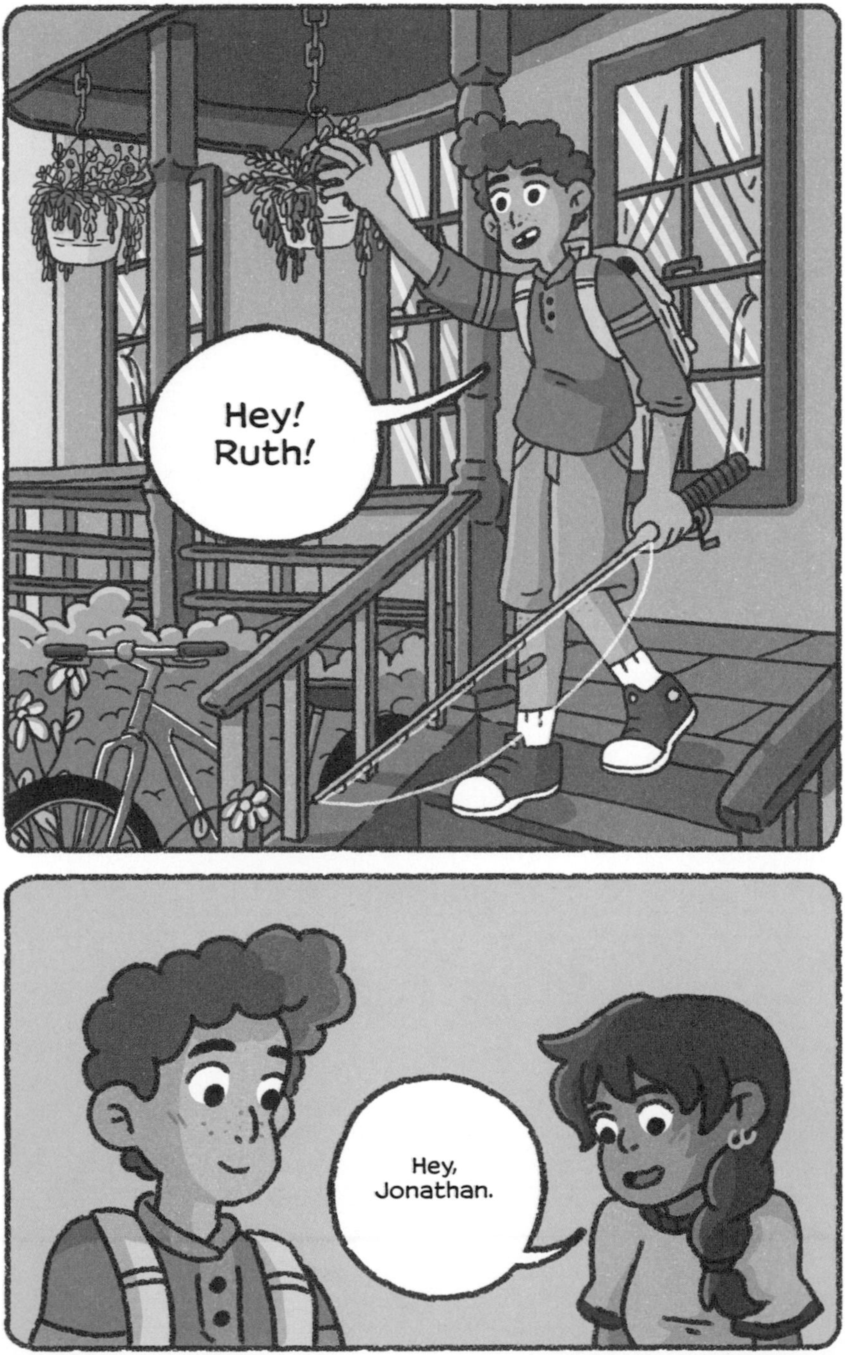
Hey! Ruth!
Hey, Jonathan.

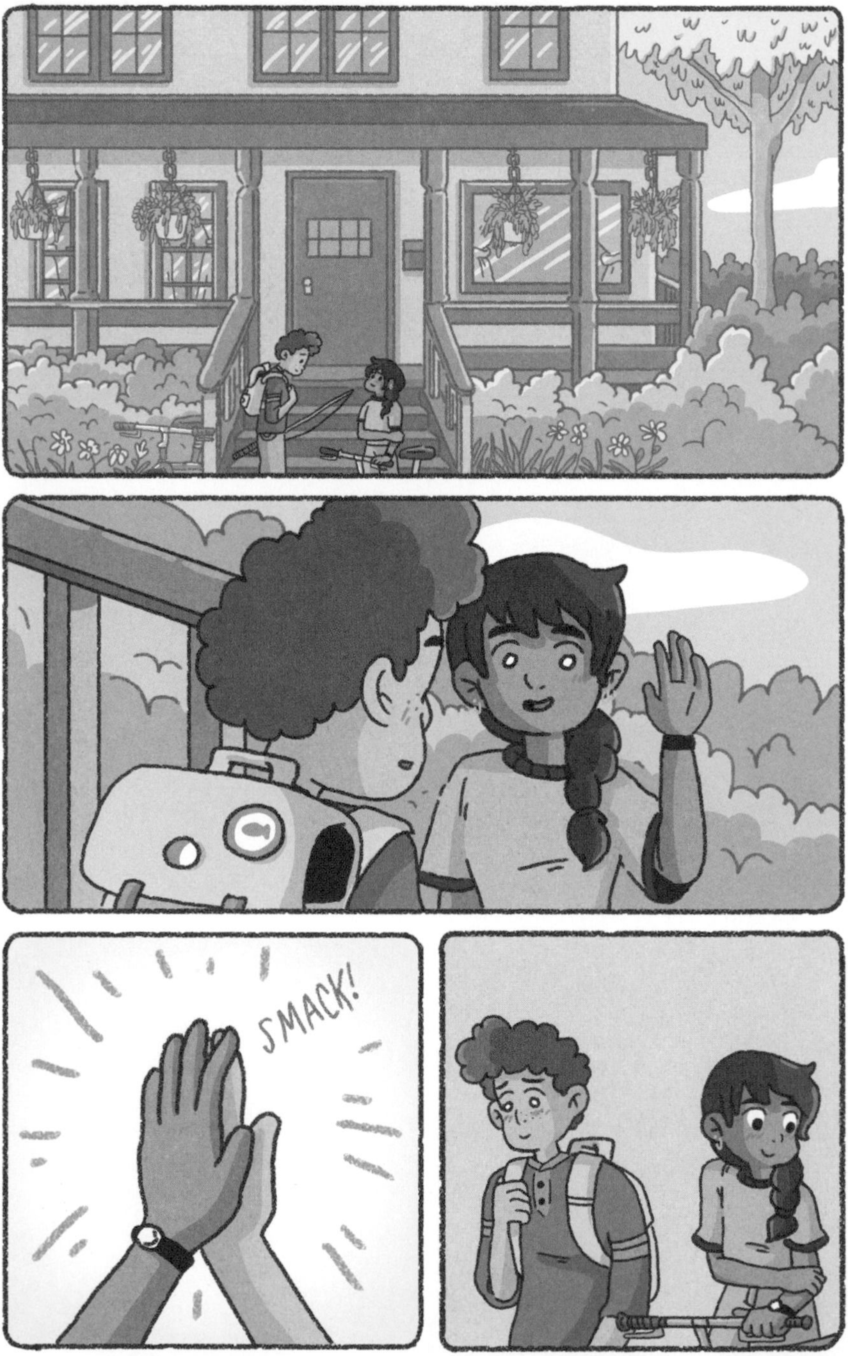
SMACK!

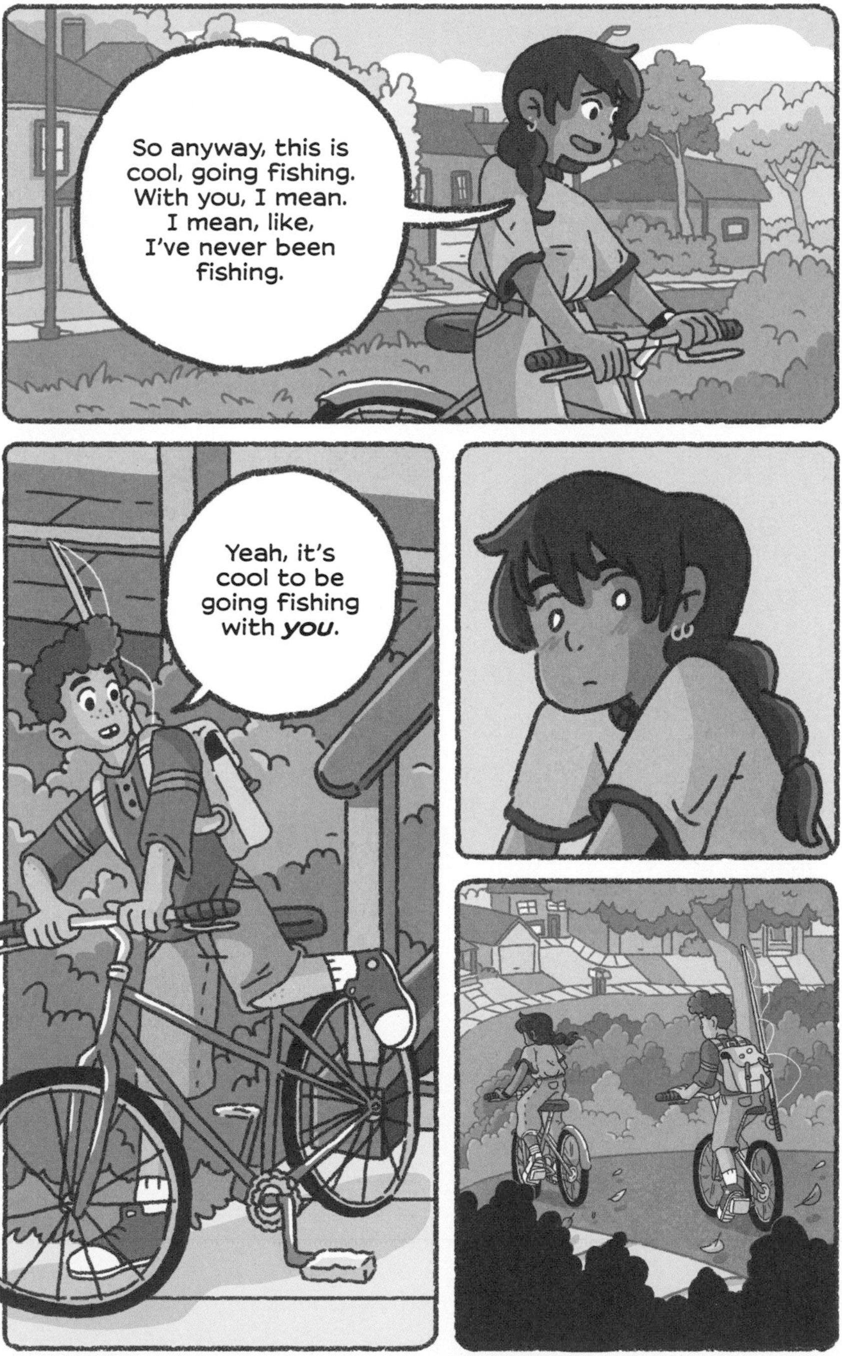
So anyway, this is cool, going fishing. With you, I mean. I mean, like, I've never been fishing.
Yeah, it's cool to be going fishing with *you*.

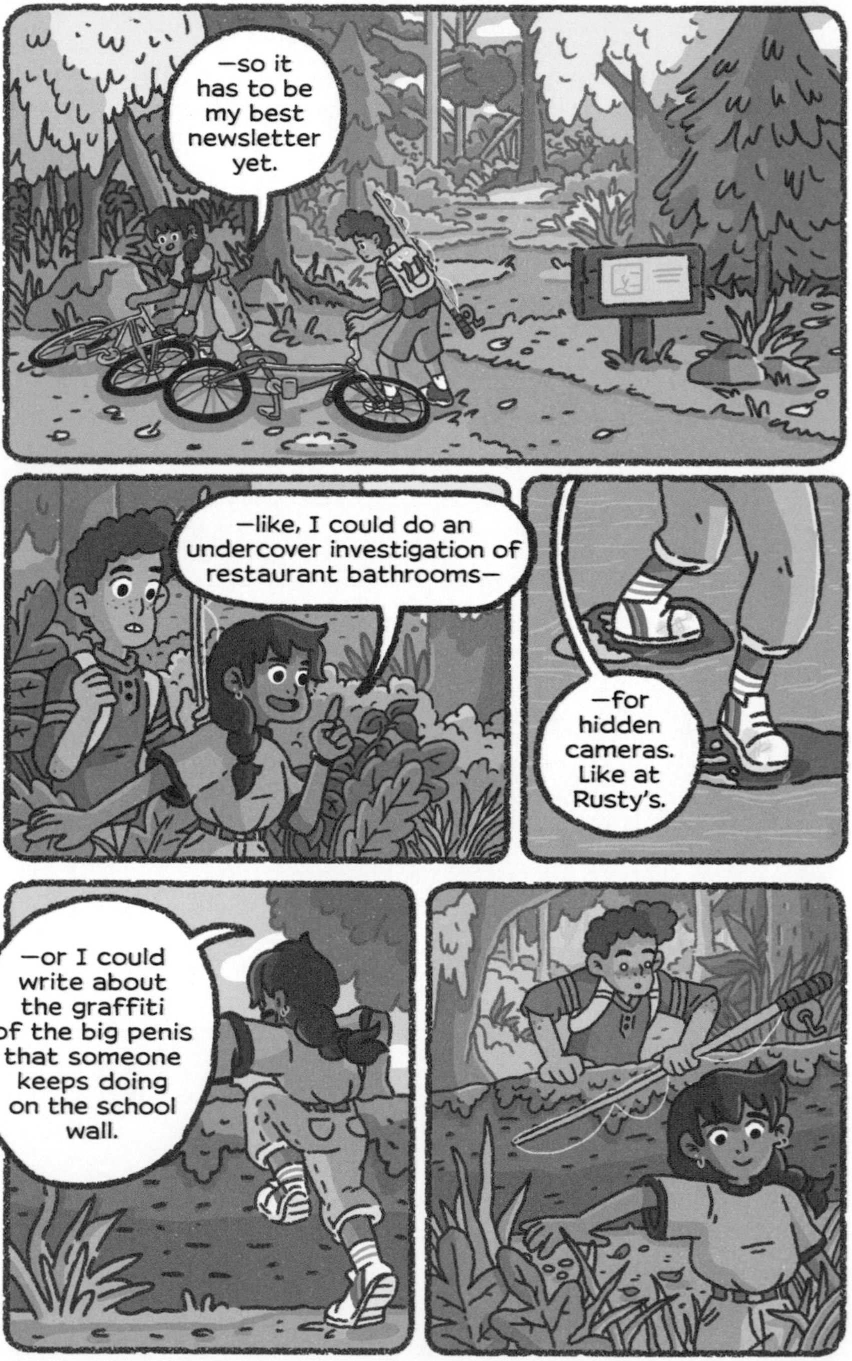
—so it has to be my best newsletter yet.
—like, I could do an undercover investigation of restaurant bathrooms—
—for hidden cameras. Like at Rusty's.
—or I could write about the graffiti of the big penis that someone keeps doing on the school wall.

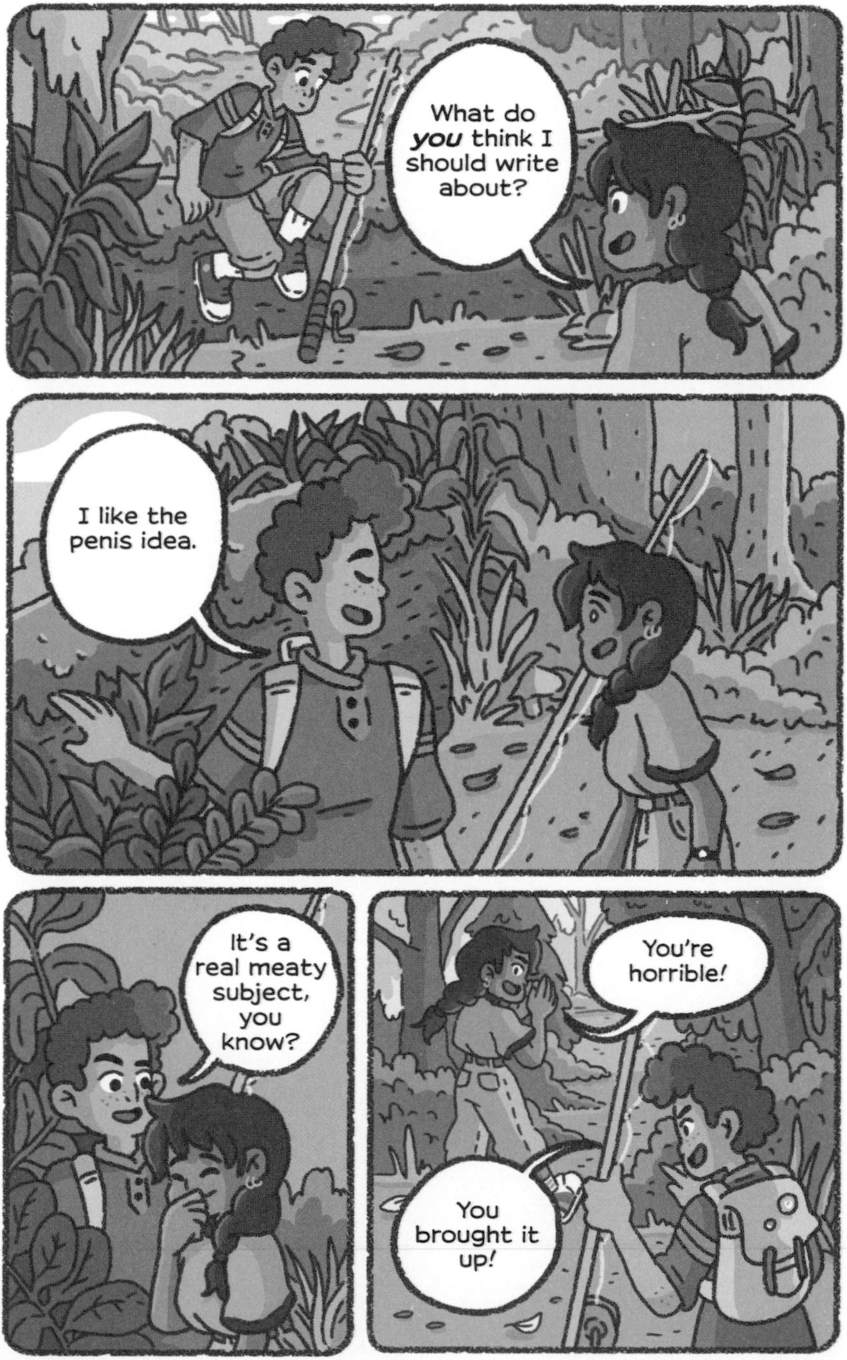
What do *you* think I should write about?
I like the penis idea.
It's a real meaty subject, you know?
You're horrible!
You brought it up!

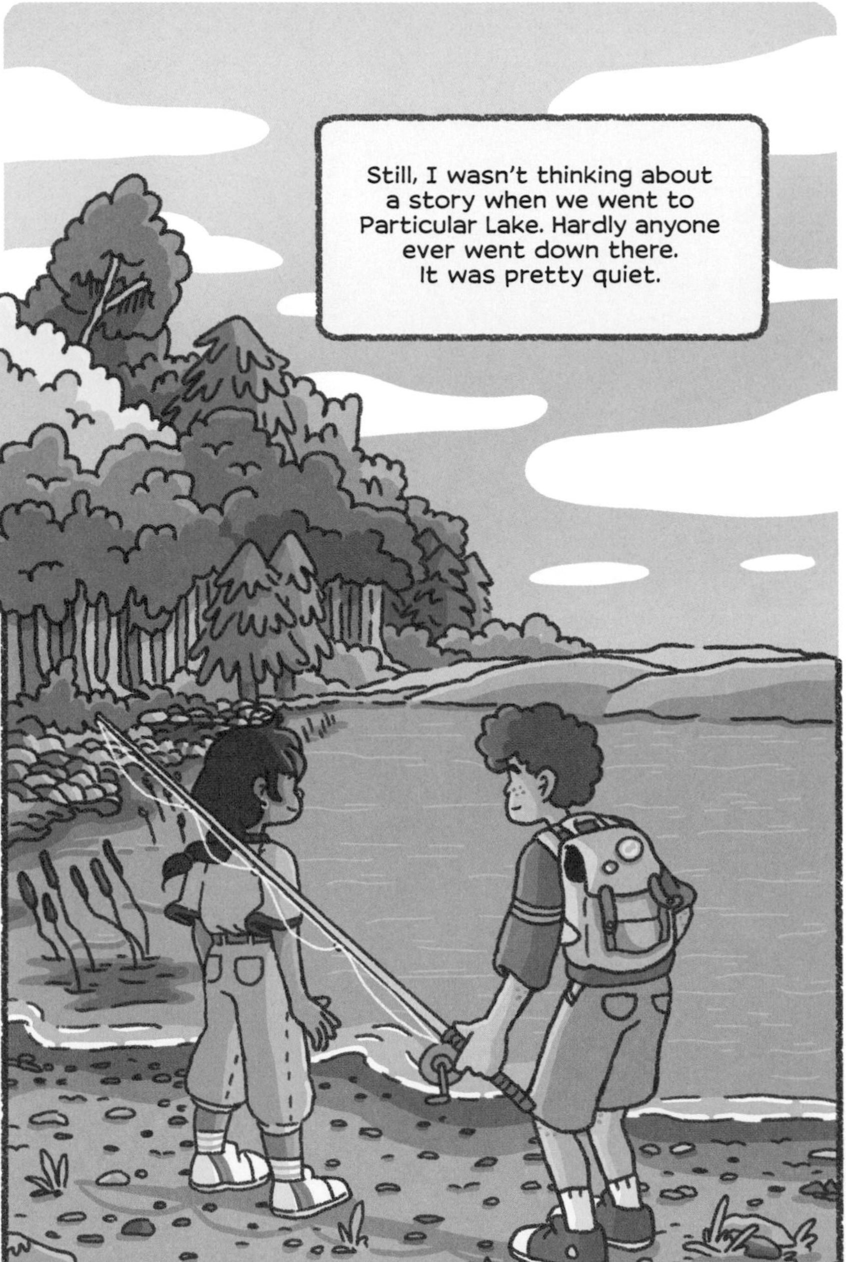
Still, I wasn't thinking about a story when we went to Particular Lake. Hardly anyone ever went down there. It was pretty quiet.

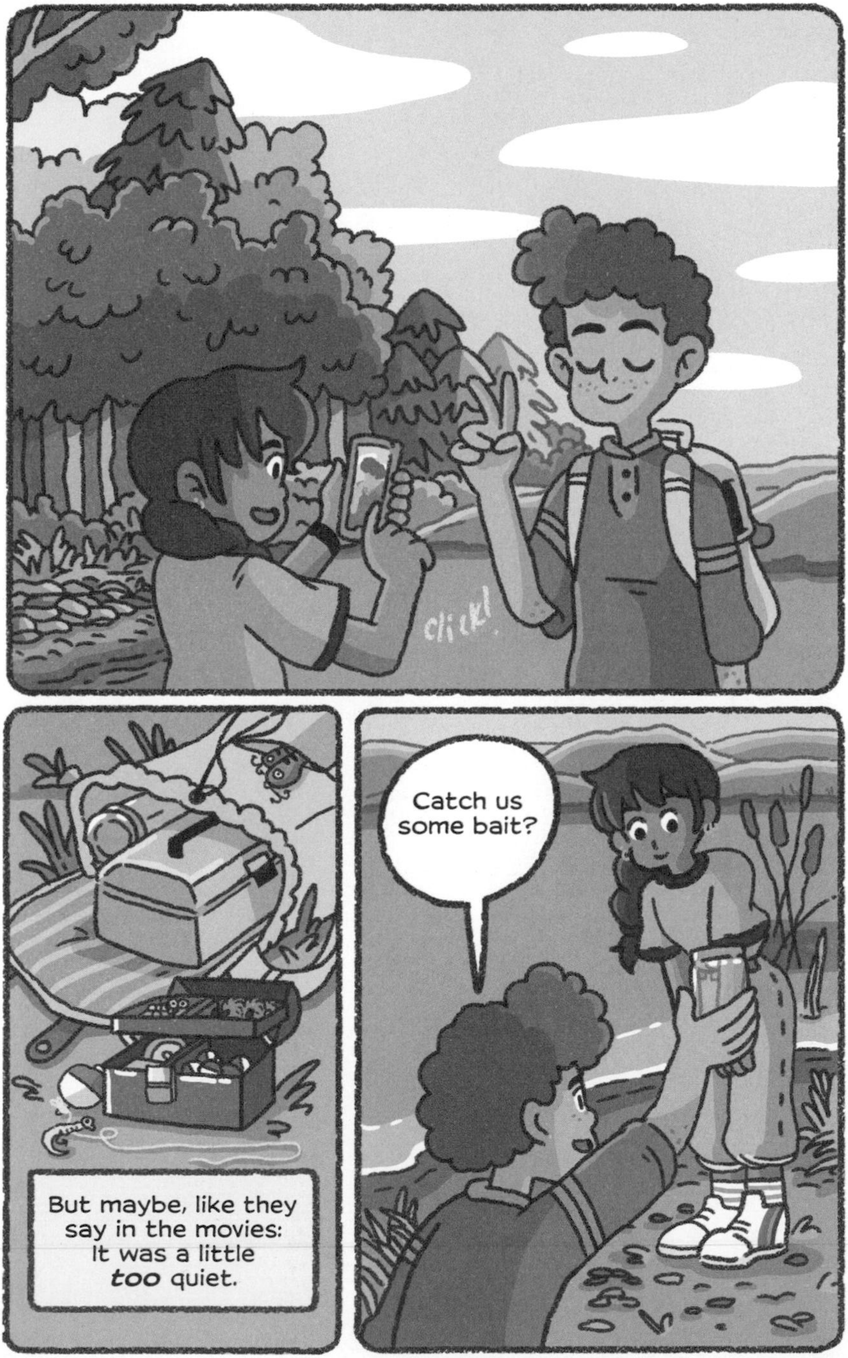
click!
But maybe, like they say in the movies: It was a little *too* quiet.
Catch us some bait?

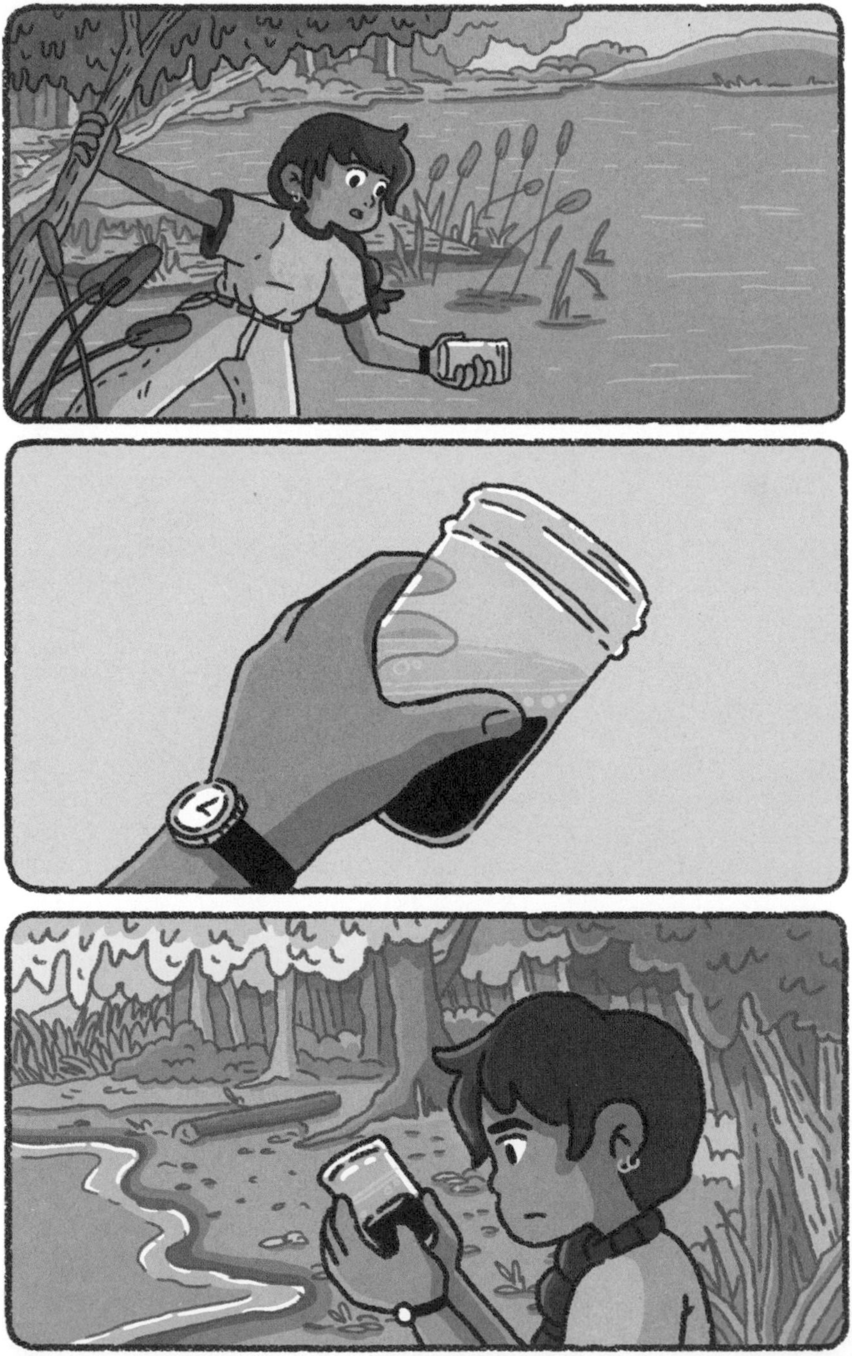

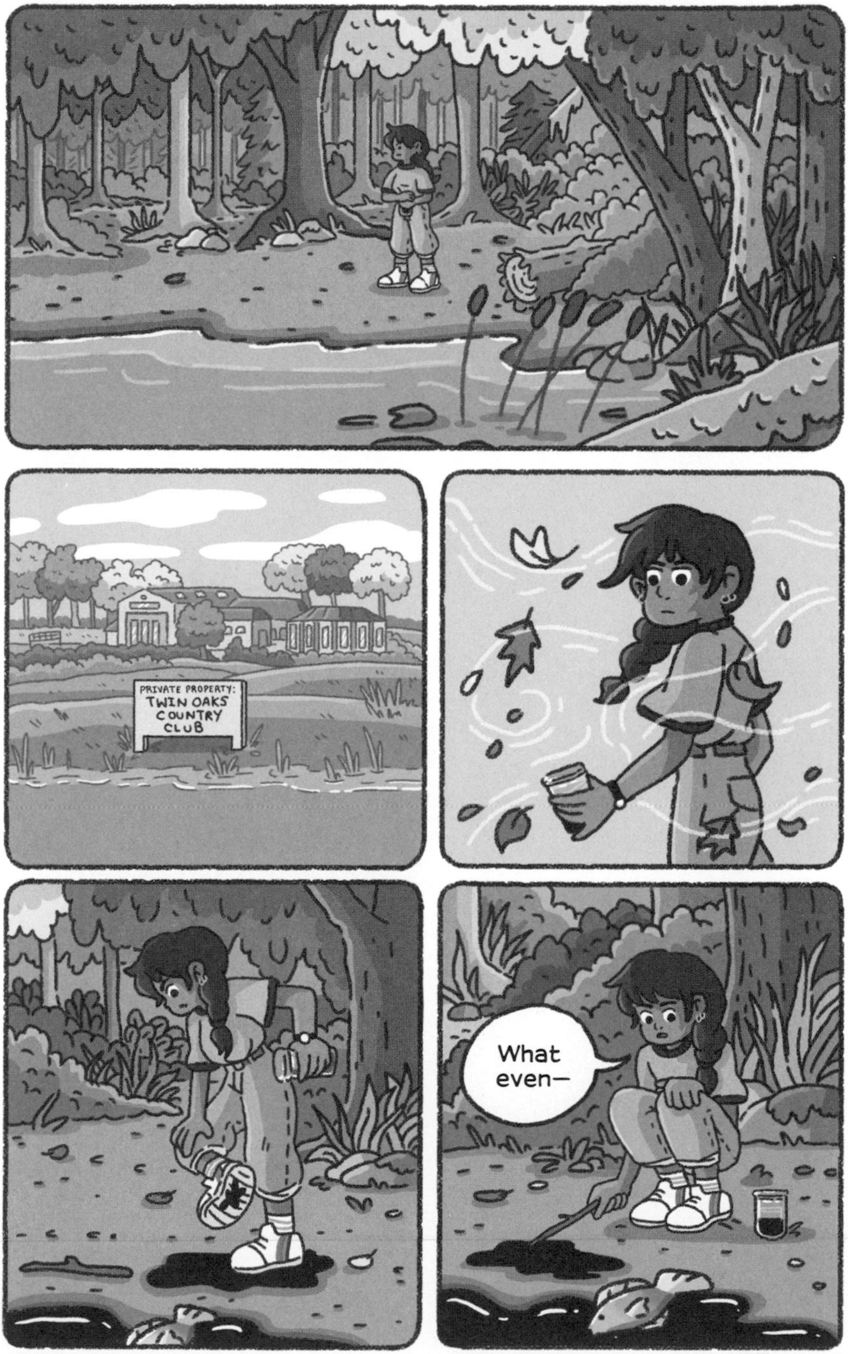
PRIVATE PROPERTY:
TWIN OAKS COUNTRY CLUB
What even—

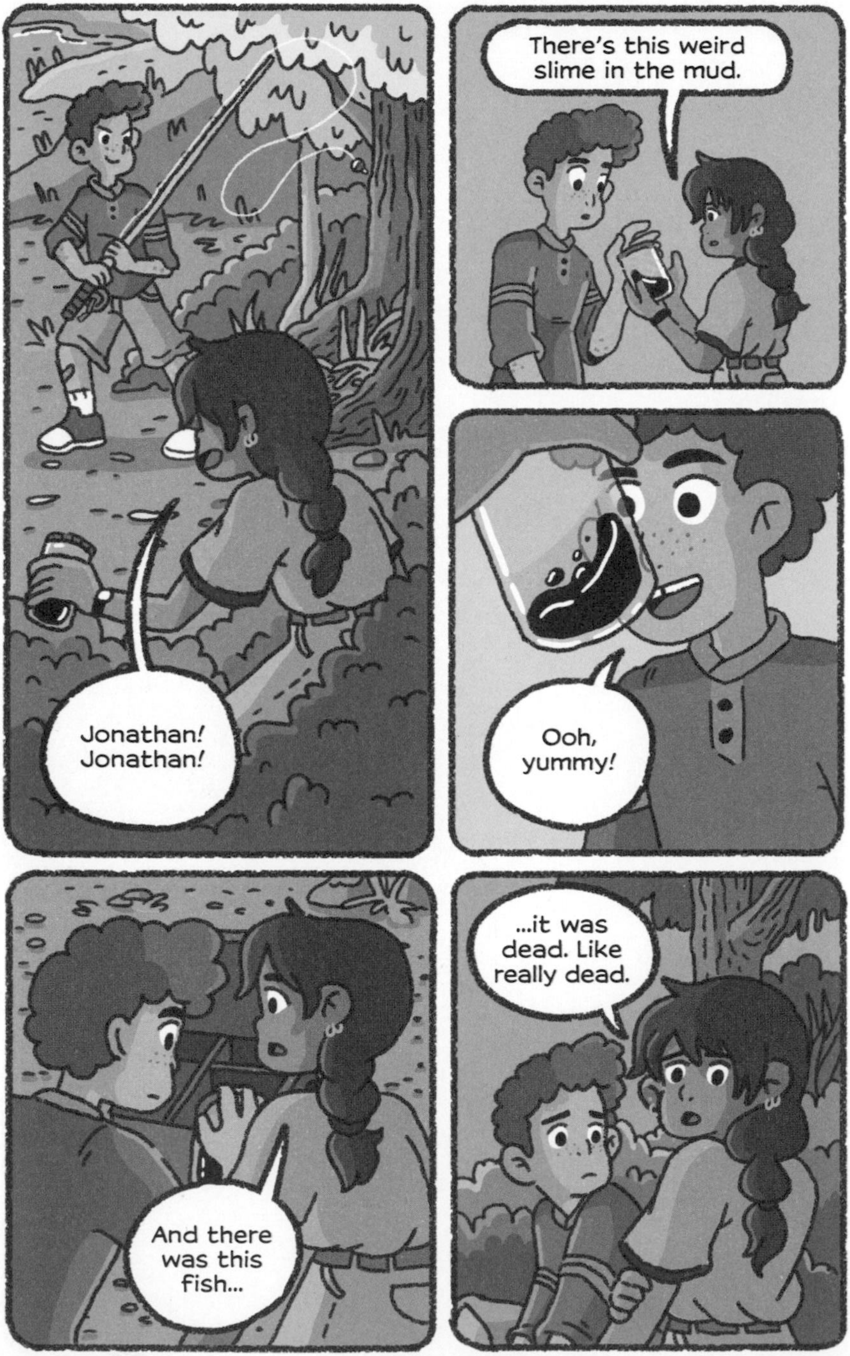
Jonathan! Jonathan!
There's this weird slime in the mud.
Ooh, yummy!
And there was this fish...
...it was dead. Like really dead.

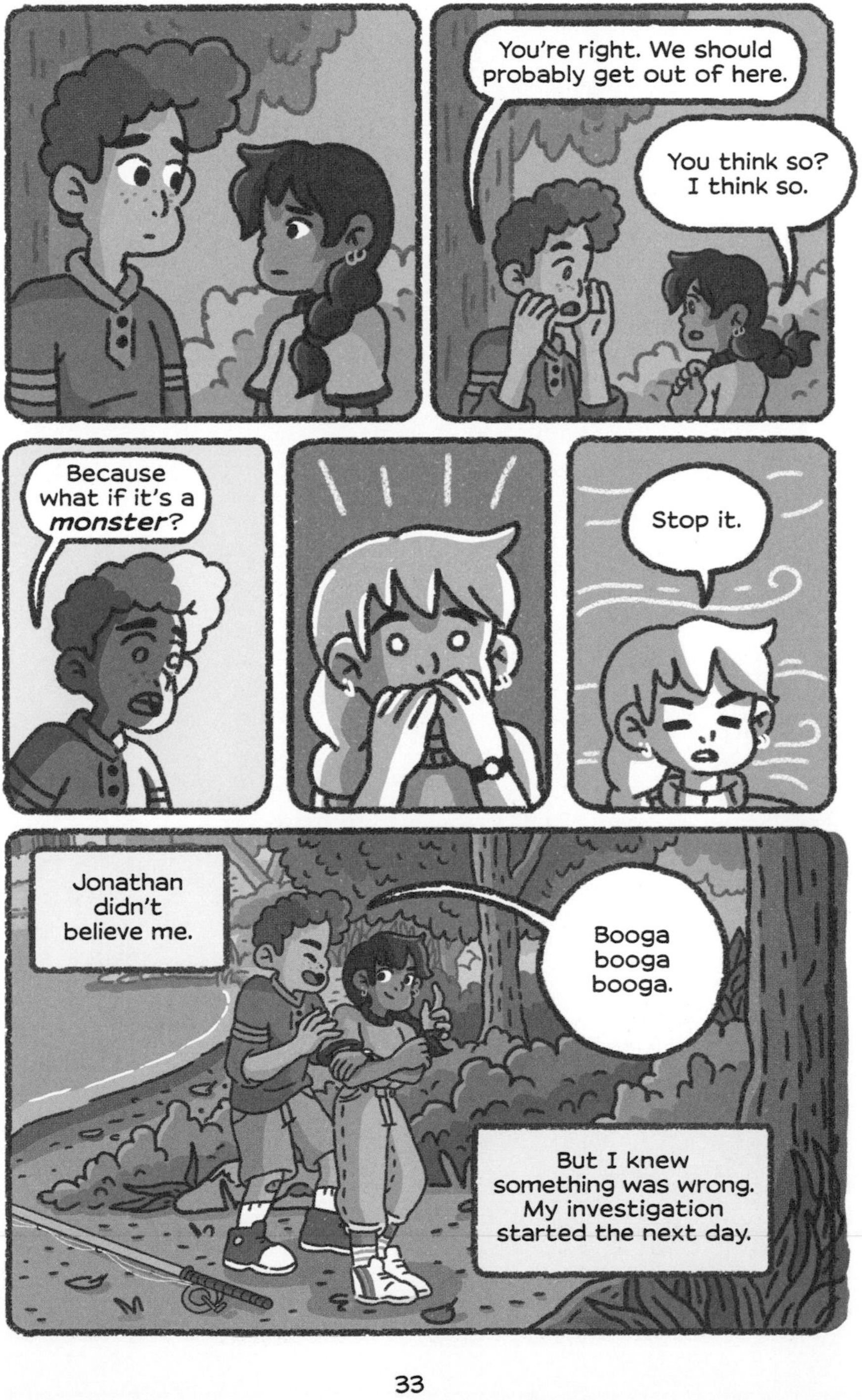
You're right. We should probably get out of here.
You think so? I think so.
Because what if it's a *monster*?
Stop it.
Jonathan didn't believe me.
Booga booga booga.
But I knew something was wrong. My investigation started the next day.

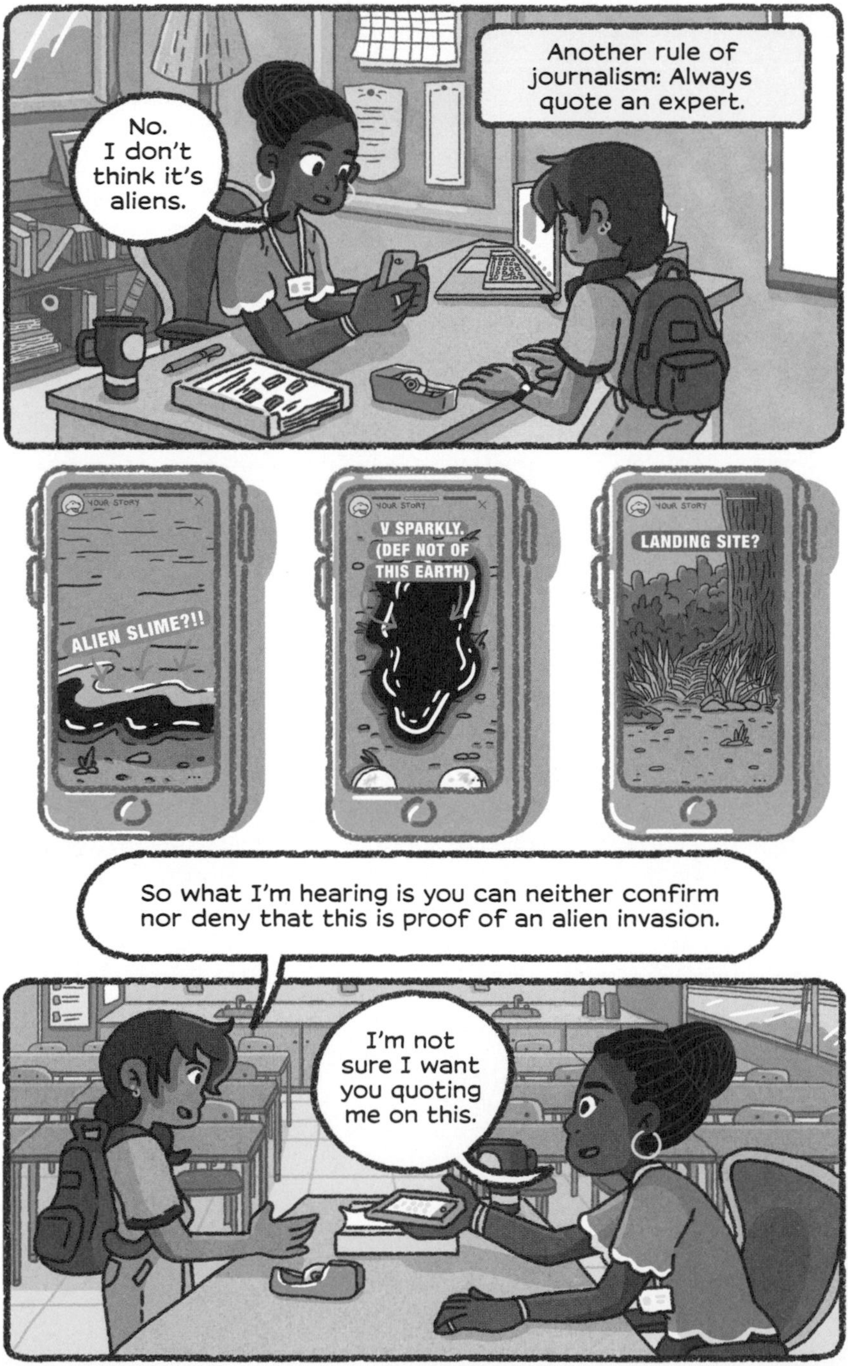
No. I don't think it's aliens.
Another rule of journalism: Always quote an expert.
YOUR STORY
ALIEN SLIME?!!
YOUR STORY
V SPARKLY. (DEF NOT OF THIS EARTH)
YOUR STORY
LANDING SITE?
So what I'm hearing is you can neither confirm nor deny that this is proof of an alien invasion.
I'm not sure I want you quoting me on this.

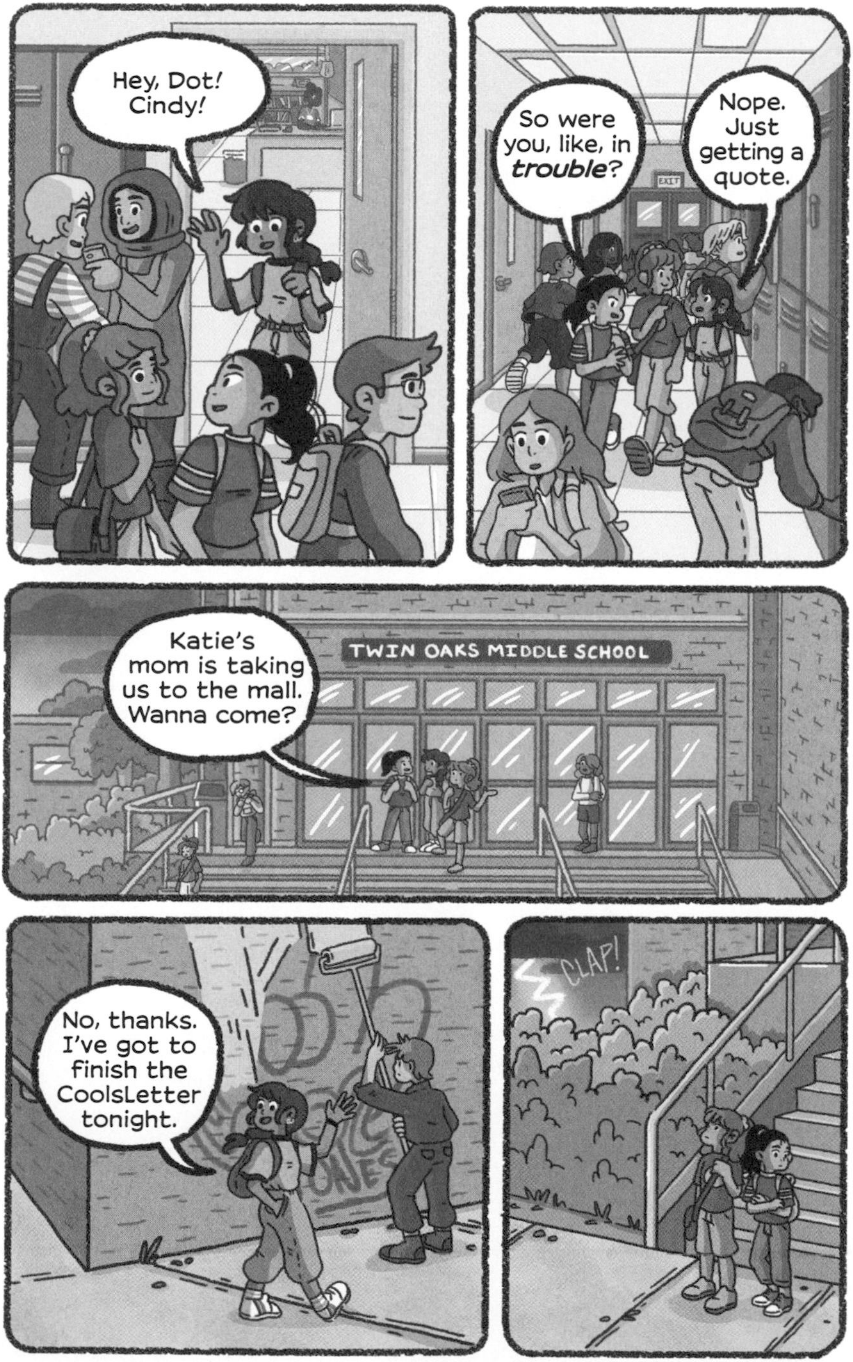
Hey, Dot! Cindy!
So were you, like, in *trouble*?
Nope. Just getting a quote.
TWIN OAKS MIDDLE SCHOOL
Katie's mom is taking us to the mall. Wanna come?
No, thanks. I've got to finish the CoolsLetter tonight.
CLAP!

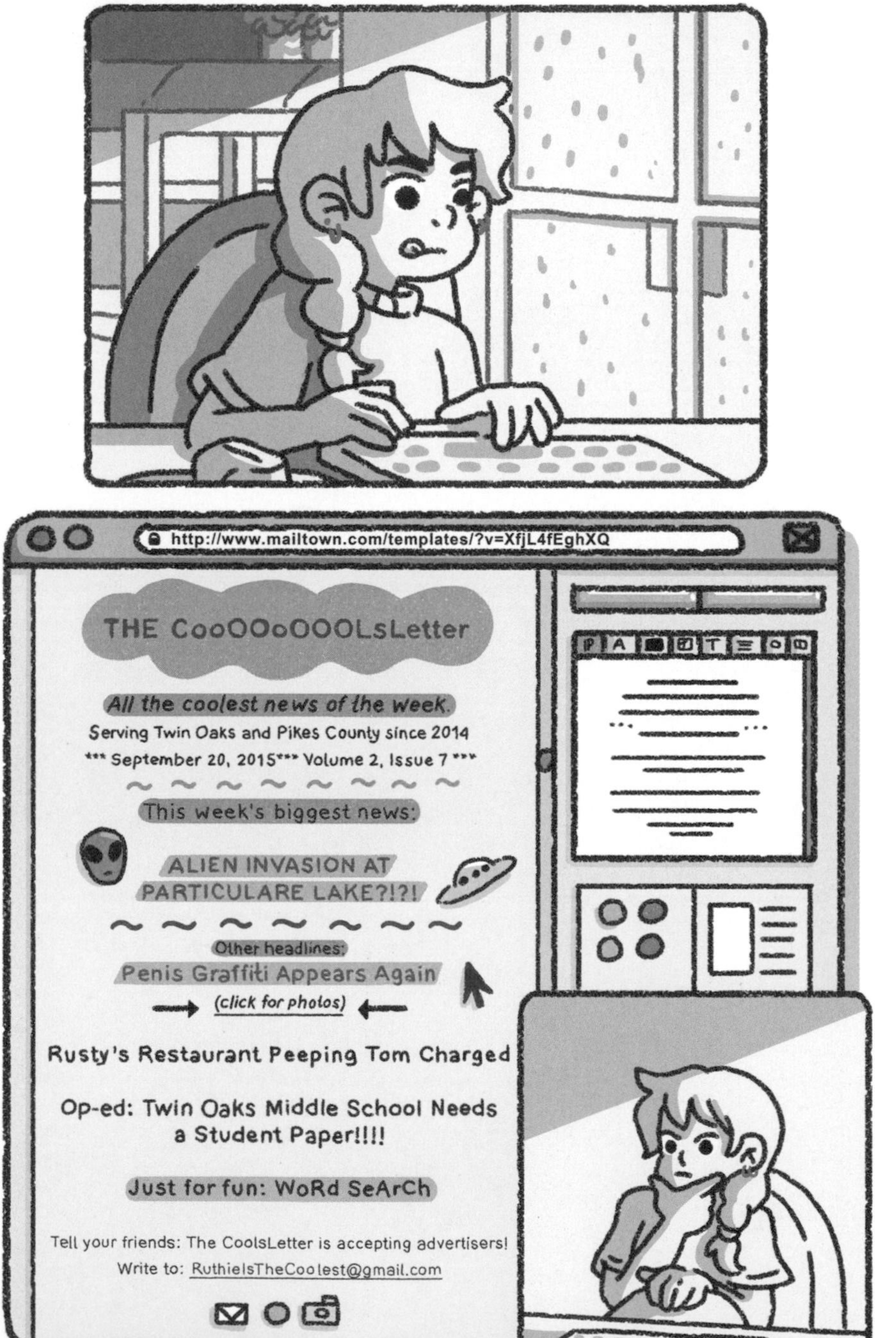

http://www.mailtown.com/templates/?v=XfjL4fEghXQ
THE CooOOoOOOLsLetter
All the coolest news of the week.
Serving Twin Oaks and Pikes County since 2014
*** September 20, 2015*** Volume 2, Issue 7 ***
This week's biggest news:
ALIEN INVASION AT PARTICULARE LAKE?!?!
Other headlines:
Penis Graffiti Appears Again
(click for photos)
Rusty's Restaurant Peeping Tom Charged
Op-ed: Twin Oaks Middle School Needs a Student Paper!!!!
Just for fun: WoRd SeArCh
Tell your friends: The CoolsLetter is accepting advertisers!
Write to: RuthieIsTheCoolest@gmail.com

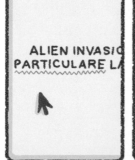

ALIEN INVASIC
PARTICULARE L

ULAR|L

Okay.

SEND ✉

CLICK!

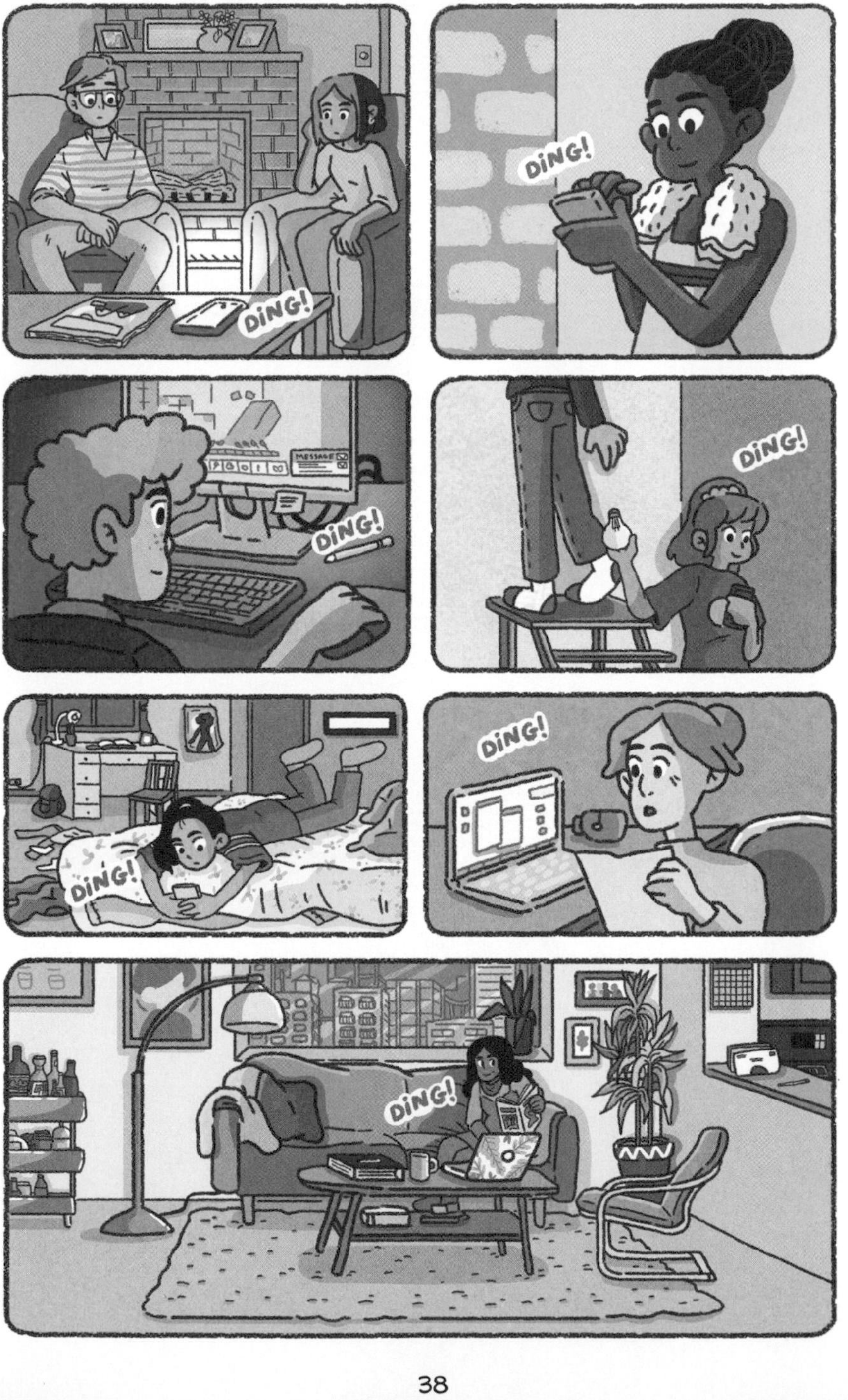
DING!
DING!
MESSAGE
DING!
DING!
DING!
DING!
DING!

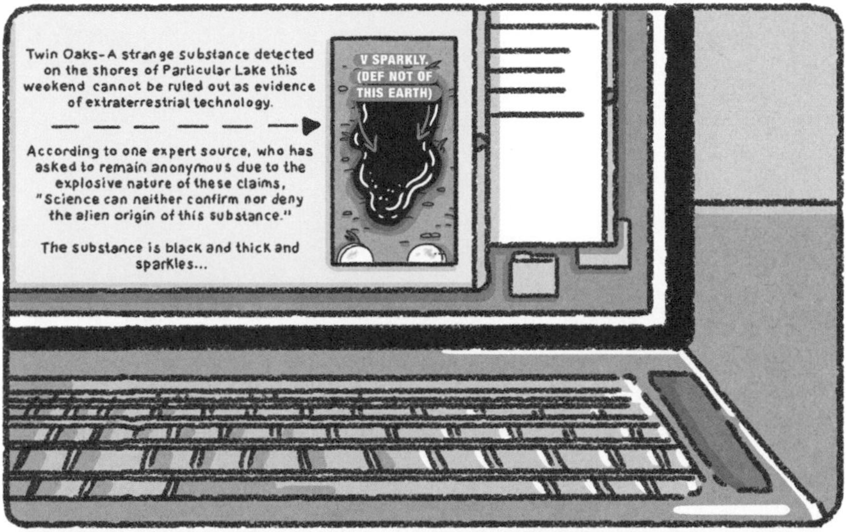
Twin Oaks- A strange substance detected on the shores of Particular Lake this weekend cannot be ruled out as evidence of extraterrestrial technology.
According to one expert source, who has asked to remain anonymous due to the explosive nature of these claims, "Science can neither confirm nor deny the alien origin of this substance."
The substance is black and thick and sparkles...
V SPARKLY. (DEF NOT OF THIS EARTH)

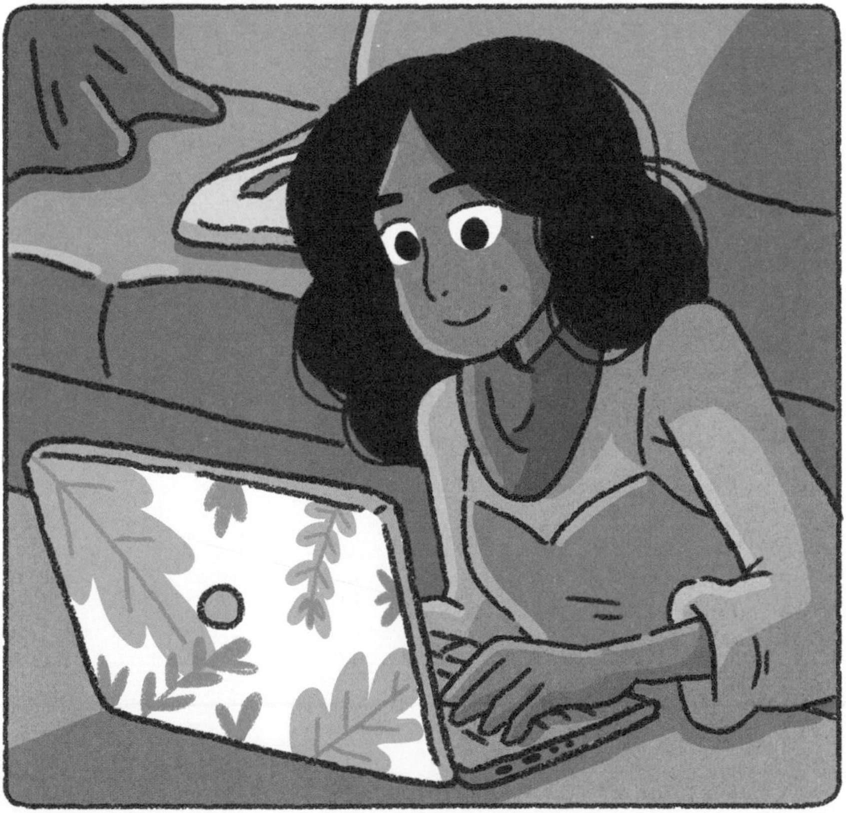

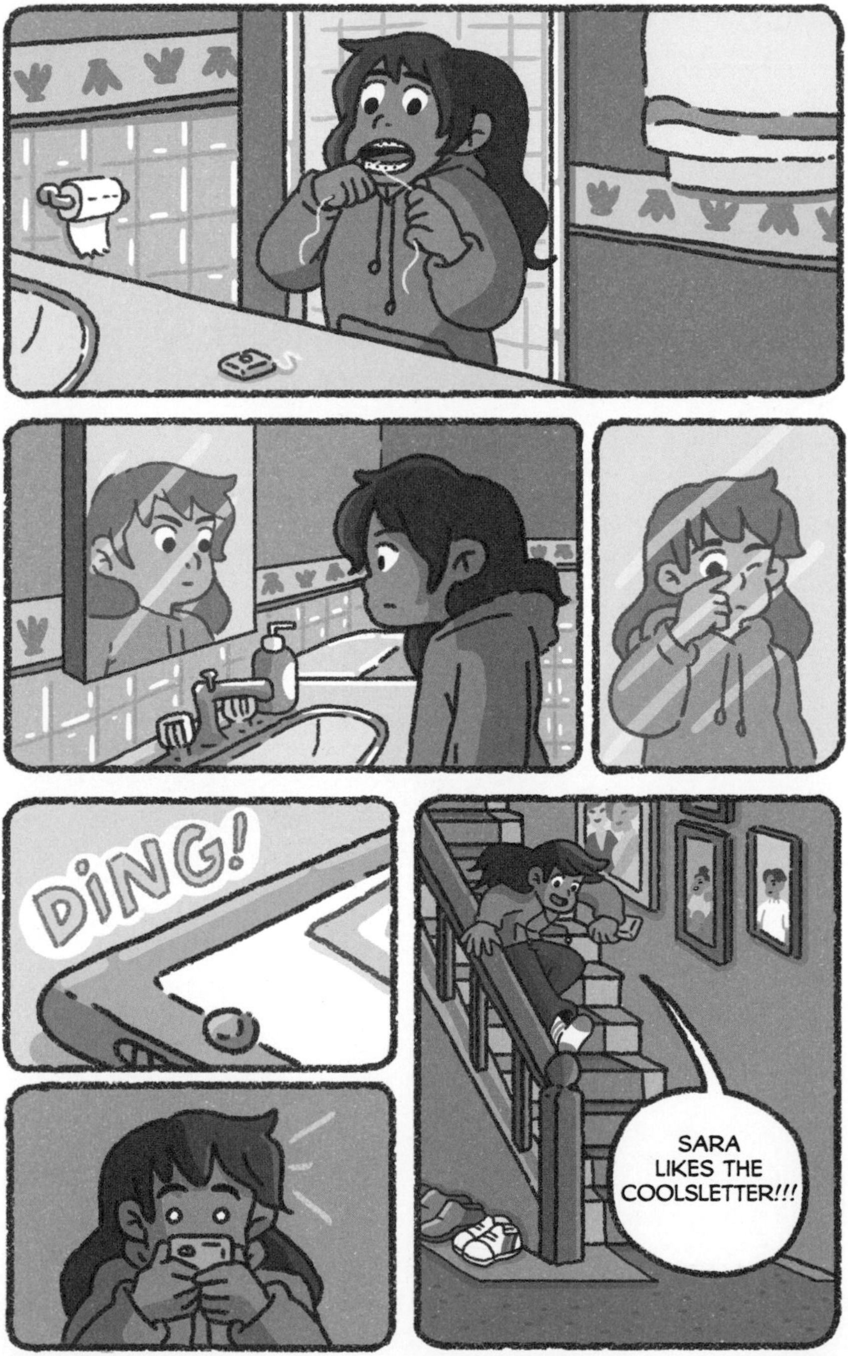
DING!
SARA
LIKES THE
COOLSLETTER!!!

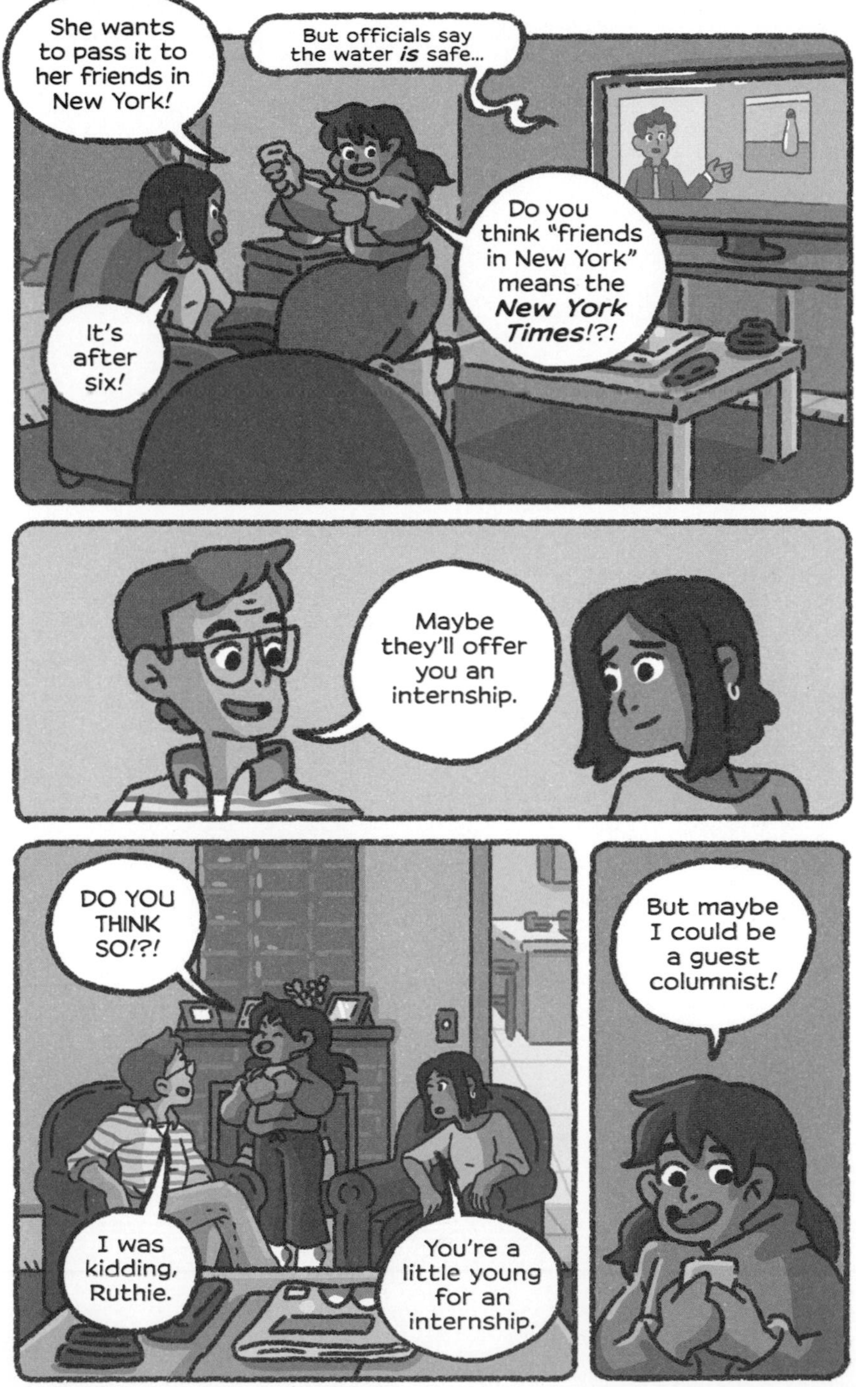
She wants to pass it to her friends in New York!
But officials say the water *is* safe...
Do you think "friends in New York" means the ***New York Times***!?!
It's after six!
Maybe they'll offer you an internship.
DO YOU THINK SO!?!
I was kidding, Ruthie.
You're a little young for an internship.
But maybe I could be a guest columnist!

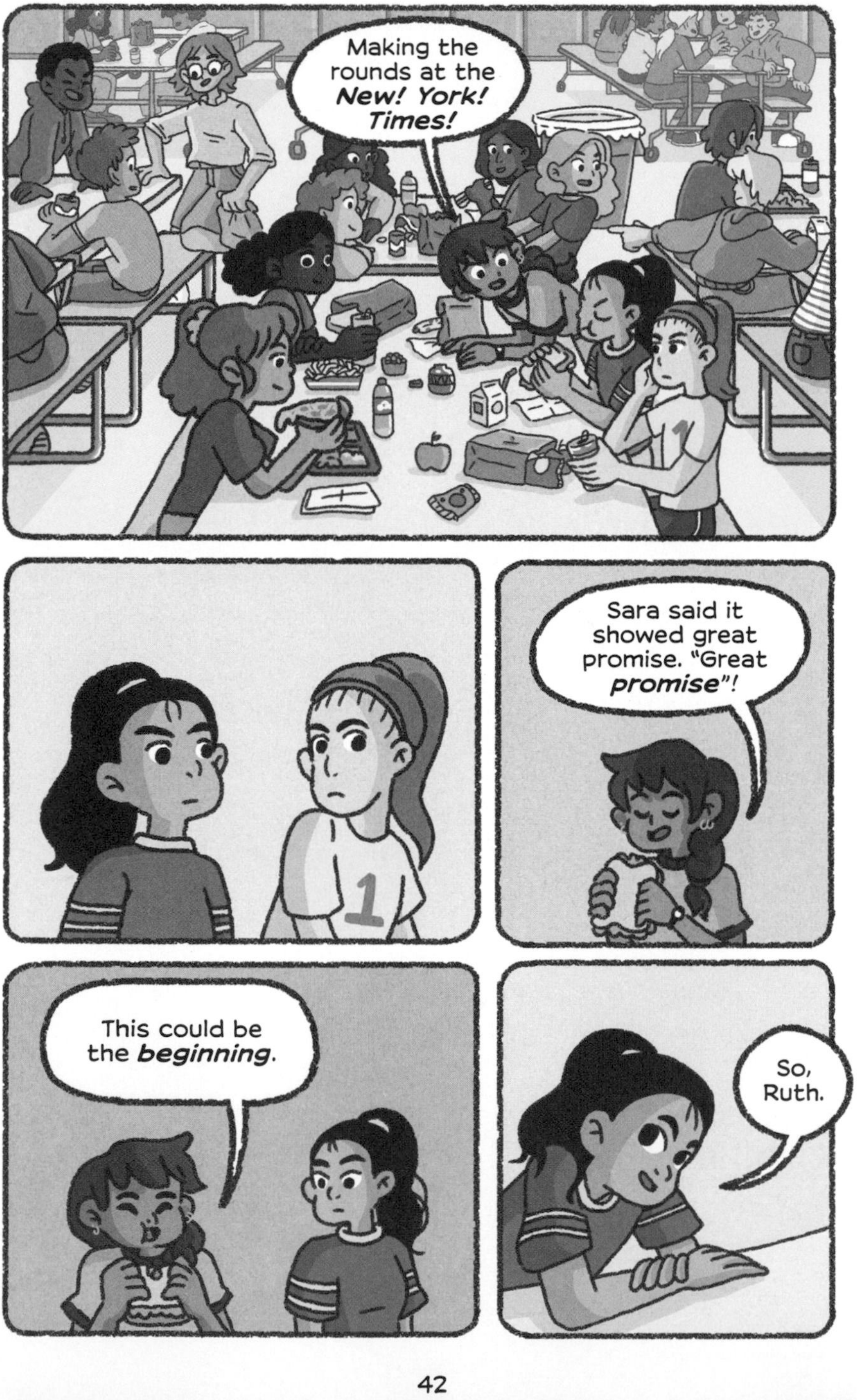
Making the rounds at the ***New! York! Times!***
Sara said it showed great promise. "Great ***promise***"!
This could be the ***beginning***.
So, Ruth.

CHAPTER 2

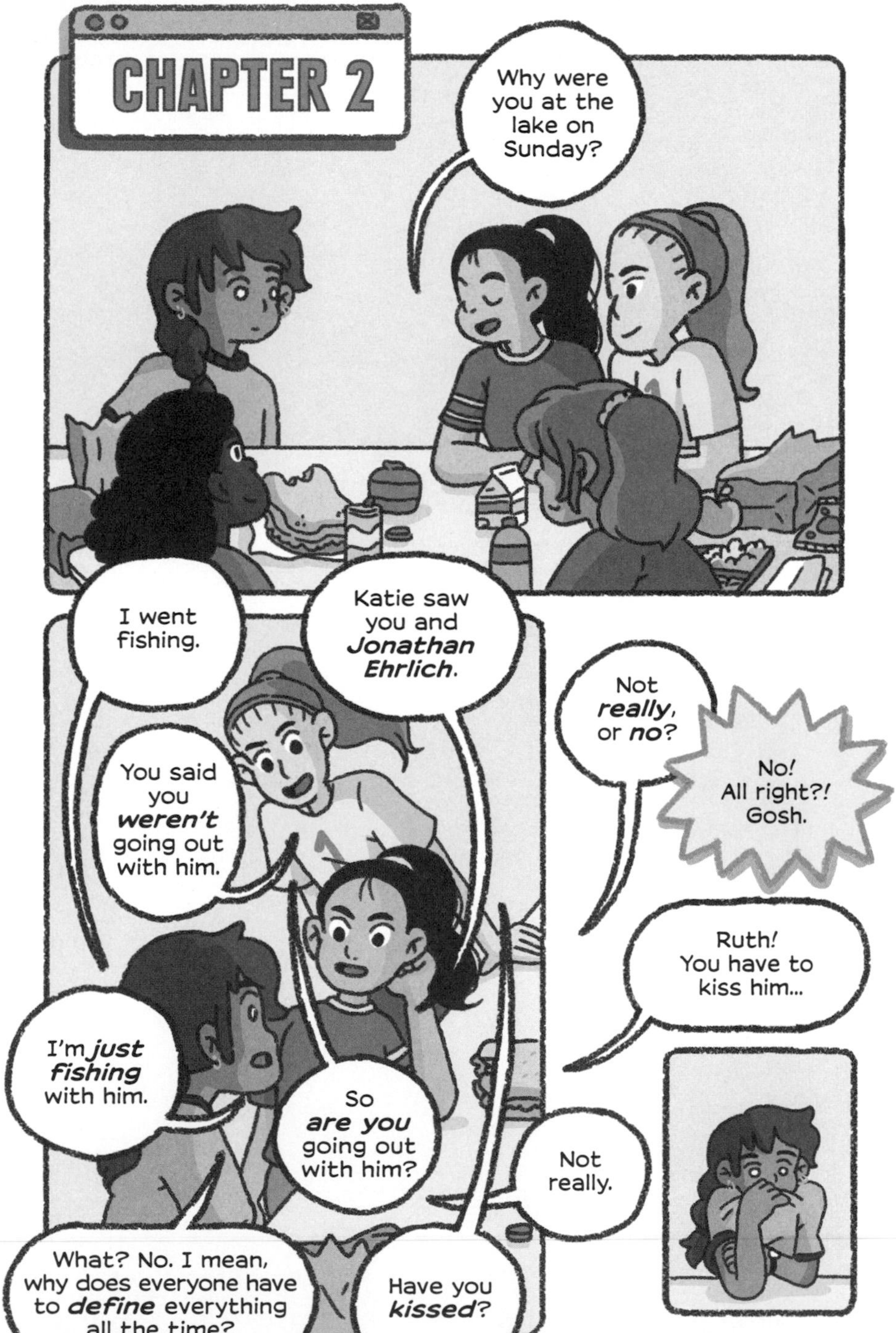
Why were you at the lake on Sunday?
I went fishing.
Katie saw you and *Jonathan Ehrlich*.
You said you *weren't* going out with him.
I'm *just fishing* with him.
So *are you* going out with him?
Not really.
Not *really*, or *no*?
No! All right?! Gosh.
Ruth! You have to kiss him...
What? No. I mean, why does everyone have to *define* everything all the time?
Have you *kissed*?

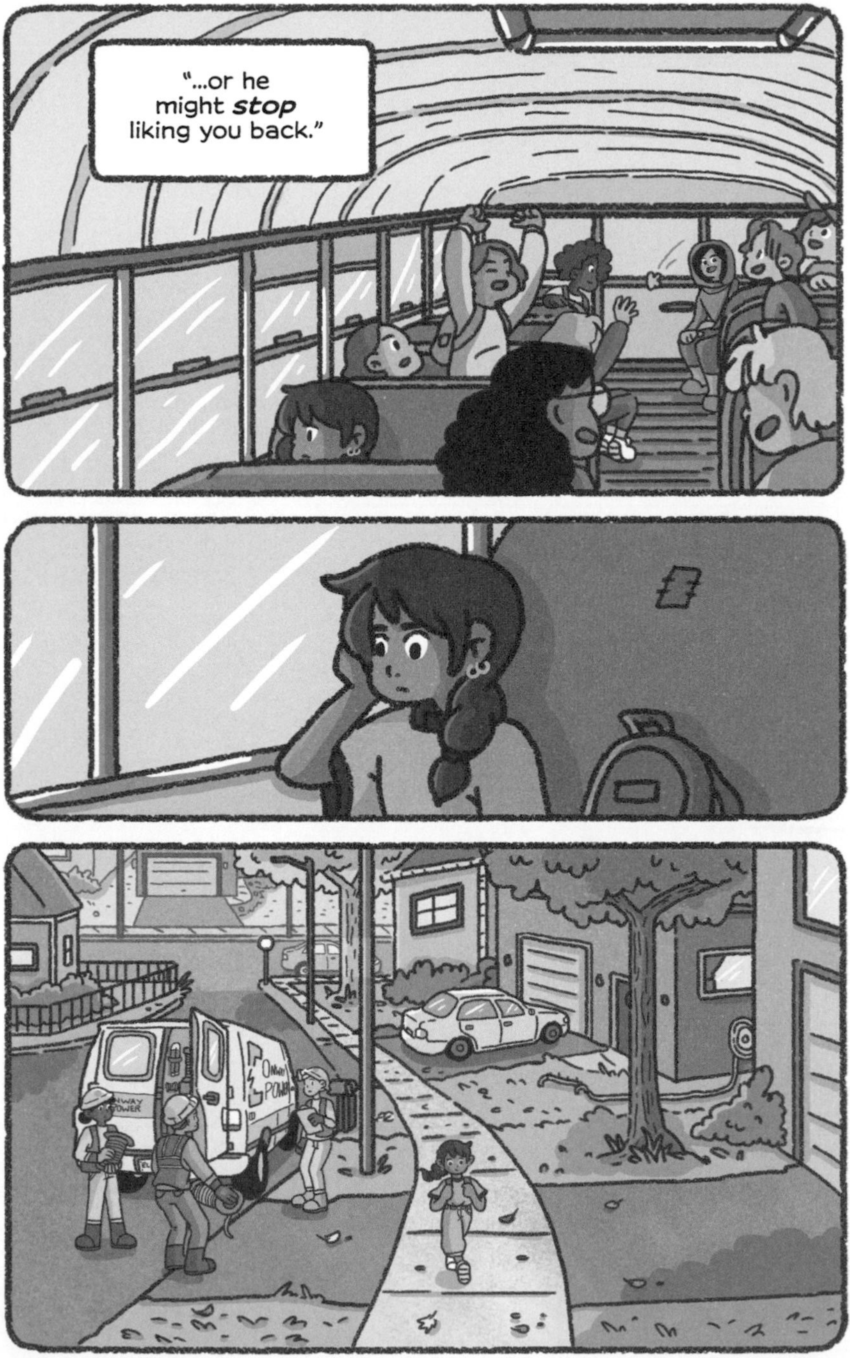
"...or he might *stop* liking you back."

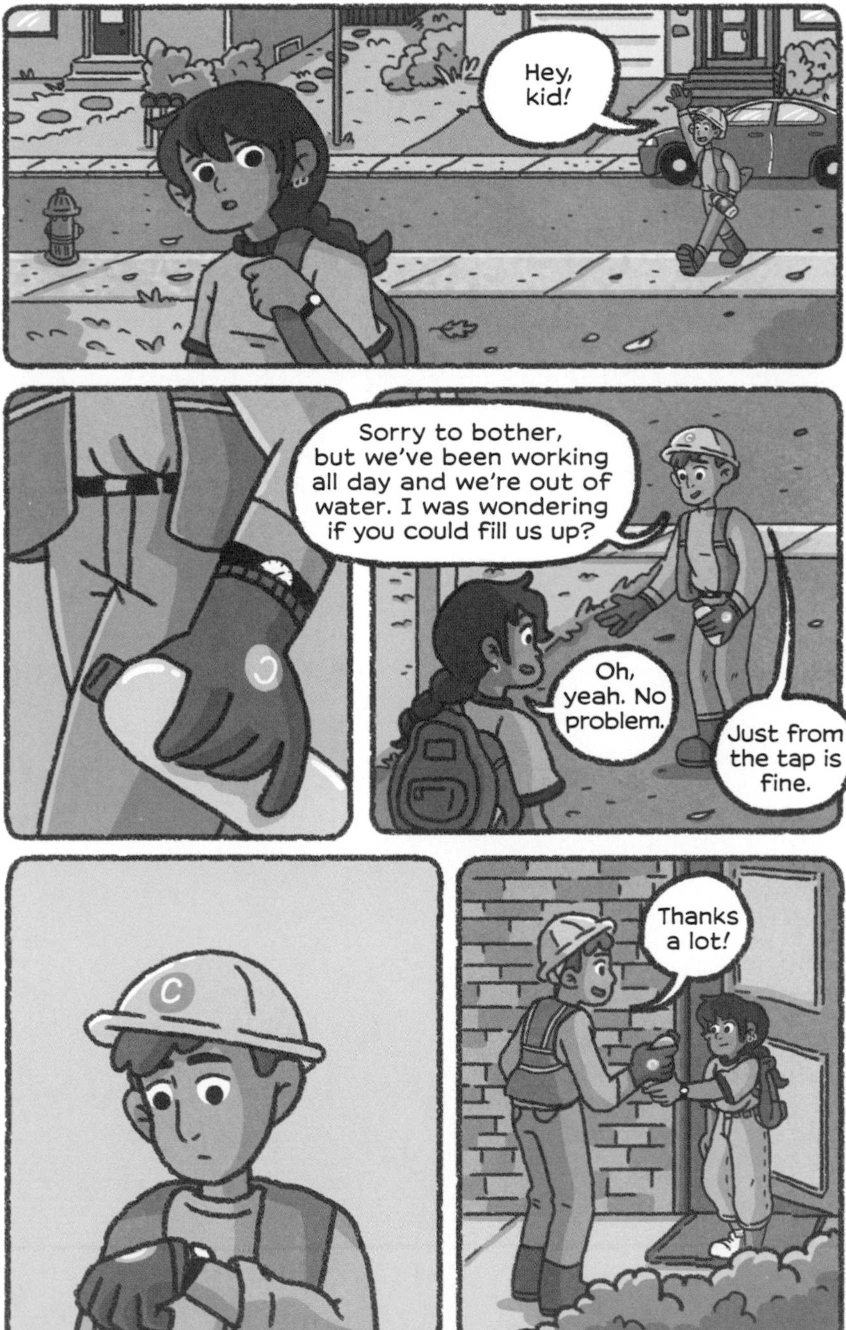
Hey, kid!
Sorry to bother, but we've been working all day and we're out of water. I was wondering if you could fill us up?
Oh, yeah. No problem.
Just from the tap is fine.
Thanks a lot!

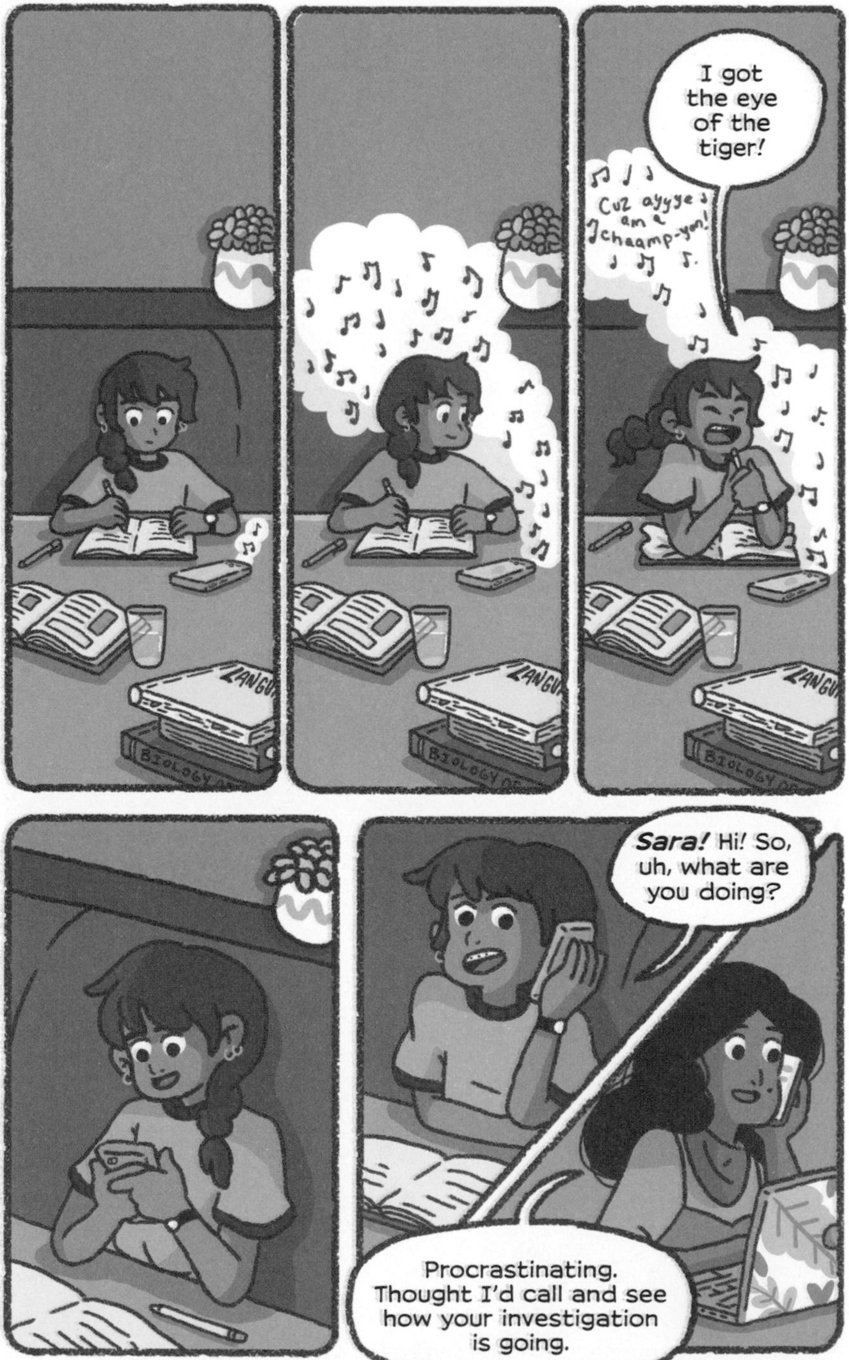
I got the eye of the tiger!
Cuz ayyye am a chaamp-yon!
BIOLOGY
Sara! Hi! So, uh, what are you doing?
Procrastinating. Thought I'd call and see how your investigation is going.

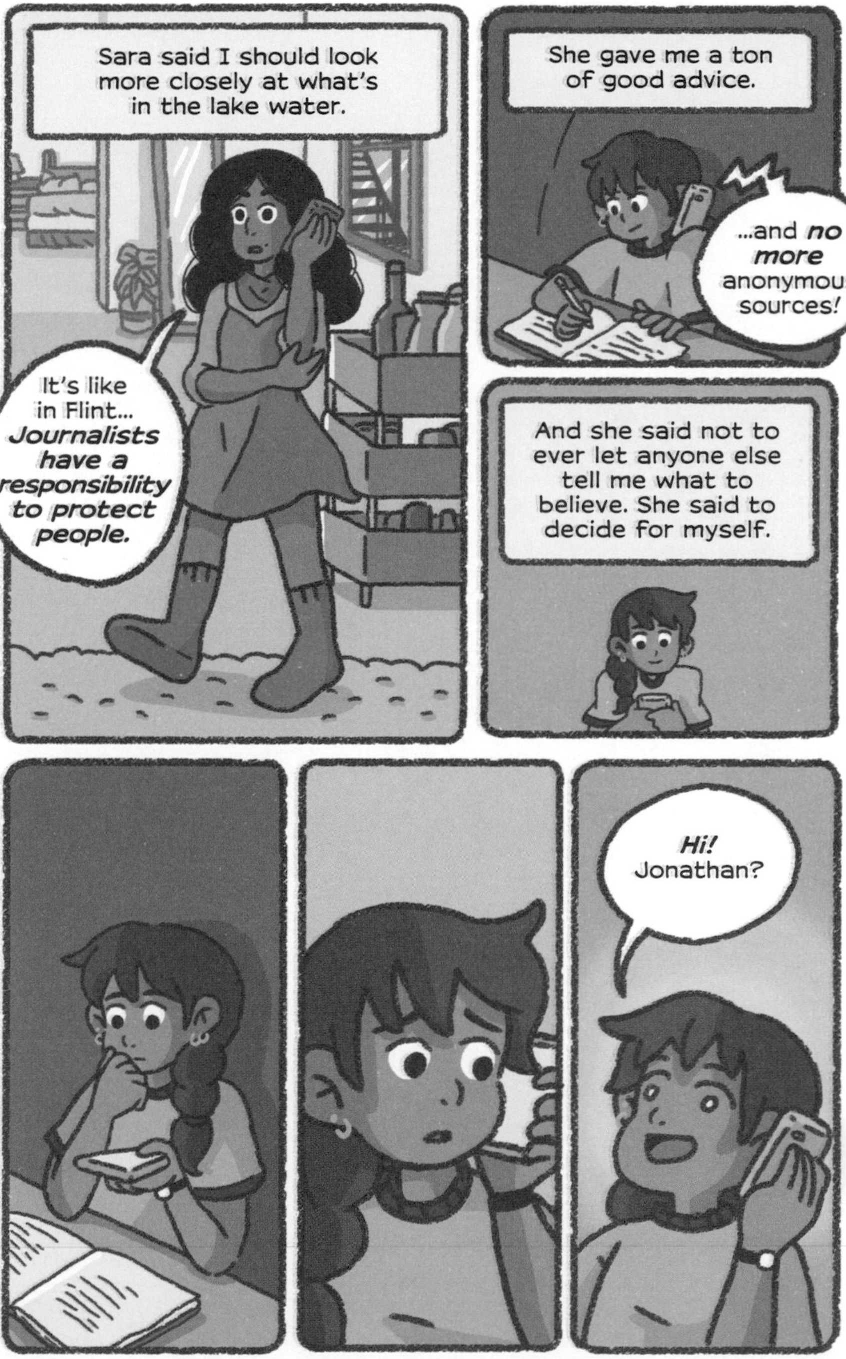
Sara said I should look more closely at what's in the lake water.
It's like in Flint... *Journalists have a responsibility to protect people.*
She gave me a ton of good advice.
...and ***no more*** anonymous sources!
And she said not to ever let anyone else tell me what to believe. She said to decide for myself.
Hi! Jonathan?

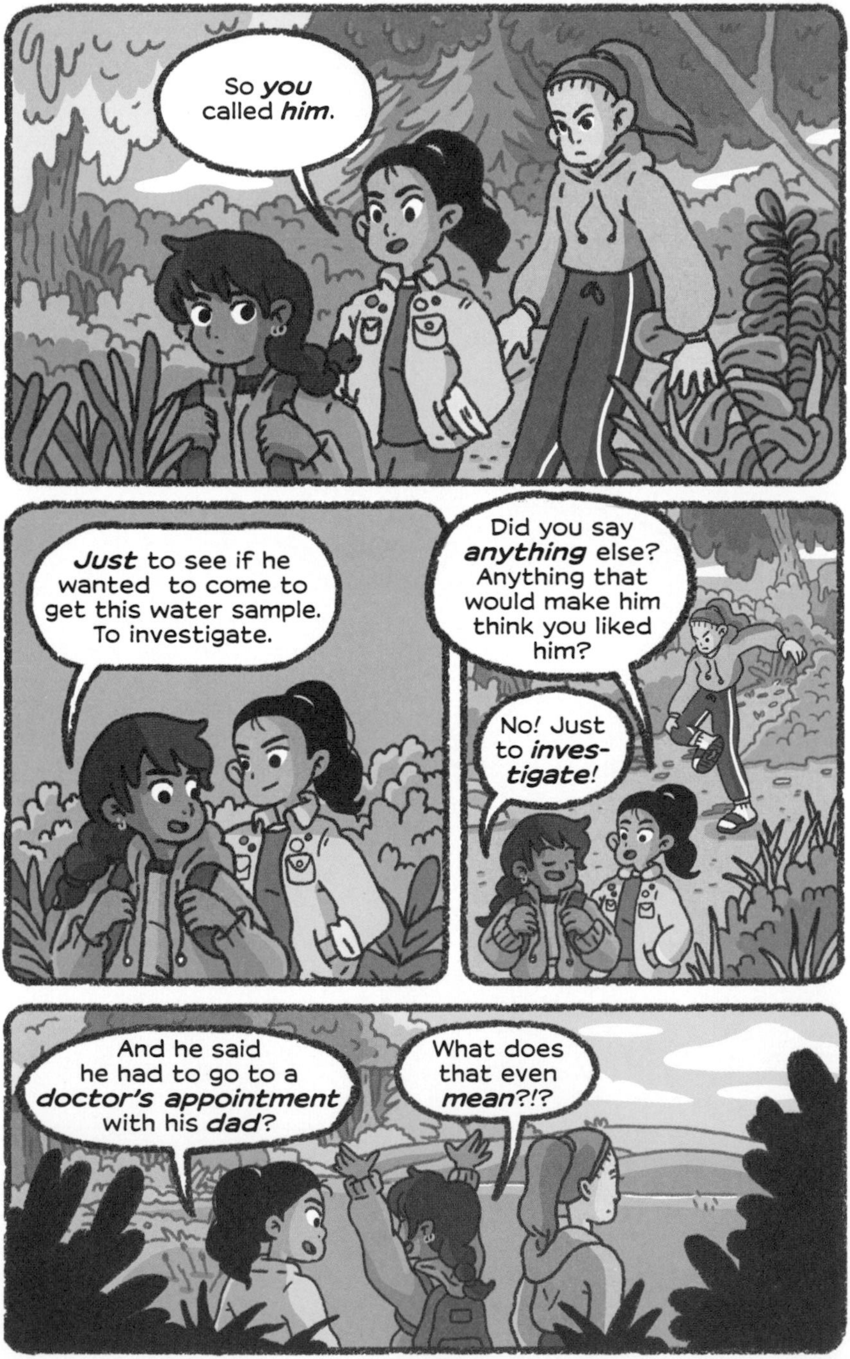
So *you* called *him*.
Just to see if he wanted to come to get this water sample. To investigate.
Did you say *anything* else? Anything that would make him think you liked him?
No! Just to *inves-tigate*!
And he said he had to go to a *doctor's appointment* with his *dad*?
What does that even *mean*?!?

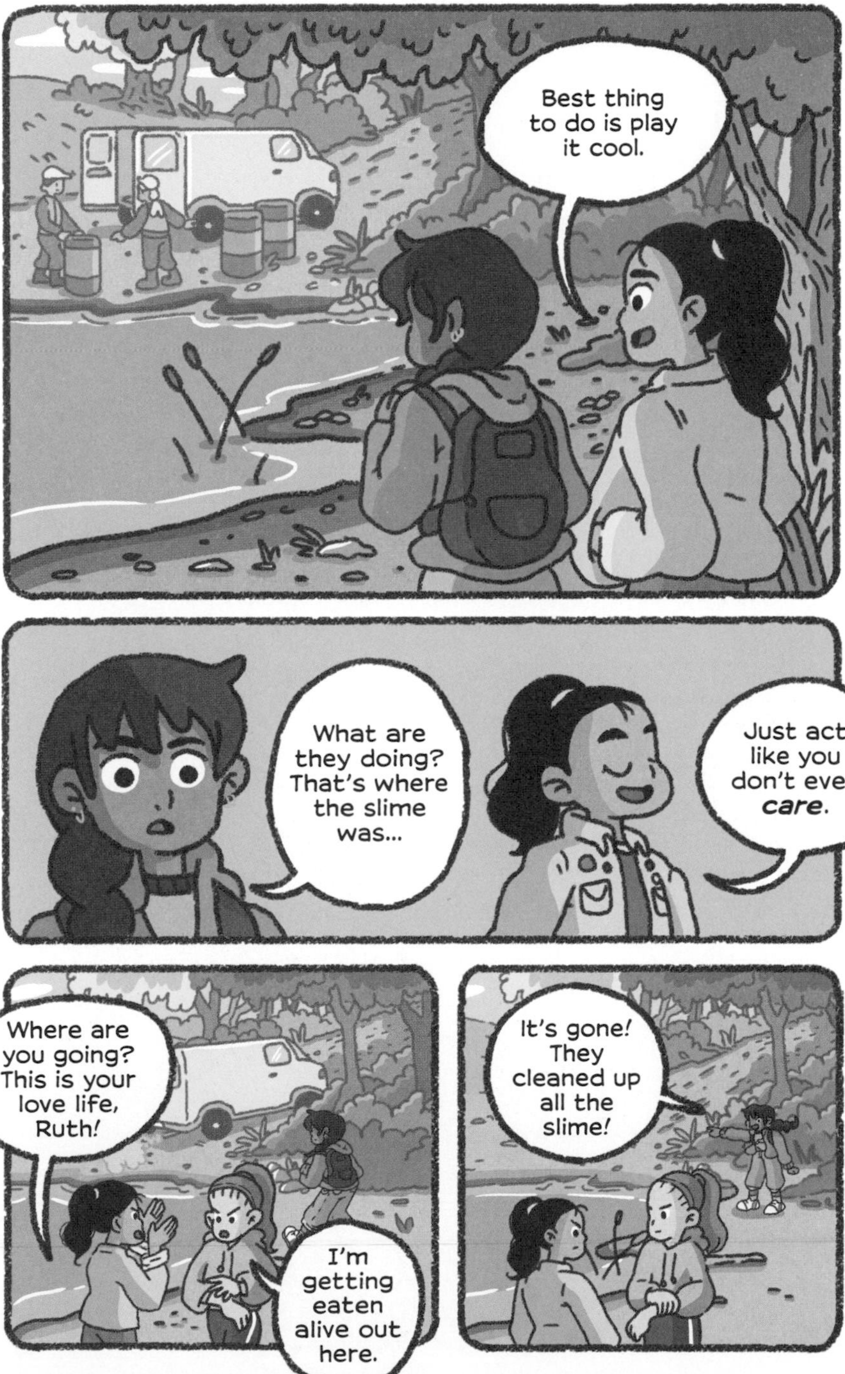
Best thing to do is play it cool.
What are they doing? That's where the slime was...
Just act like you don't even *care*.
Where are you going? This is your love life, Ruth!
I'm getting eaten alive out here.
It's gone! They cleaned up all the slime!

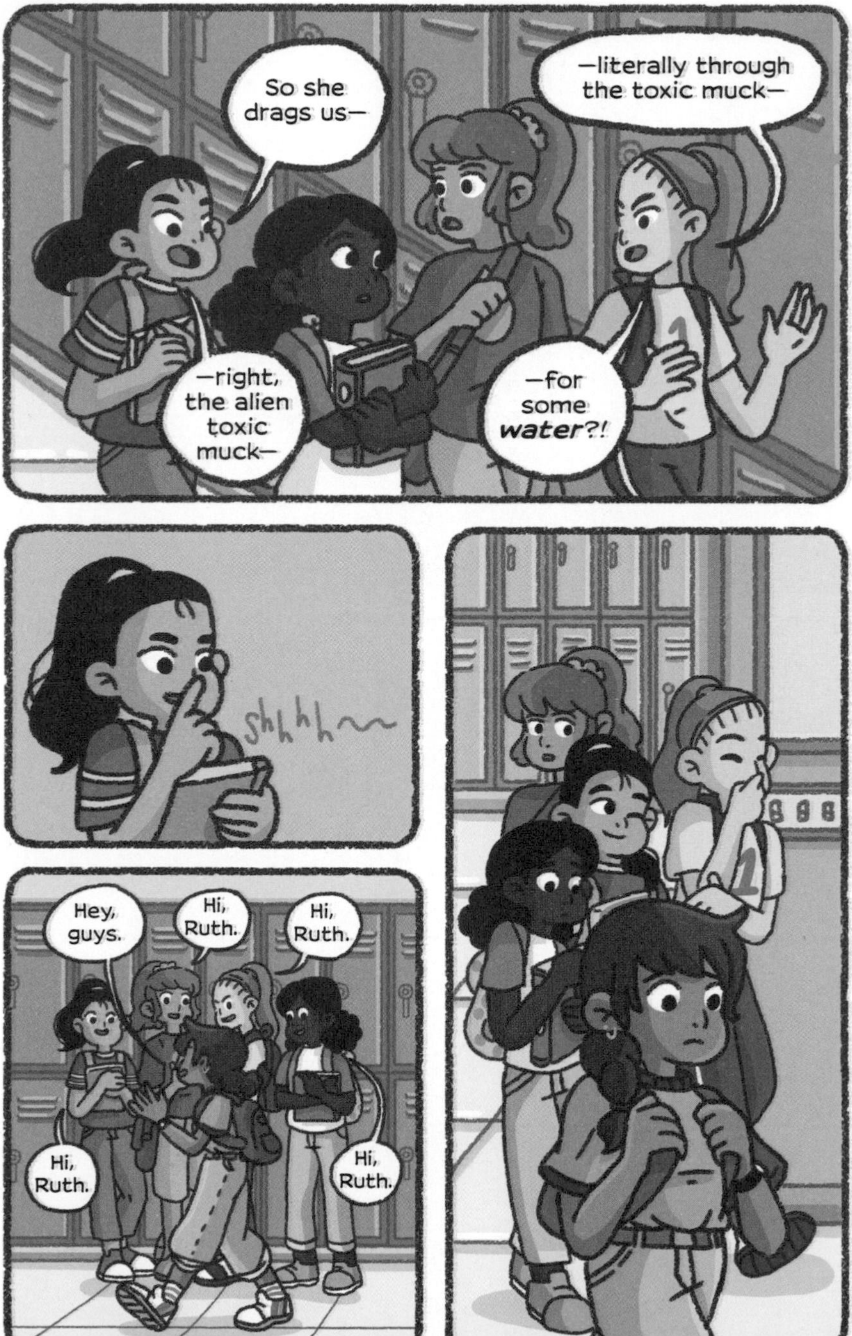
So she drags us—
—literally through the toxic muck—
—right, the alien toxic muck—
—for some *water*?!
shhhhh~~
Hey, guys.
Hi, Ruth.
Hi, Ruth.
Hi, Ruth.
Hi, Ruth.

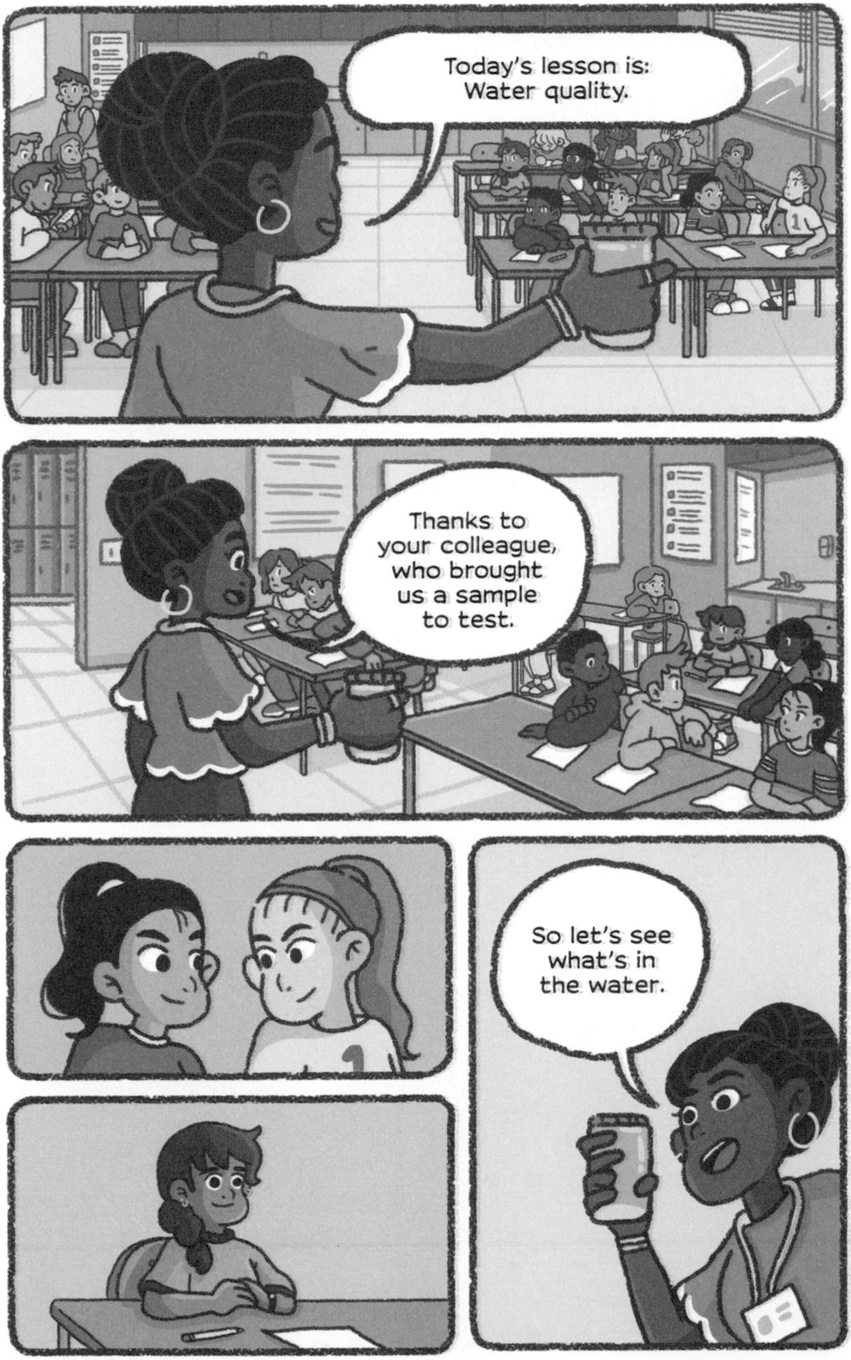
Today's lesson is: Water quality.
Thanks to your colleague, who brought us a sample to test.
So let's see what's in the water.

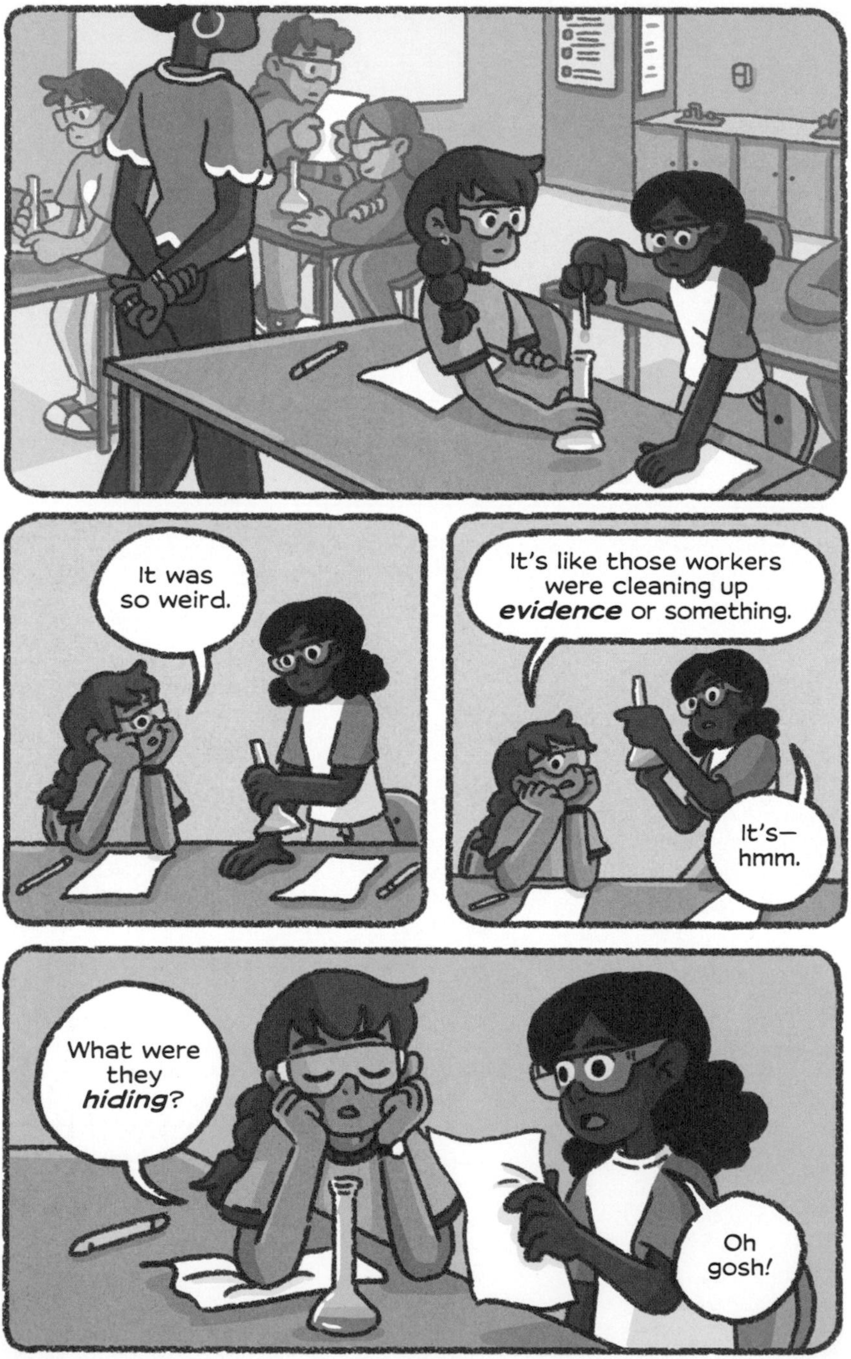
It was so weird.
It's like those workers were cleaning up *evidence* or something.
It's—hmm.
What were they *hiding*?
Oh gosh!

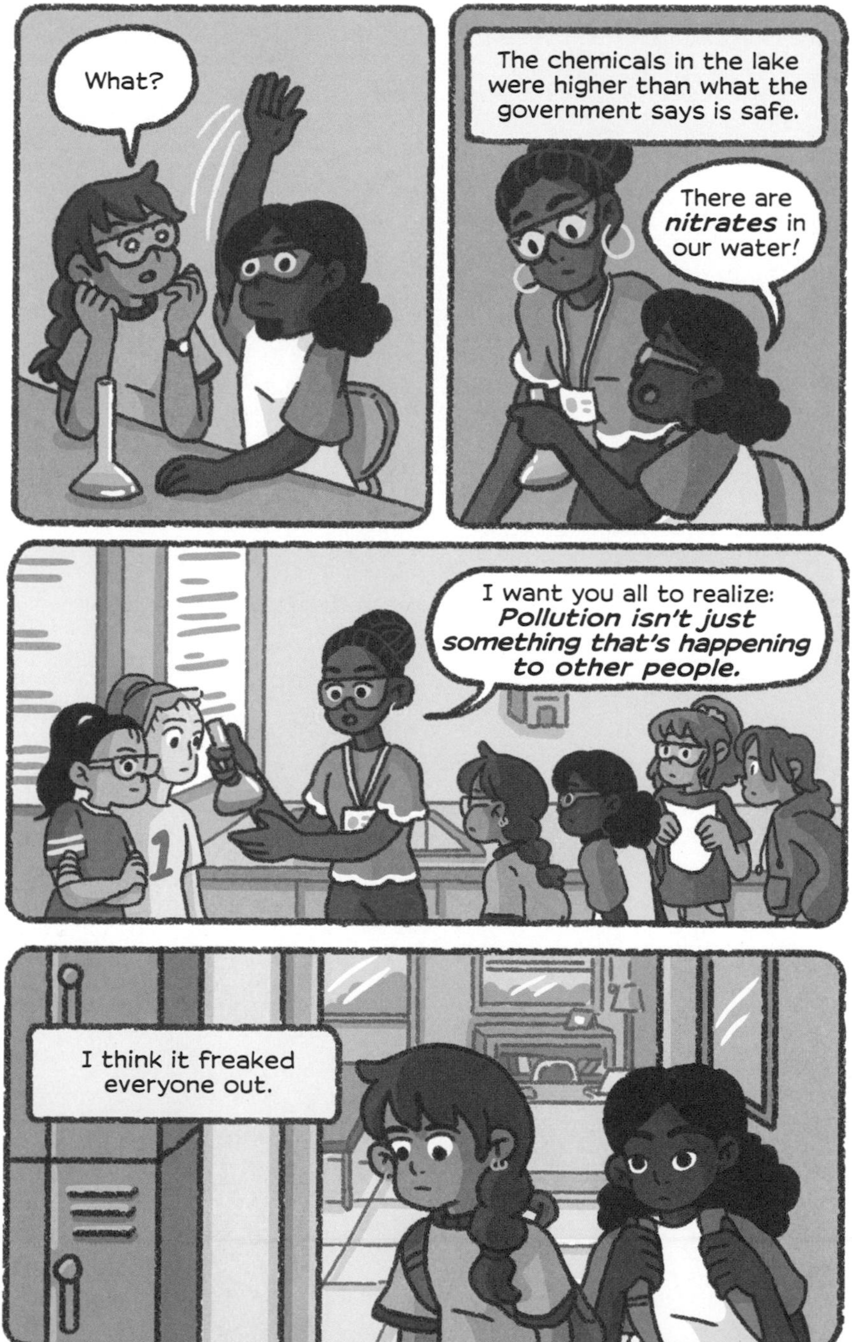
What?
The chemicals in the lake were higher than what the government says is safe.
There are *nitrates* in our water!
I want you all to realize: ***Pollution isn't just something that's happening to other people.***
I think it freaked everyone out.

I felt weird about it.

On one hand, I was right: There was something in the lake.

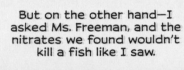

But on the other hand—I asked Ms. Freeman, and the nitrates we found wouldn't kill a fish like I saw.

Of course I knew it wasn't aliens.

ruthis

But *somebody* was hiding *something*.

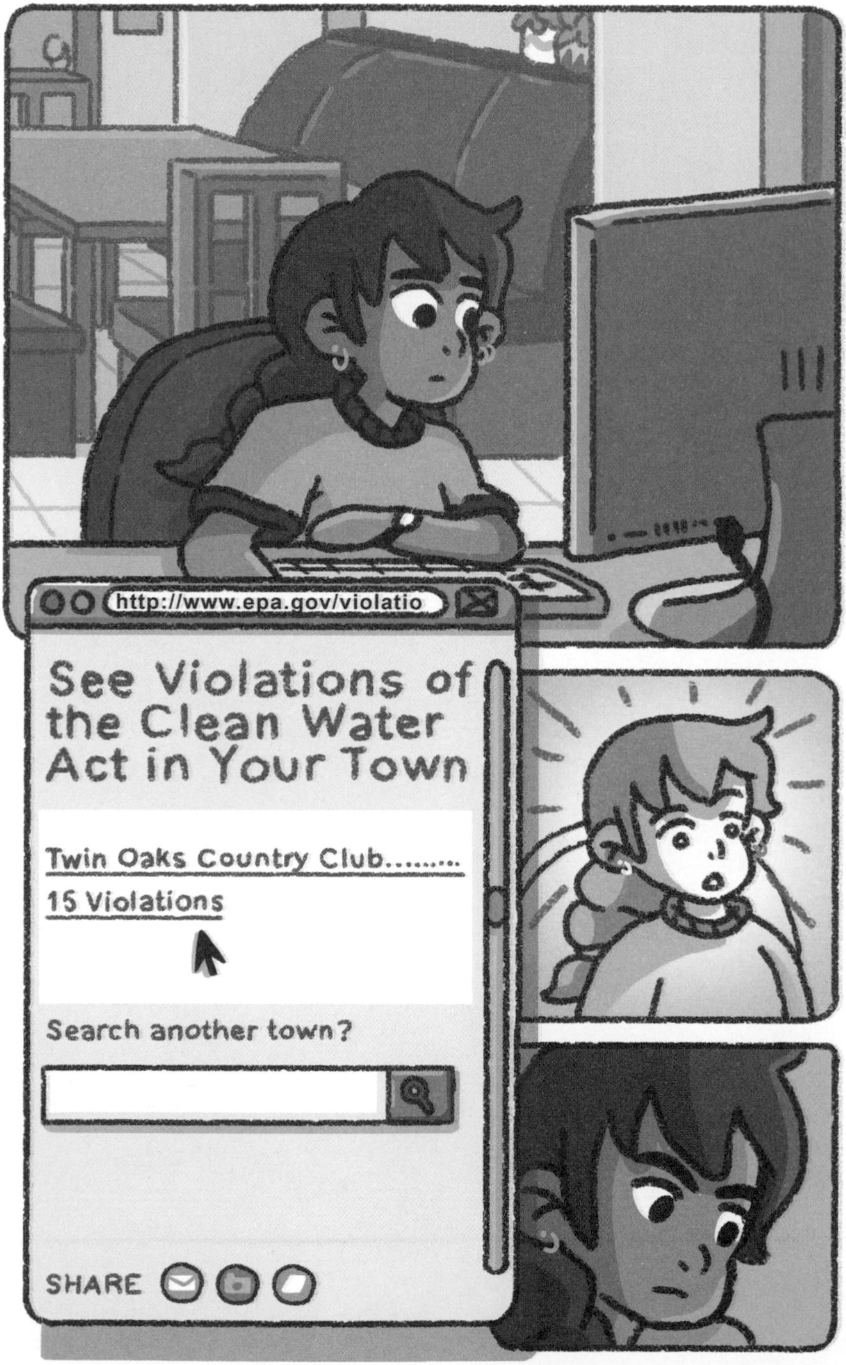
http://www.epa.gov/violatio
See Violations of the Clean Water Act in Your Town
Twin Oaks Country Club.........
15 Violations
Search another town?
SHARE

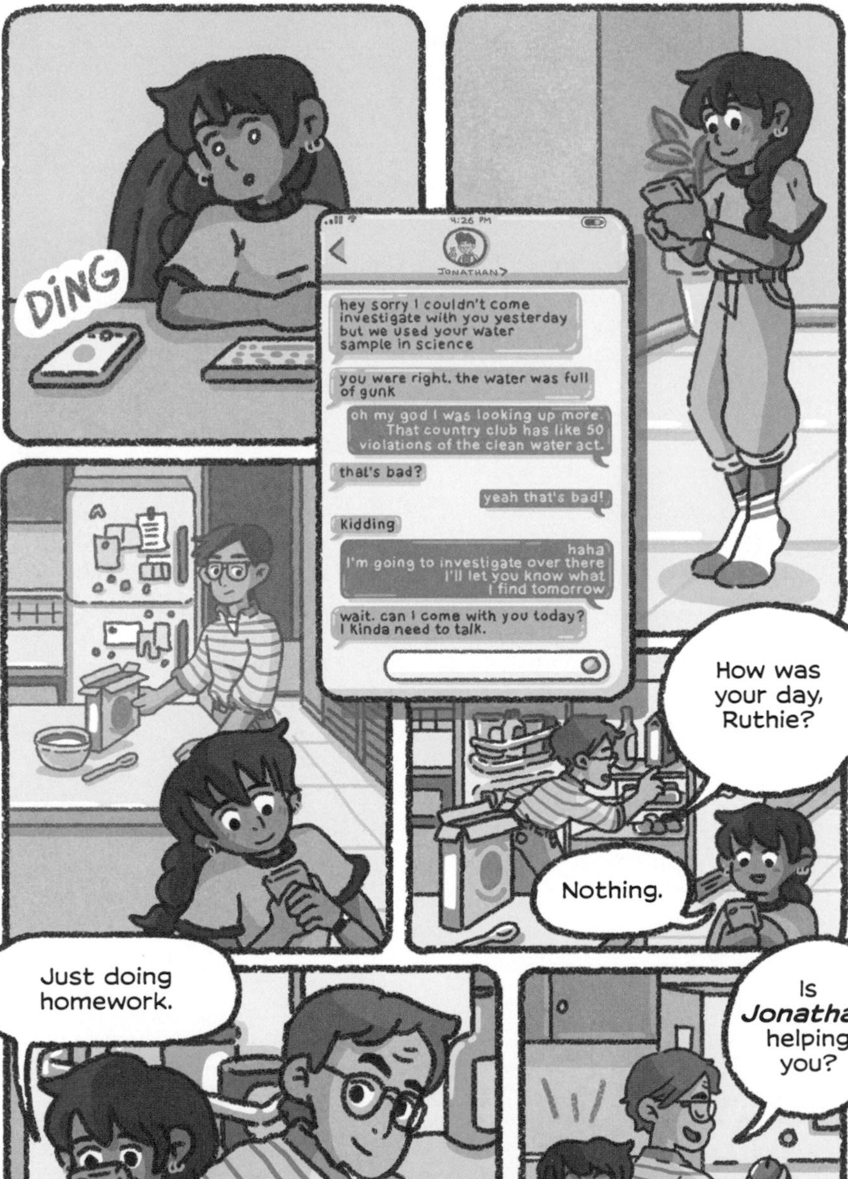
DING
4:26 PM
JONATHAN
hey sorry I couldn't come investigate with you yesterday but we used your water sample in science
you were right. the water was full of gunk
oh my god I was looking up more. That country club has like 50 violations of the clean water act.
that's bad?
yeah that's bad!
Kidding
haha
I'm going to investigate over there
I'll let you know what I find tomorrow
wait. can I come with you today? I kinda need to talk.
How was your day, Ruthie?
Nothing.
Just doing homework.
Is *Jonathan* helping you?

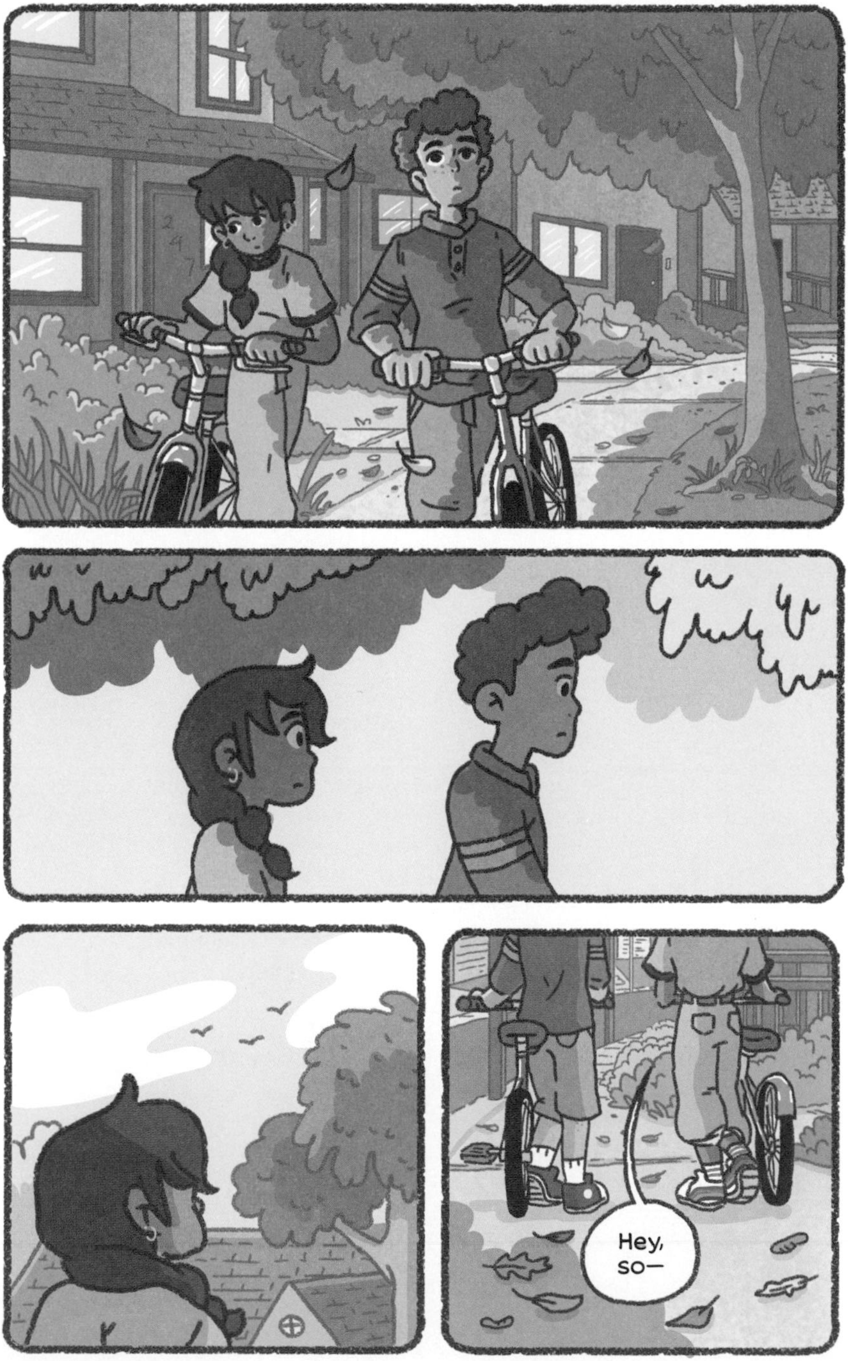
Hey,
so—

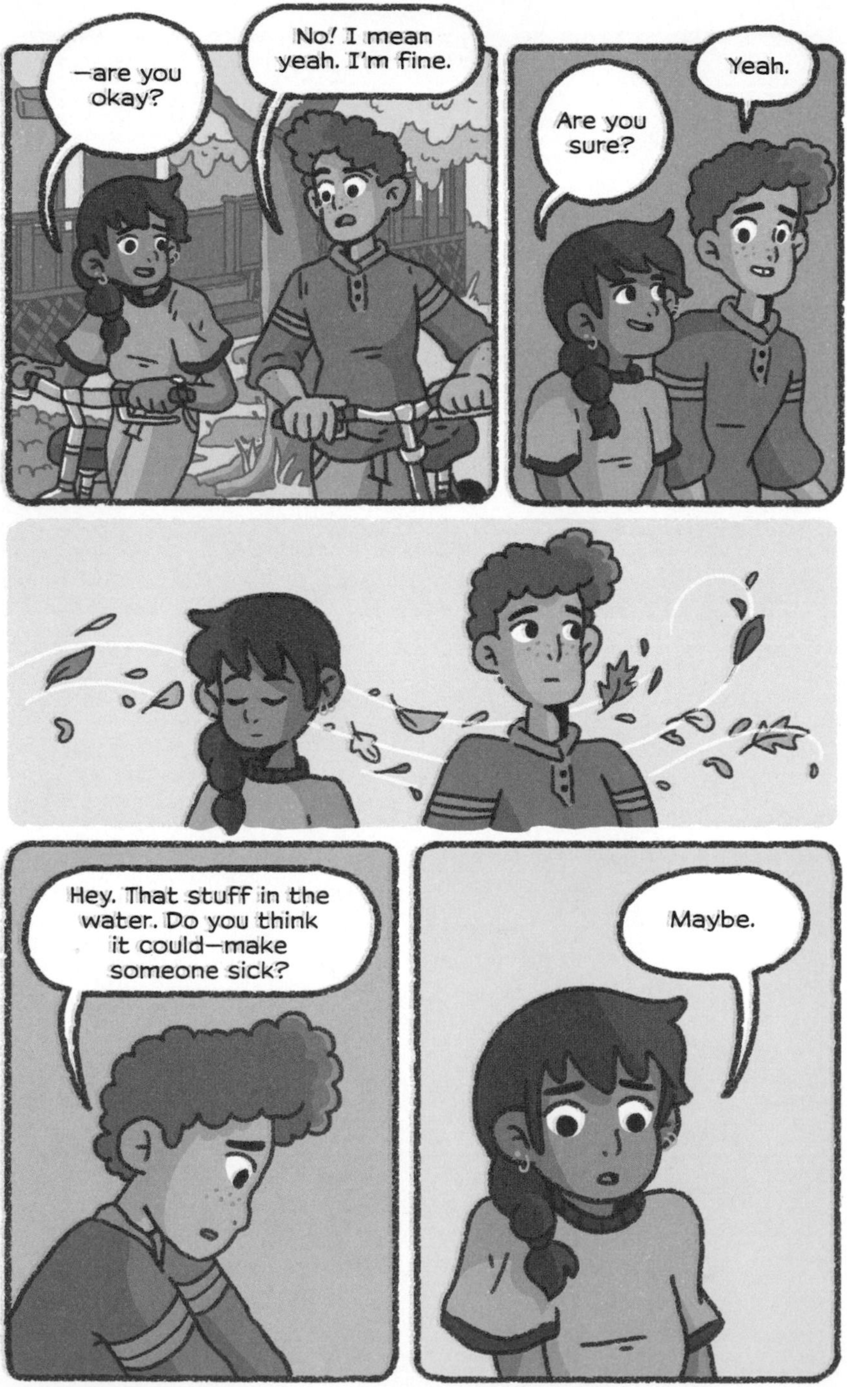
—are you okay?
No! I mean yeah. I'm fine.
Are you sure?
Yeah.
Hey. That stuff in the water. Do you think it could—make someone sick?
Maybe.

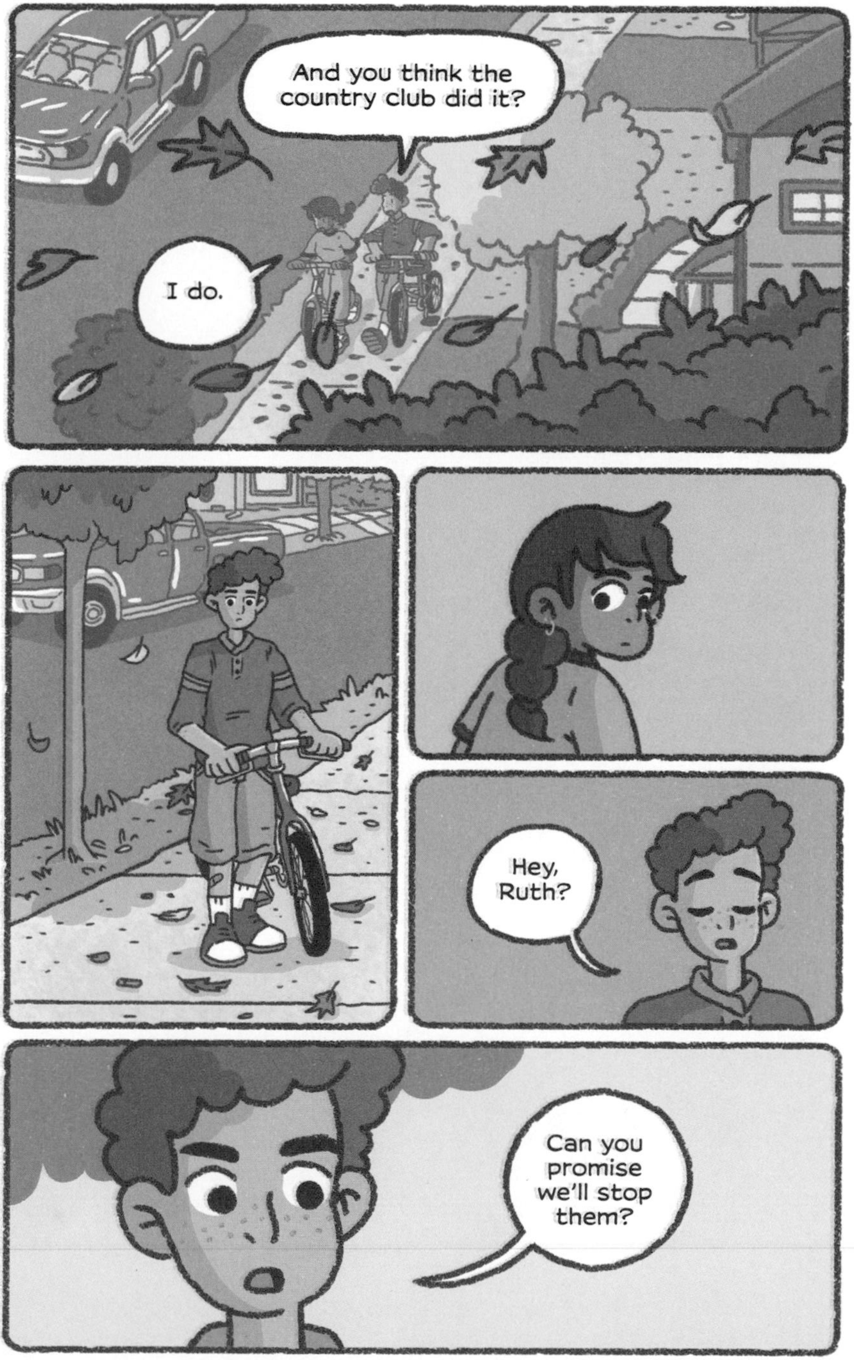
And you think the country club did it?
I do.
Hey, Ruth?
Can you promise we'll stop them?

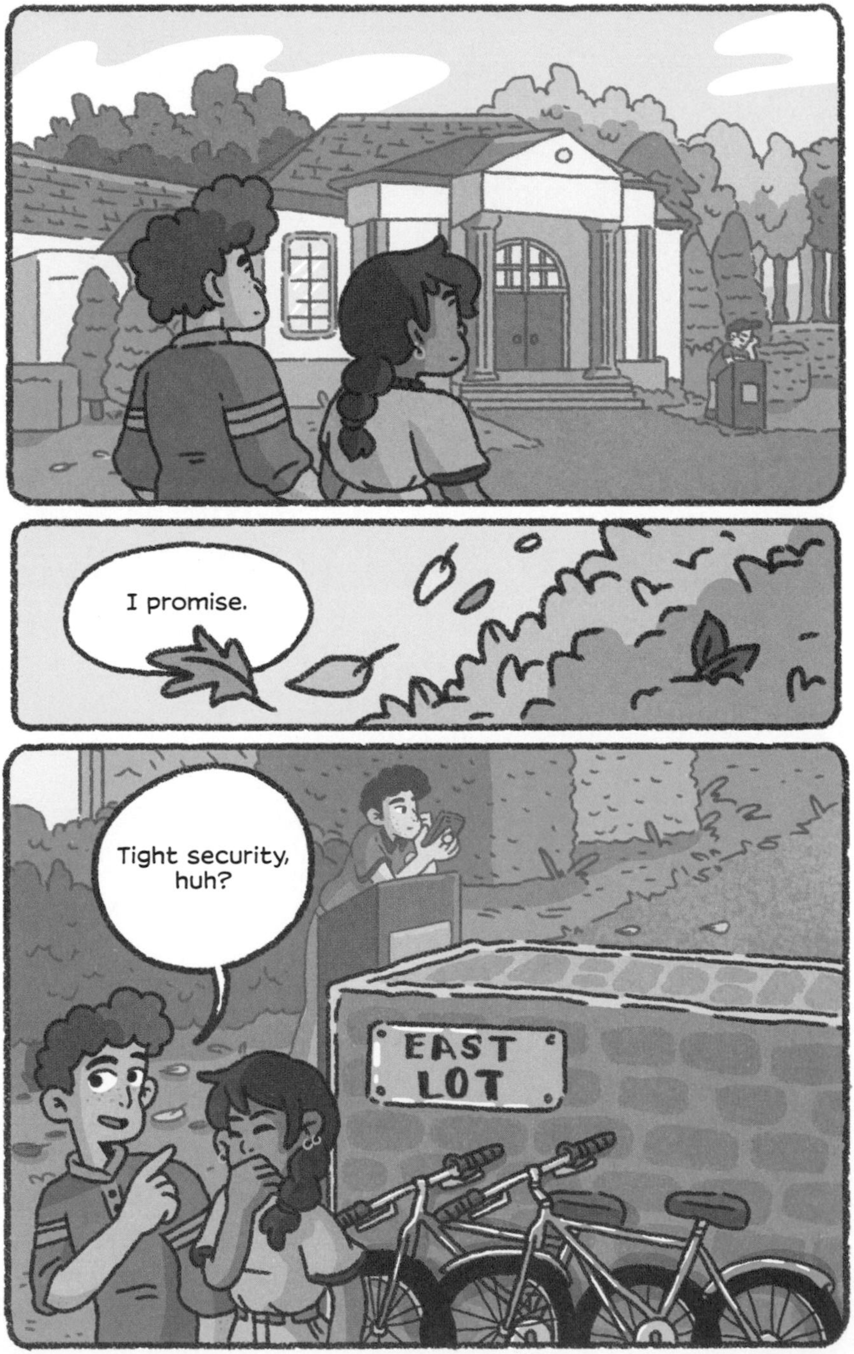
I promise.
Tight security, huh?
EAST LOT

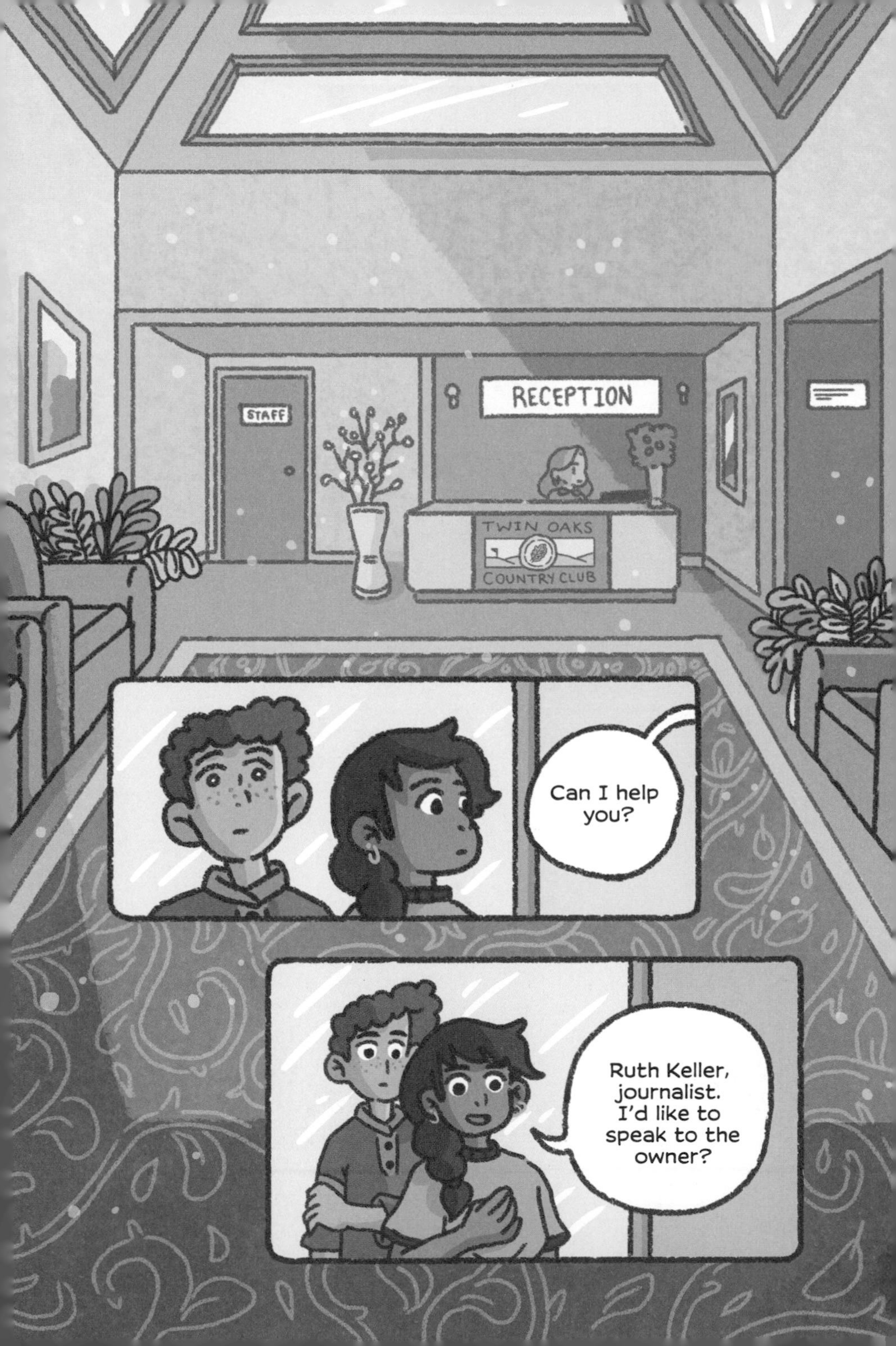
STAFF
RECEPTION
TWIN OAKS
COUNTRY CLUB
Can I help you?
Ruth Keller, journalist. I'd like to speak to the owner?

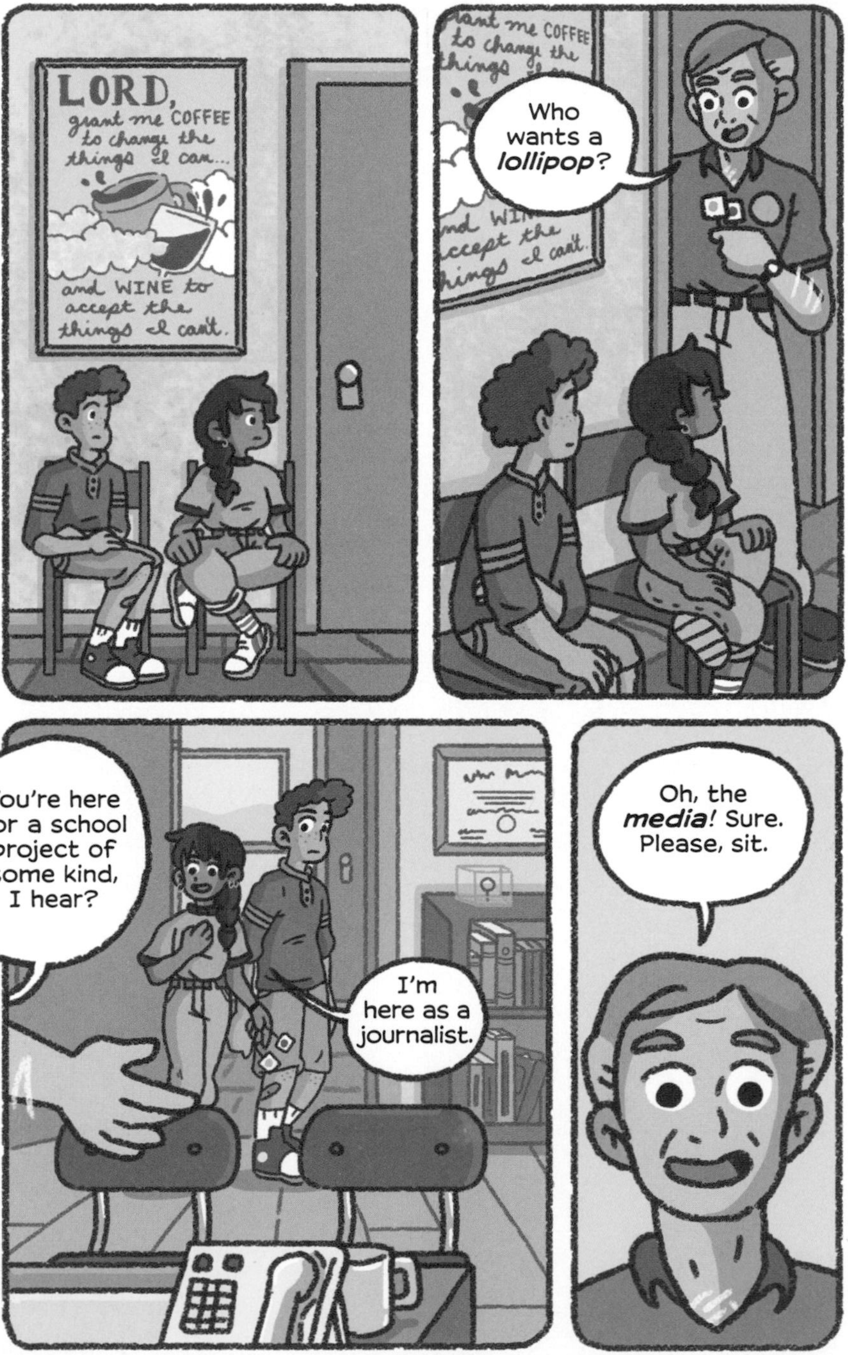
LORD,
grant me COFFEE to change the things I can...
and WINE to accept the things I can't.
Who wants a *lollipop*?
You're here for a school project of some kind, I hear?
I'm here as a journalist.
Oh, the *media*! Sure. Please, sit.

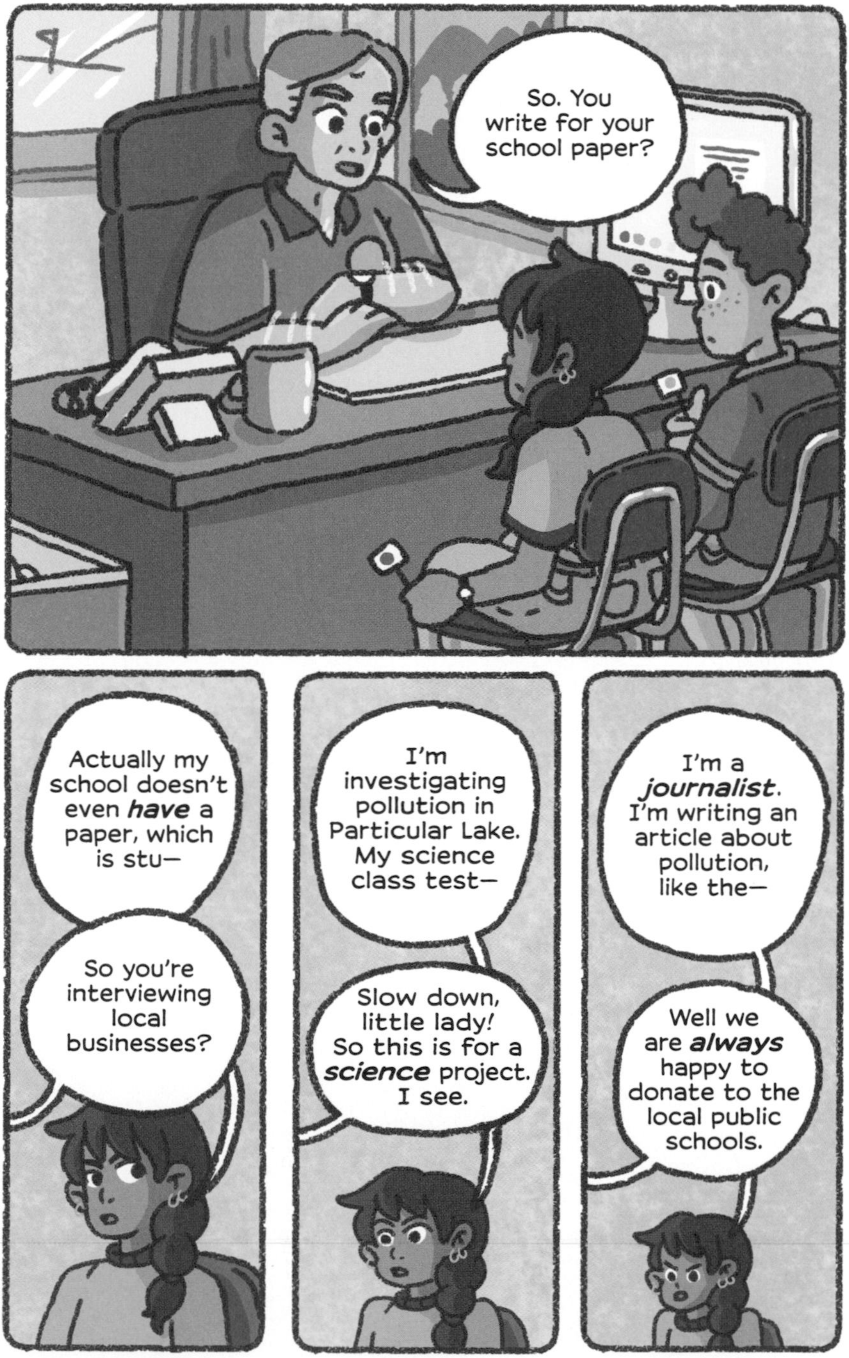
So. You write for your school paper?
Actually my school doesn't even *have* a paper, which is stu—
So you're interviewing local businesses?
I'm investigating pollution in Particular Lake. My science class test—
Slow down, little lady! So this is for a *science* project. I see.
I'm a *journalist*. I'm writing an article about pollution, like the—
Well we are *always* happy to donate to the local public schools.

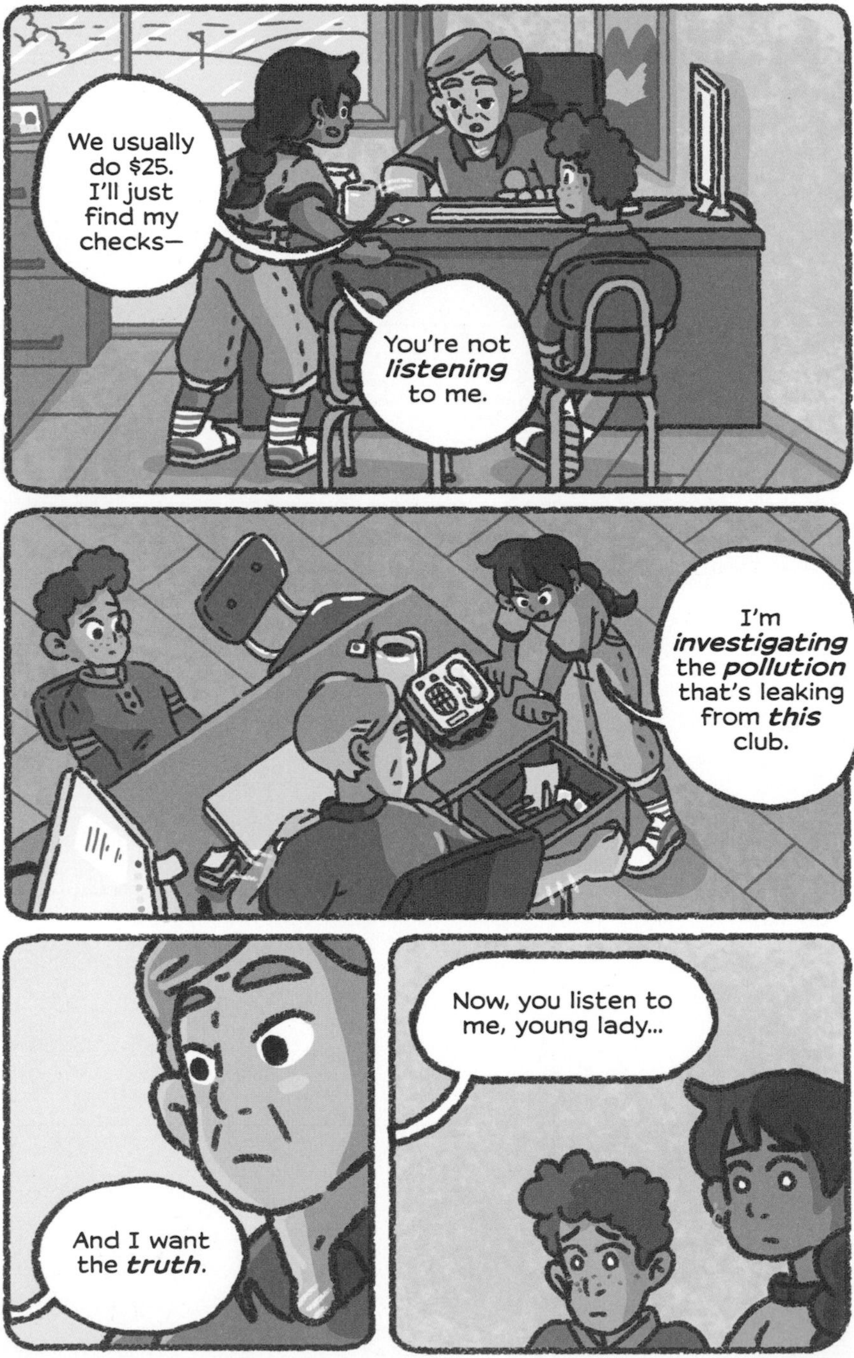
We usually do $25. I'll just find my checks—
You're not *listening* to me.
I'm *investigating* the *pollution* that's leaking from *this* club.
Now, you listen to me, young lady...
And I want the *truth*.

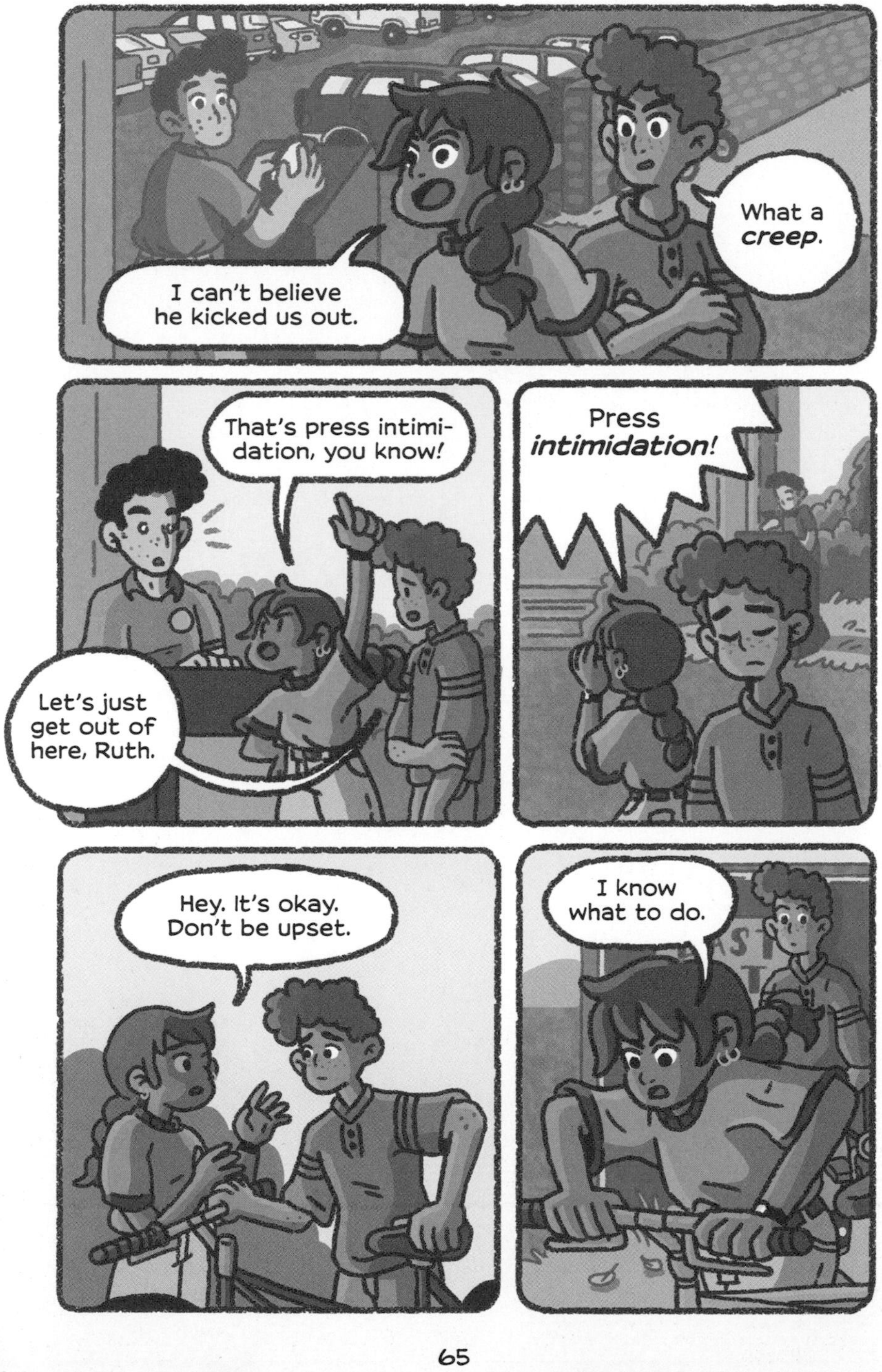
I can't believe he kicked us out.
What a *creep*.
That's press intimi-dation, you know!
Let's just get out of here, Ruth.
Press *intimidation*!
Hey. It's okay. Don't be upset.
I know what to do.

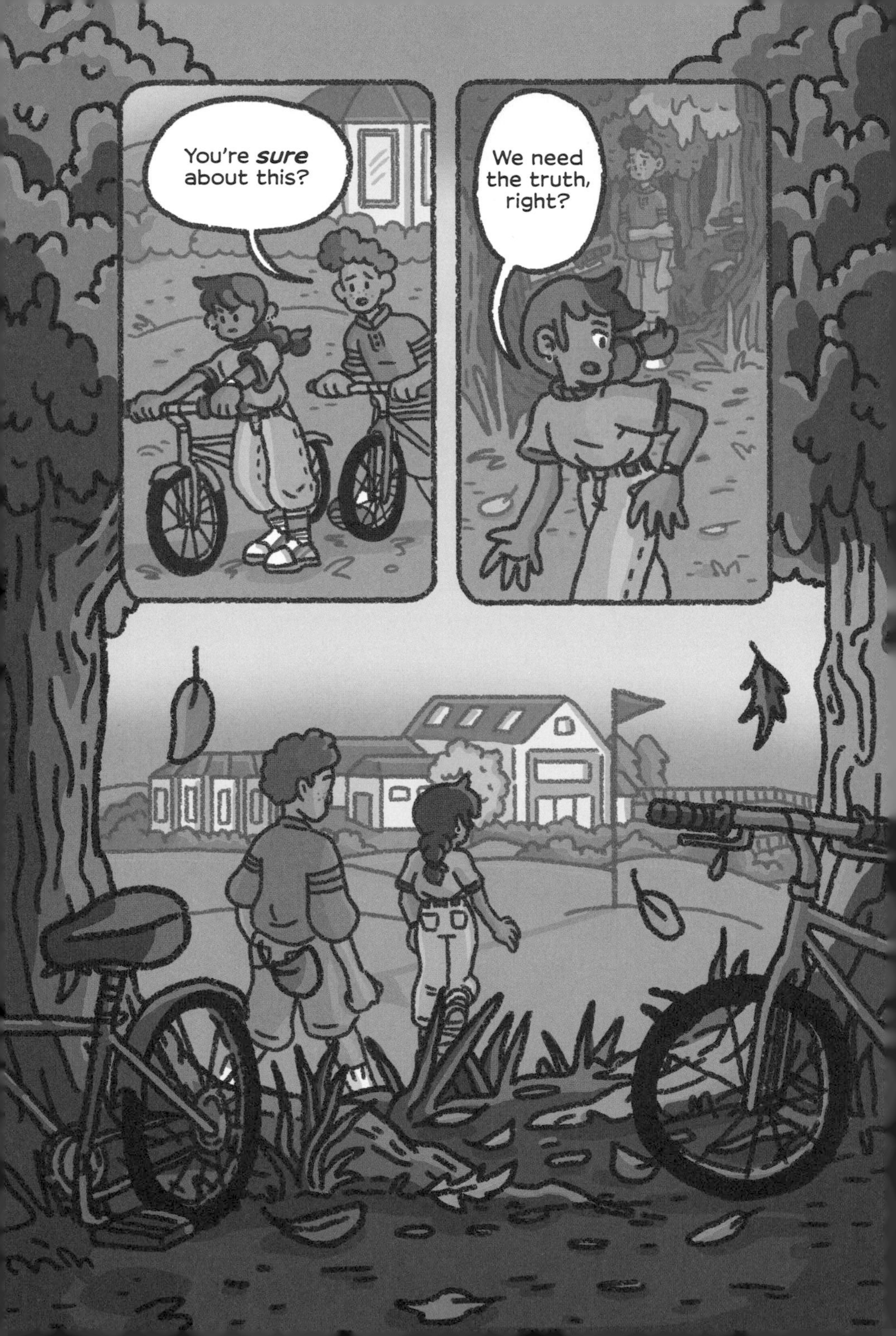
You're *sure* about this?
We need the truth, right?

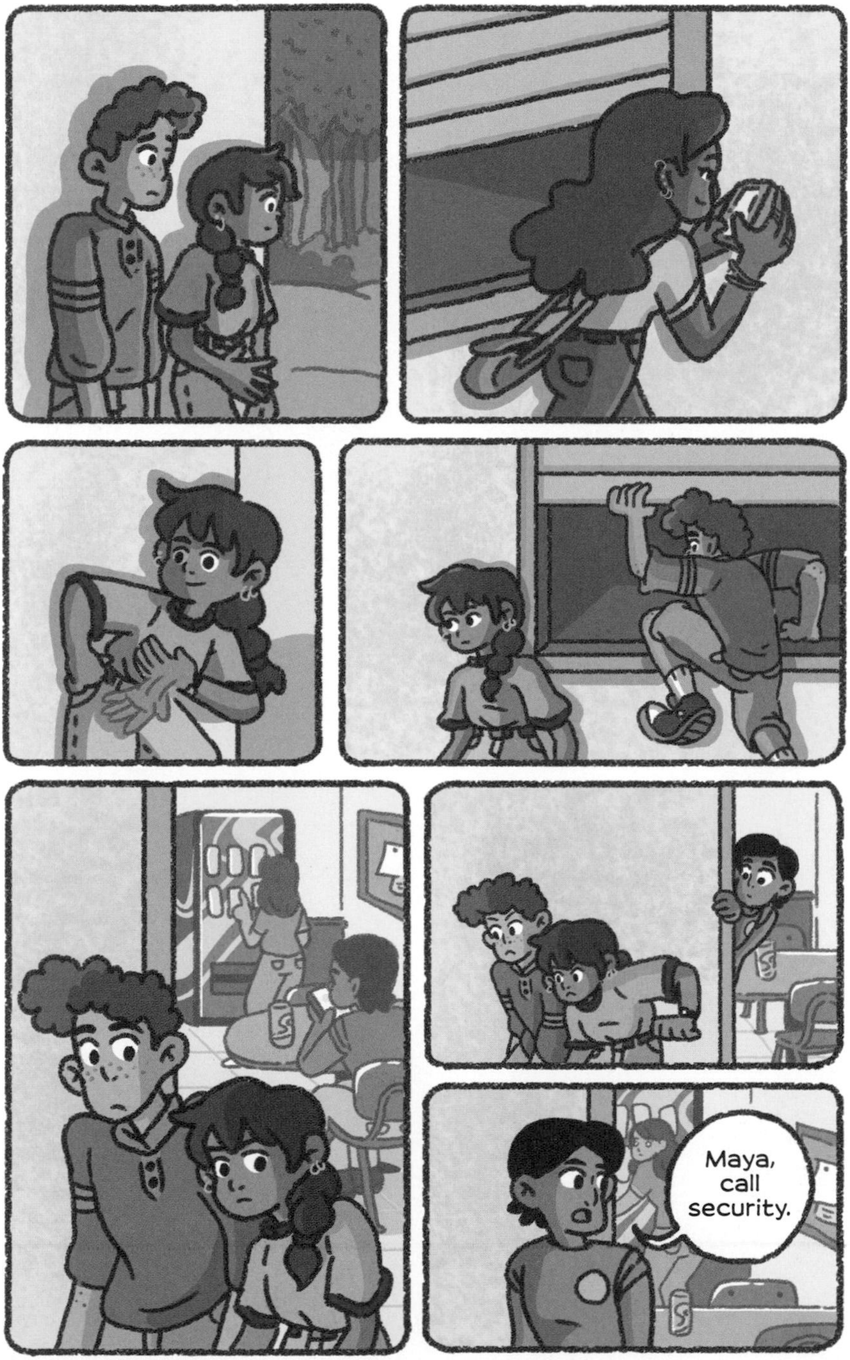
Maya,
call
security.

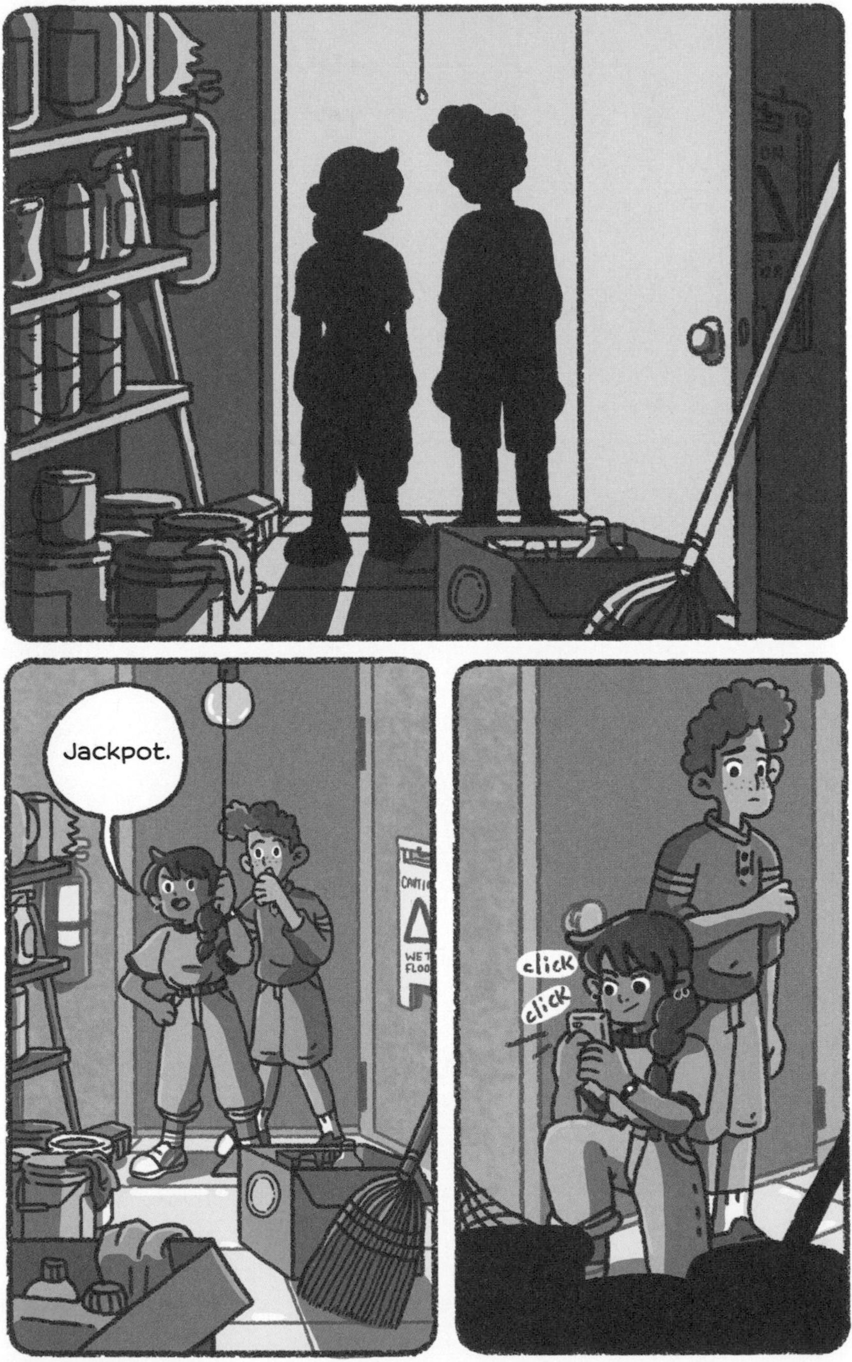
Jackpot.
click
click

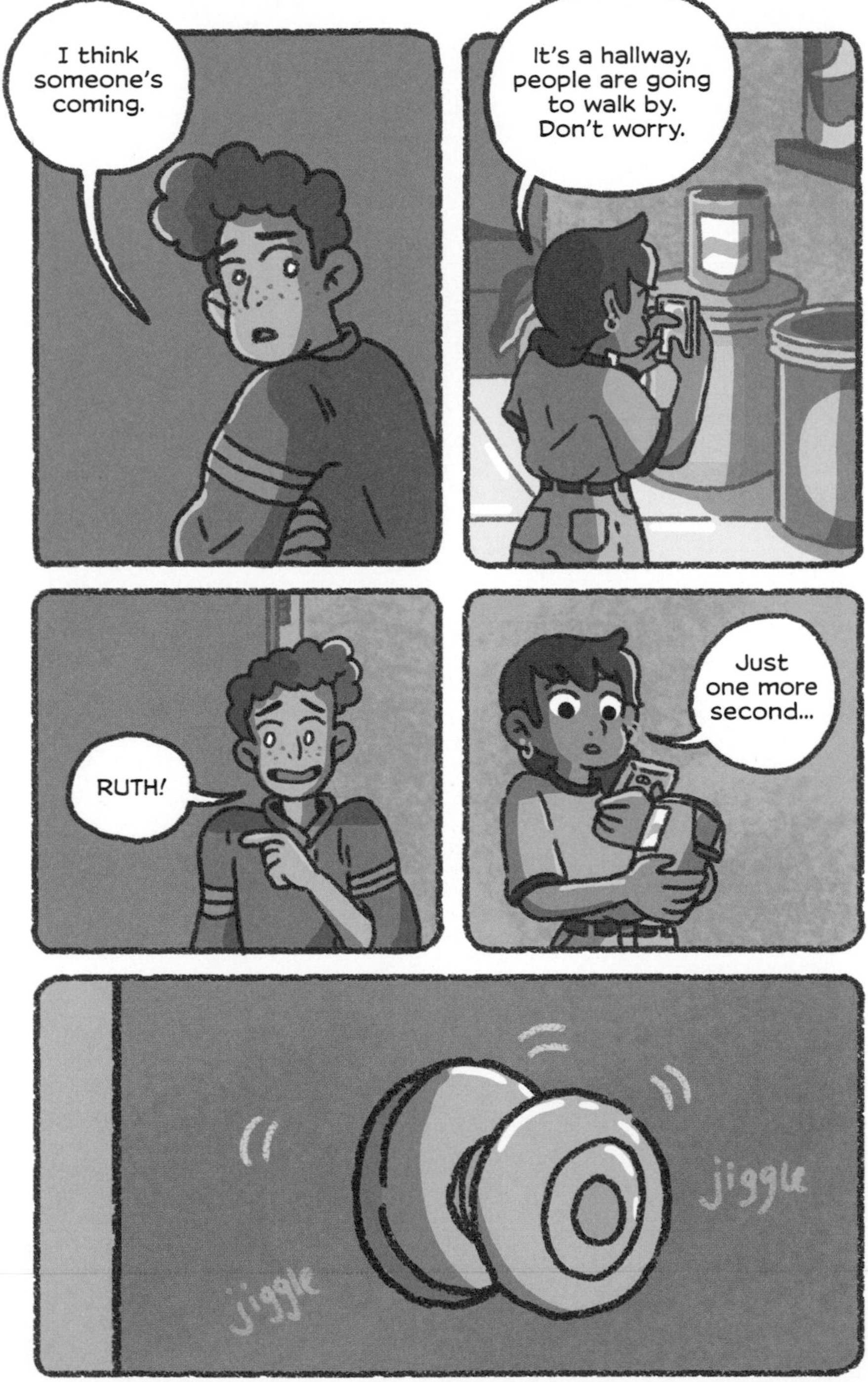
I think someone's coming.
It's a hallway, people are going to walk by. Don't worry.
RUTH!
Just one more second...
jiggle
jiggle

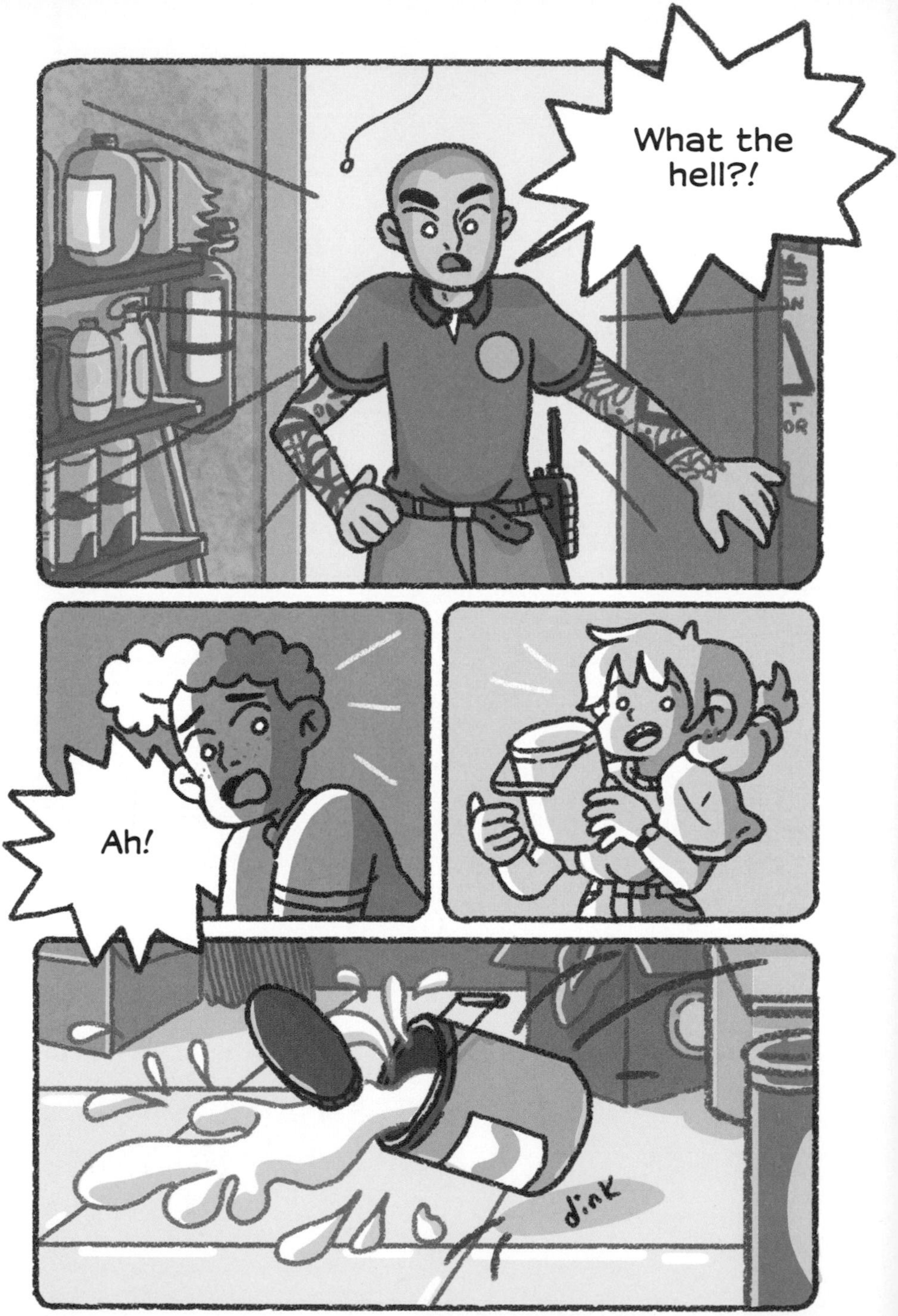
What the hell?!
Ah!
dink

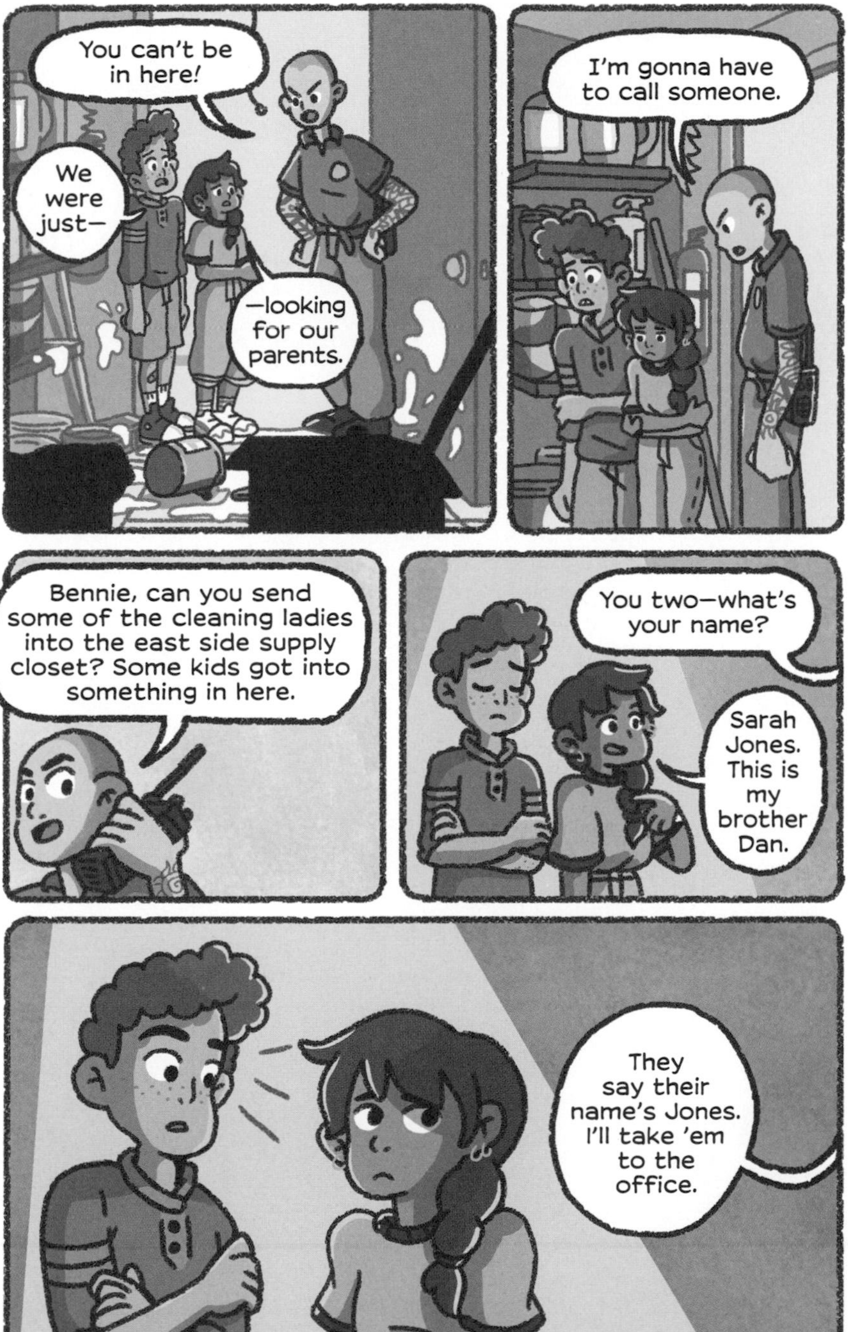
You can't be in here!
We were just—
—looking for our parents.
I'm gonna have to call someone.
Bennie, can you send some of the cleaning ladies into the east side supply closet? Some kids got into something in here.
You two—what's your name?
Sarah Jones. This is my brother Dan.
They say their name's Jones. I'll take 'em to the office.

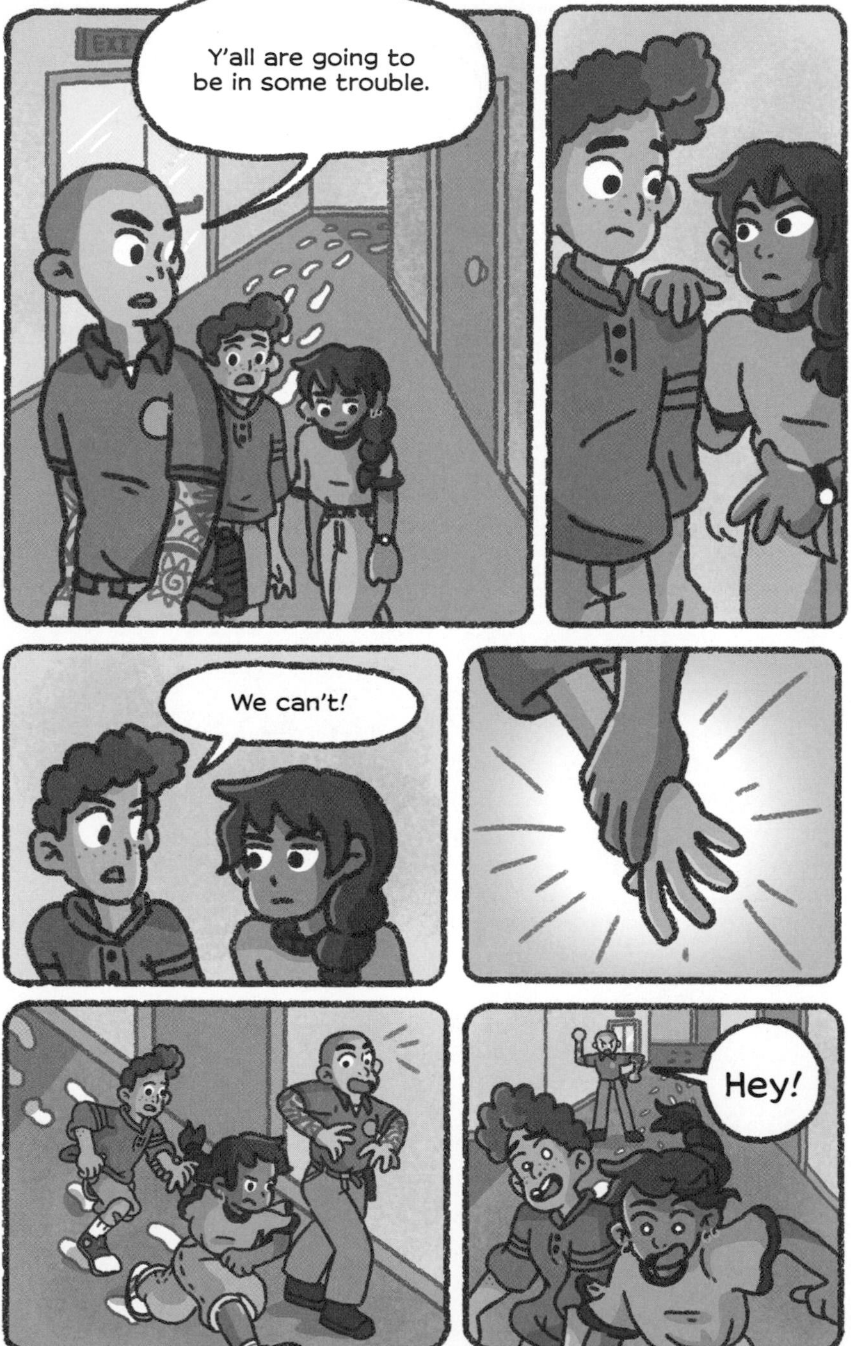
EXIT
Y'all are going to be in some trouble.
We can't!
Hey!

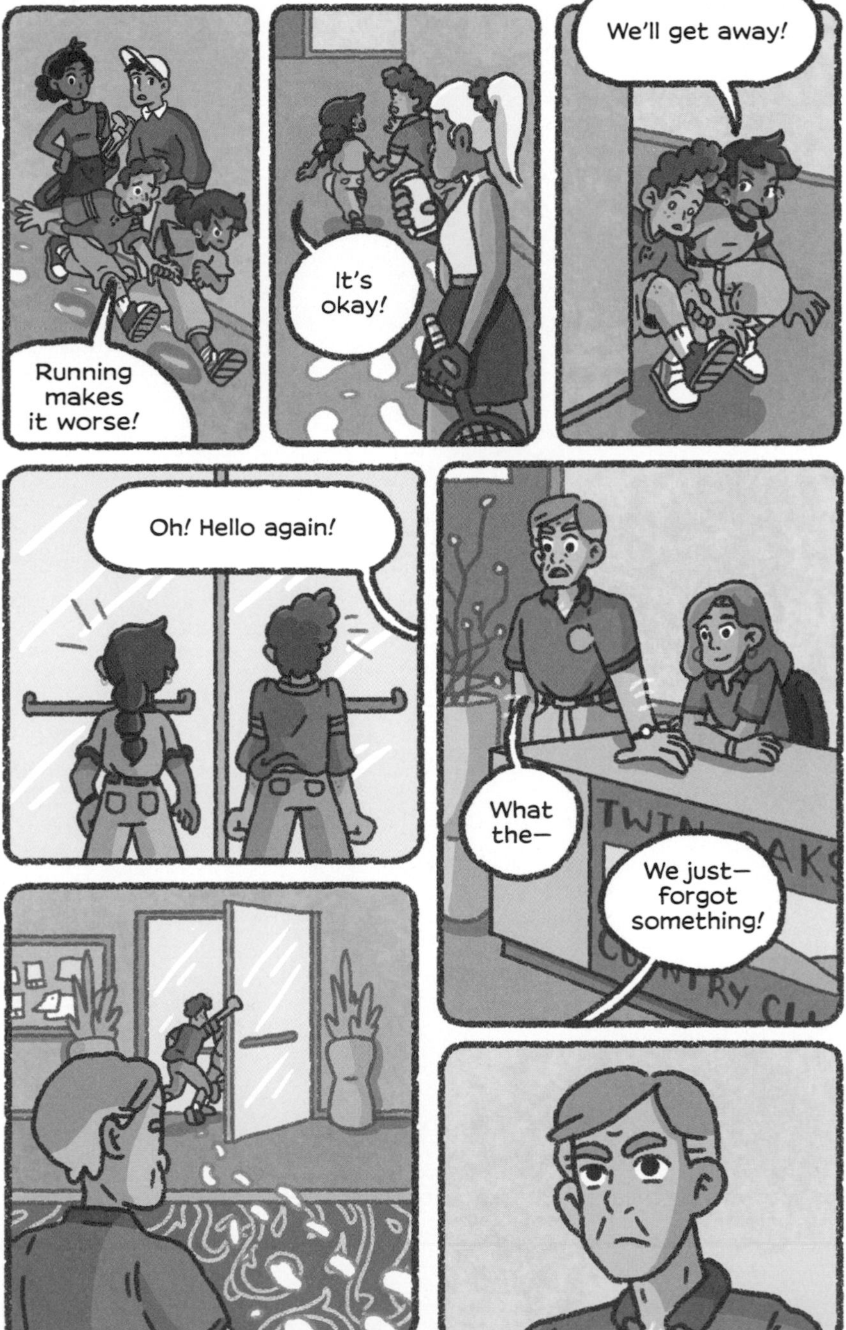
Running makes it worse!
It's okay!
We'll get away!
Oh! Hello again!
What the—
We just— forgot something!

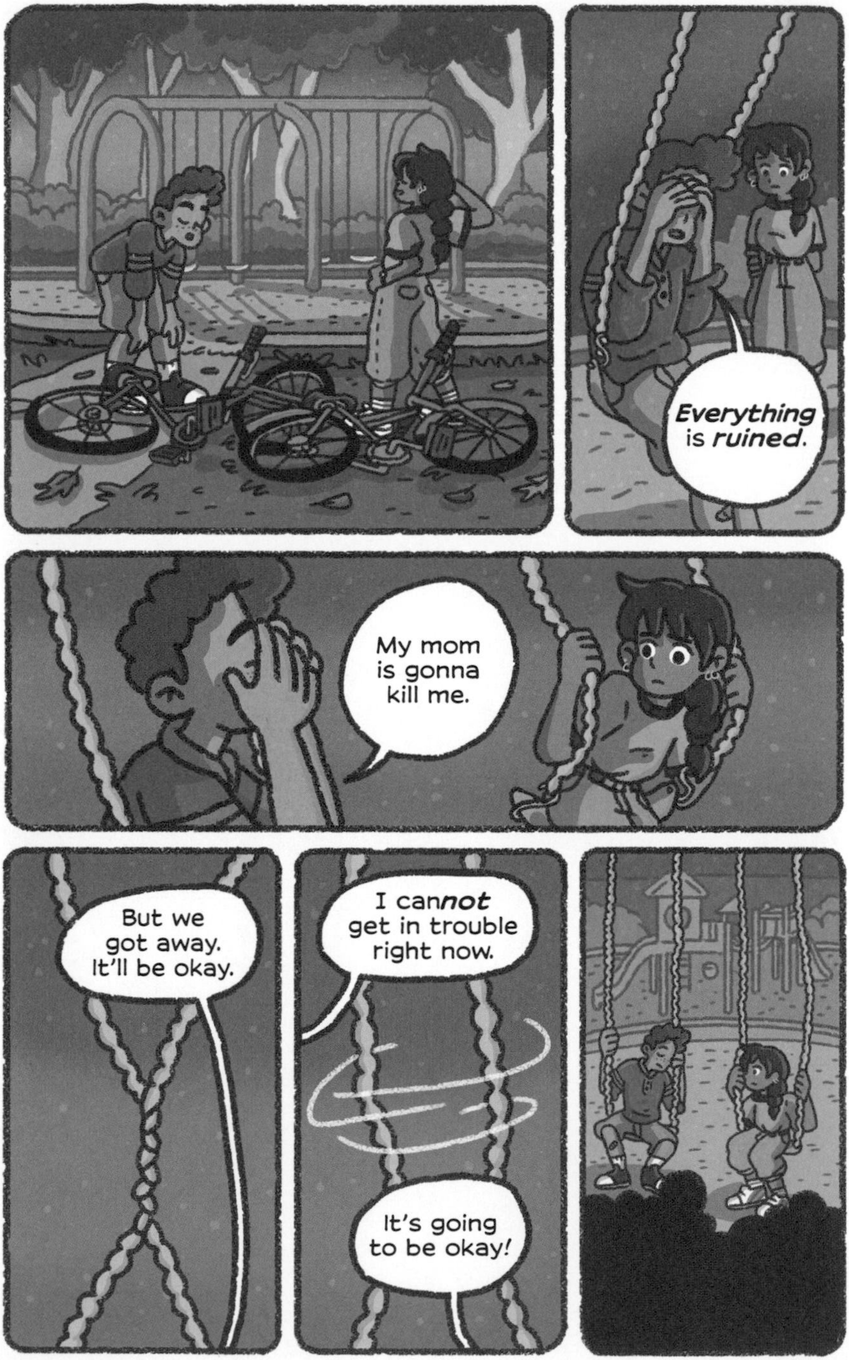
Everything is ruined.
My mom is gonna kill me.
But we got away. It'll be okay.
I can**not** get in trouble right now.
It's going to be okay!

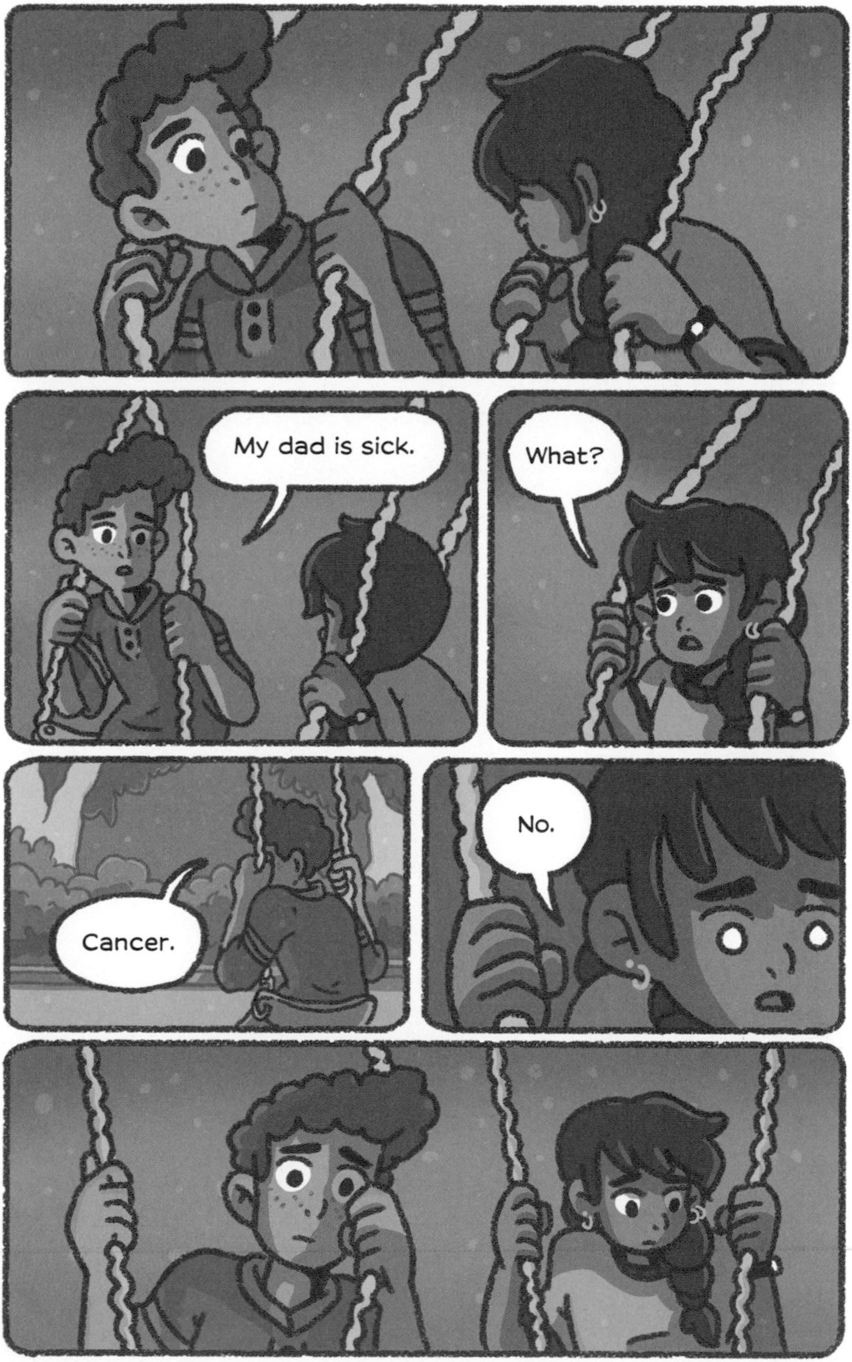
My dad is sick.
What?
Cancer.
No.

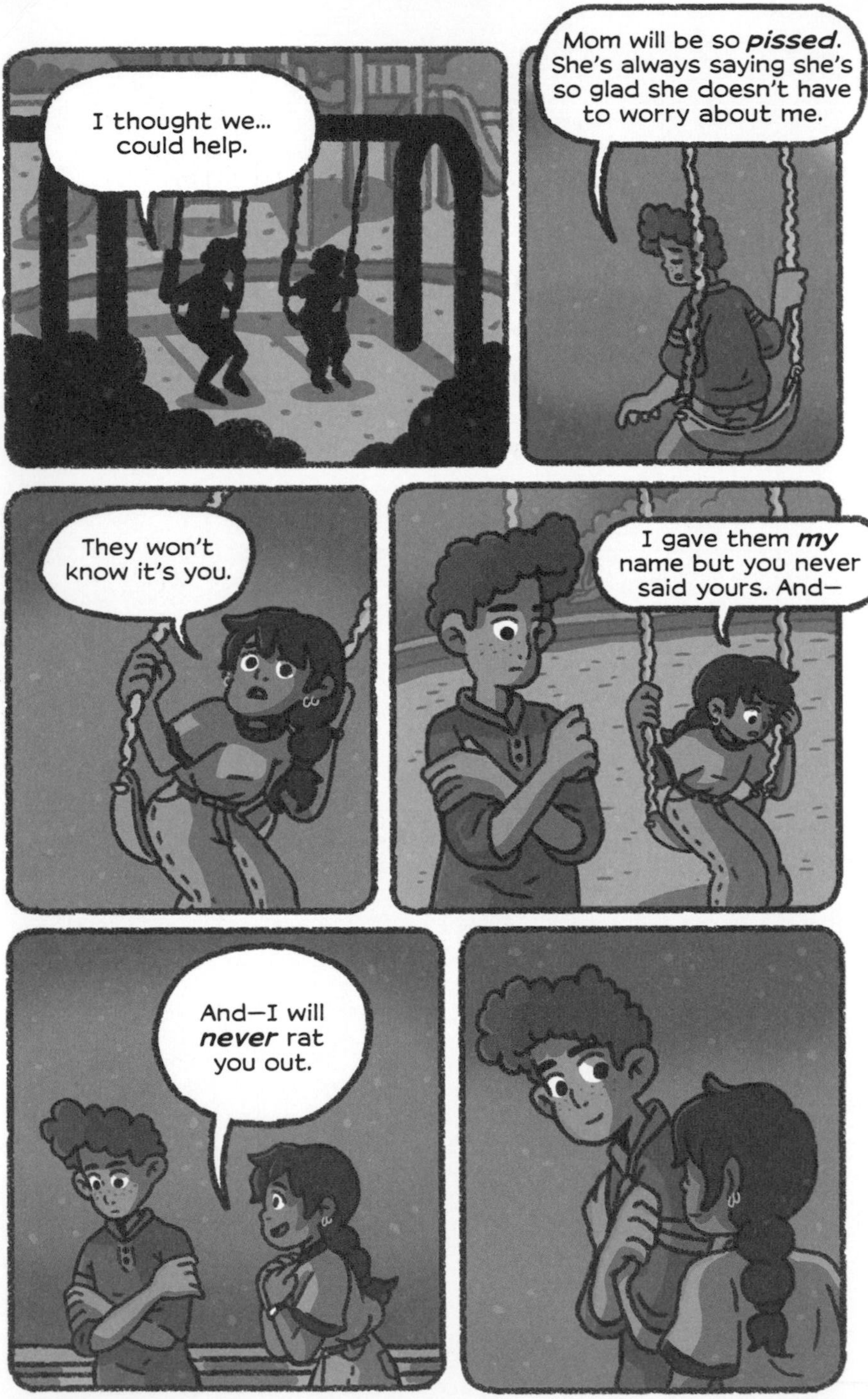
I thought we... could help.
Mom will be so **pissed**. She's always saying she's so glad she doesn't have to worry about me.
They won't know it's you.
I gave them **my** name but you never said yours. And—
And—I will **never** rat you out.

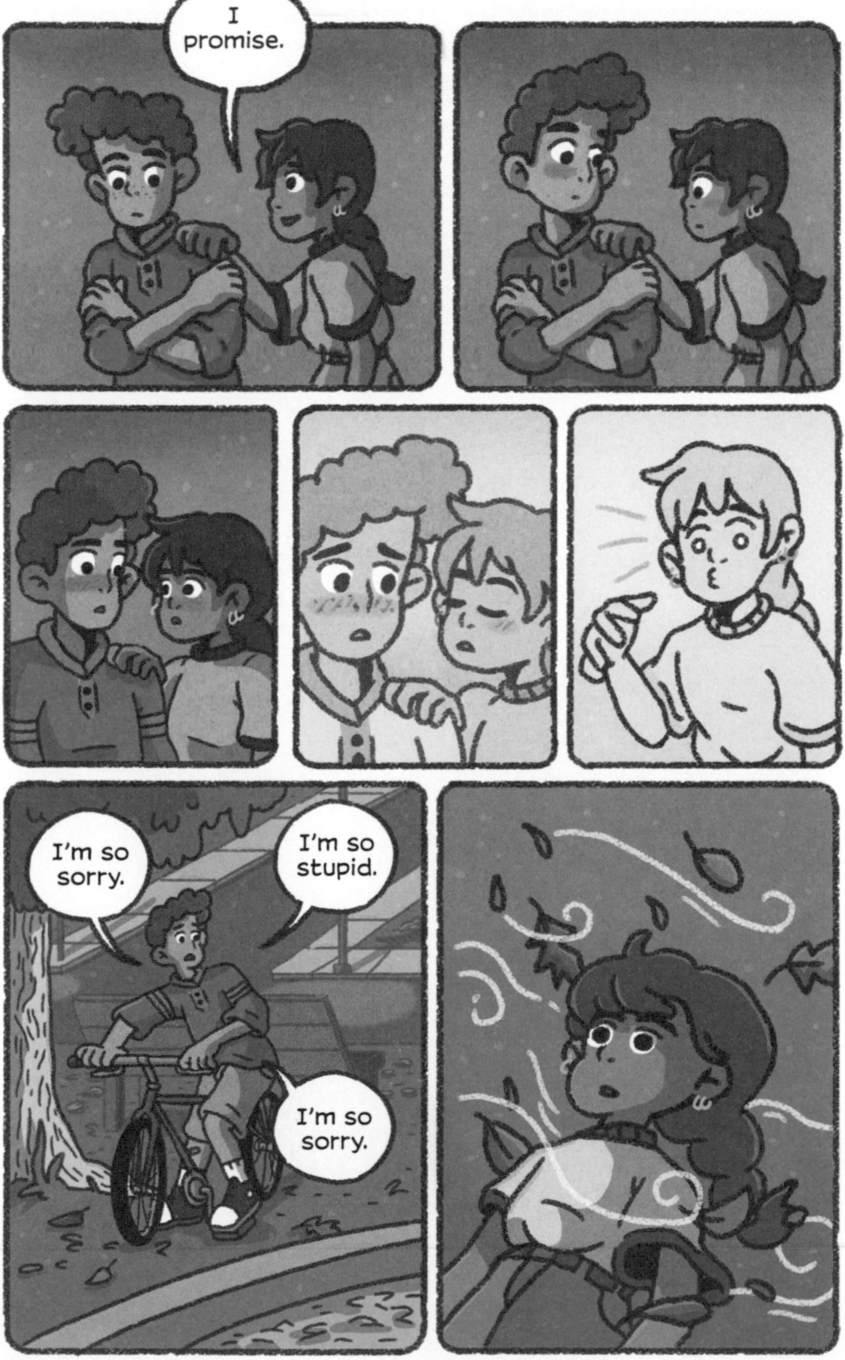
I promise.
I'm so sorry.
I'm so stupid.
I'm so sorry.

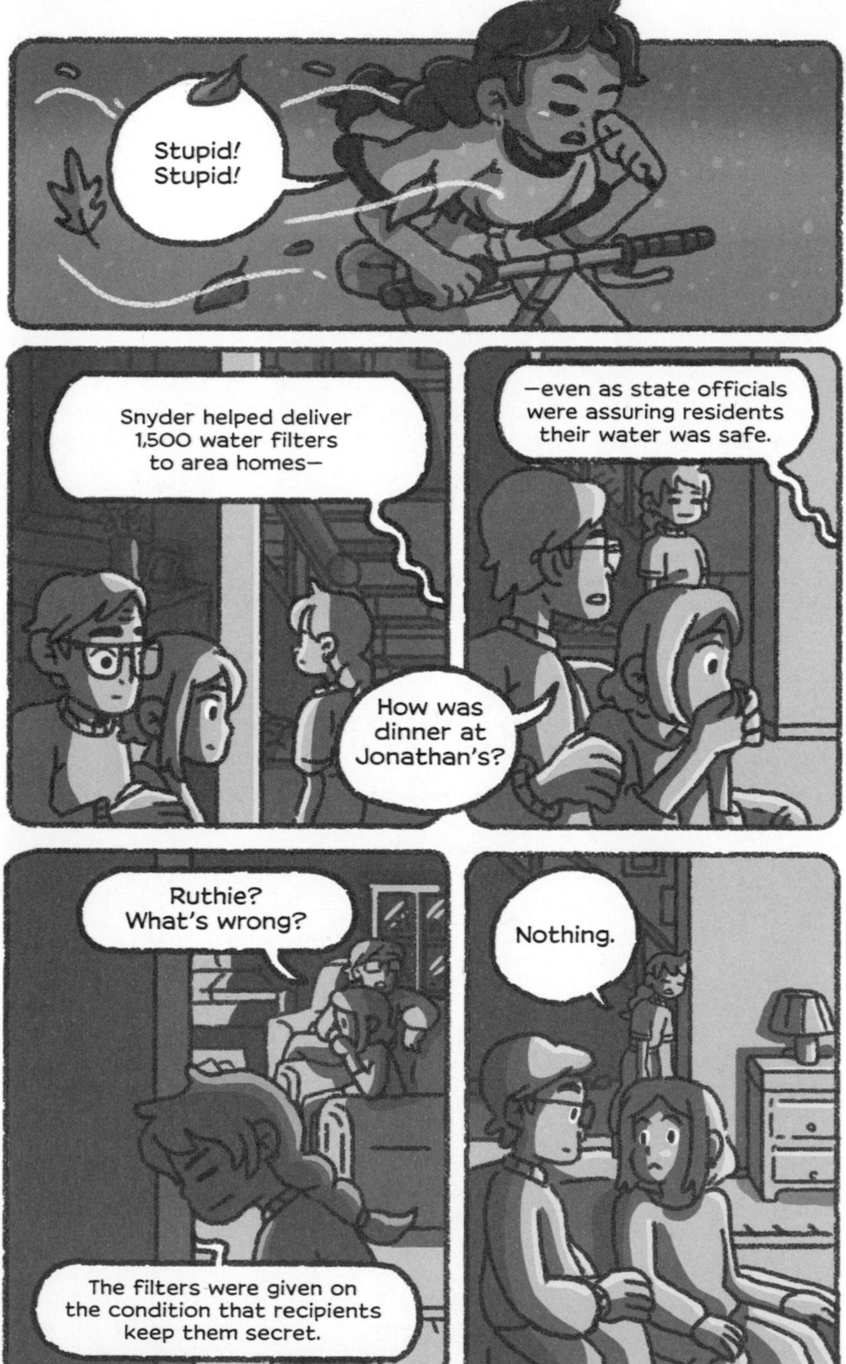
Stupid!
Stupid!
Snyder helped deliver 1,500 water filters to area homes—
How was dinner at Jonathan's?
—even as state officials were assuring residents their water was safe.
Ruthie? What's wrong?
The filters were given on the condition that recipients keep them secret.
Nothing.

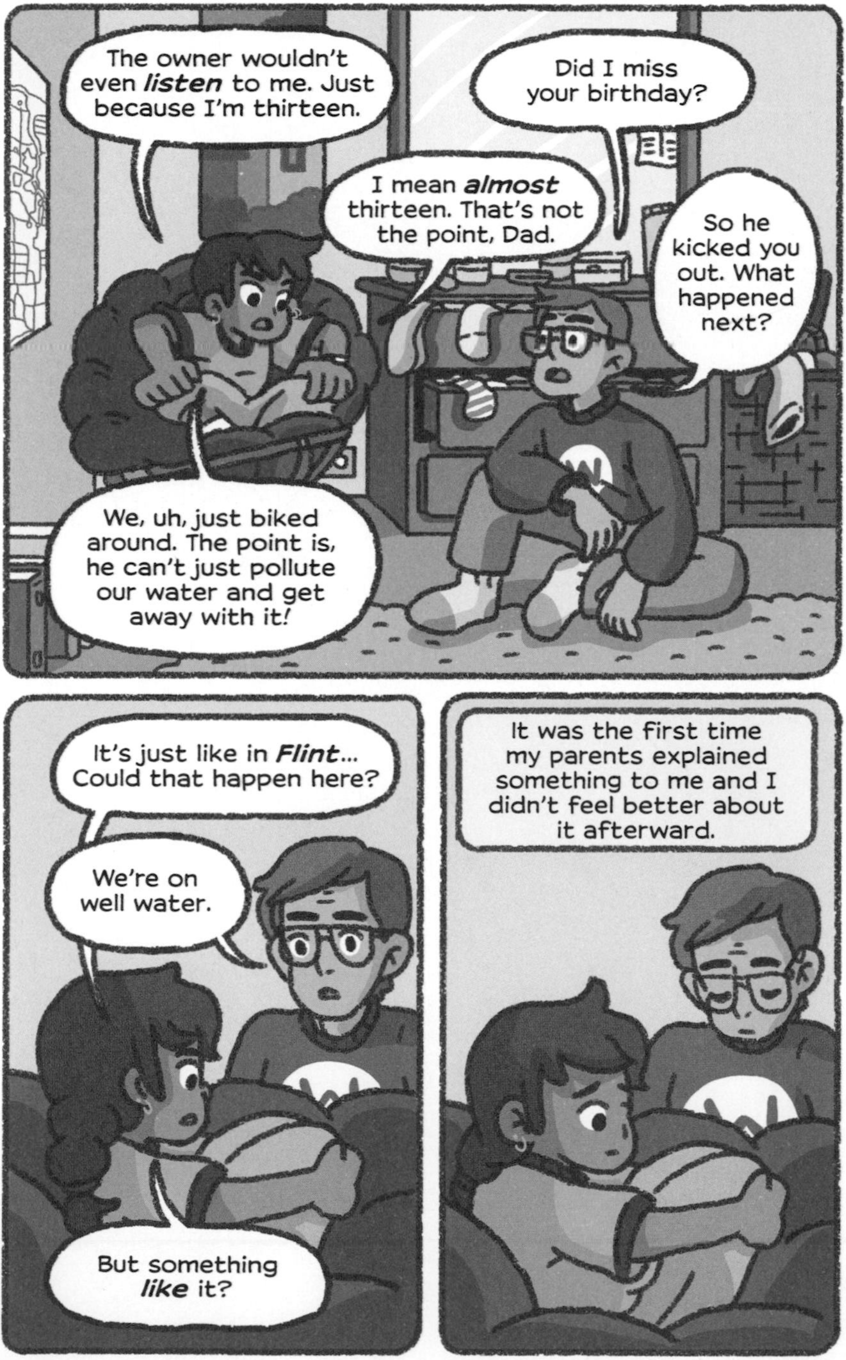
The owner wouldn't even *listen* to me. Just because I'm thirteen.
Did I miss your birthday?
I mean *almost* thirteen. That's not the point, Dad.
So he kicked you out. What happened next?
We, uh, just biked around. The point is, he can't just pollute our water and get away with it!
It's just like in *Flint*... Could that happen here?
We're on well water.
But something *like* it?
It was the first time my parents explained something to me and I didn't feel better about it afterward.

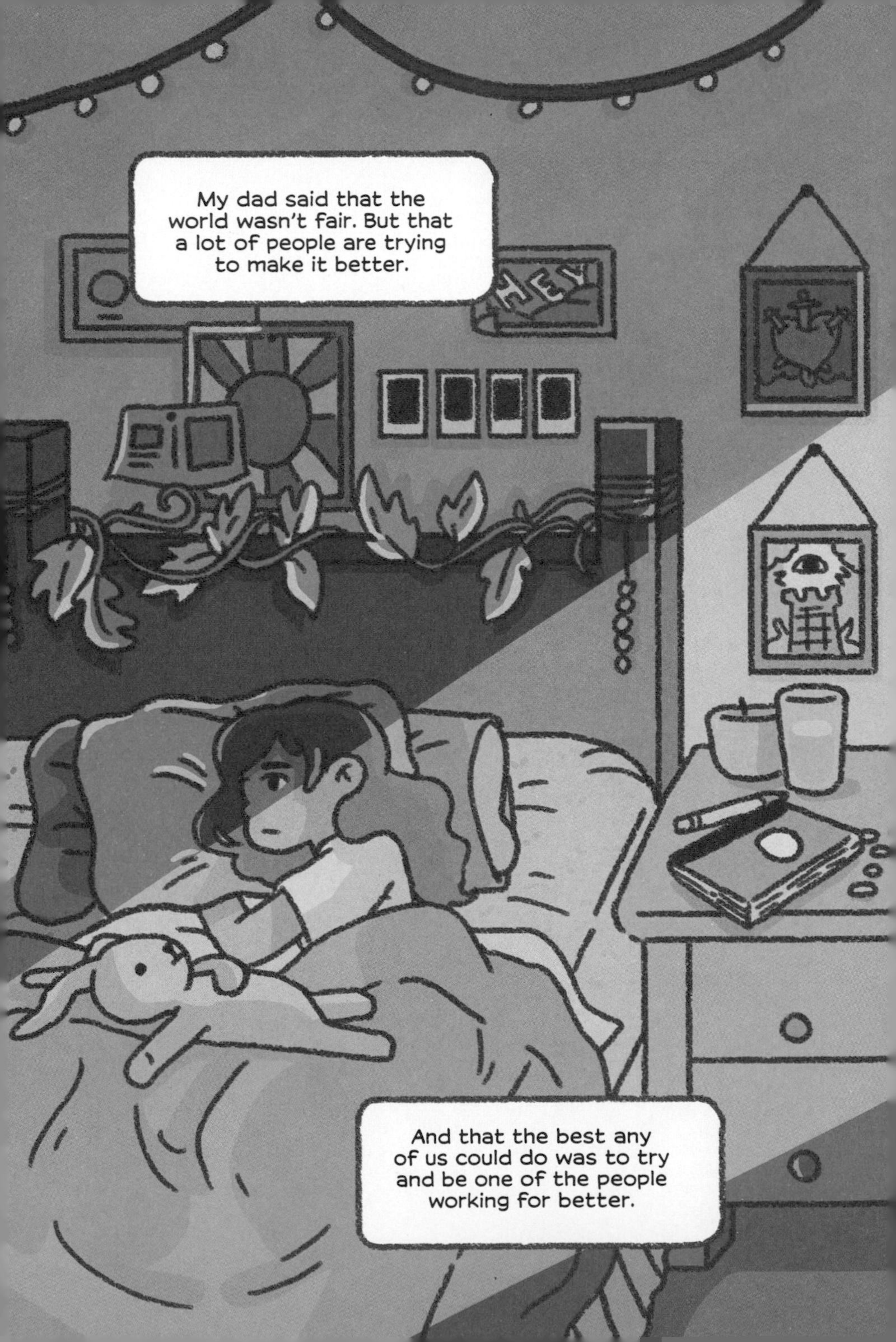
My dad said that the world wasn't fair. But that a lot of people are trying to make it better.
HEY
And that the best any of us could do was to try and be one of the people working for better.

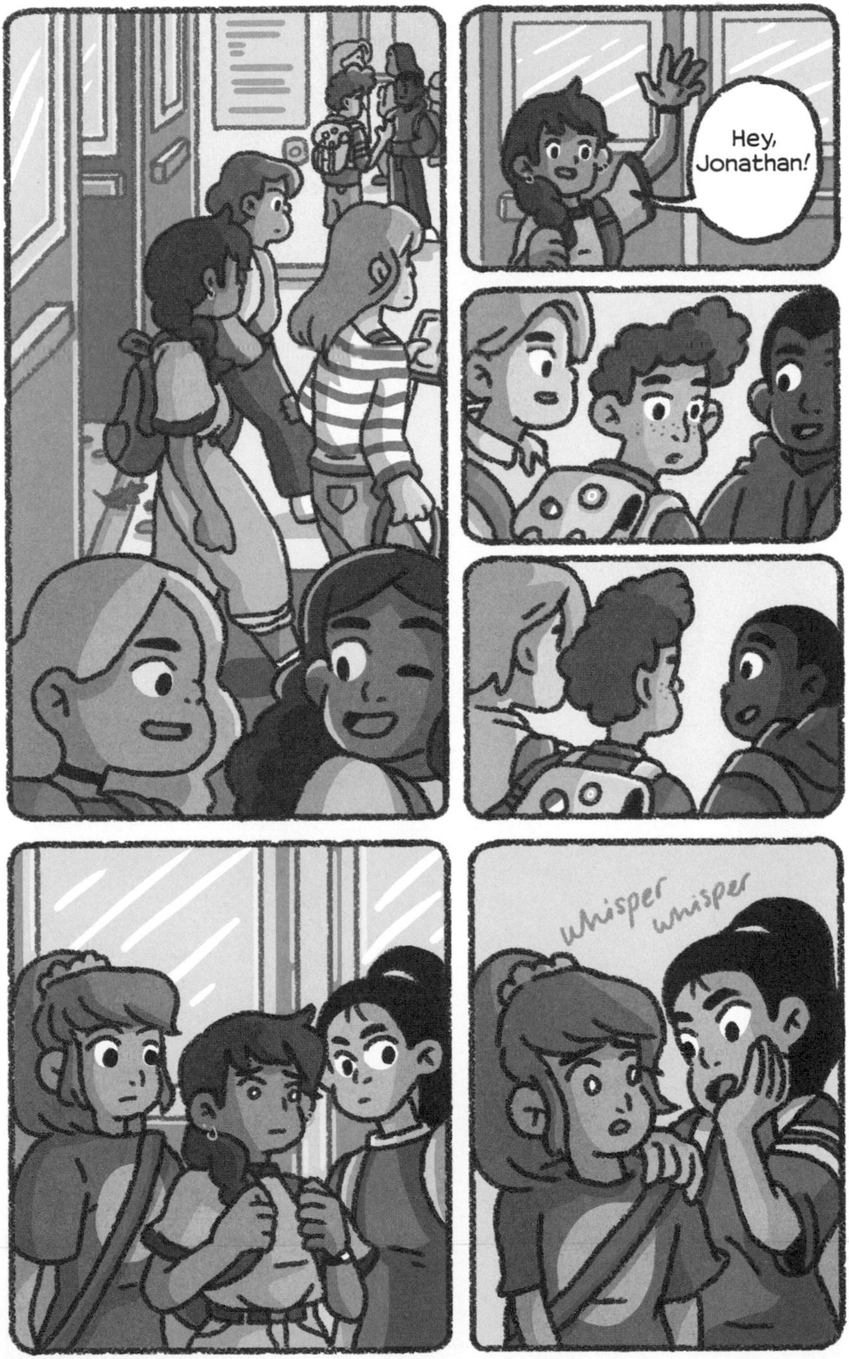
Hey, Jonathan!
whisper whisper

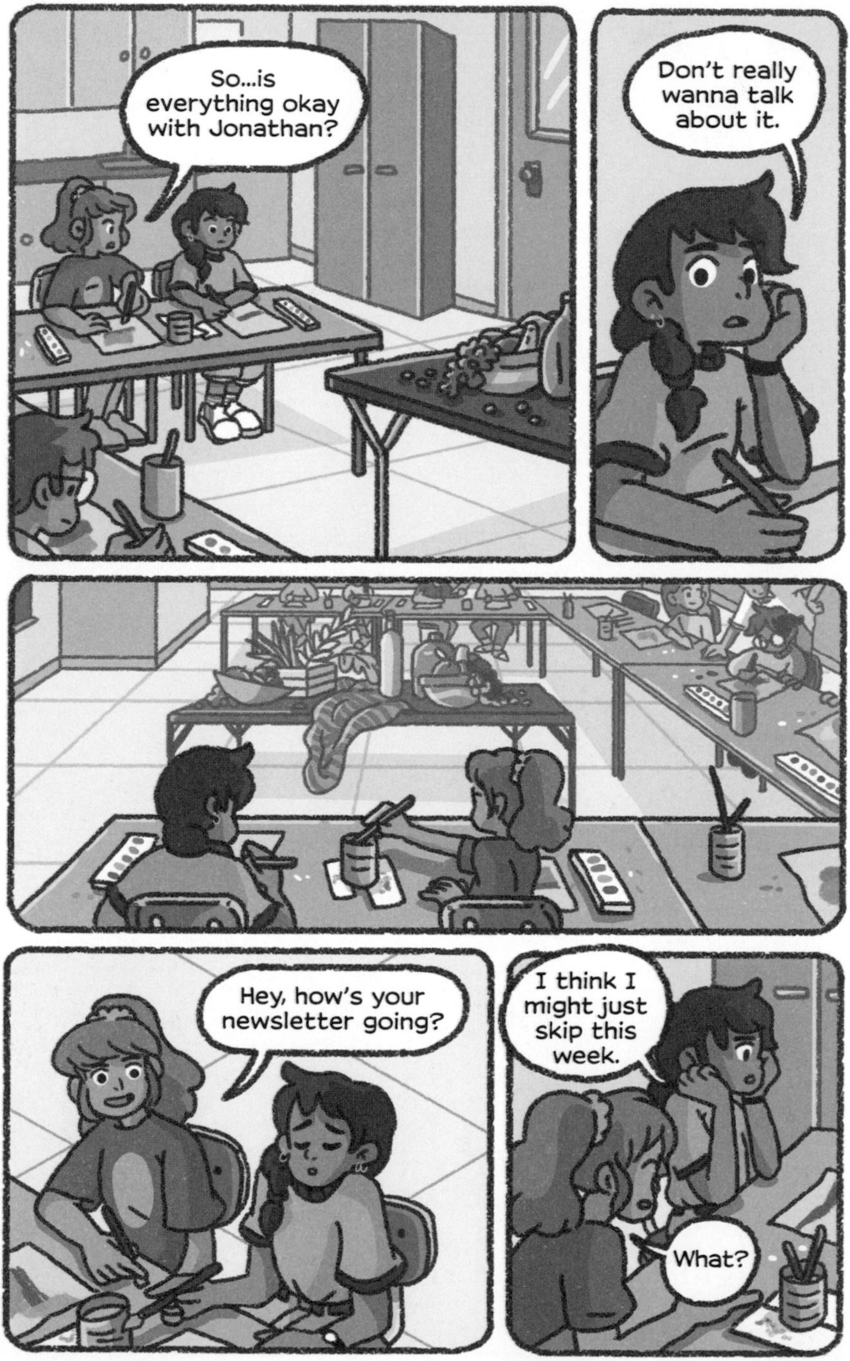
So...is everything okay with Jonathan?
Don't really wanna talk about it.
Hey, how's your newsletter going?
I think I might just skip this week.
What?

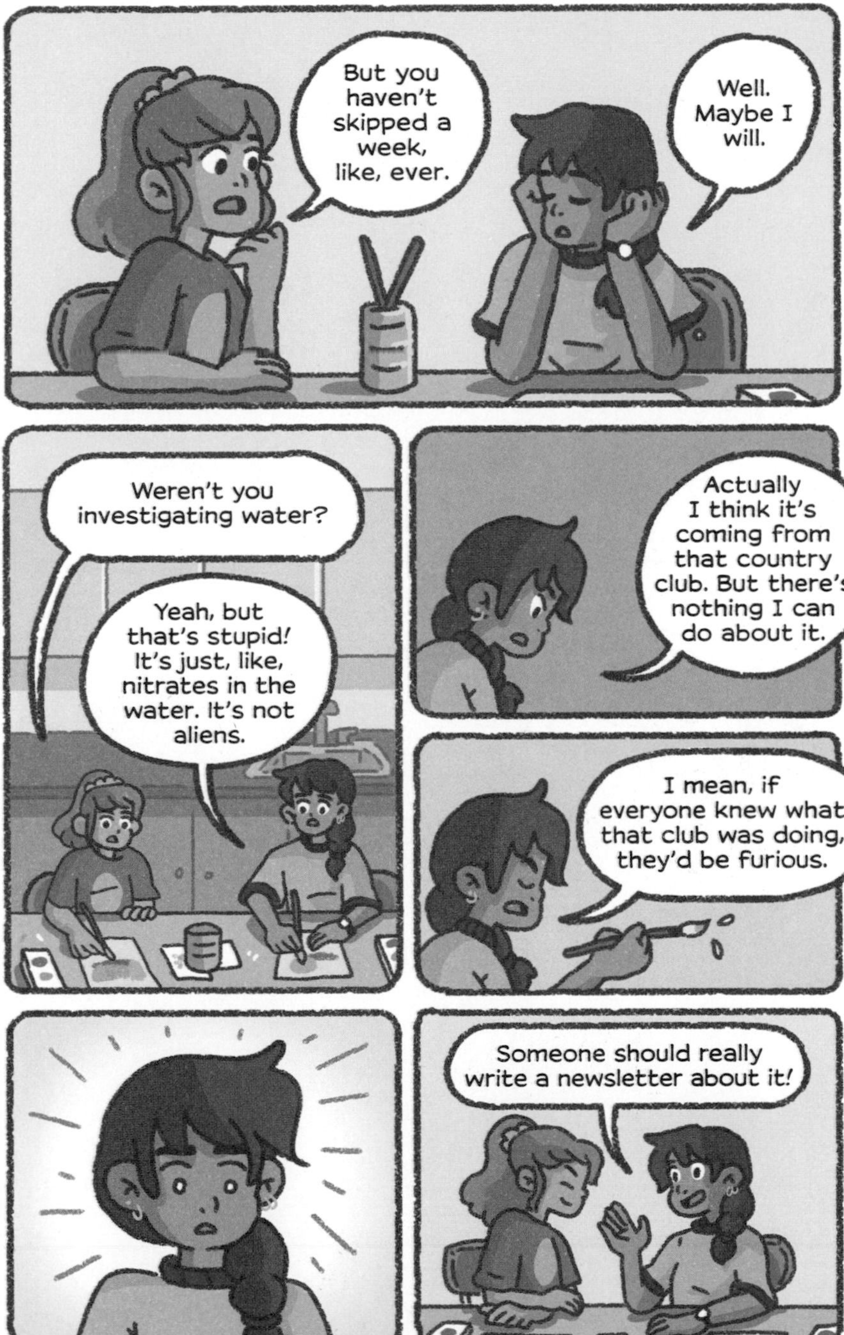
But you haven't skipped a week, like, ever.
Well. Maybe I will.
Weren't you investigating water?
Yeah, but that's stupid! It's just, like, nitrates in the water. It's not aliens.
Actually I think it's coming from that country club. But there's nothing I can do about it.
I mean, if everyone knew what that club was doing, they'd be furious.
Someone should really write a newsletter about it!

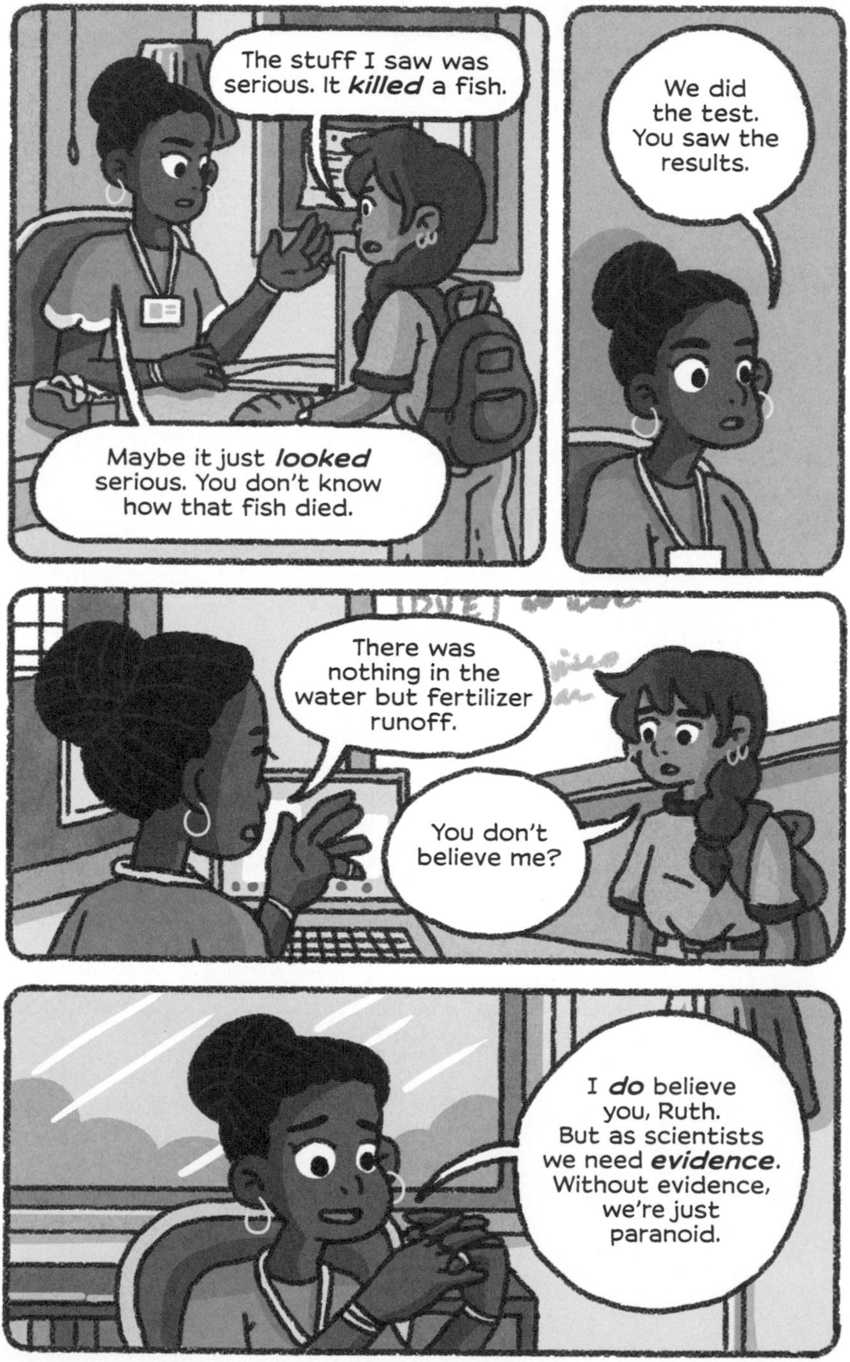
The stuff I saw was serious. It ***killed*** a fish.
Maybe it just ***looked*** serious. You don't know how that fish died.
We did the test. You saw the results.
There was nothing in the water but fertilizer runoff.
You don't believe me?
I ***do*** believe you, Ruth. But as scientists we need ***evidence***. Without evidence, we're just paranoid.

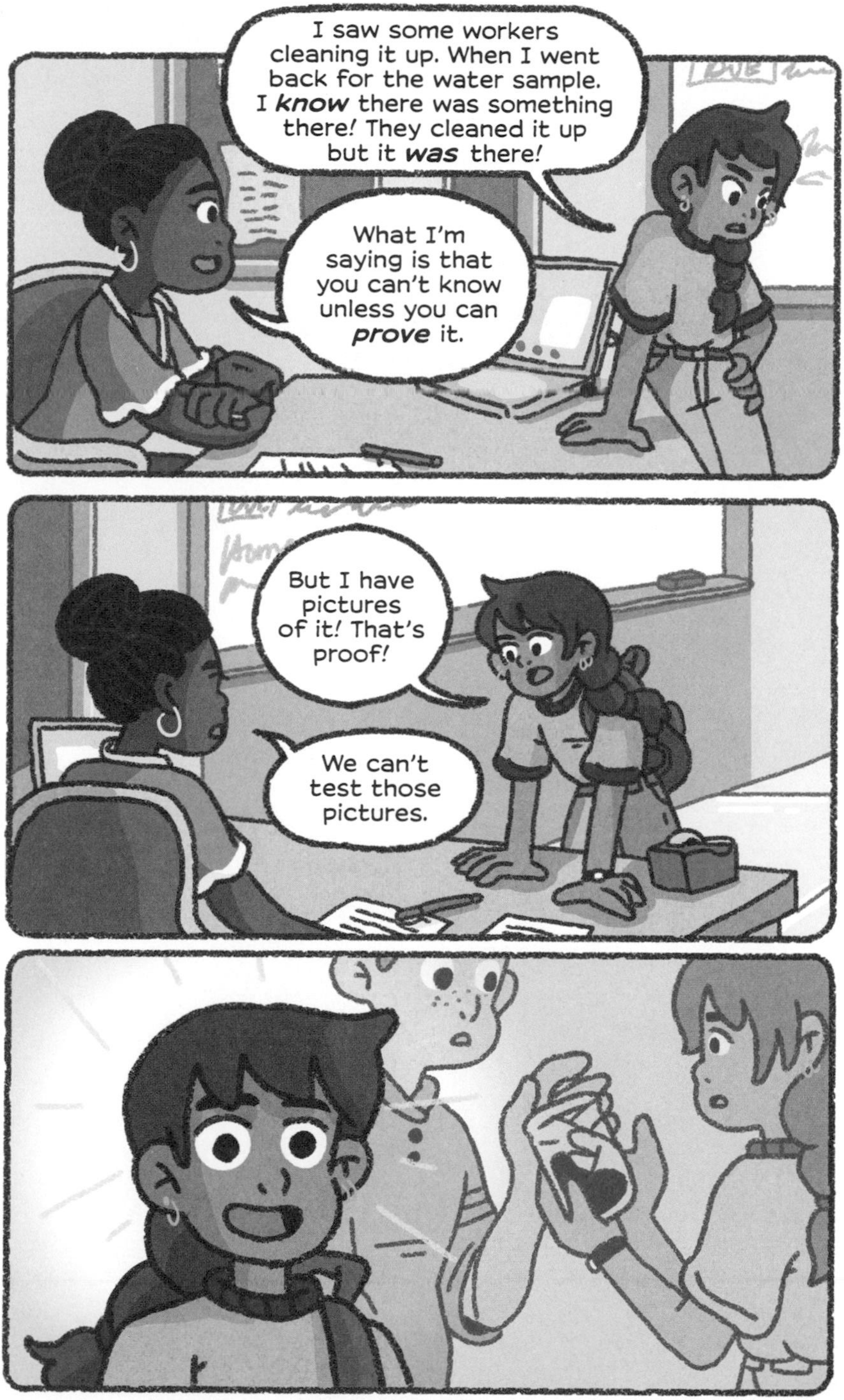
I saw some workers cleaning it up. When I went back for the water sample. I *know* there was something there! They cleaned it up but it *was* there!
What I'm saying is that you can't know unless you can *prove* it.
But I have pictures of it! That's proof!
We can't test those pictures.

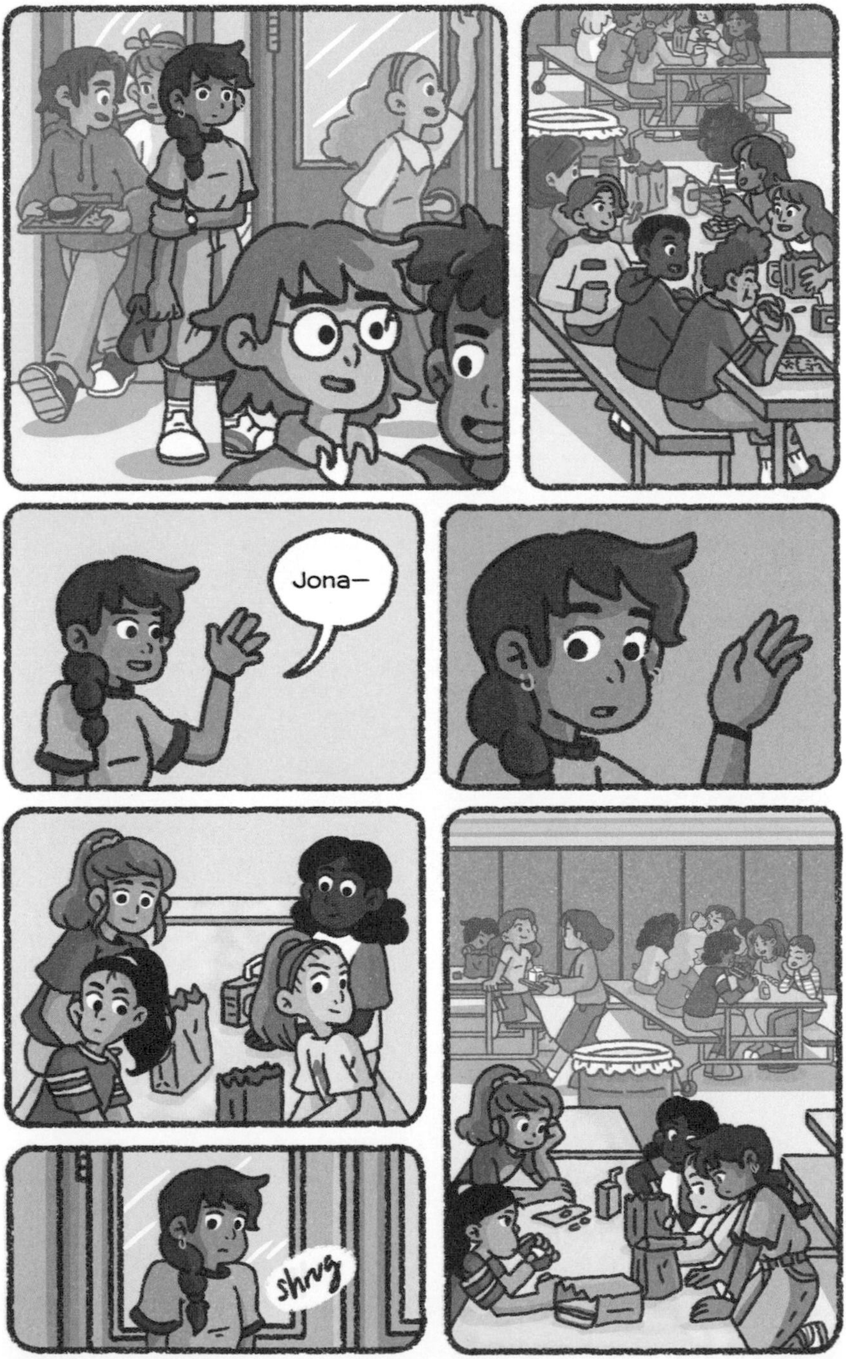
Jona—
shrug

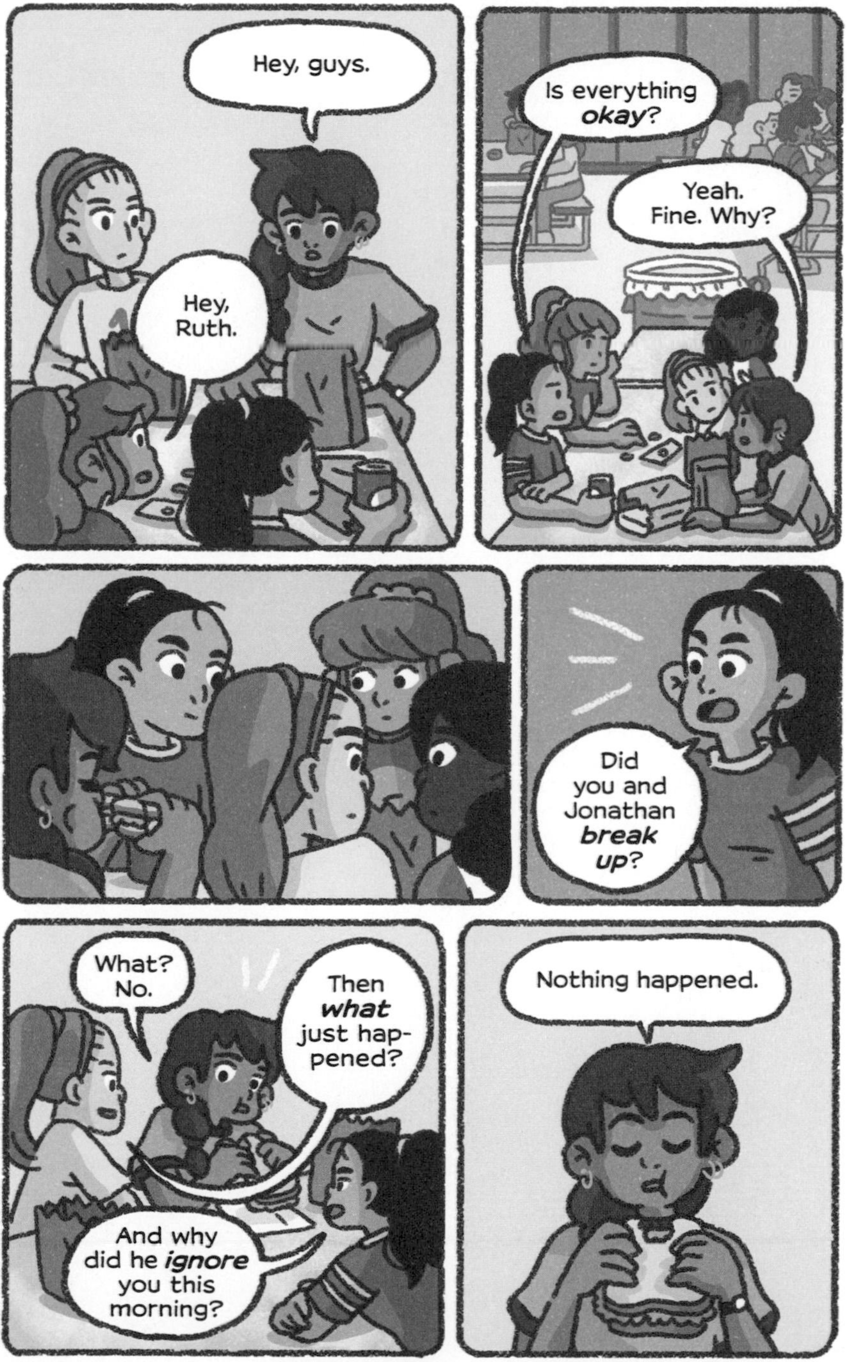
Hey, guys.
Hey, Ruth.
Is everything *okay*?
Yeah. Fine. Why?
Did you and Jonathan *break up*?
What? No.
Then *what* just happened?
And why did he *ignore* you this morning?
Nothing happened.

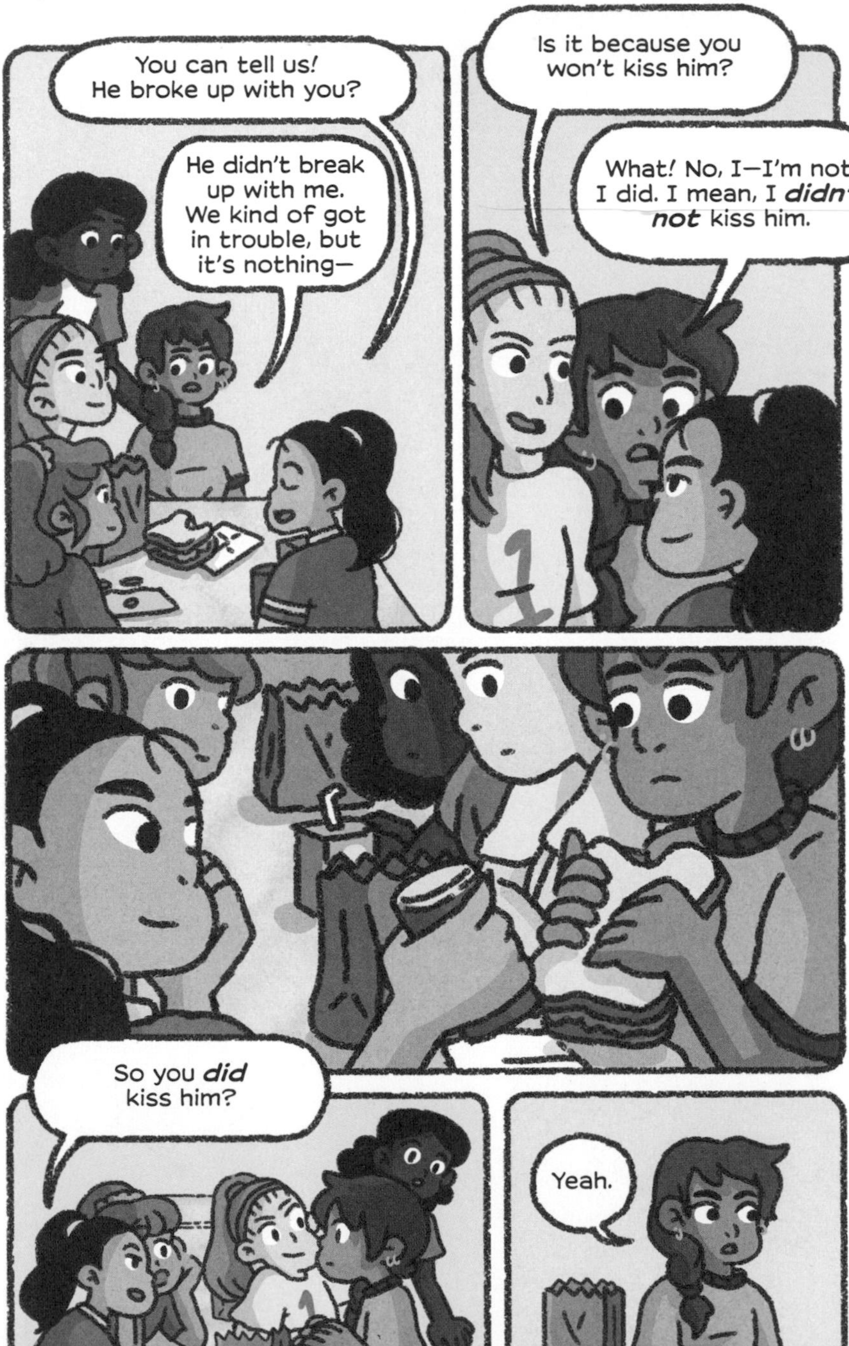
You can tell us! He broke up with you?
He didn't break up with me. We kind of got in trouble, but it's nothing—
Is it because you won't kiss him?
What! No, I—I'm not, I did. I mean, I ***didn't not*** kiss him.
So you ***did*** kiss him?
Yeah.

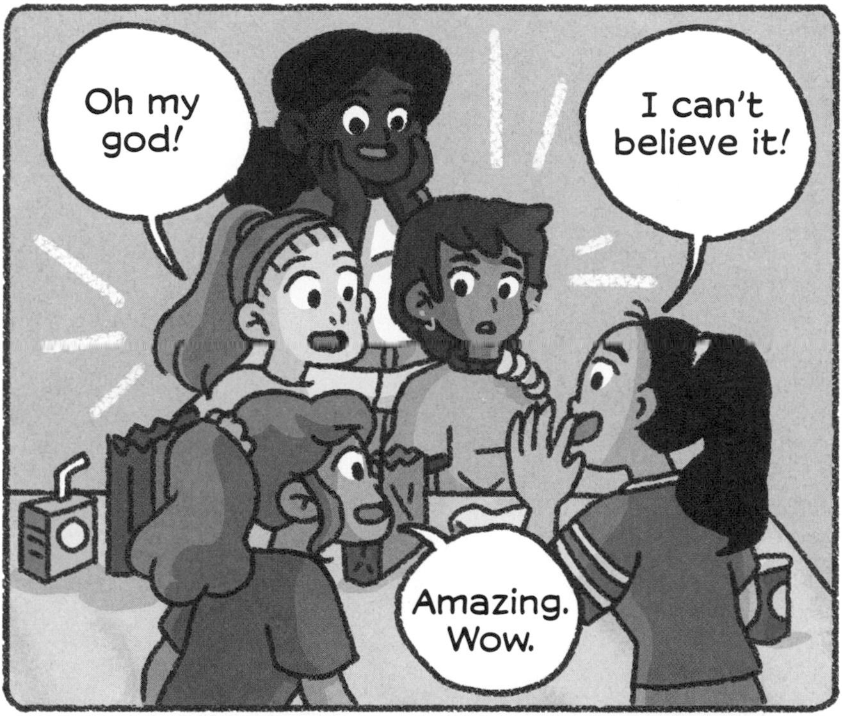
Oh my god!
I can't believe it!
Amazing. Wow.

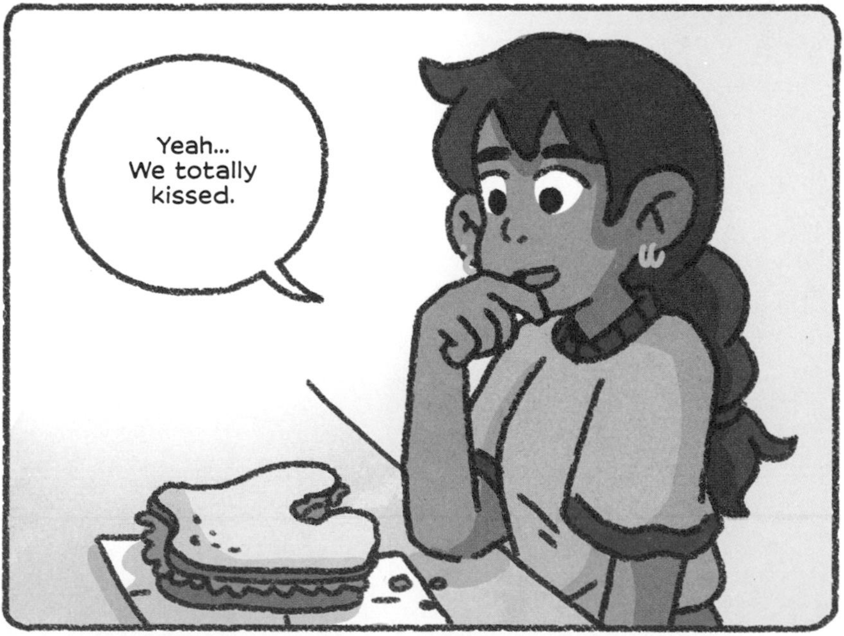
Yeah... We totally kissed.

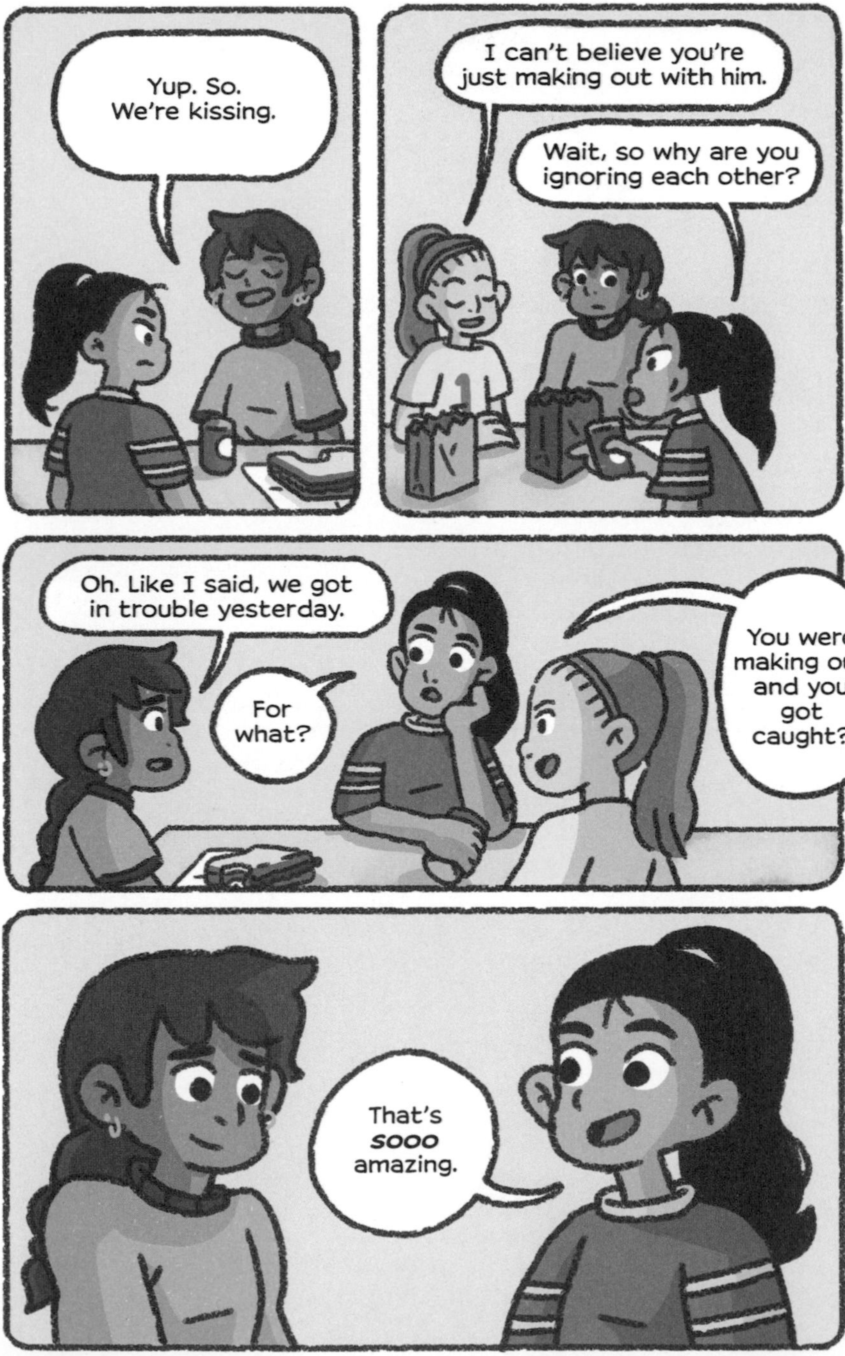
Yup. So.
We're kissing.
I can't believe you're just making out with him.
Wait, so why are you ignoring each other?
Oh. Like I said, we got in trouble yesterday.
For what?
You were making out and you got caught?
That's *sooo* amazing.

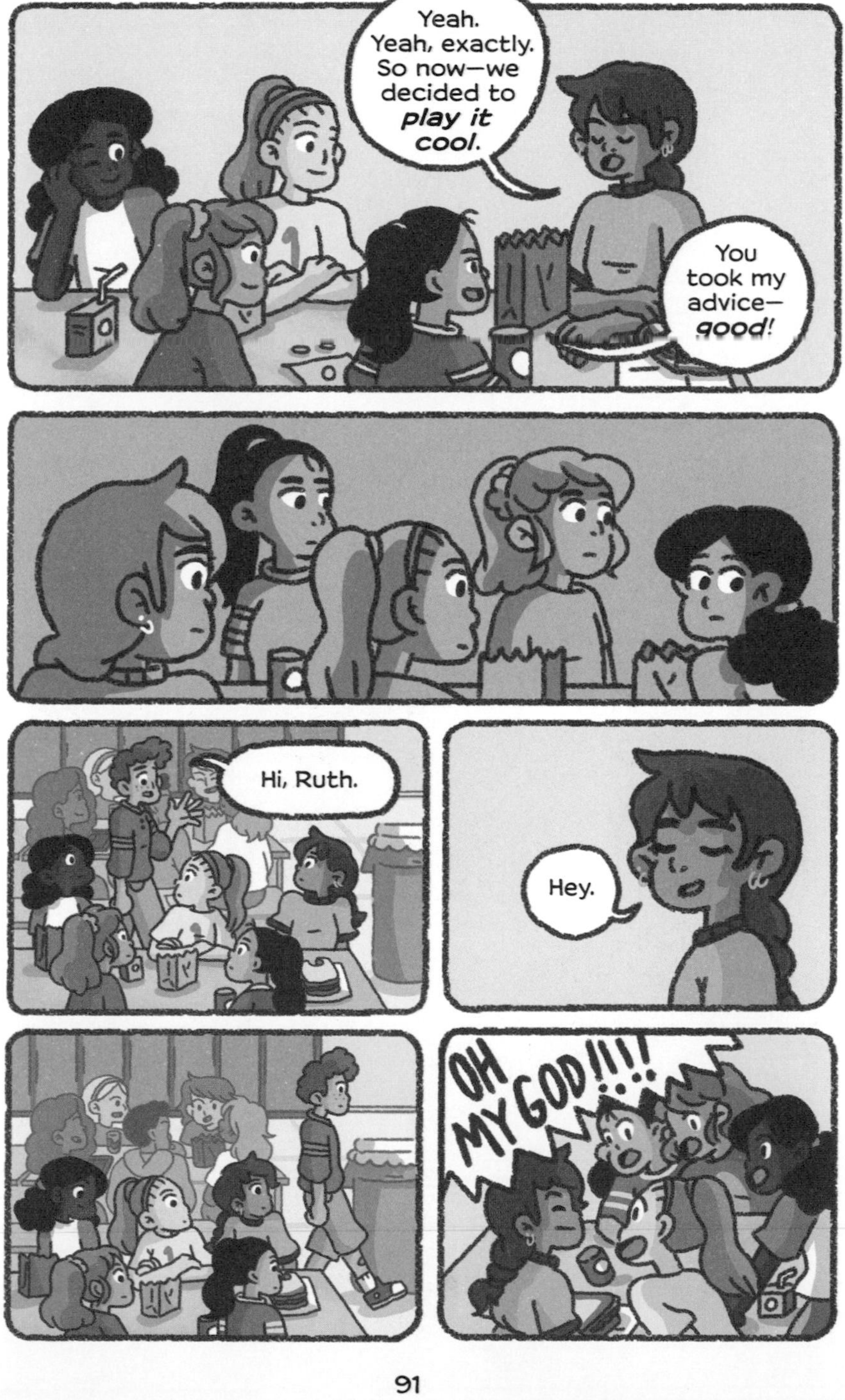
Yeah. Yeah, exactly. So now—we decided to *play it cool*.
You took my advice—*good*!
Hi, Ruth.
Hey.
OH MY GOD!!!!

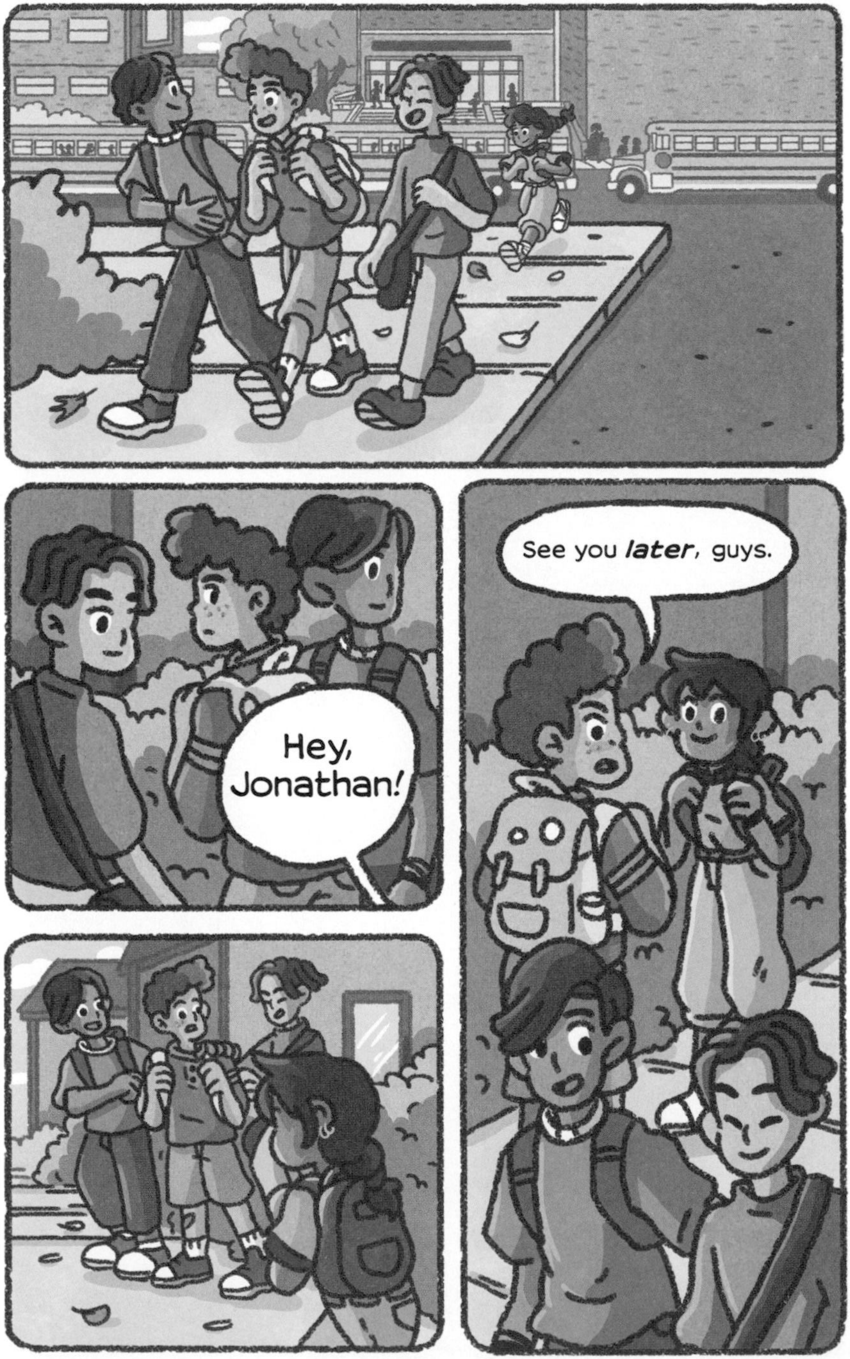
Hey, Jonathan!
See you *later*, guys.

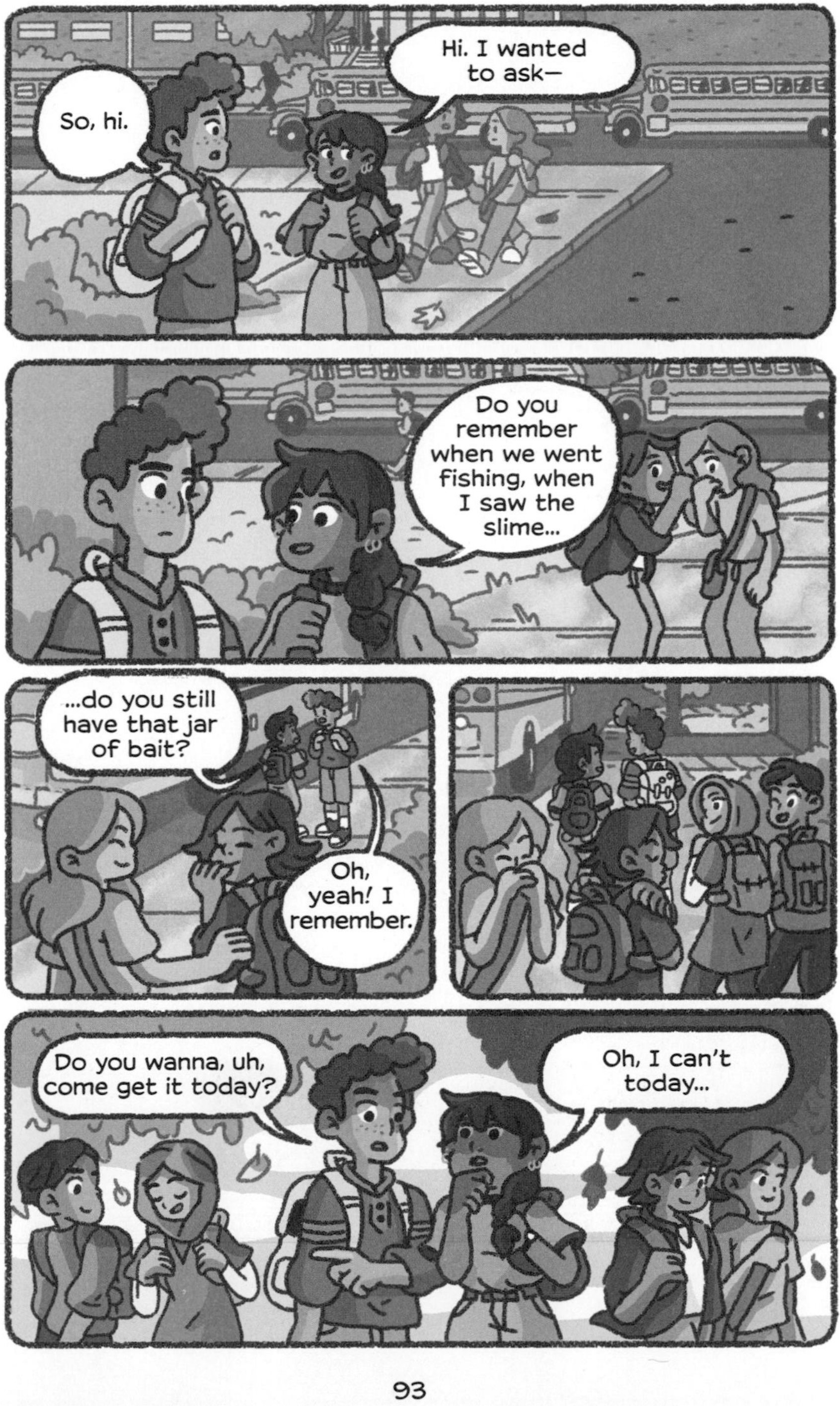
So, hi.
Hi. I wanted to ask—
Do you remember when we went fishing, when I saw the slime...
...do you still have that jar of bait?
Oh, yeah! I remember.
Do you wanna, uh, come get it today?
Oh, I can't today...

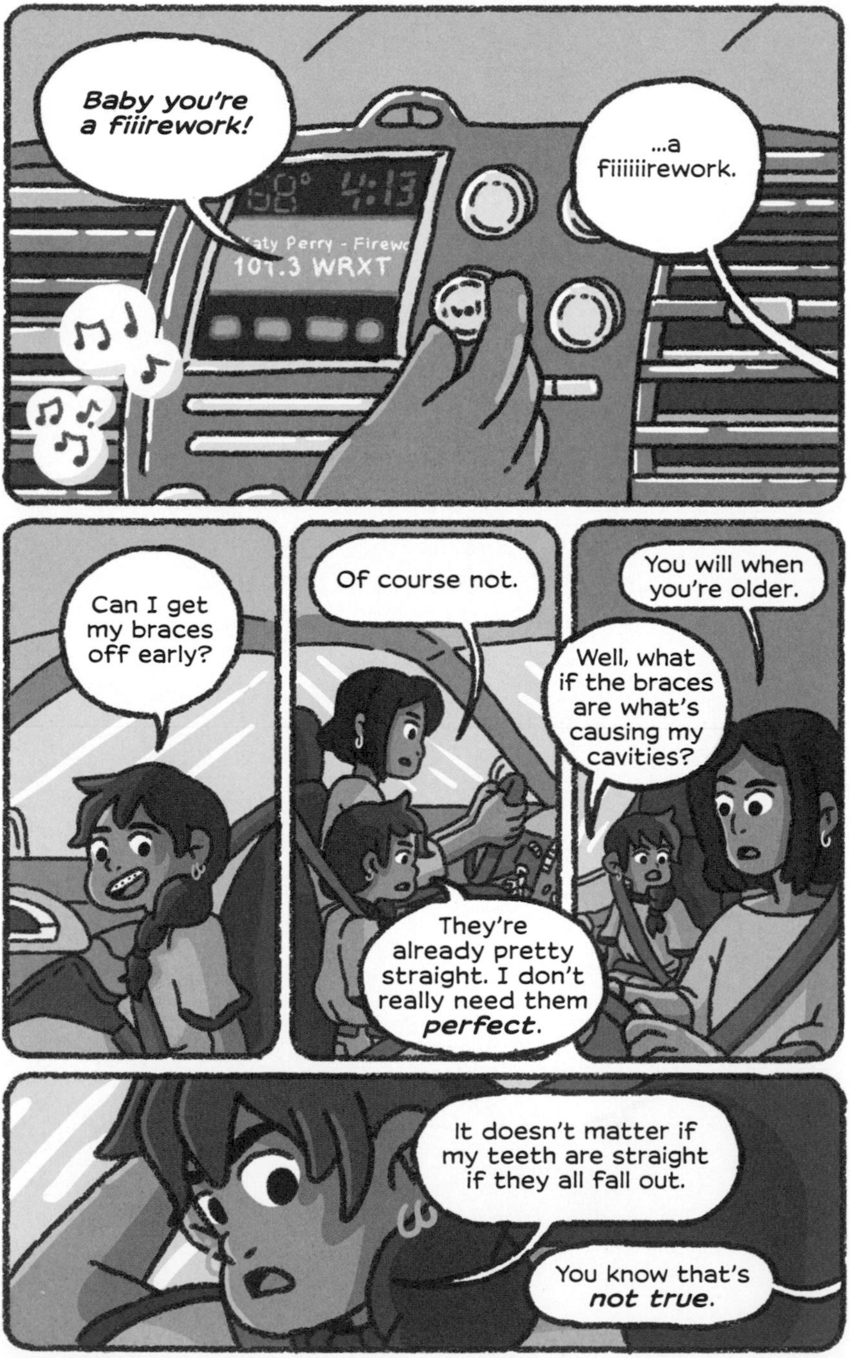

Baby you're a fiiirework!
...a fiiiiiirework.
Katy Perry - Firewo
101.3 WRXT
Can I get my braces off early?
Of course not.
They're already pretty straight. I don't really need them ***perfect***.
You will when you're older.
Well, what if the braces are what's causing my cavities?
It doesn't matter if my teeth are straight if they all fall out.
You know that's ***not true***.

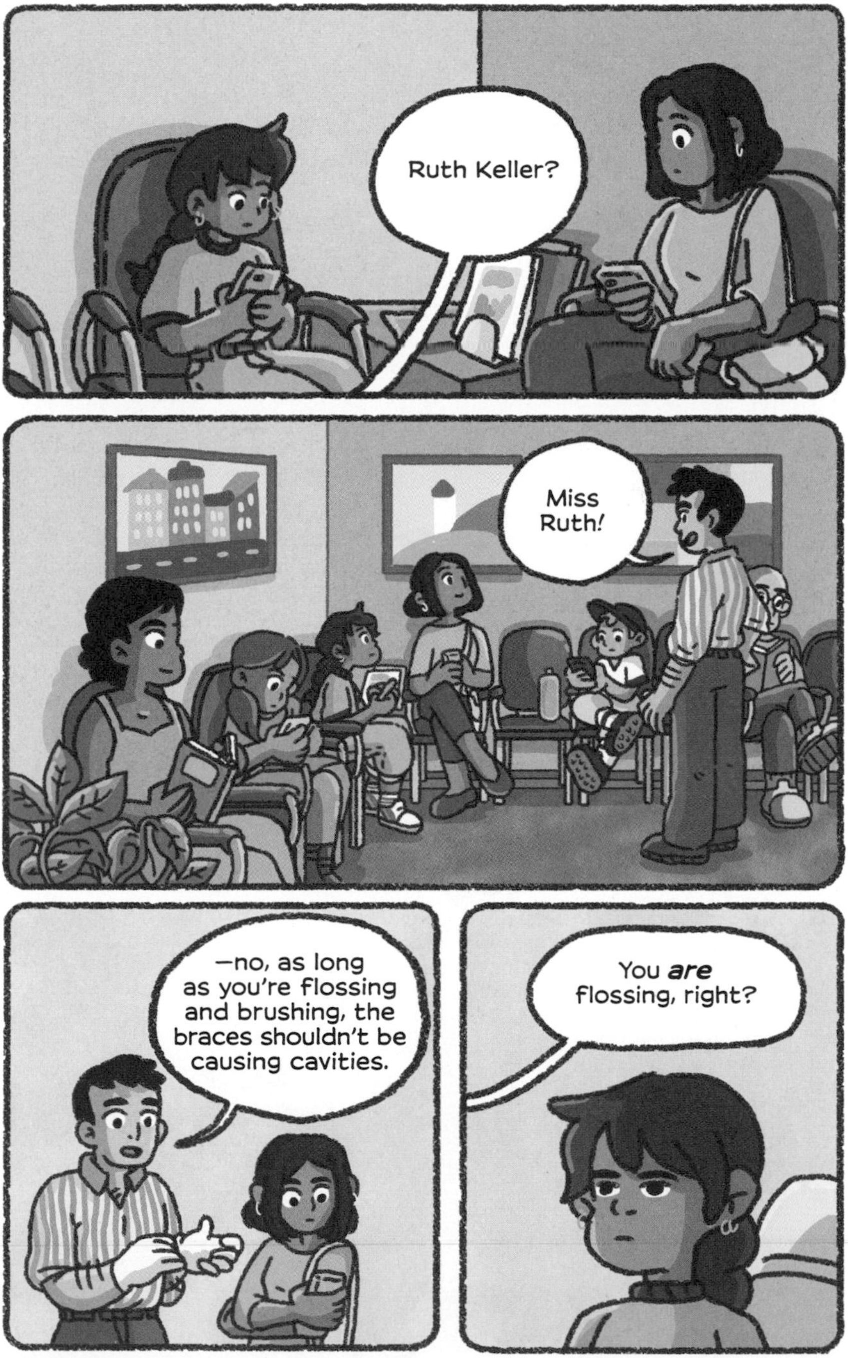
Ruth Keller?
Miss Ruth!
—no, as long as you're flossing and brushing, the braces shouldn't be causing cavities.
You ***are*** flossing, right?

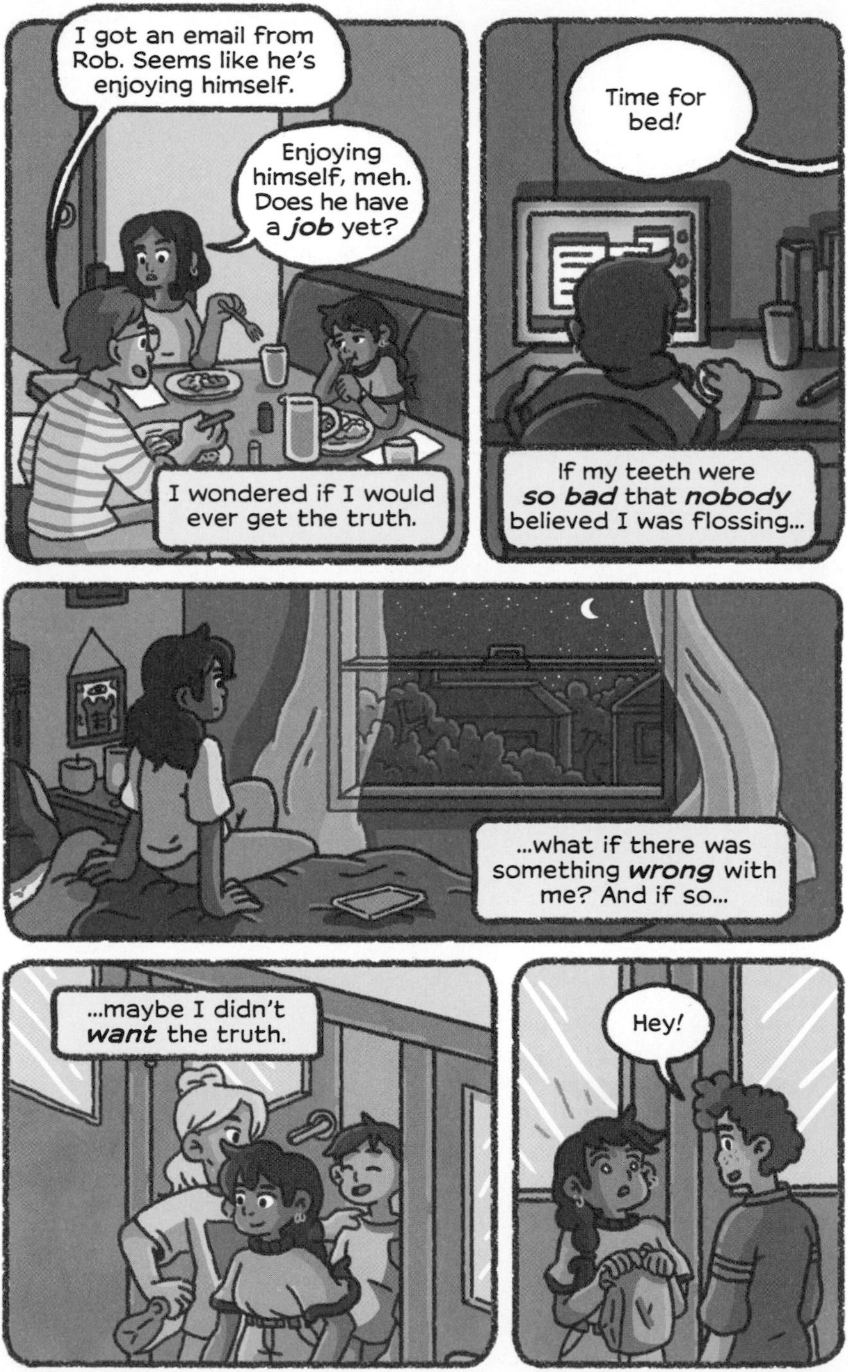
I got an email from Rob. Seems like he's enjoying himself.
Enjoying himself, meh. Does he have a *job* yet?
I wondered if I would ever get the truth.
Time for bed!
If my teeth were ***so bad*** that ***nobody*** believed I was flossing...
...what if there was something ***wrong*** with me? And if so...
...maybe I didn't ***want*** the truth.
Hey!

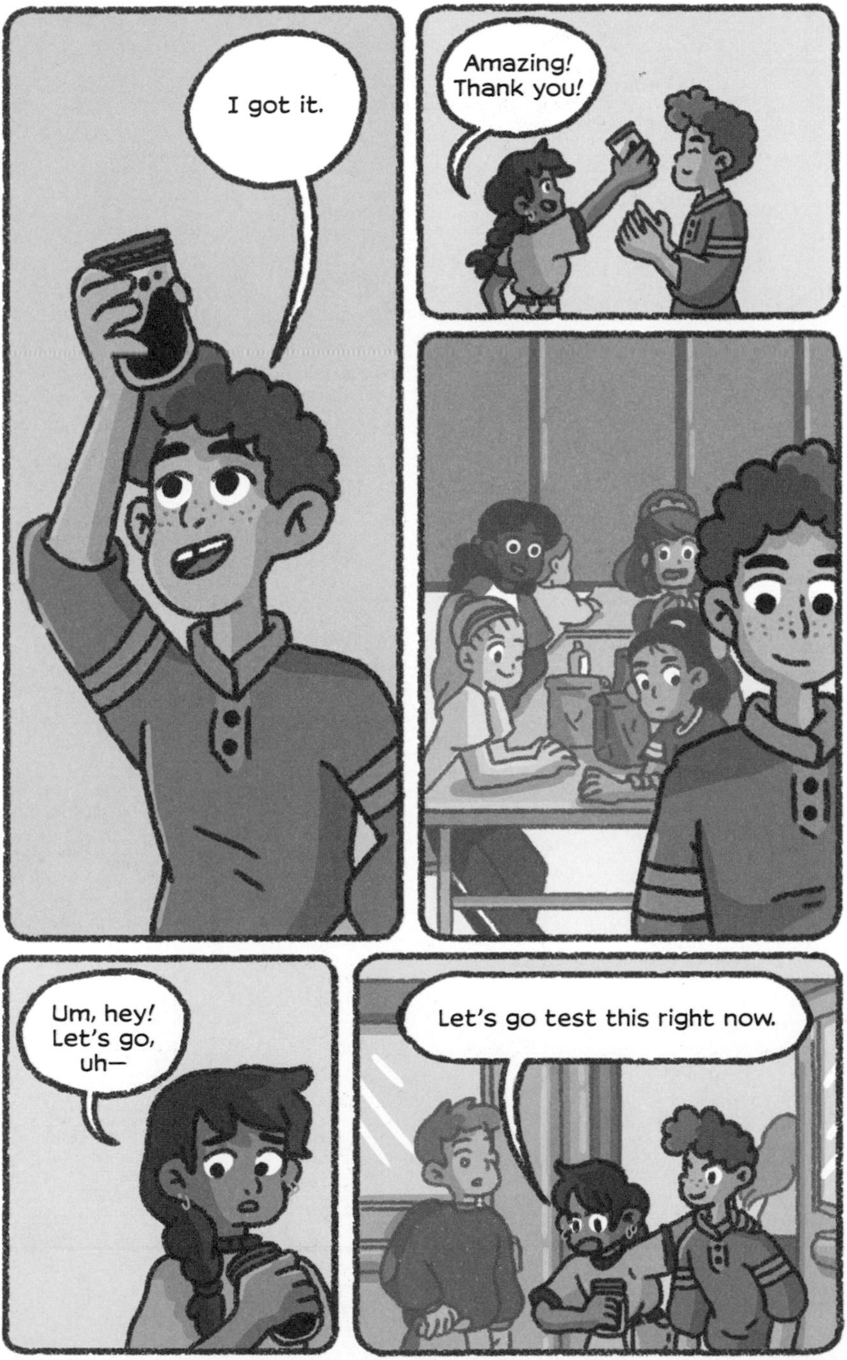
I got it.
Amazing! Thank you!
Um, hey! Let's go, uh—
Let's go test this right now.

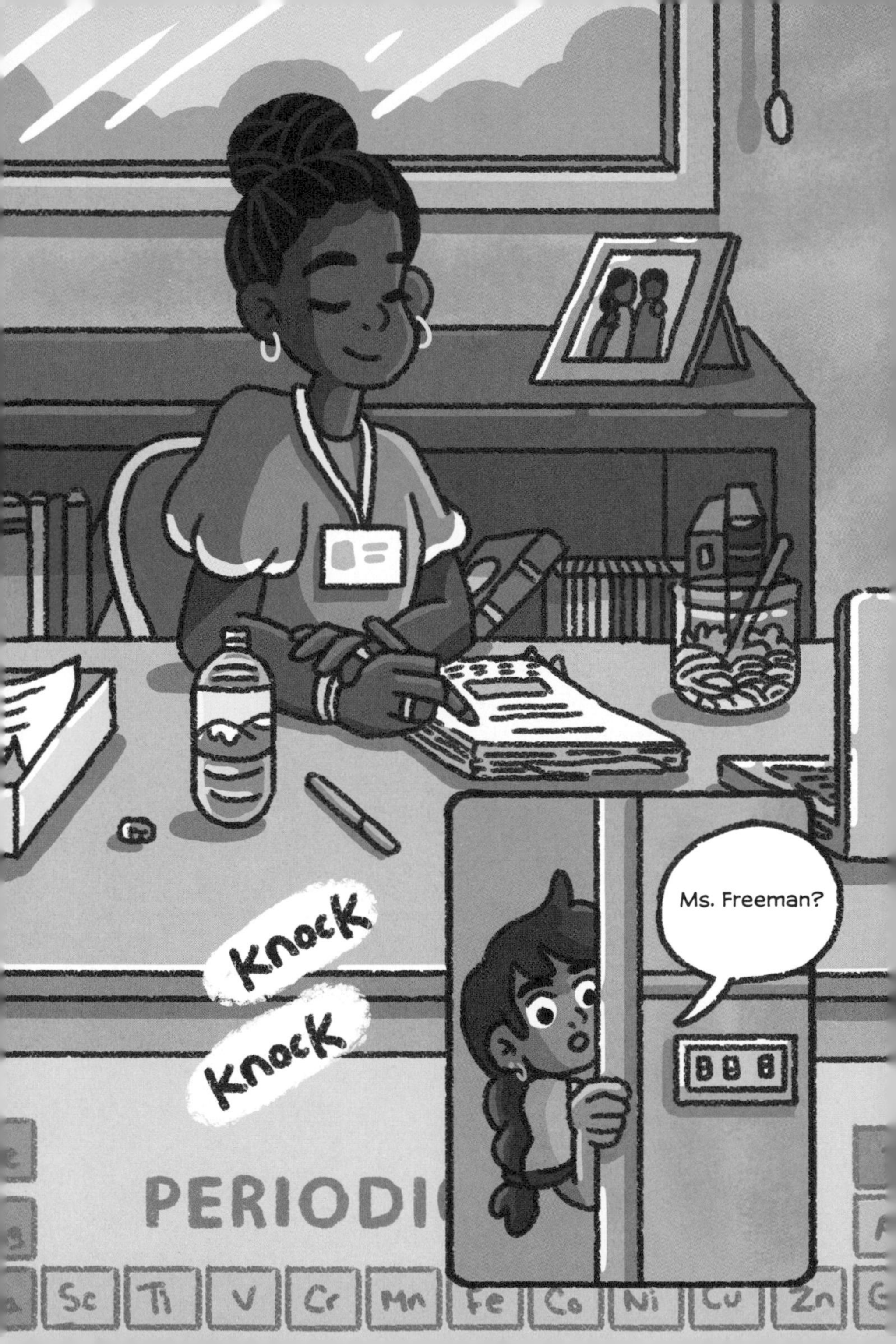
Knock
Knock
Ms. Freeman?
PERIODI
Sc
Ti
V
Cr
Mn
Fe
Co
Ni
Cu
Zn

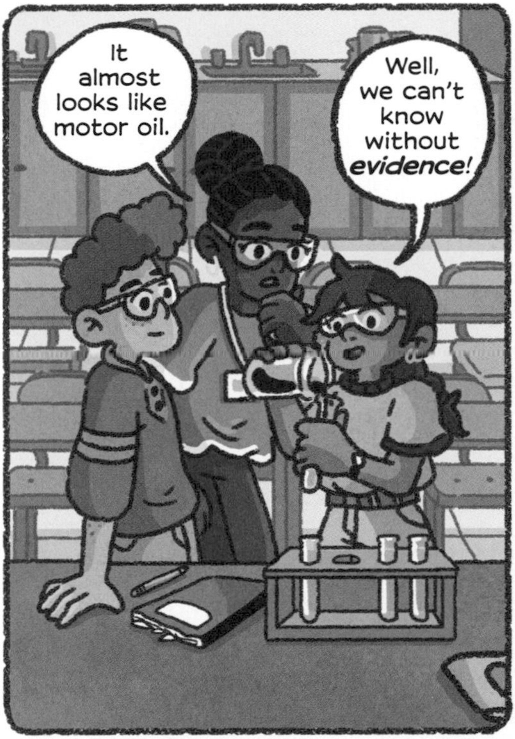
It almost looks like motor oil.
Well, we can't know without *evidence*!

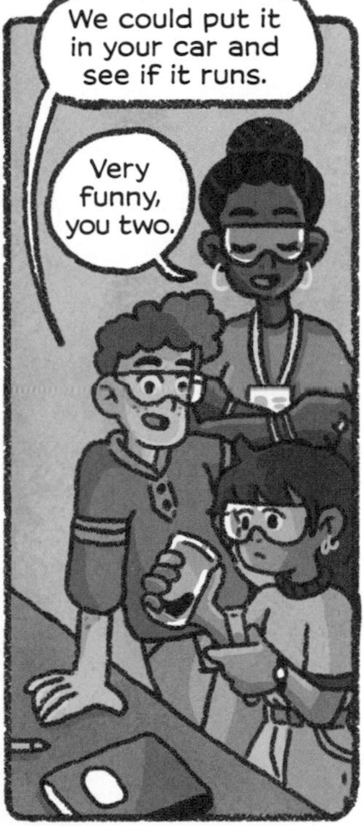
We could put it in your car and see if it runs.
Very funny, you two.

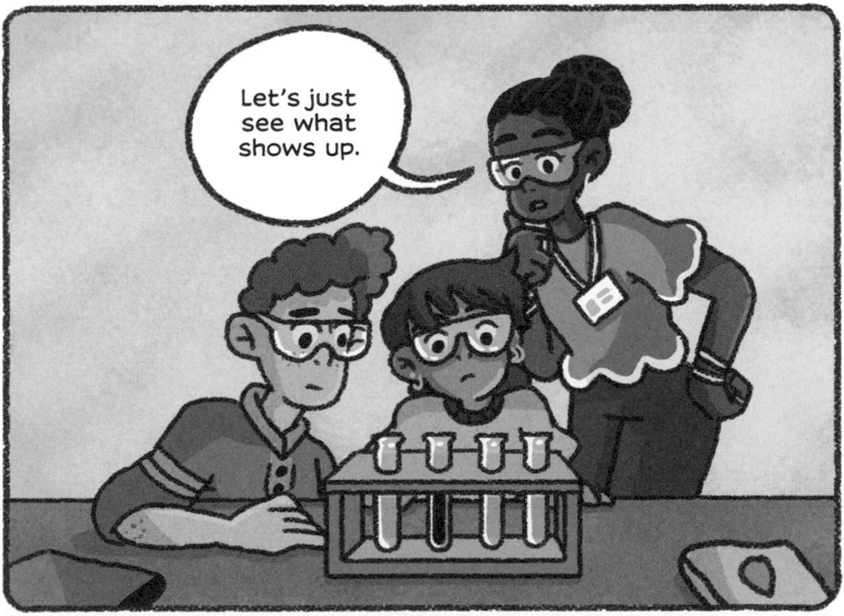
Let's just see what shows up.

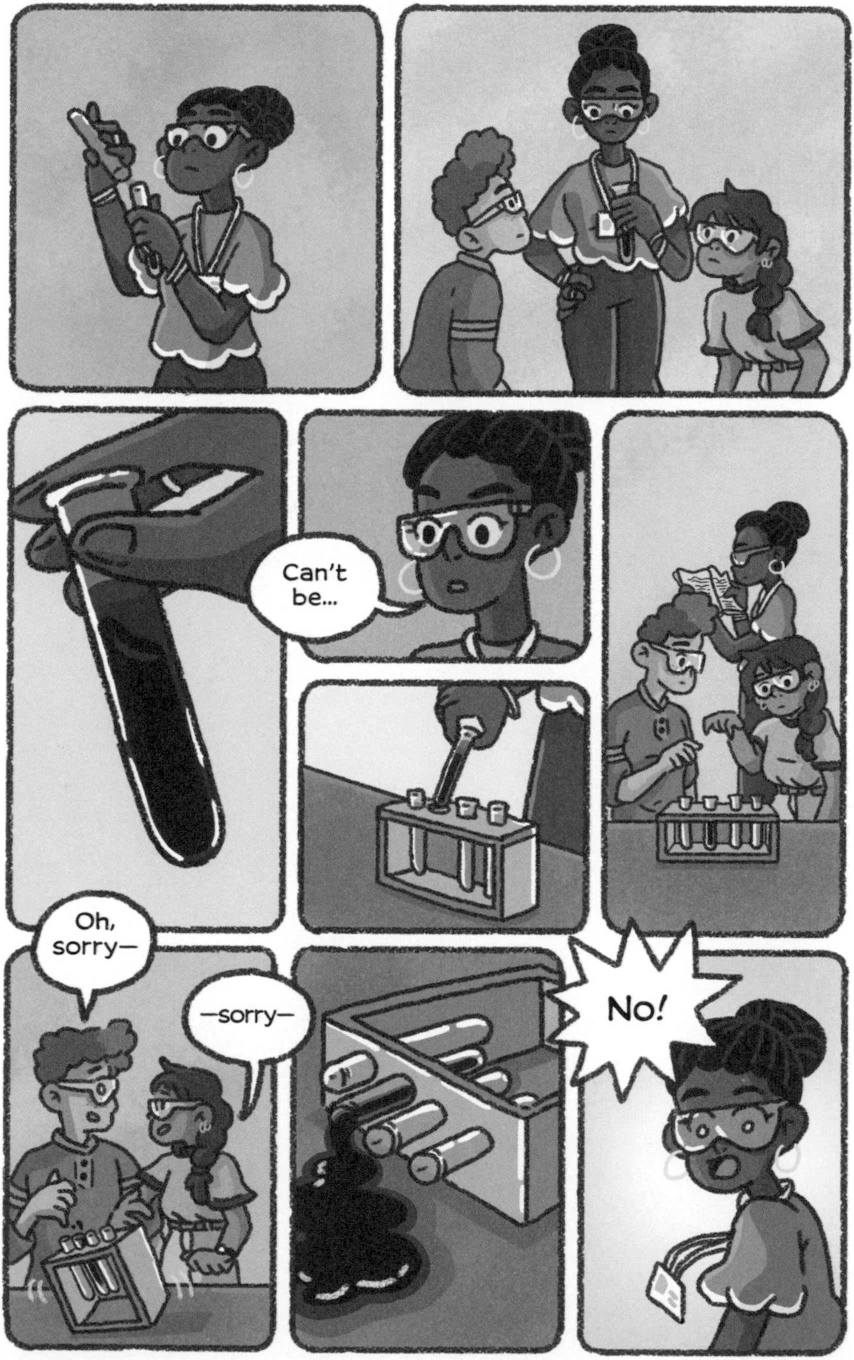
Can't be...
Oh, sorry—
—sorry—
No!

Ruth and Jonathan, walk out of the room and go wash your hands. Right. Now.

It *can't* be...

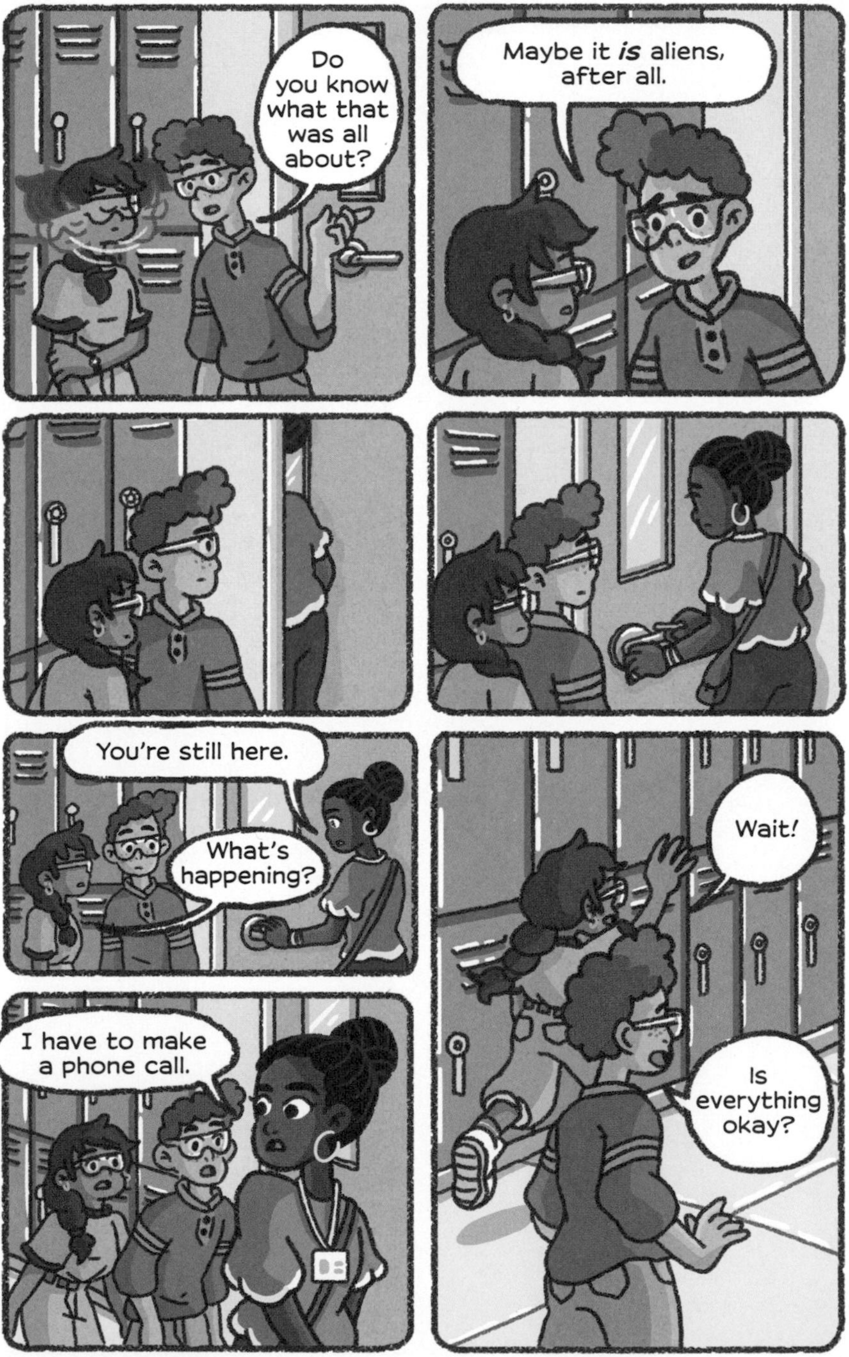
Do you know what that was all about?
Maybe it *is* aliens, after all.
You're still here.
What's happening?
I have to make a phone call.
Wait!
Is everything okay?

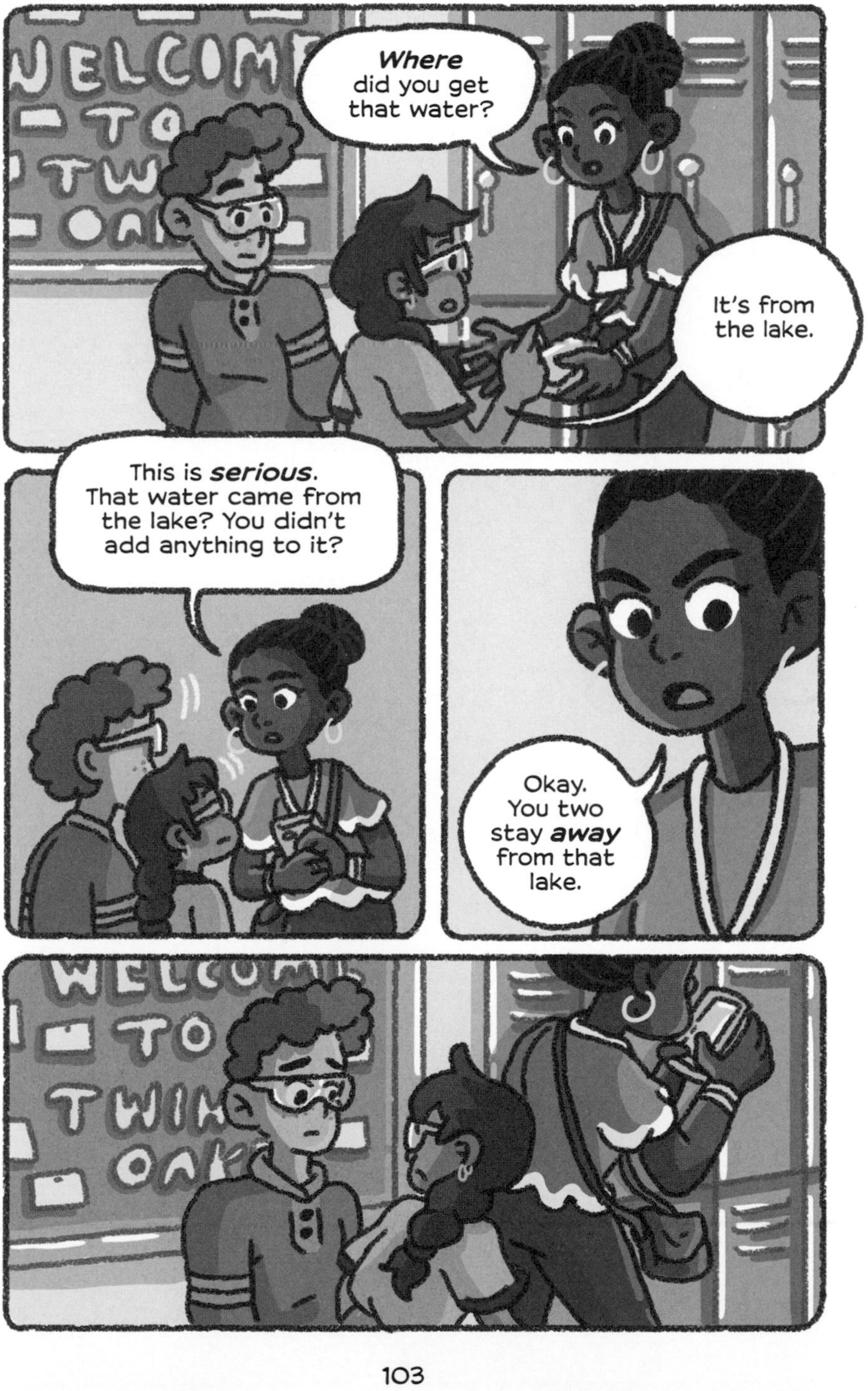
Where did you get that water?
It's from the lake.
This is *serious*. That water came from the lake? You didn't add anything to it?
Okay. You two stay *away* from that lake.

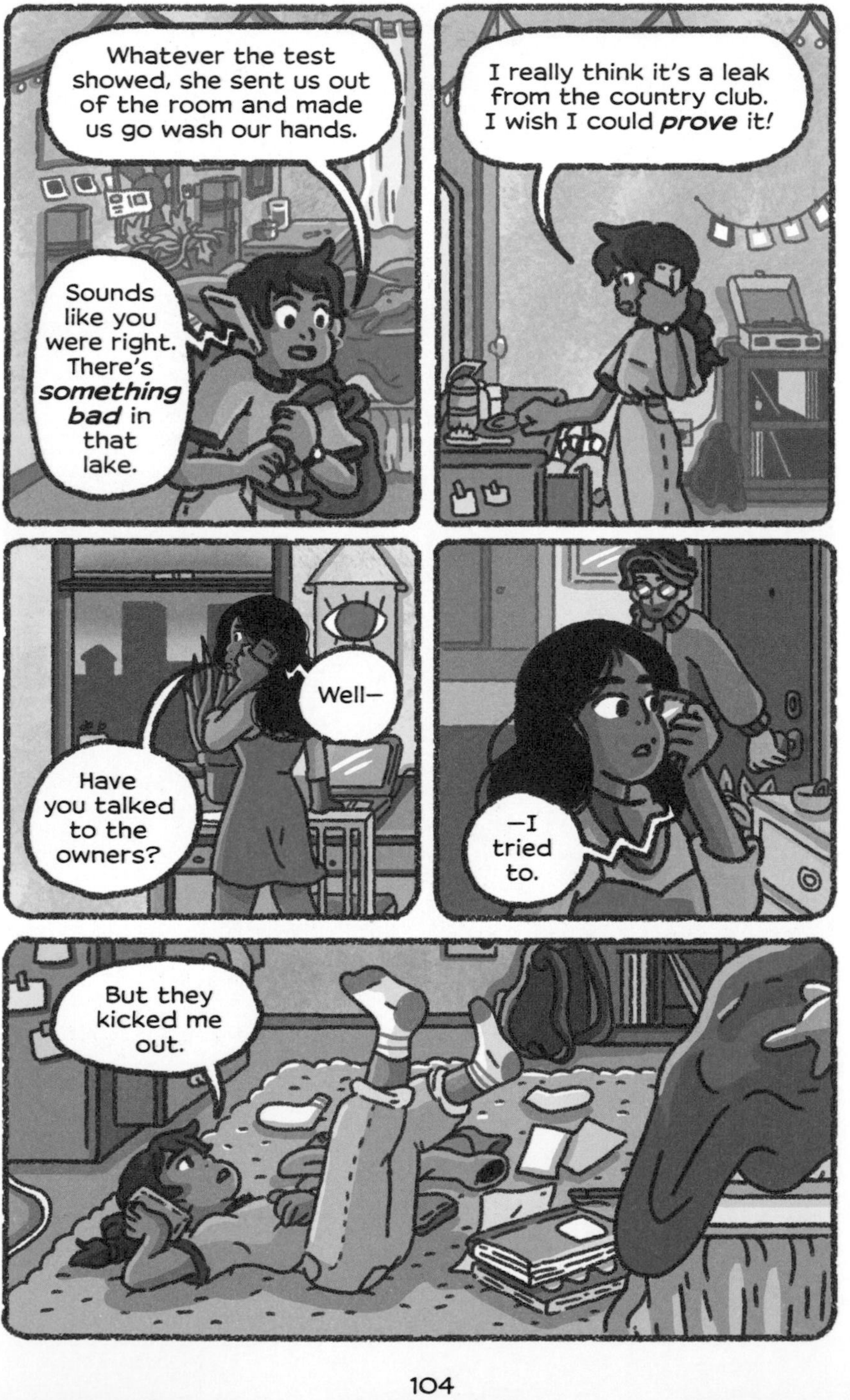
Whatever the test showed, she sent us out of the room and made us go wash our hands.
Sounds like you were right. There's ***something bad*** in that lake.
I really think it's a leak from the country club. I wish I could ***prove*** it!
Well—
Have you talked to the owners?
—I tried to.
But they kicked me out.

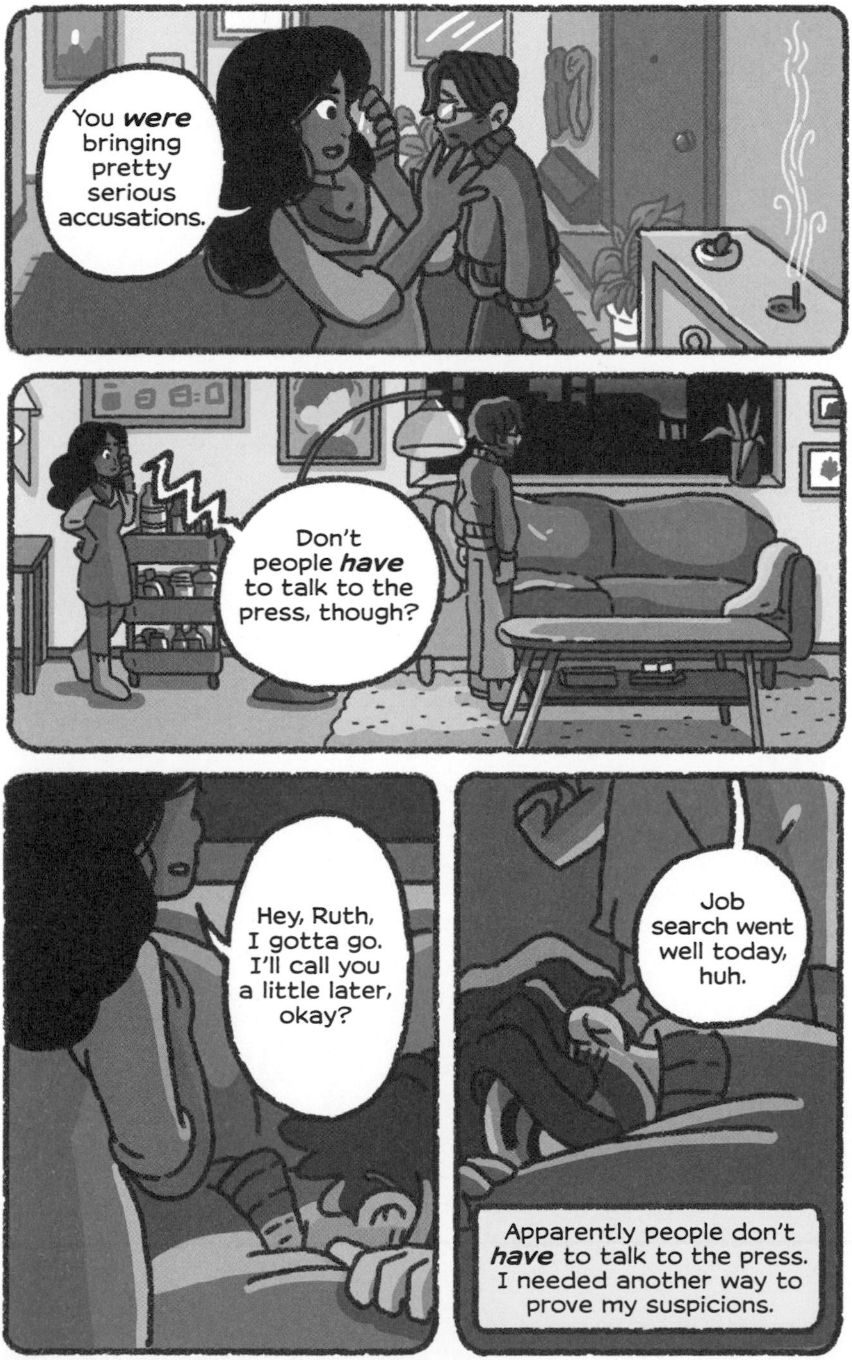
You ***were*** bringing pretty serious accusations.
Don't people ***have*** to talk to the press, though?
Hey, Ruth, I gotta go. I'll call you a little later, okay?
Job search went well today, huh.
Apparently people don't ***have*** to talk to the press. I needed another way to prove my suspicions.

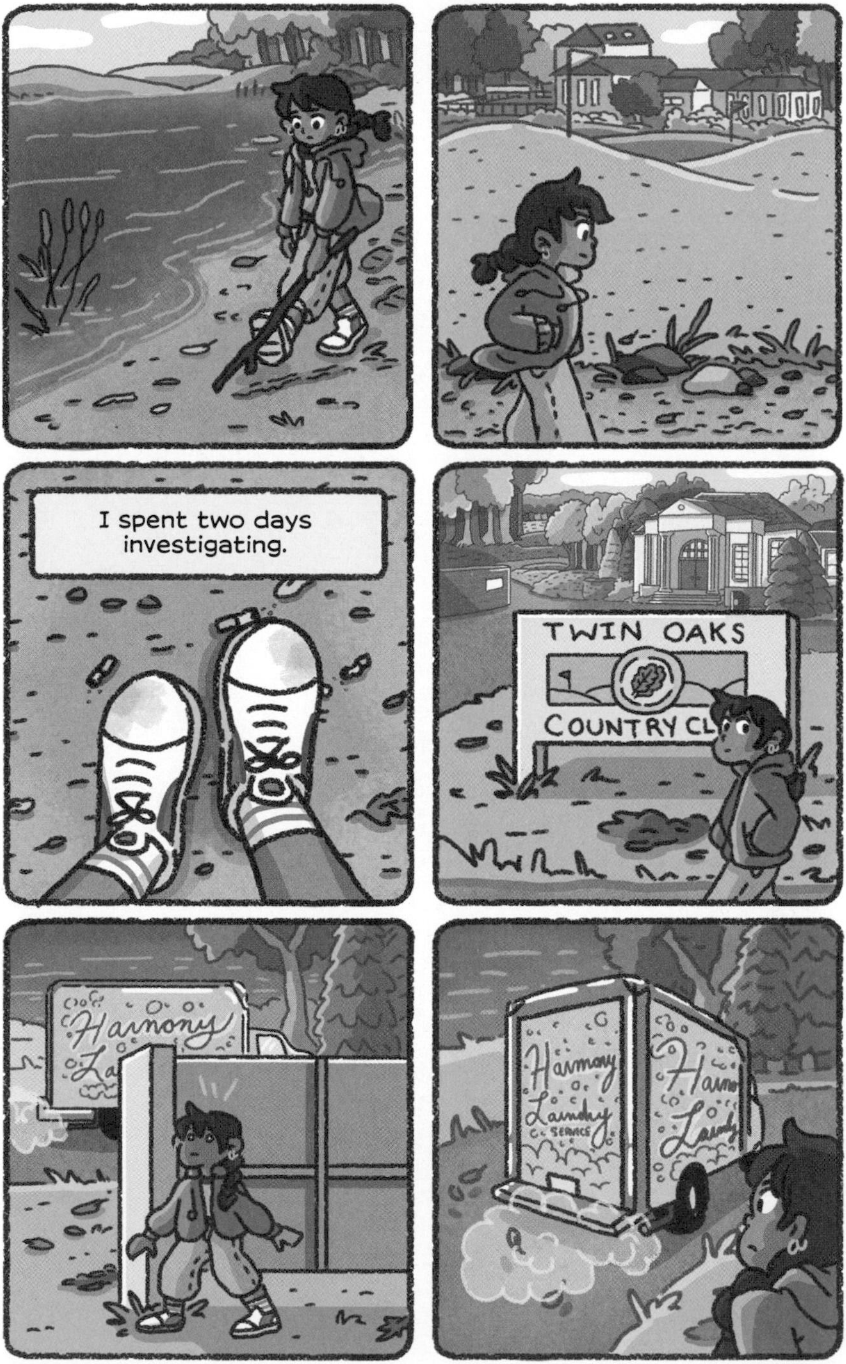
I spent two days investigating.
TWIN OAKS
COUNTRY CL
Harmony
Harmony Laundry SERVICE

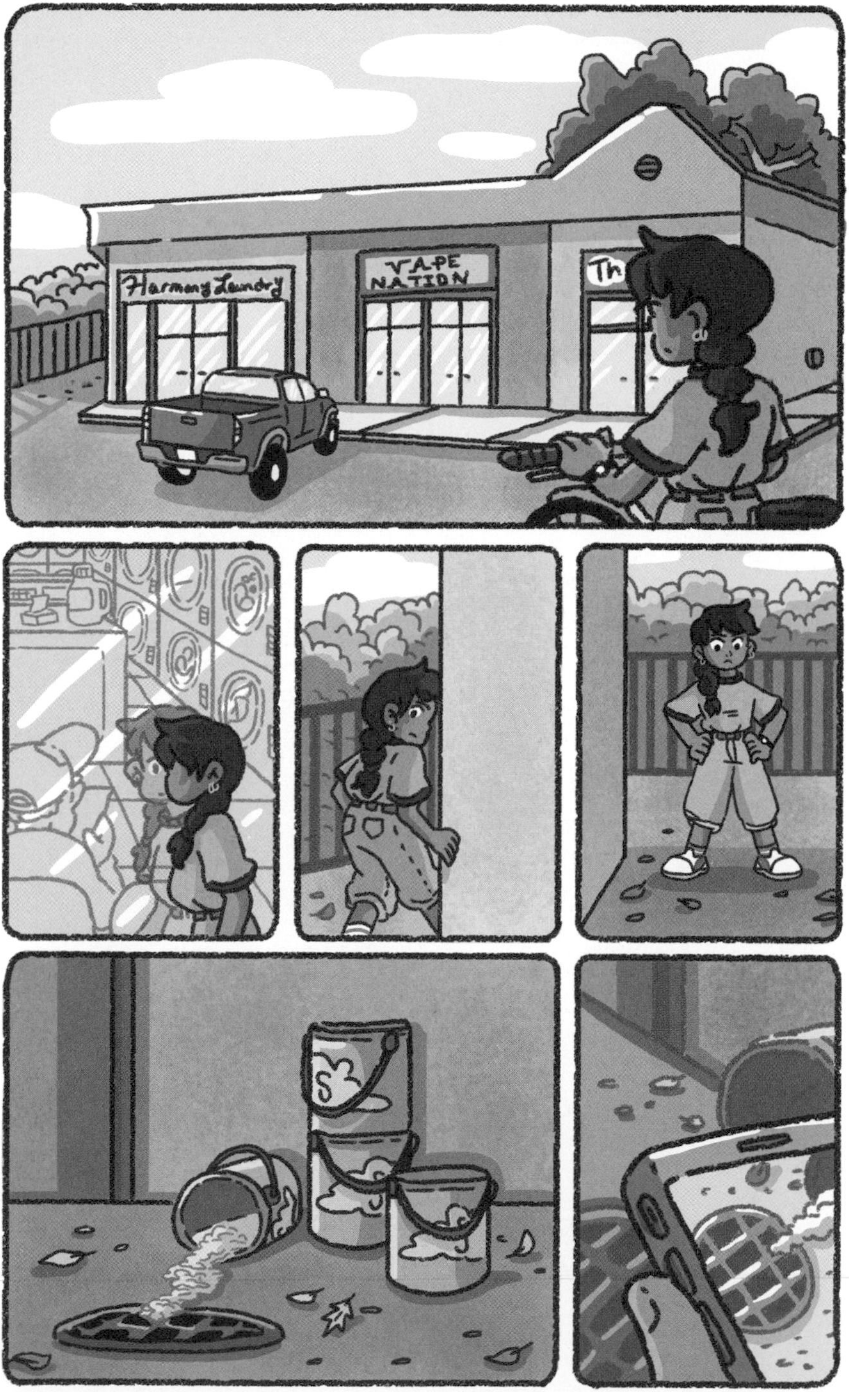
Harmony Laundry
VAPE NATION
Th

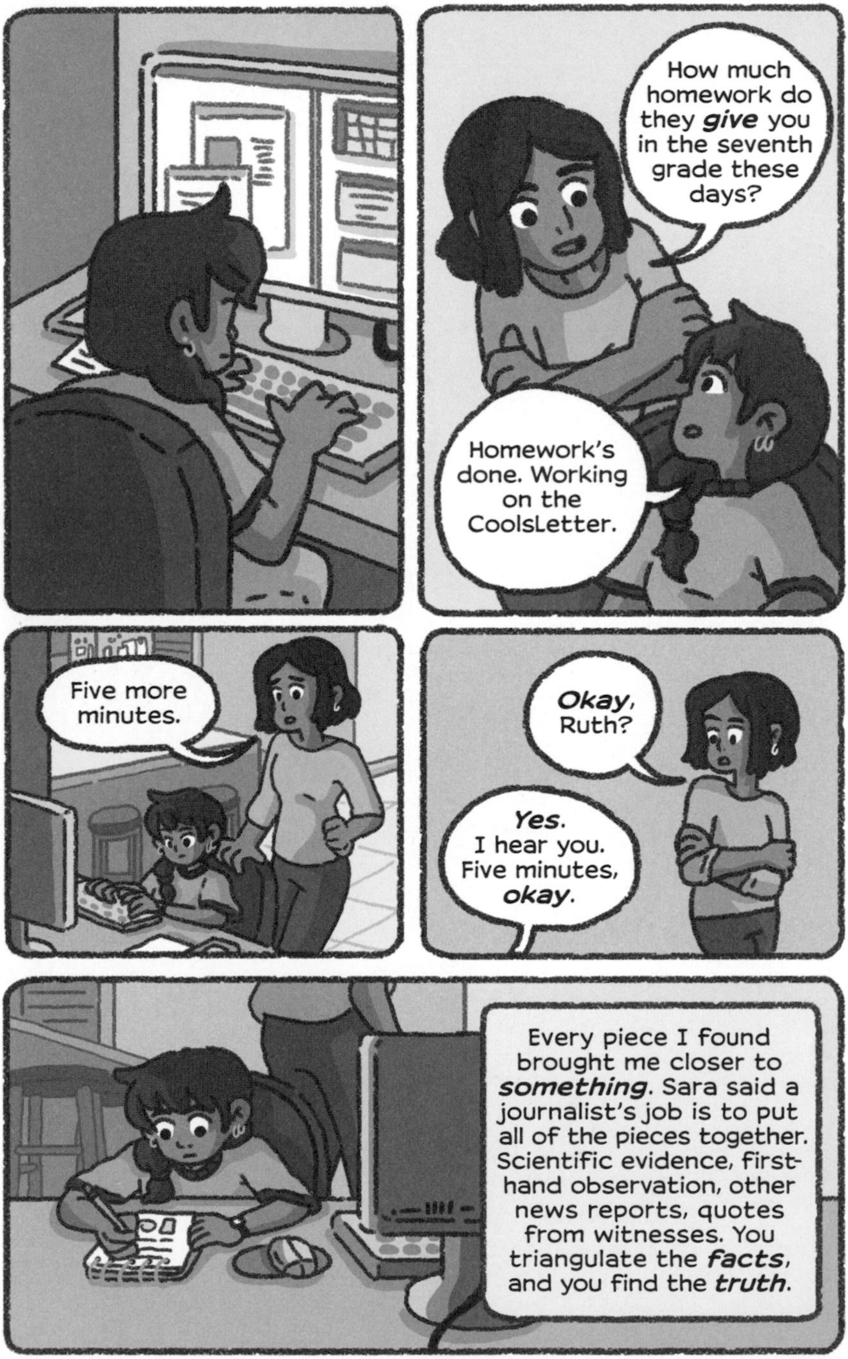
How much homework do they *give* you in the seventh grade these days?
Homework's done. Working on the CoolsLetter.
Five more minutes.
Okay, Ruth?
Yes. I hear you. Five minutes, *okay*.
Every piece I found brought me closer to *something*. Sara said a journalist's job is to put all of the pieces together. Scientific evidence, first-hand observation, other news reports, quotes from witnesses. You triangulate the *facts*, and you find the *truth*.

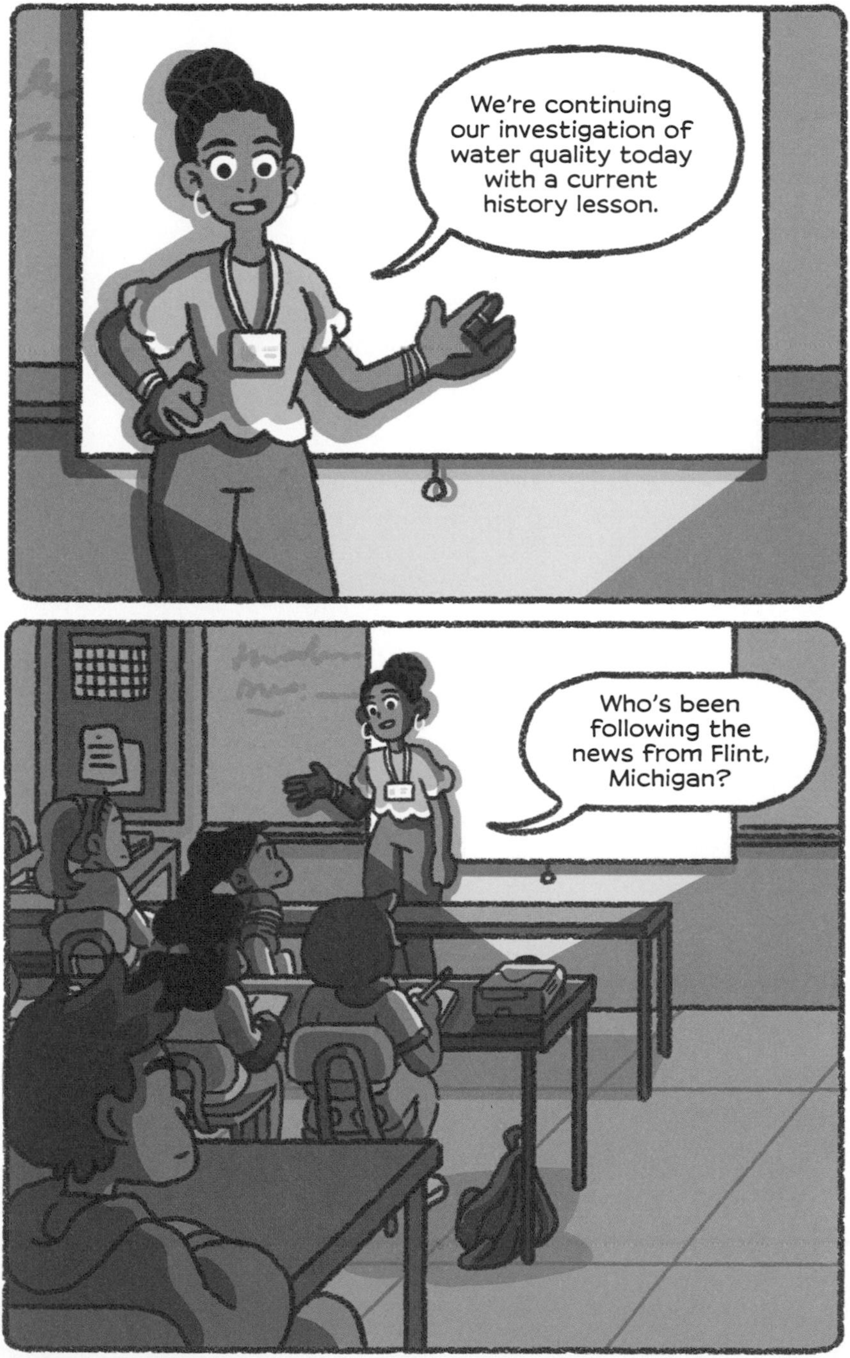
We're continuing our investigation of water quality today with a current history lesson.
Who's been following the news from Flint, Michigan?

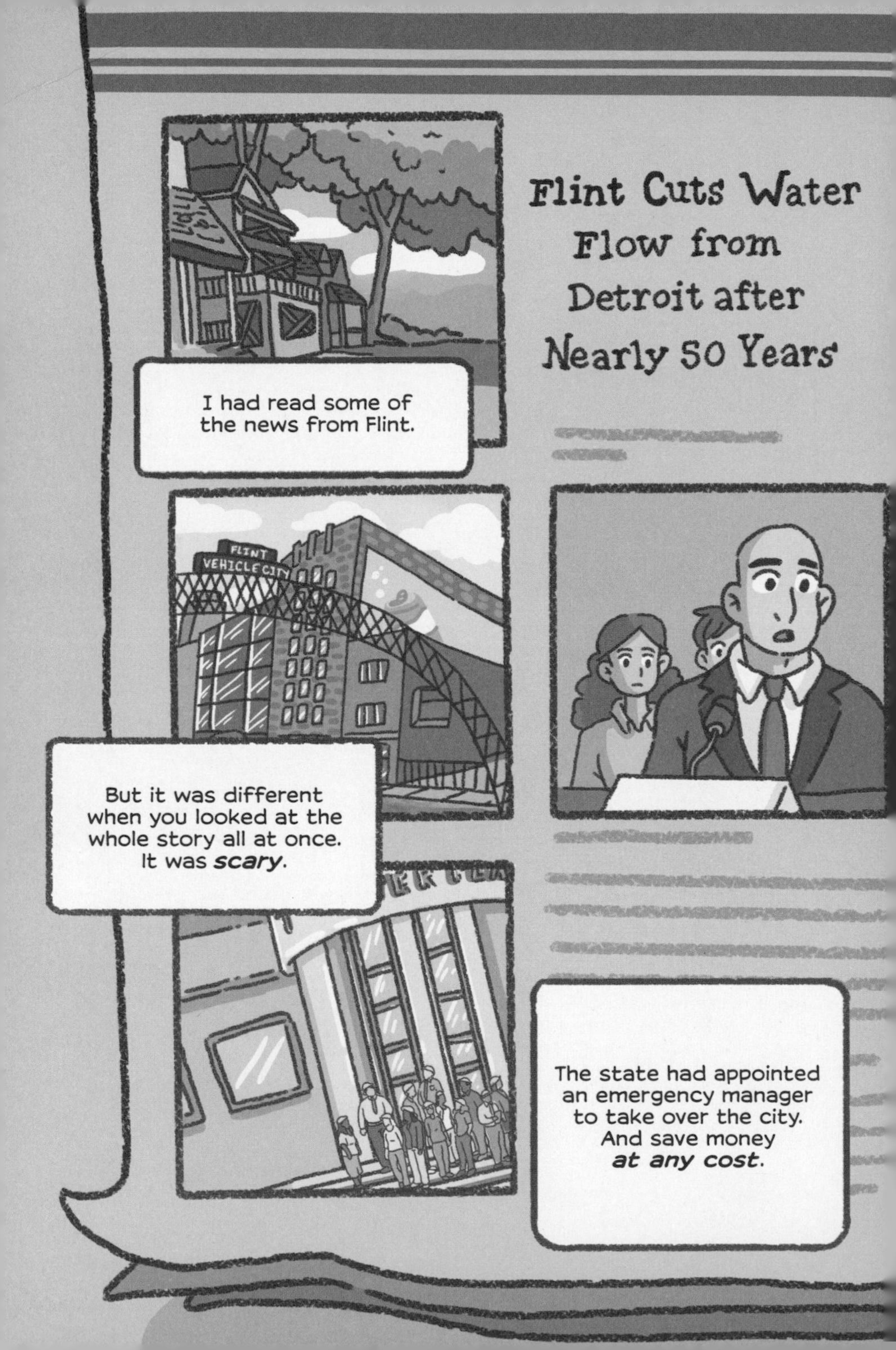
Flint Cuts Water Flow from Detroit after Nearly 50 Years
I had read some of the news from Flint.
FLINT VEHICLE CITY
But it was different when you looked at the whole story all at once. It was *scary*.
The state had appointed an emergency manager to take over the city. And save money ***at any cost***.

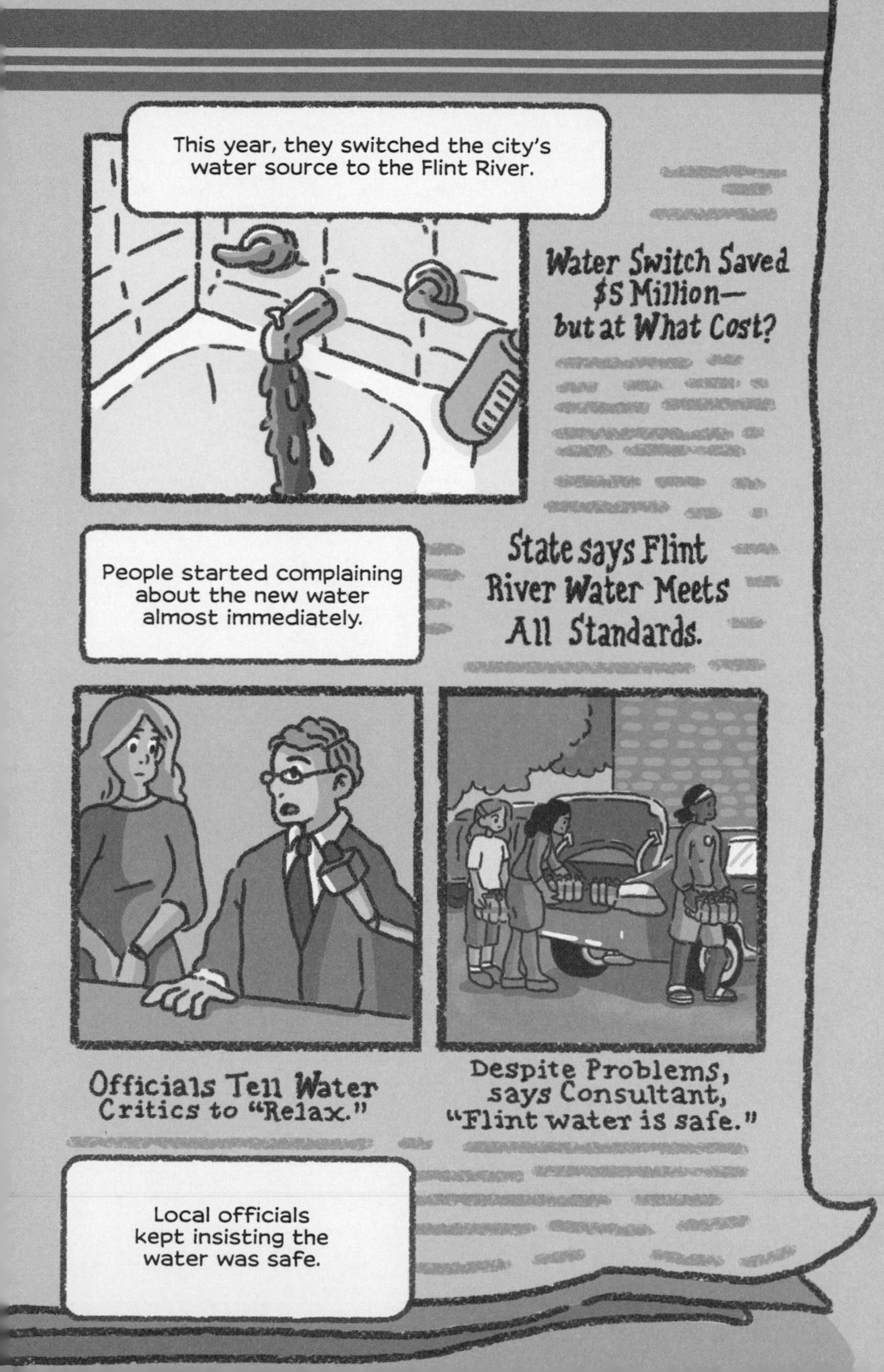

This year, they switched the city's water source to the Flint River.
Water Switch Saved $5 Million—but at What Cost?
People started complaining about the new water almost immediately.
State says Flint River Water Meets All Standards.
Officials Tell Water Critics to "Relax."
Despite Problems, says Consultant, "Flint water is safe."
Local officials kept insisting the water was safe.

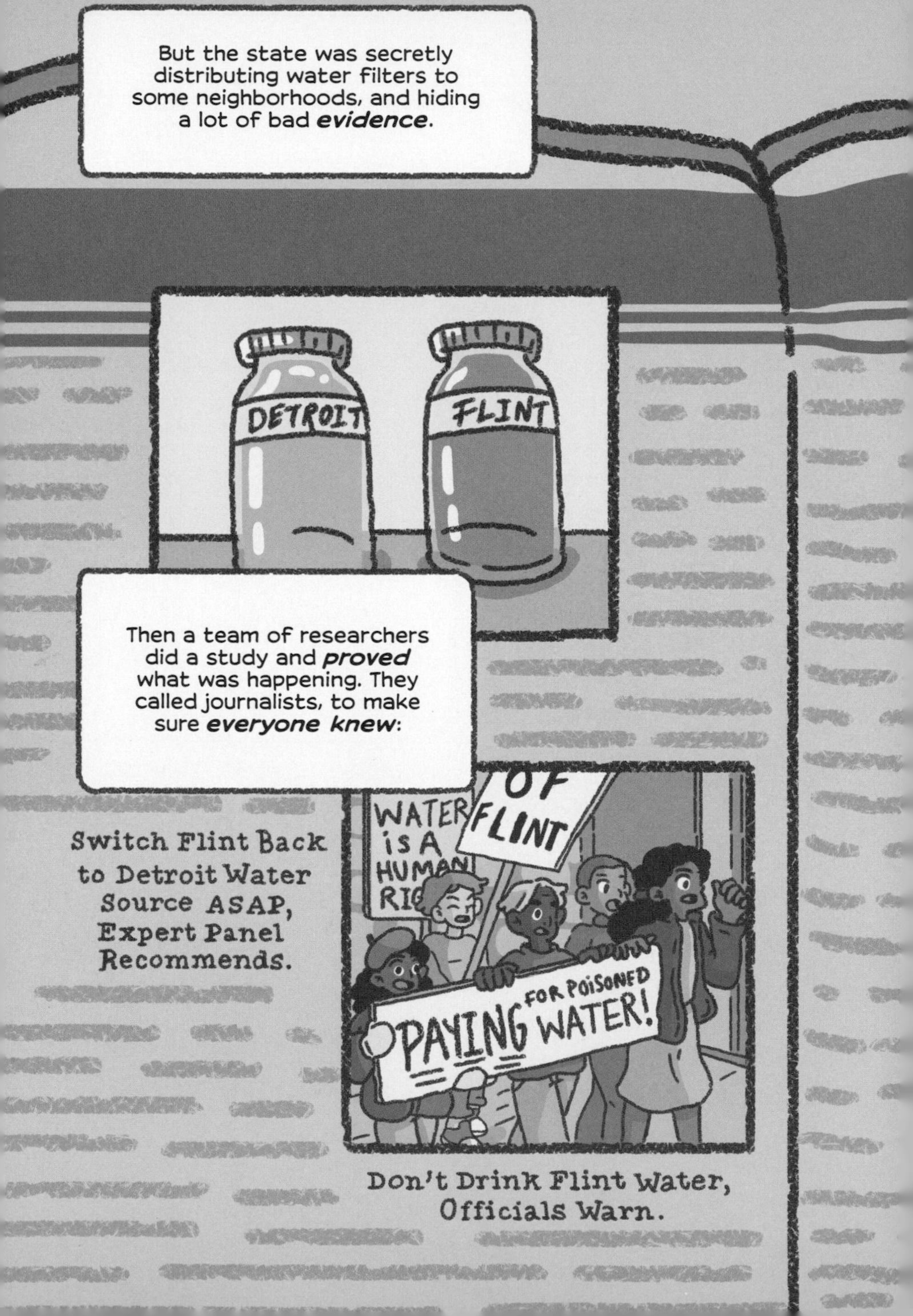
But the state was secretly distributing water filters to some neighborhoods, and hiding a lot of bad *evidence*.
DETROIT
FLINT
Then a team of researchers did a study and *proved* what was happening. They called journalists, to make sure *everyone knew*:
Switch Flint Back to Detroit Water Source ASAP, Expert Panel Recommends.
WATER is A HUMAN RIG
OF FLINT
PAYING FOR POISONED WATER!
Don't Drink Flint Water, Officials Warn.

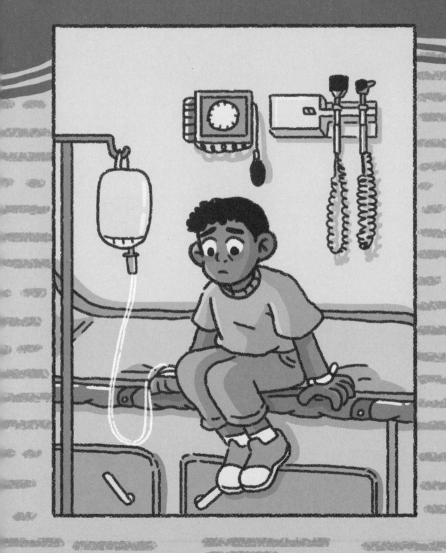

Thousands of *children* in Flint were poisoned by lead in the water.

I felt so stupid. Here I was complaining about a little pond.

Riiiiiinnggg

Did we do that lesson because of the water test yesterday?

Well, that lake isn't drinking water.

But what you found is dangerous stuff.

—but it's bad.

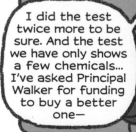

I did the test twice more to be sure. And the test we have only shows a few chemicals... I've asked Principal Walker for funding to buy a better one—

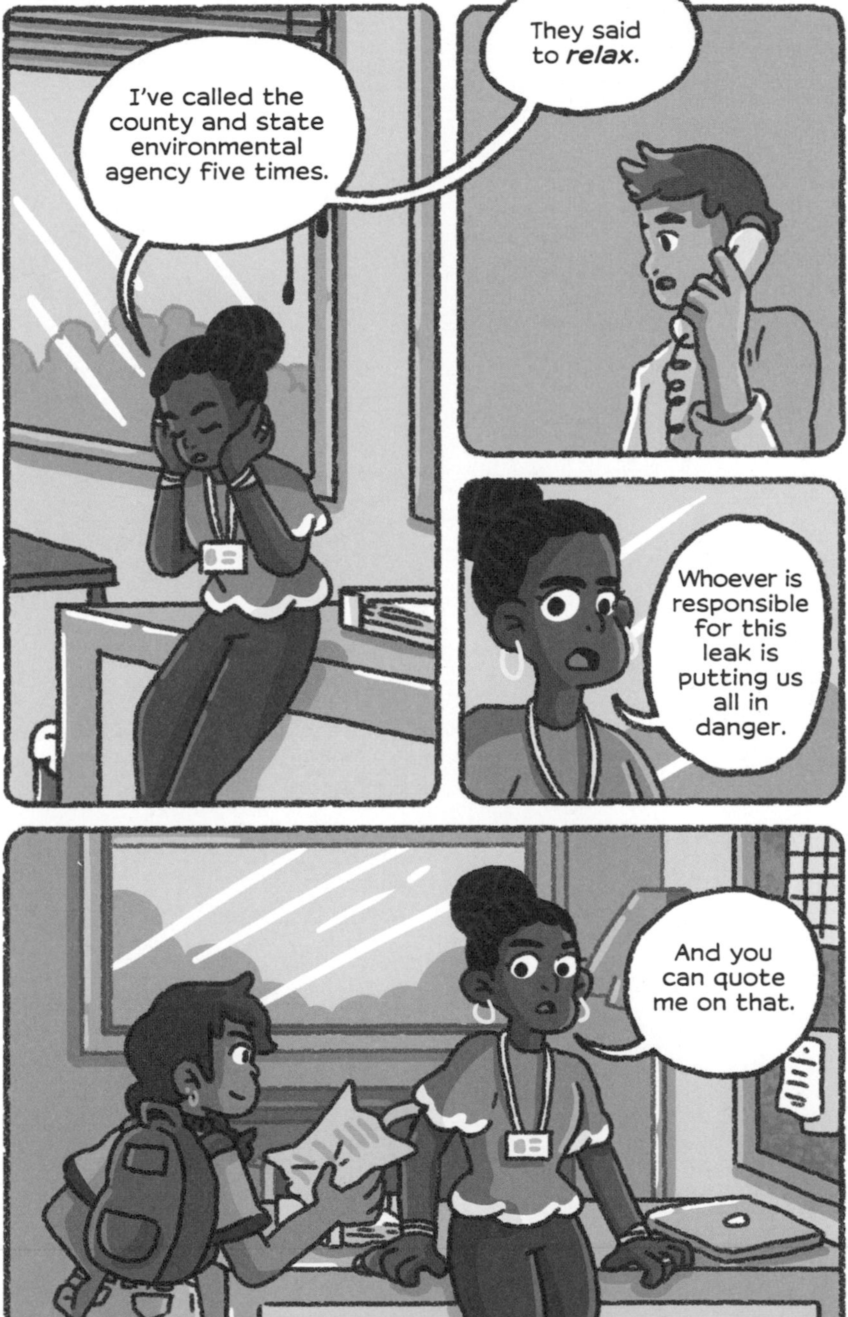
I've called the county and state environmental agency five times.
They said to *relax*.
Whoever is responsible for this leak is putting us all in danger.
And you can quote me on that.

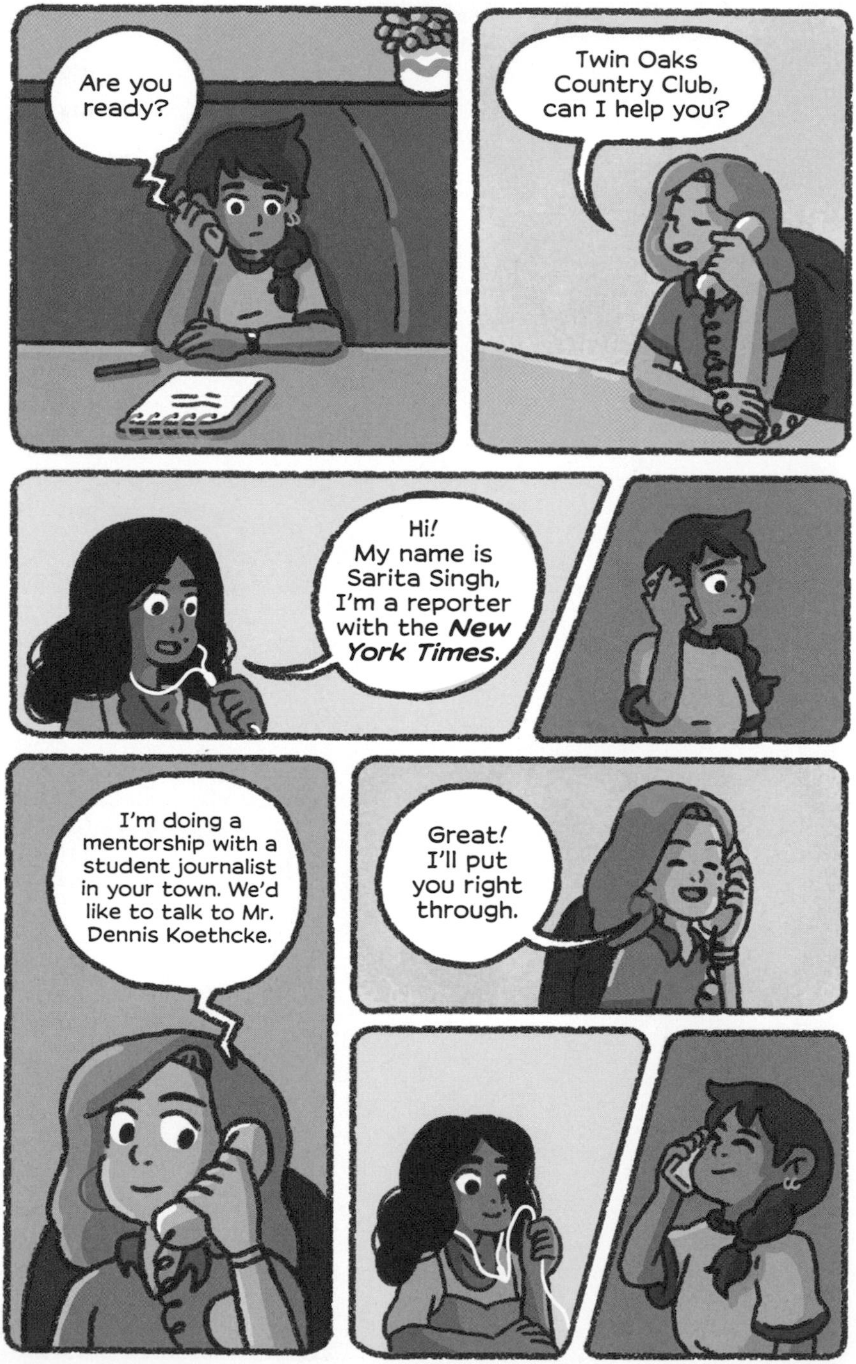
Are you ready?
Twin Oaks Country Club, can I help you?
Hi! My name is Sarita Singh, I'm a reporter with the *New York Times*.
I'm doing a mentorship with a student journalist in your town. We'd like to talk to Mr. Dennis Koethcke.
Great! I'll put you right through.

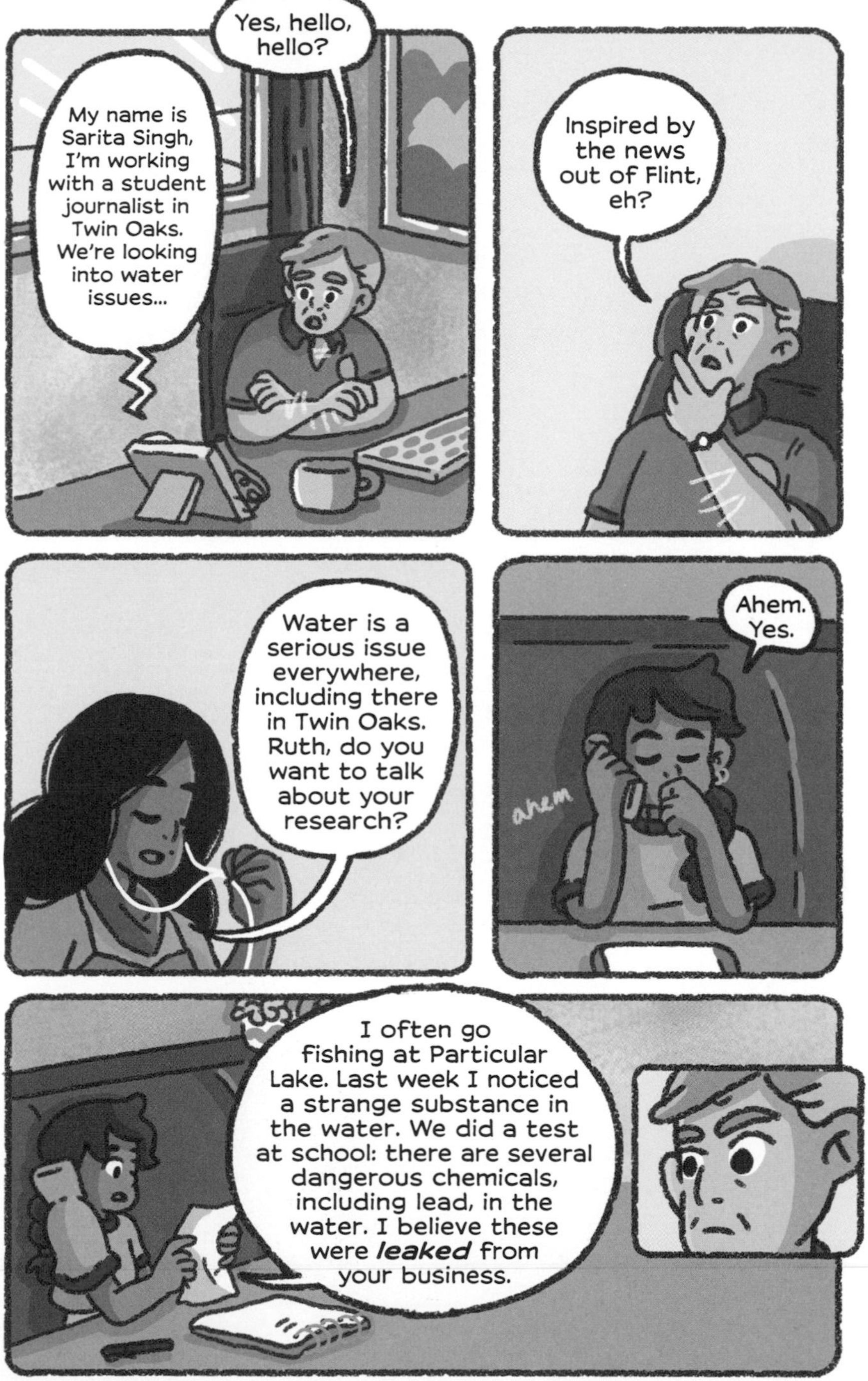
Yes, hello, hello?
My name is Sarita Singh, I'm working with a student journalist in Twin Oaks. We're looking into water issues...
Inspired by the news out of Flint, eh?
Water is a serious issue everywhere, including there in Twin Oaks. Ruth, do you want to talk about your research?
Ahem. Yes.
ahem
I often go fishing at Particular Lake. Last week I noticed a strange substance in the water. We did a test at school: there are several dangerous chemicals, including lead, in the water. I believe these were *leaked* from your business.

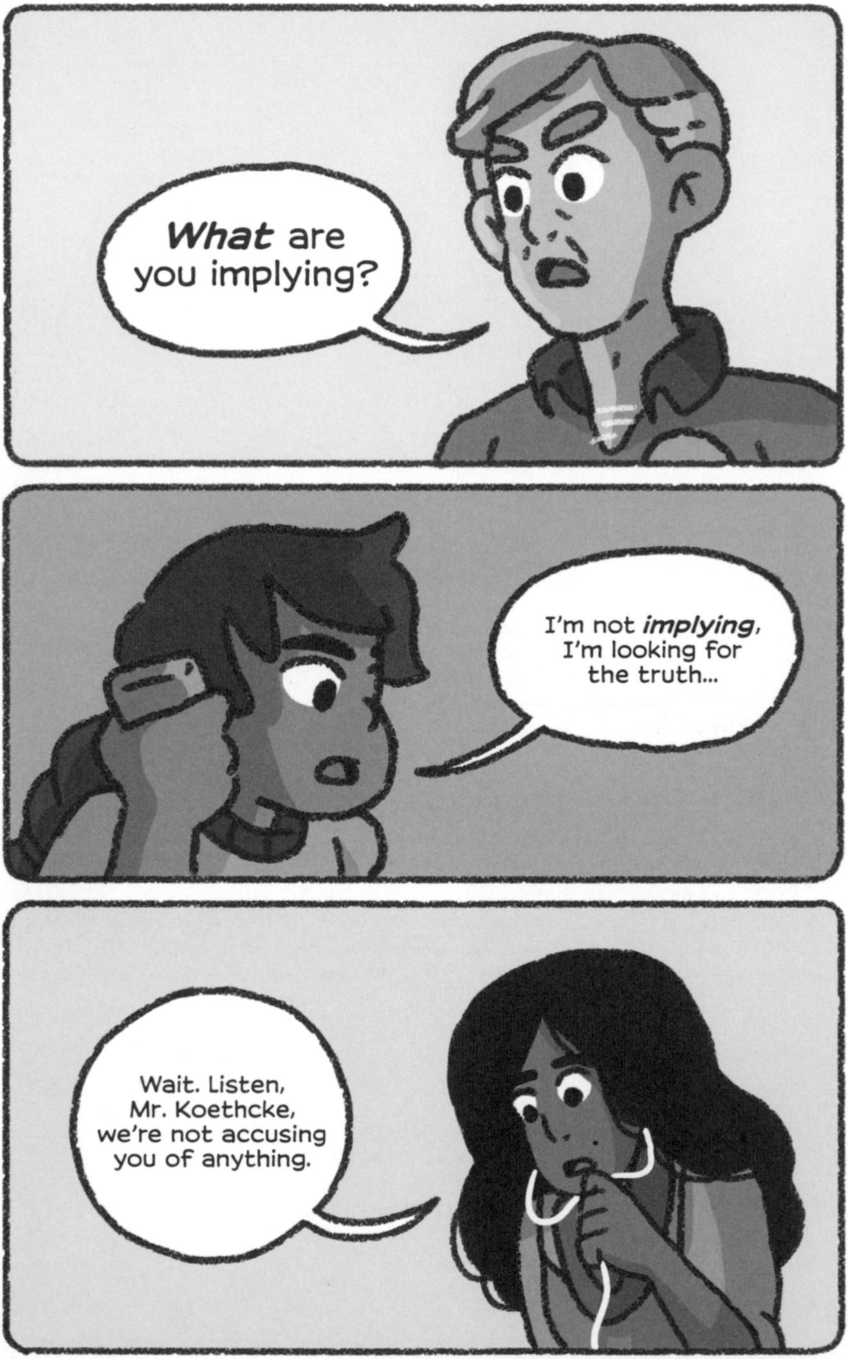
What are you implying?
I'm not *implying*, I'm looking for the truth...
Wait. Listen, Mr. Koethcke, we're not accusing you of anything.

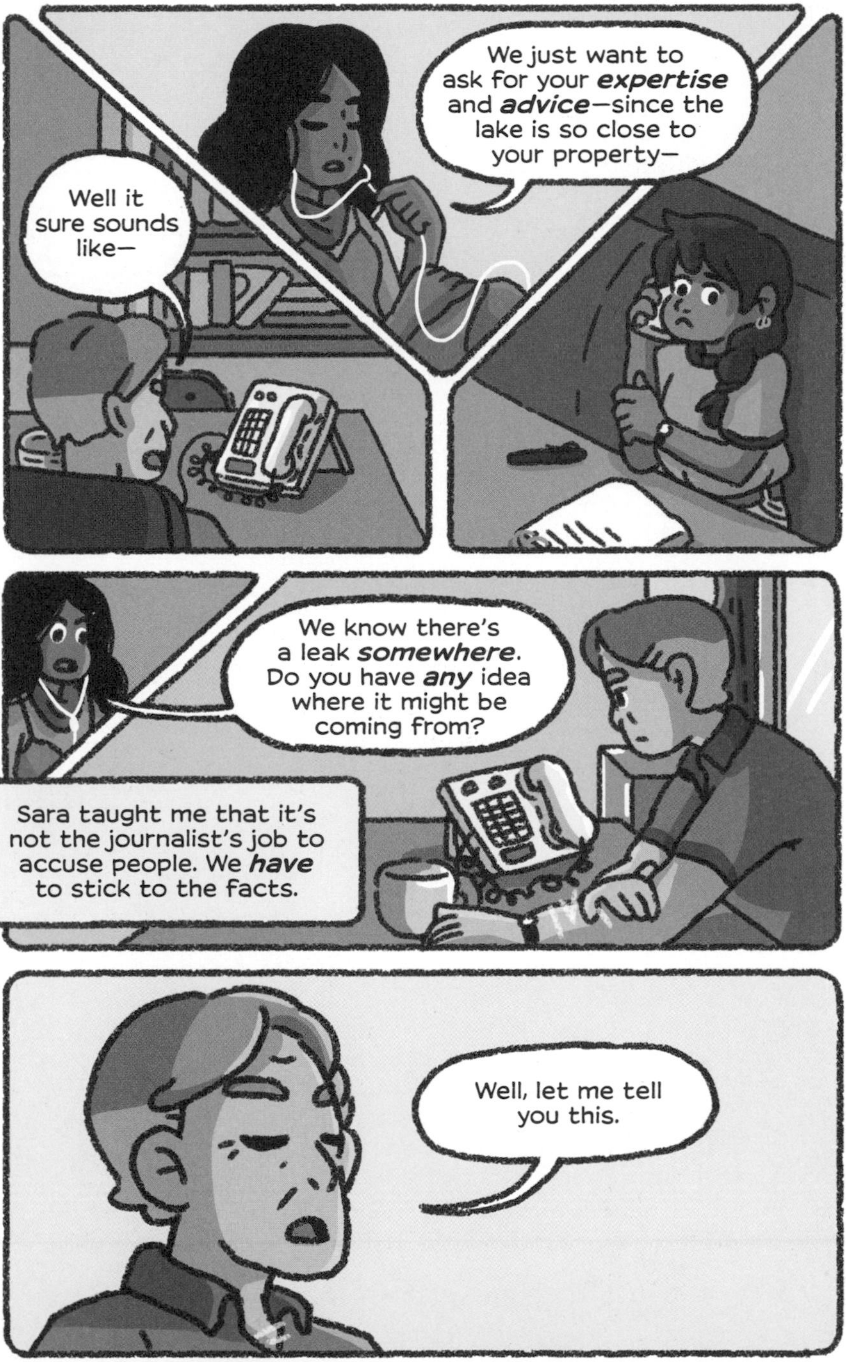
We just want to ask for your *expertise* and *advice*—since the lake is so close to your property—
Well it sure sounds like—
We know there's a leak *somewhere*. Do you have *any* idea where it might be coming from?
Sara taught me that it's not the journalist's job to accuse people. We *have* to stick to the facts.
Well, let me tell you this.

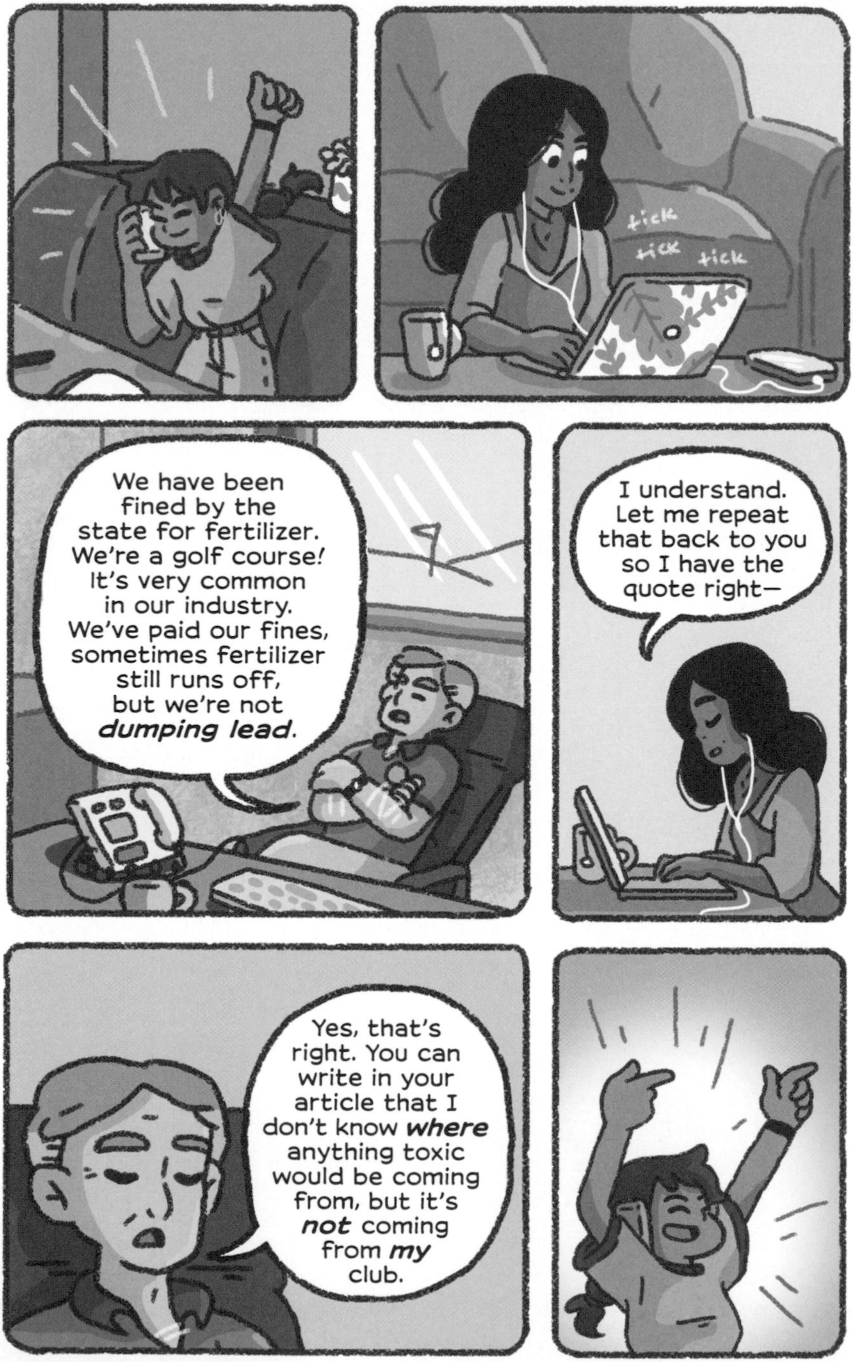
tick
tick
tick
We have been fined by the state for fertilizer. We're a golf course! It's very common in our industry. We've paid our fines, sometimes fertilizer still runs off, but we're not ***dumping lead***.
I understand. Let me repeat that back to you so I have the quote right—
Yes, that's right. You can write in your article that I don't know ***where*** anything toxic would be coming from, but it's ***not*** coming from ***my*** club.

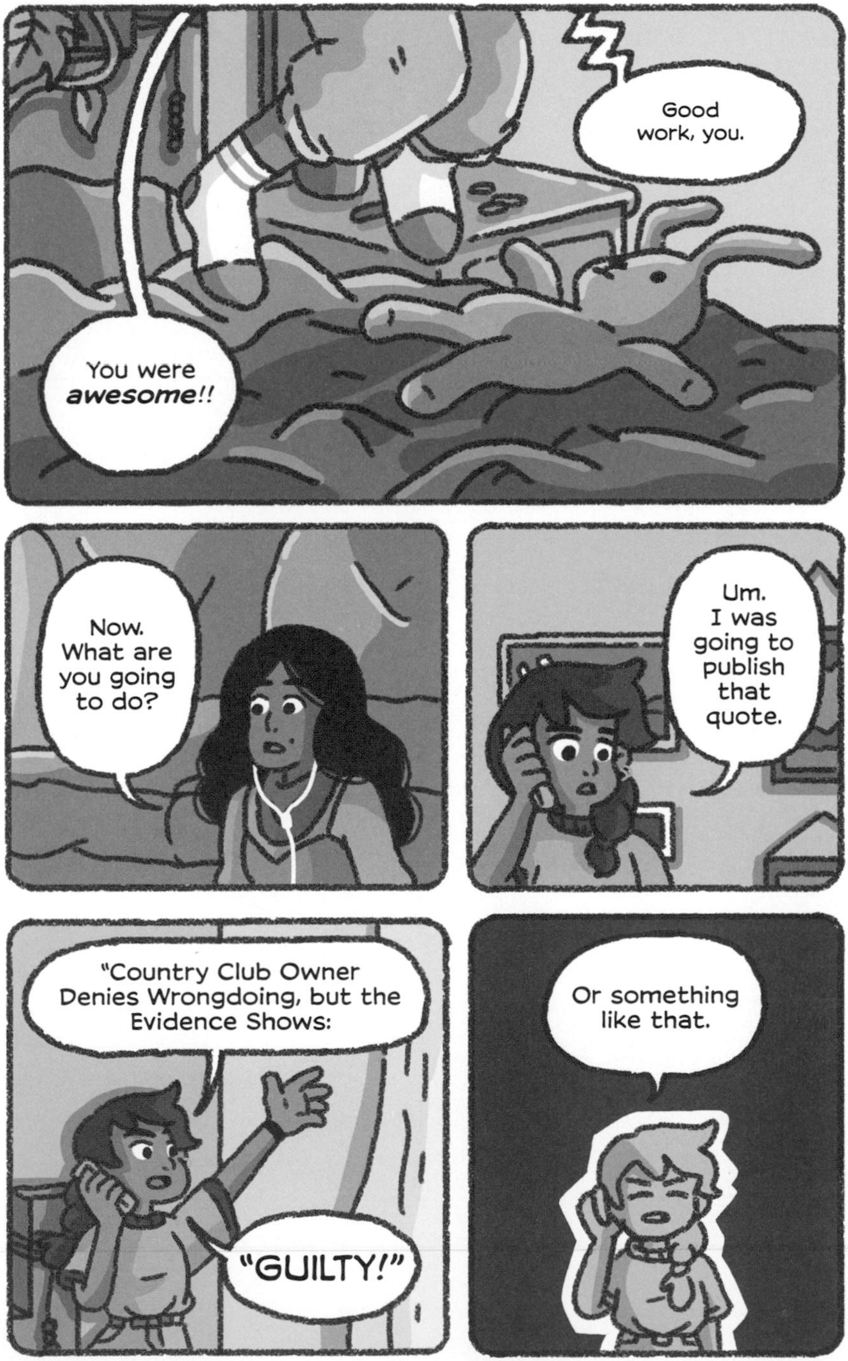
Good work, you.
You were *awesome*!!
Now. What are you going to do?
Um. I was going to publish that quote.
"Country Club Owner Denies Wrongdoing, but the Evidence Shows:
"GUILTY!"
Or something like that.

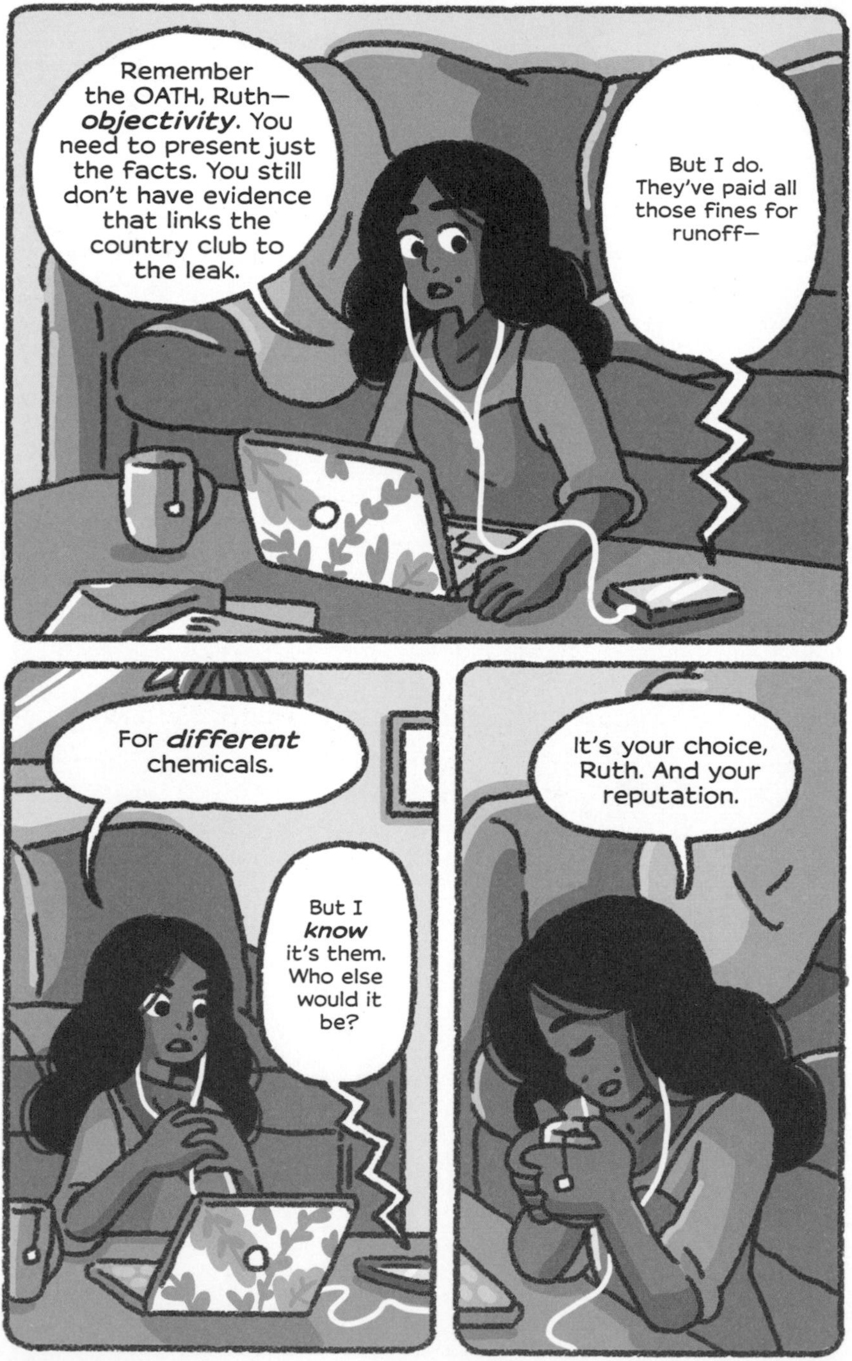
Remember the OATH, Ruth—*objectivity*. You need to present just the facts. You still don't have evidence that links the country club to the leak.
But I do. They've paid all those fines for runoff—
For *different* chemicals.
But I *know* it's them. Who else would it be?
It's your choice, Ruth. And your reputation.

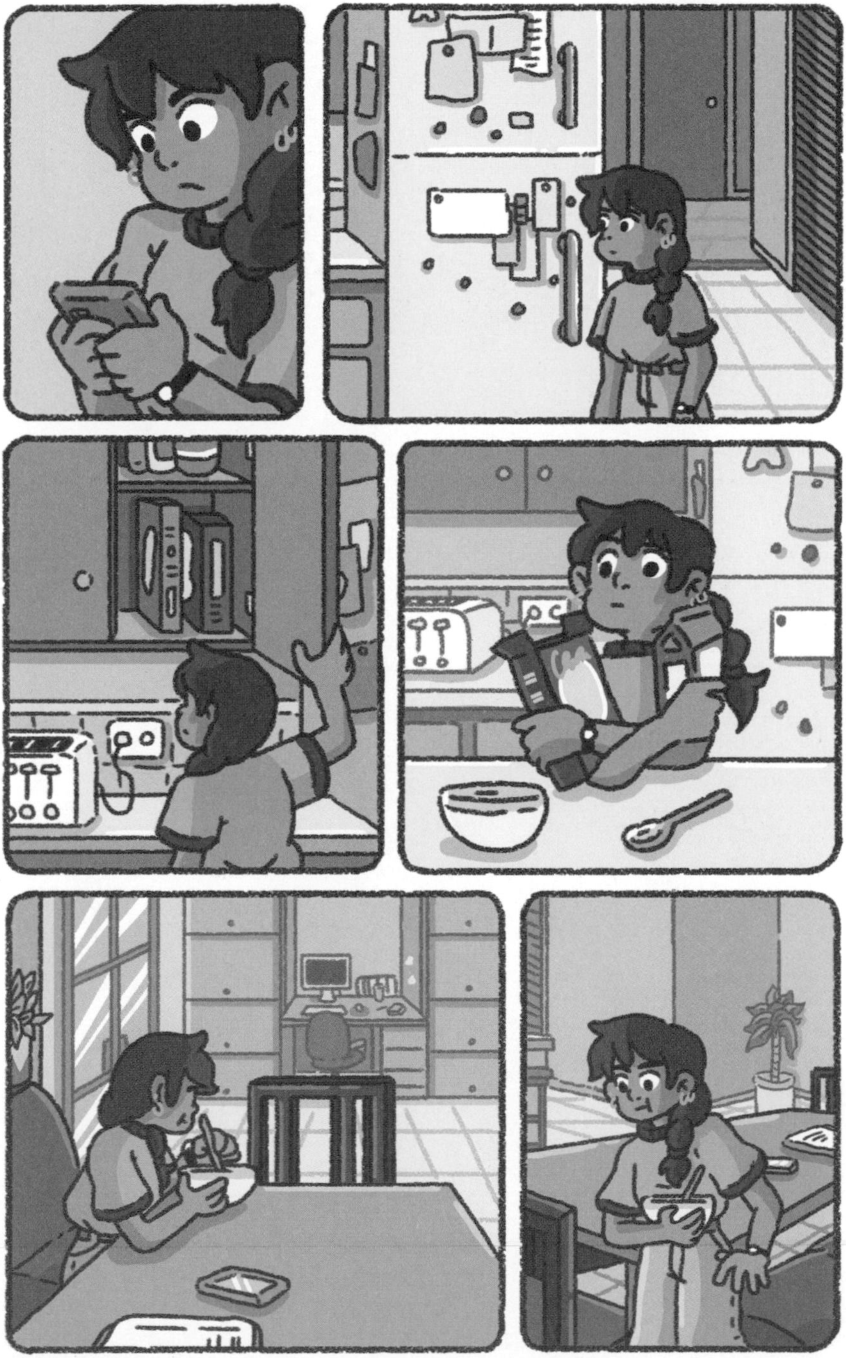

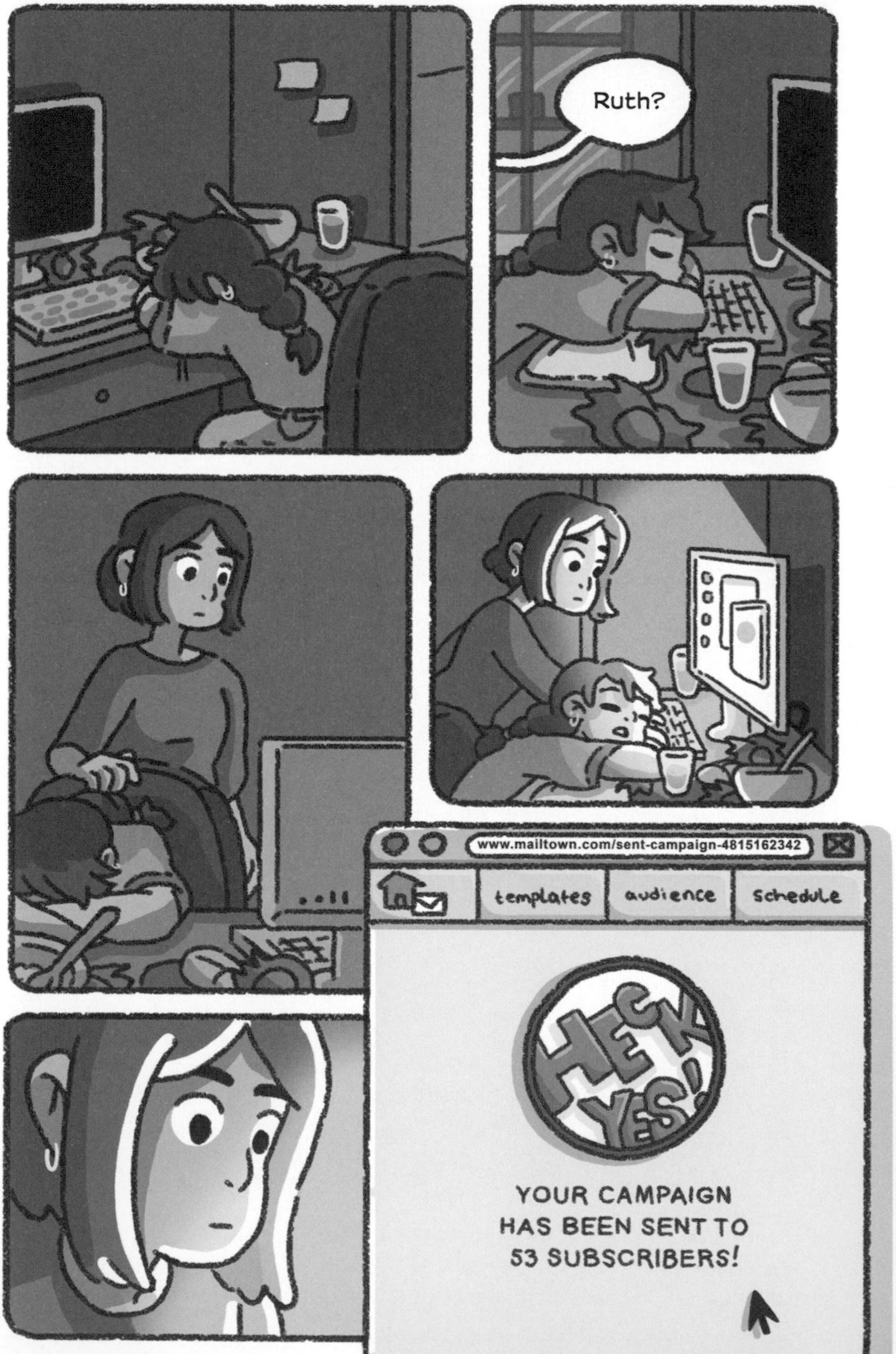
Ruth?
www.mailtown.com/sent-campaign-4815162342
templates
audience
schedule
HECK YES!
YOUR CAMPAIGN
HAS BEEN SENT TO
53 SUBSCRIBERS!

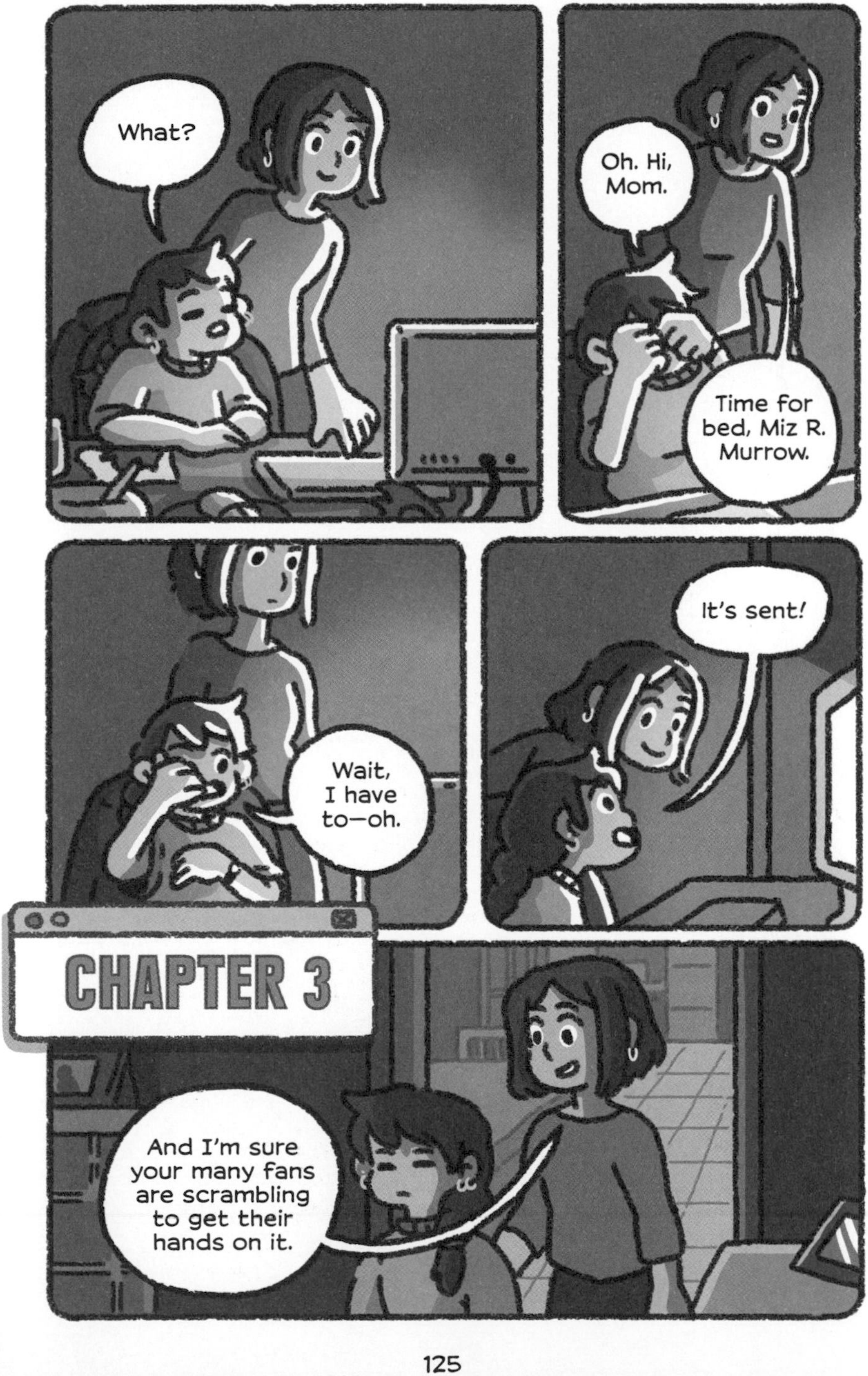
What?
Oh. Hi, Mom.
Time for bed, Miz R. Murrow.
Wait, I have to—oh.
It's sent!
CHAPTER 3
And I'm sure your many fans are scrambling to get their hands on it.

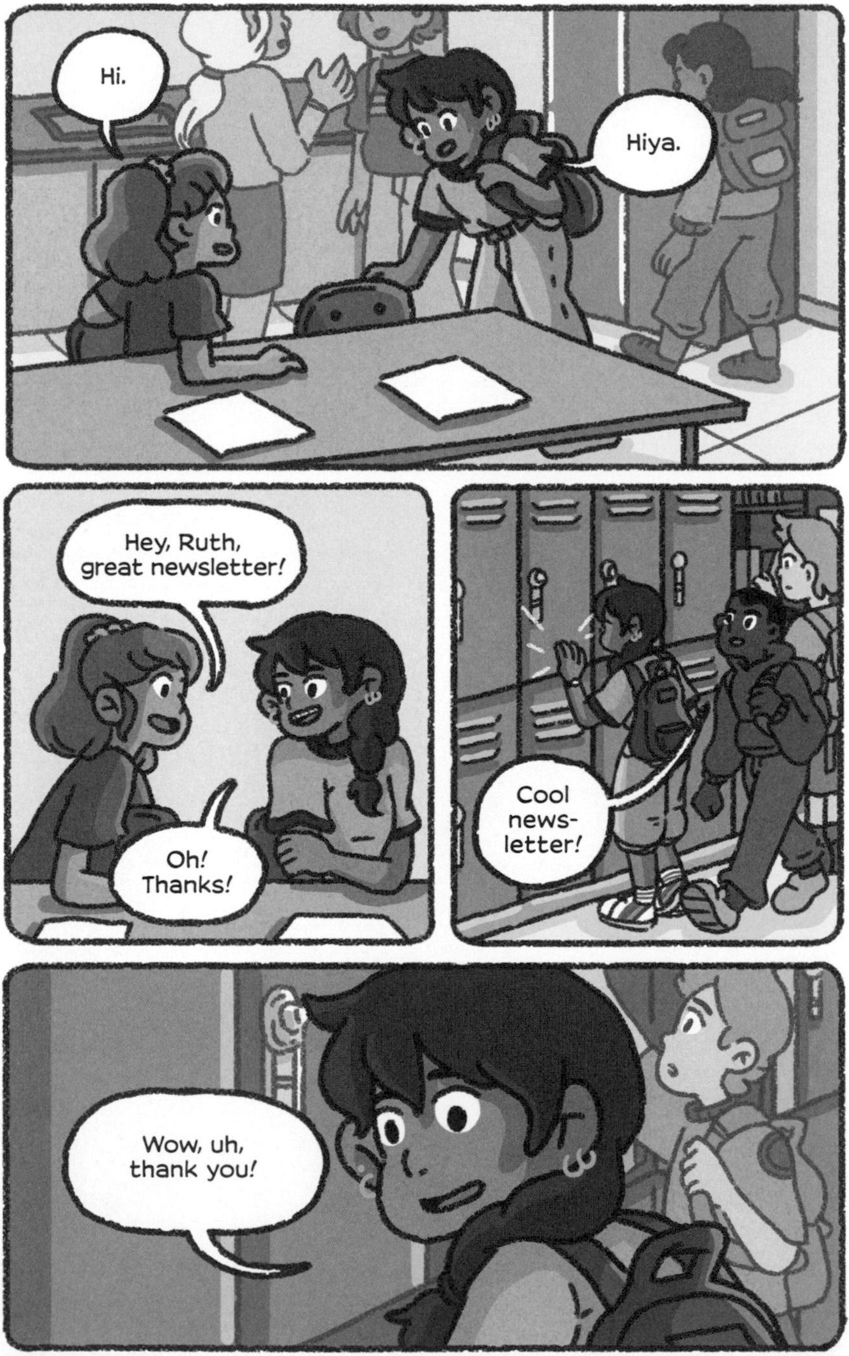
Hi.
Hiya.
Hey, Ruth, great newsletter!
Oh! Thanks!
Cool news-letter!
Wow, uh, thank you!

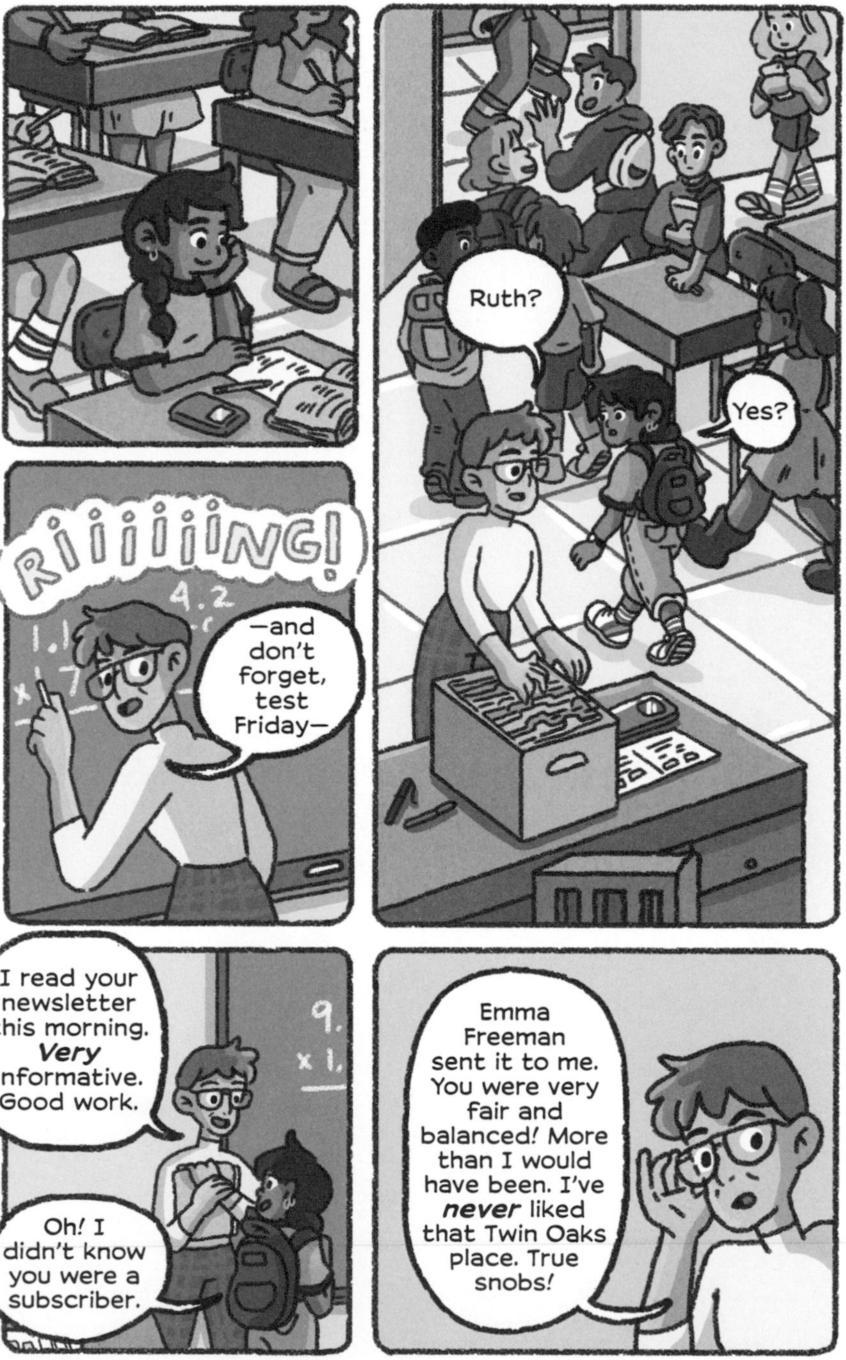
RIIIIING!
—and don't forget, test Friday—
Ruth?
Yes?
I read your newsletter this morning. ***Very*** informative. Good work.
Oh! I didn't know you were a subscriber.
Emma Freeman sent it to me. You were very fair and balanced! More than I would have been. I've ***never*** liked that Twin Oaks place. True snobs!

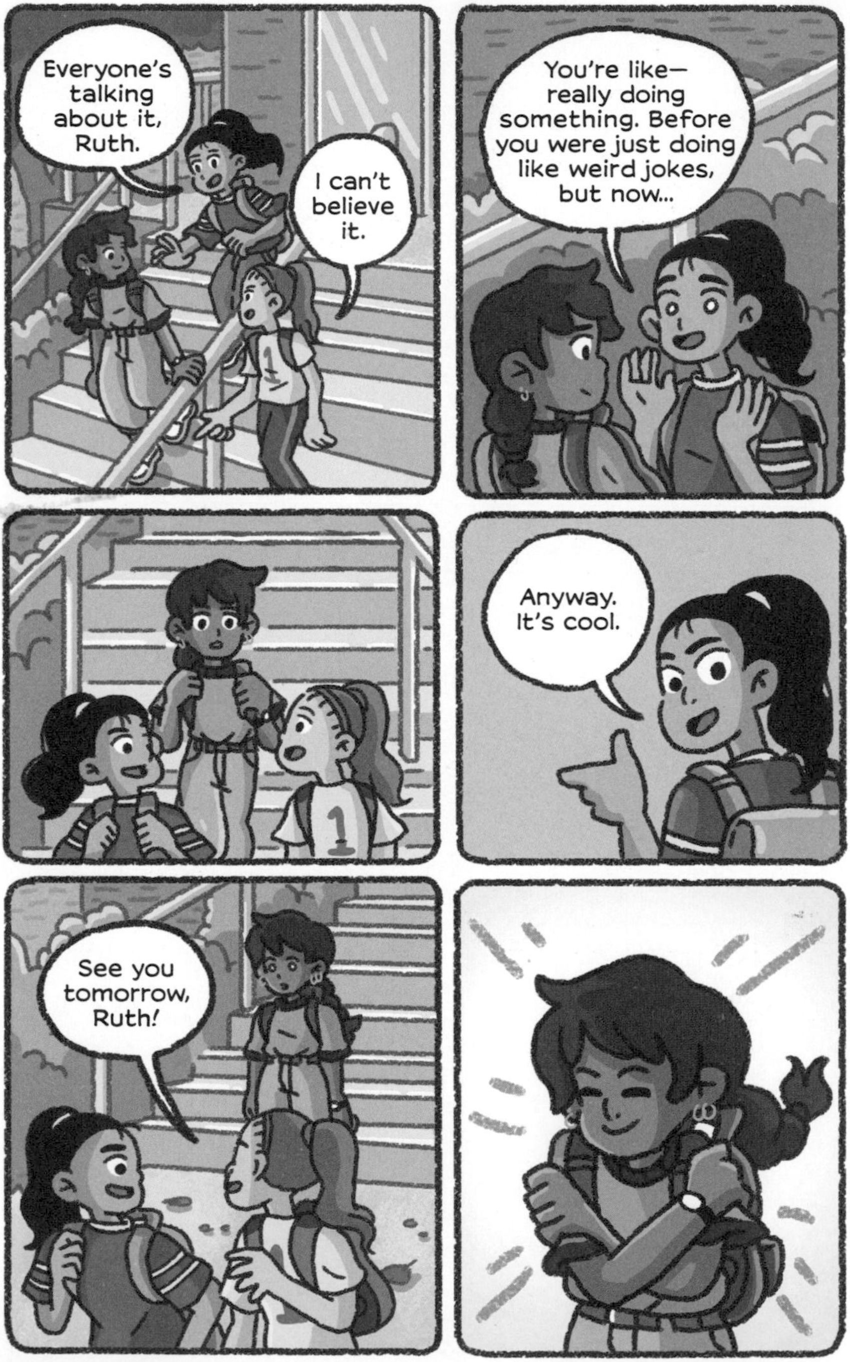
Everyone's talking about it, Ruth.
I can't believe it.
You're like— really doing something. Before you were just doing like weird jokes, but now...
Anyway. It's cool.
See you tomorrow, Ruth!

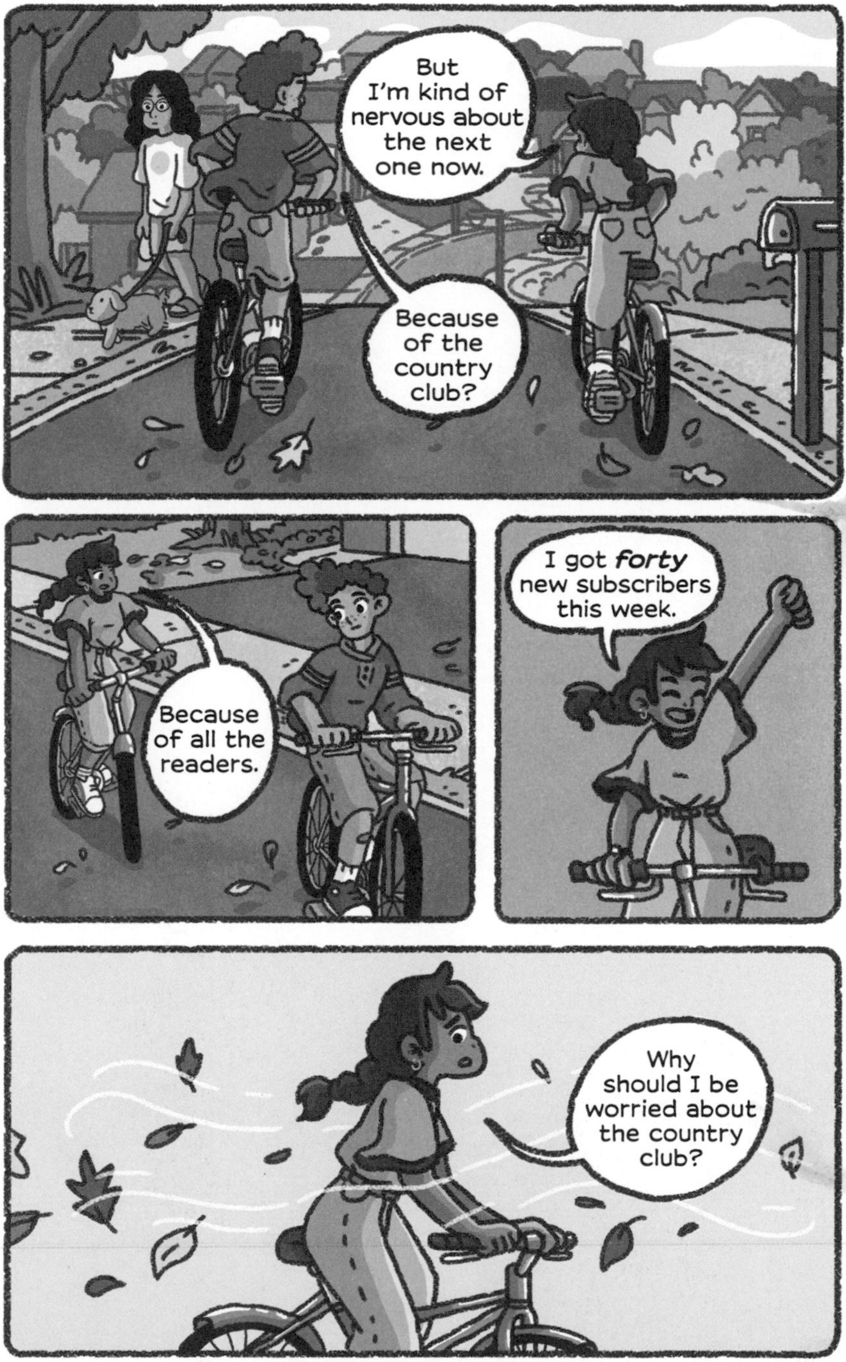
But I'm kind of nervous about the next one now.
Because of the country club?
Because of all the readers.
I got *forty* new subscribers this week.
Why should I be worried about the country club?

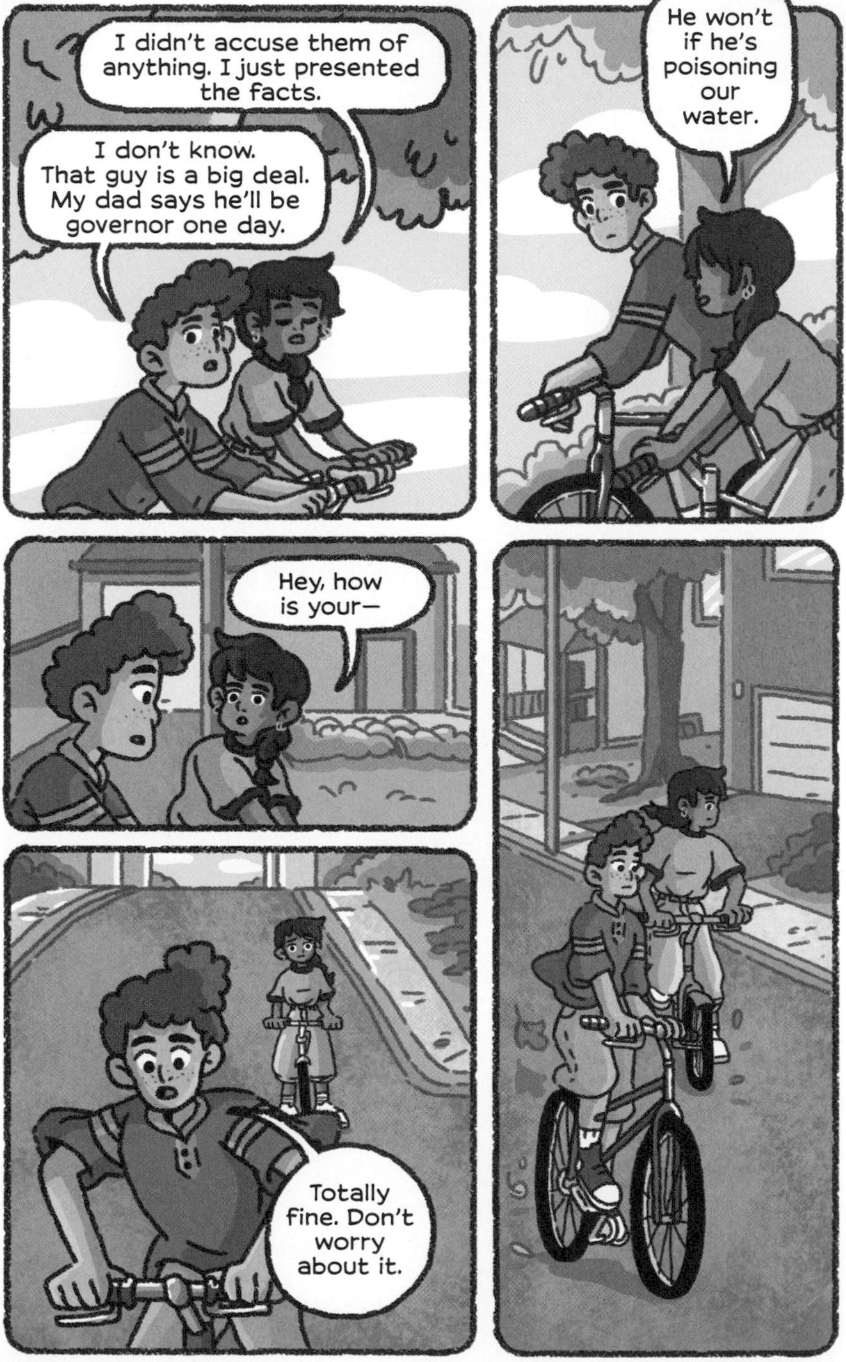
I didn't accuse them of anything. I just presented the facts.
I don't know. That guy is a big deal. My dad says he'll be governor one day.
He won't if he's poisoning our water.
Hey, how is your—
Totally fine. Don't worry about it.

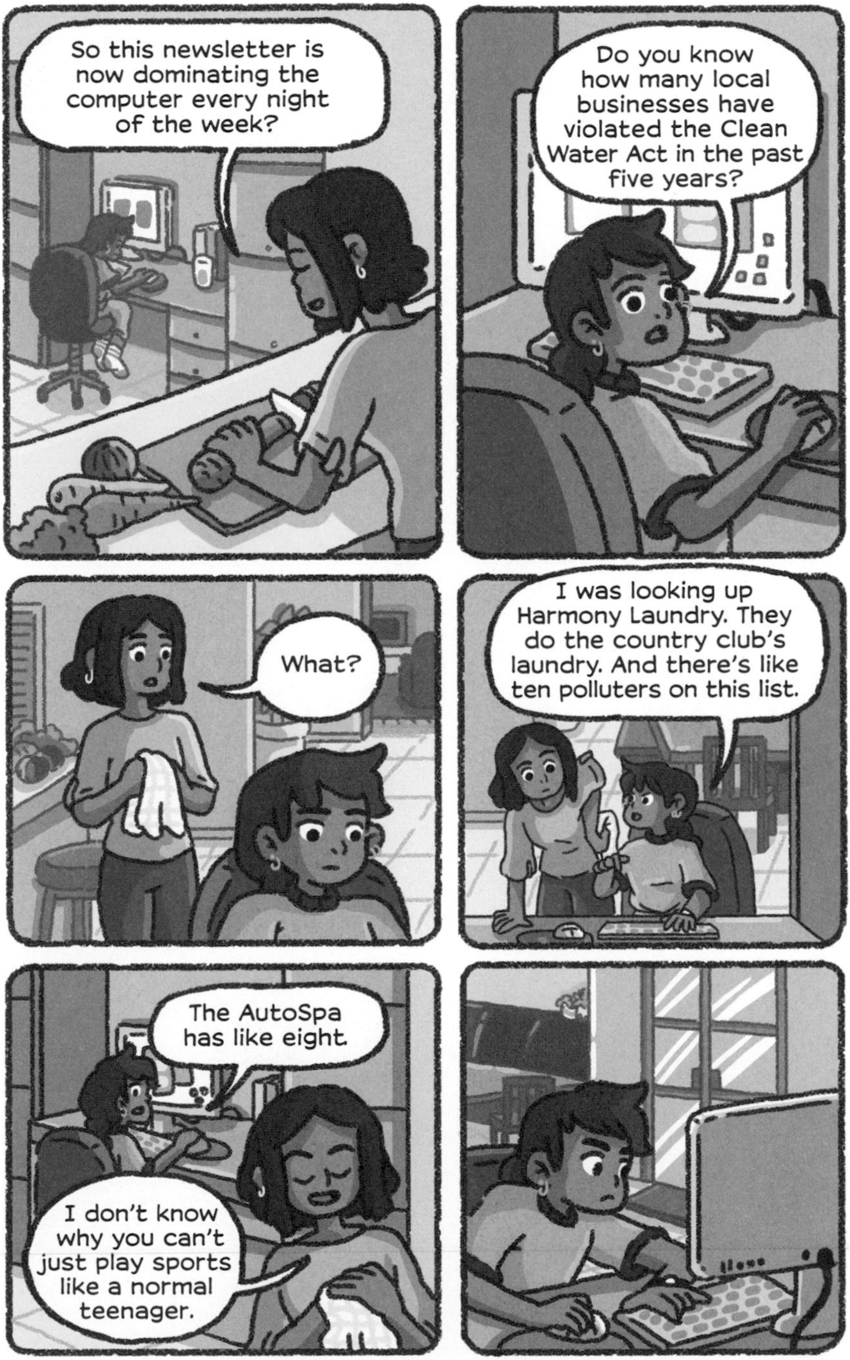
So this newsletter is now dominating the computer every night of the week?
Do you know how many local businesses have violated the Clean Water Act in the past five years?
What?
I was looking up Harmony Laundry. They do the country club's laundry. And there's like ten polluters on this list.
The AutoSpa has like eight.
I don't know why you can't just play sports like a normal teenager.

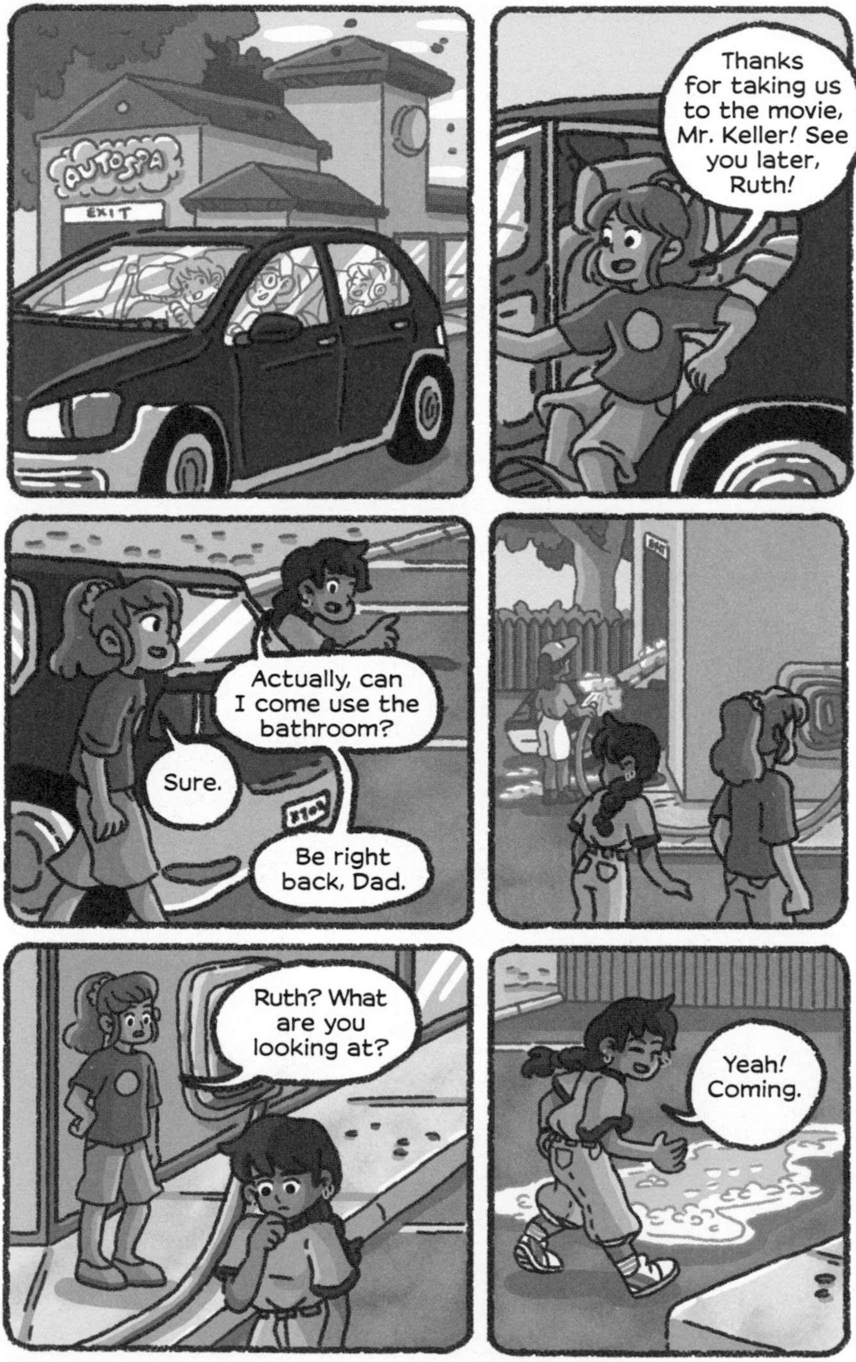
AUTOSPA
EXIT
Thanks for taking us to the movie, Mr. Keller! See you later, Ruth!
Actually, can I come use the bathroom?
Sure.
Be right back, Dad.
Ruth? What are you looking at?
Yeah! Coming.

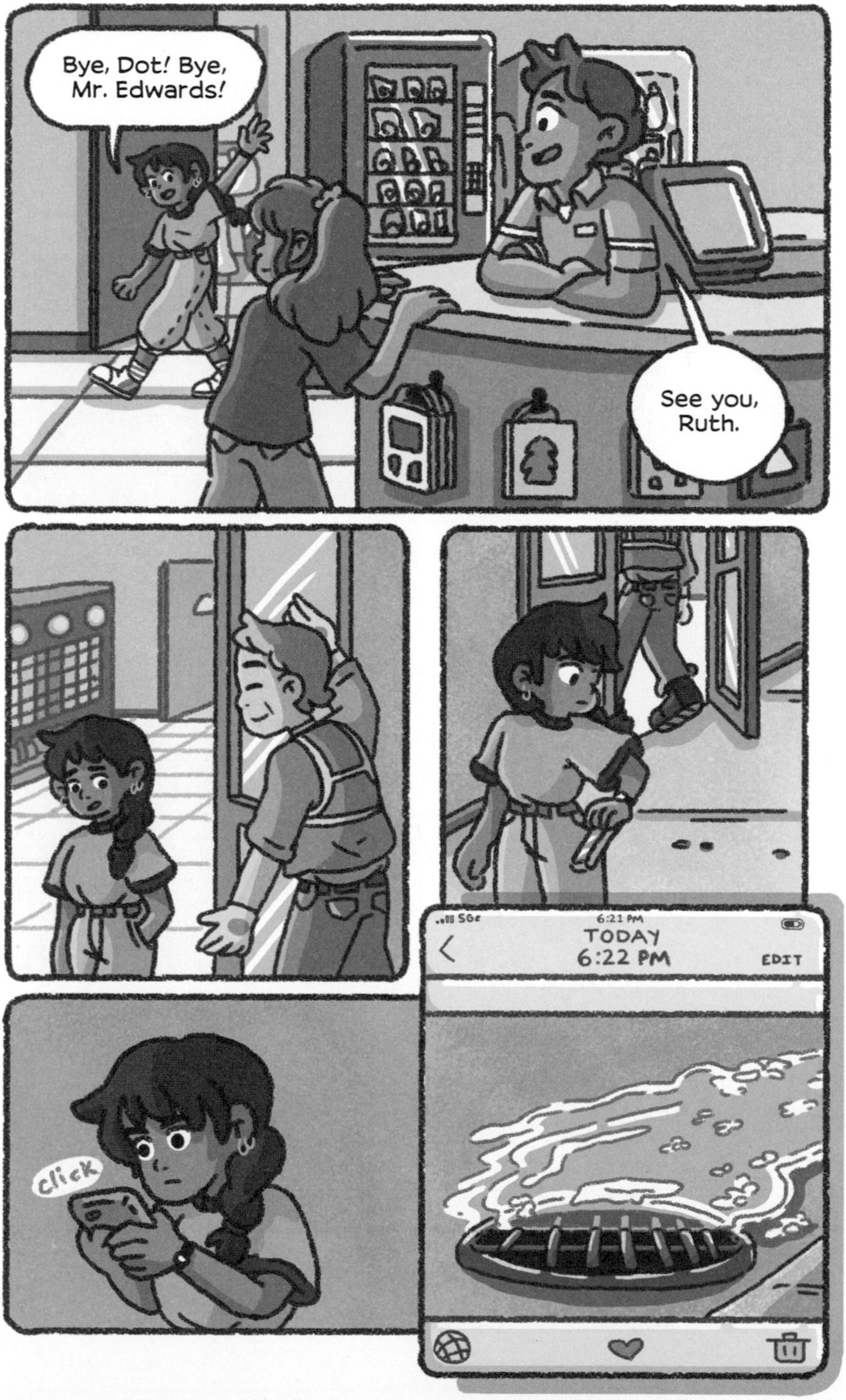

Bye, Dot! Bye, Mr. Edwards!
See you, Ruth.
6:21 PM
TODAY
6:22 PM
EDIT
click

Ruth! Can I talk to you?

So—I forwarded your newsletter to a couple of people at the county, and to the *Daily Record*.

Oh. Thanks! Yeah, I got a bunch of new subscribers.

Better than that, you got a reaction.

DEAR MS. FREEMAN,

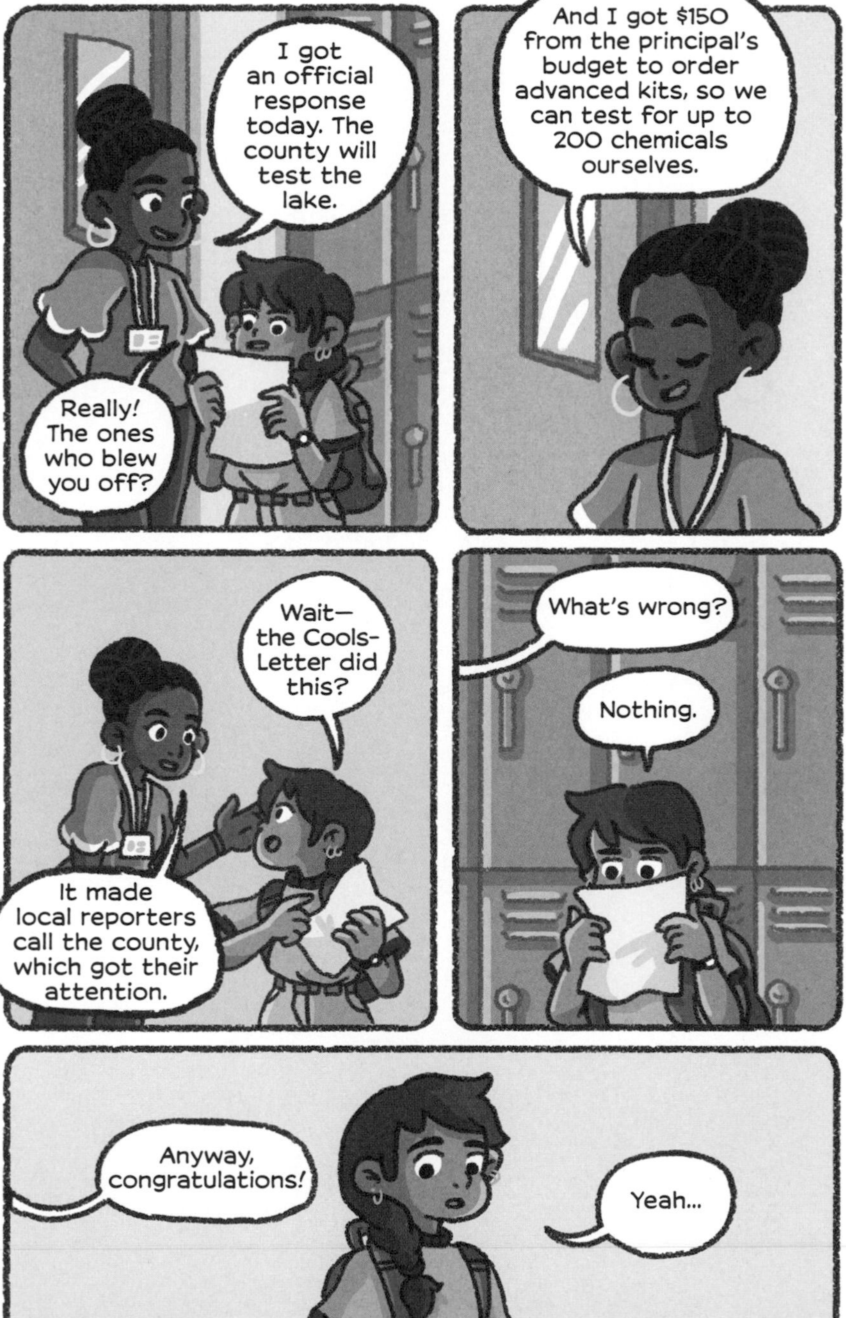
I got an official response today. The county will test the lake.
Really! The ones who blew you off?
And I got $150 from the principal's budget to order advanced kits, so we can test for up to 200 chemicals ourselves.
Wait—the Cools-Letter did this?
It made local reporters call the county, which got their attention.
What's wrong?
Nothing.
Anyway, congratulations!
Yeah...

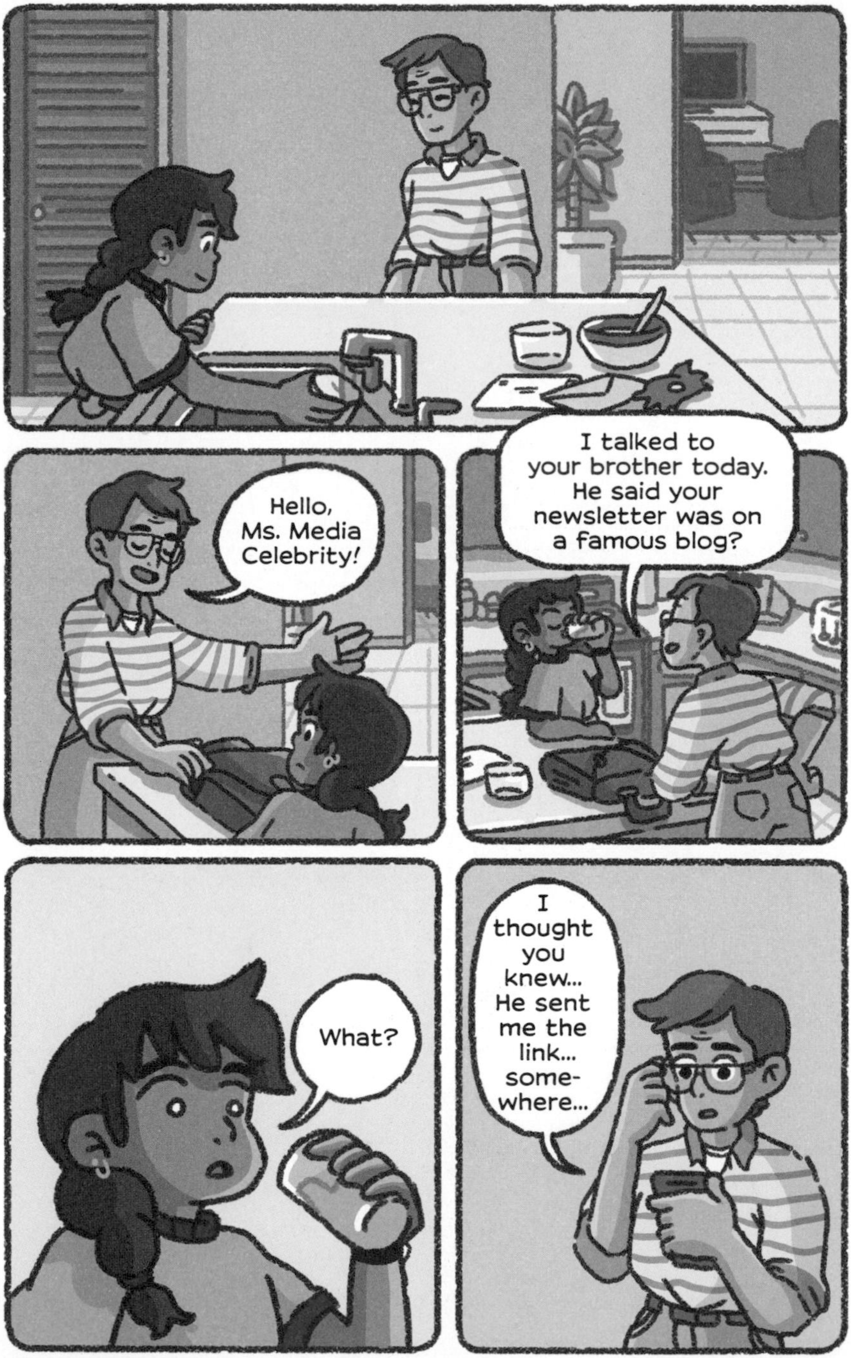
Hello, Ms. Media Celebrity!
I talked to your brother today. He said your newsletter was on a famous blog?
What?
I thought you knew... He sent me the link... some-where...

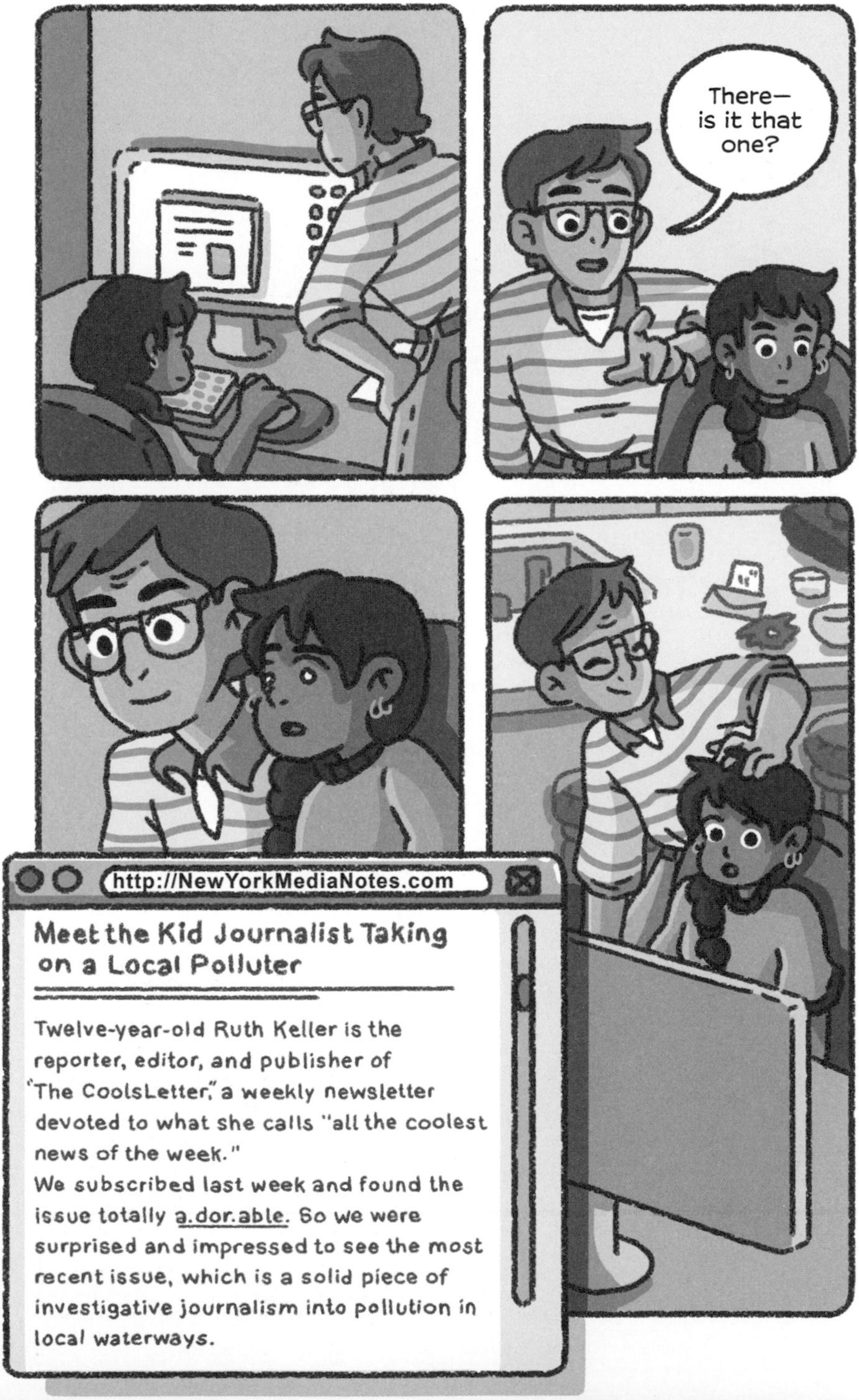
There—
is it that one?
http://NewYorkMediaNotes.com
Meet the Kid Journalist Taking on a Local Polluter
Twelve-year-old Ruth Keller is the reporter, editor, and publisher of "The CoolsLetter," a weekly newsletter devoted to what she calls "all the coolest news of the week."
We subscribed last week and found the issue totally a.dor.able. So we were surprised and impressed to see the most recent issue, which is a solid piece of investigative journalism into pollution in local waterways.

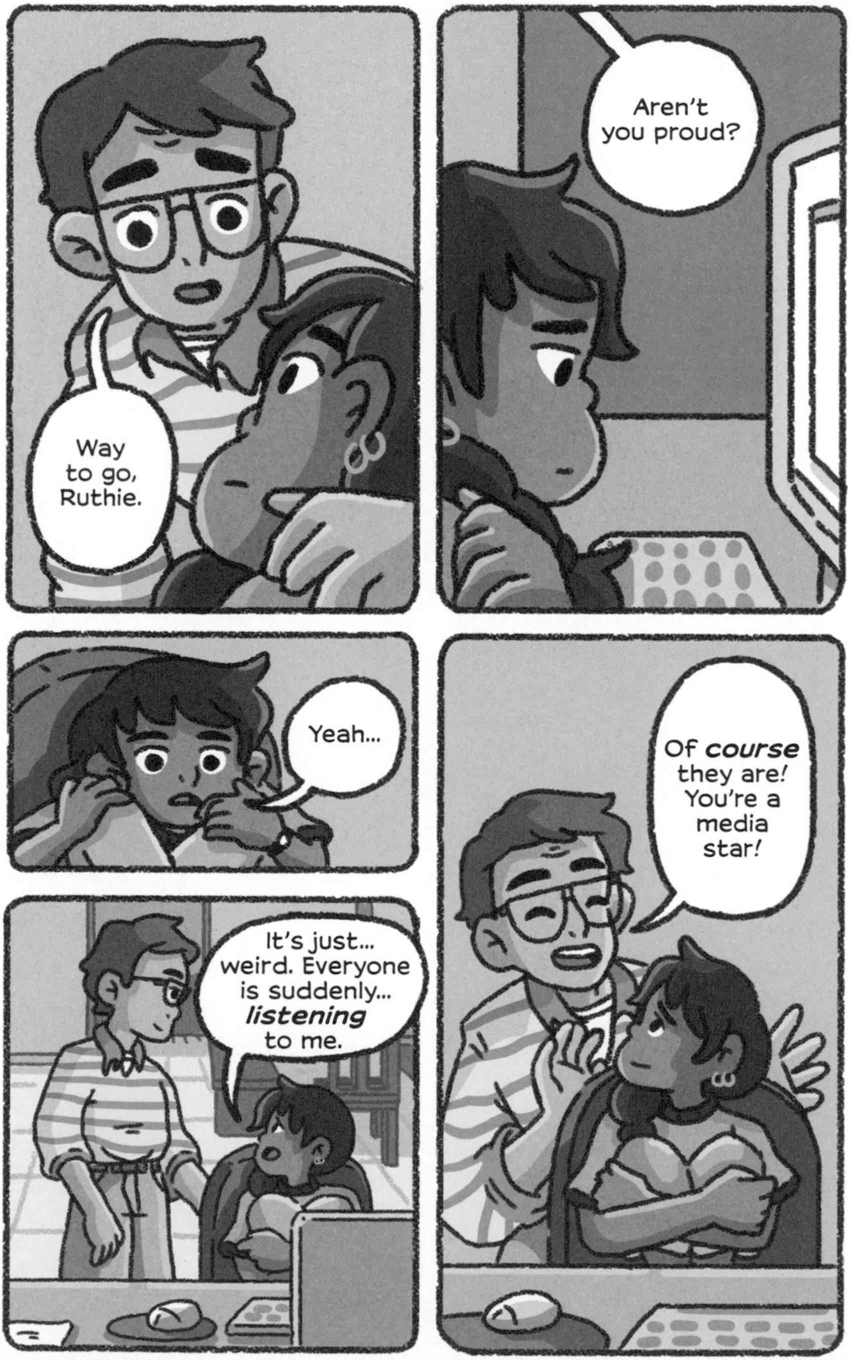
Way to go, Ruthie.
Aren't you proud?
Yeah...
It's just... weird. Everyone is suddenly... *listening* to me.
Of *course* they are! You're a media star!

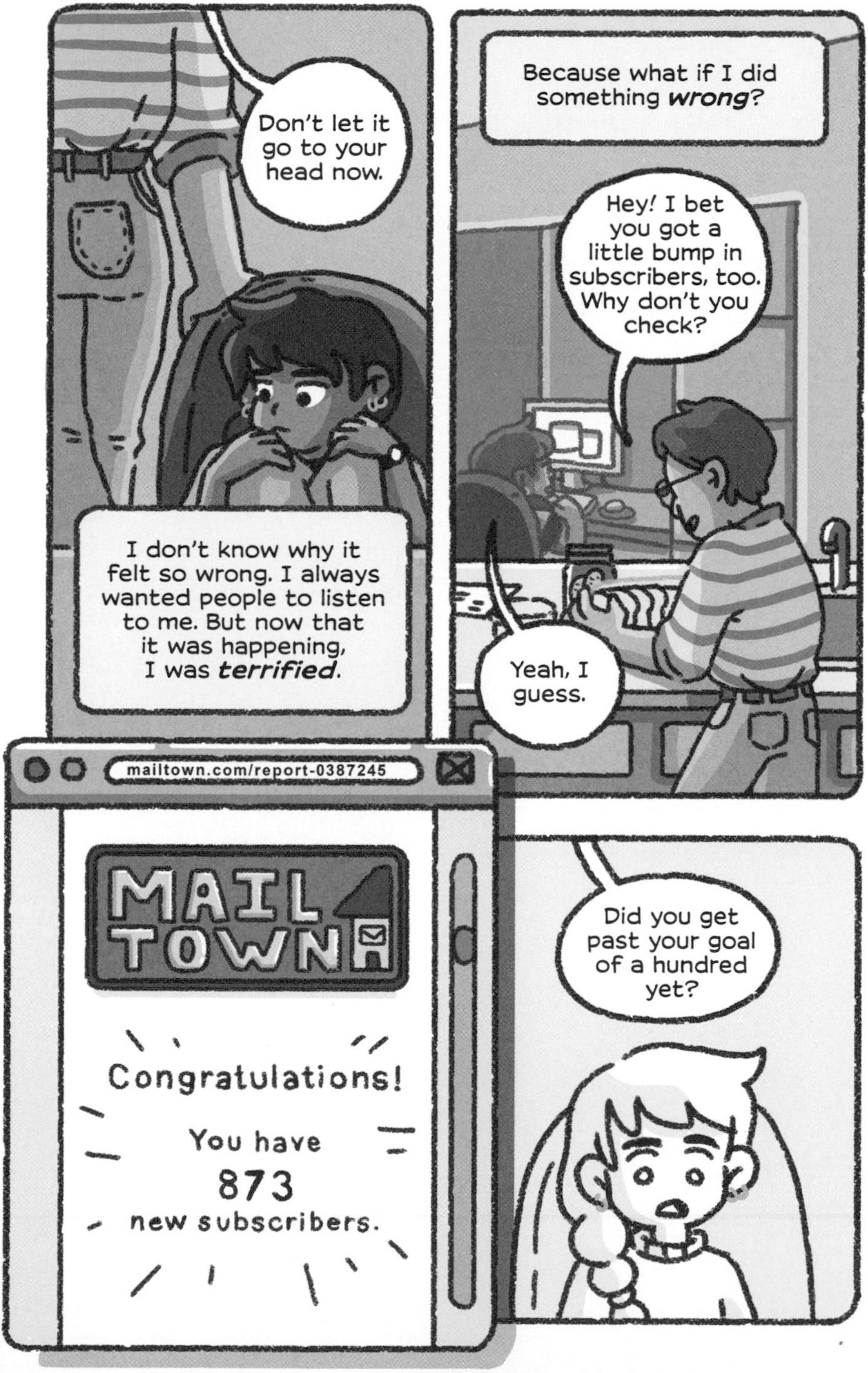
Don't let it go to your head now.
I don't know why it felt so wrong. I always wanted people to listen to me. But now that it was happening, I was *terrified*.
Because what if I did something *wrong*?
Hey! I bet you got a little bump in subscribers, too. Why don't you check?
Yeah, I guess.
mailtown.com/report-0387245
MAIL TOWN
Congratulations!
You have
873
new subscribers.
Did you get past your goal of a hundred yet?

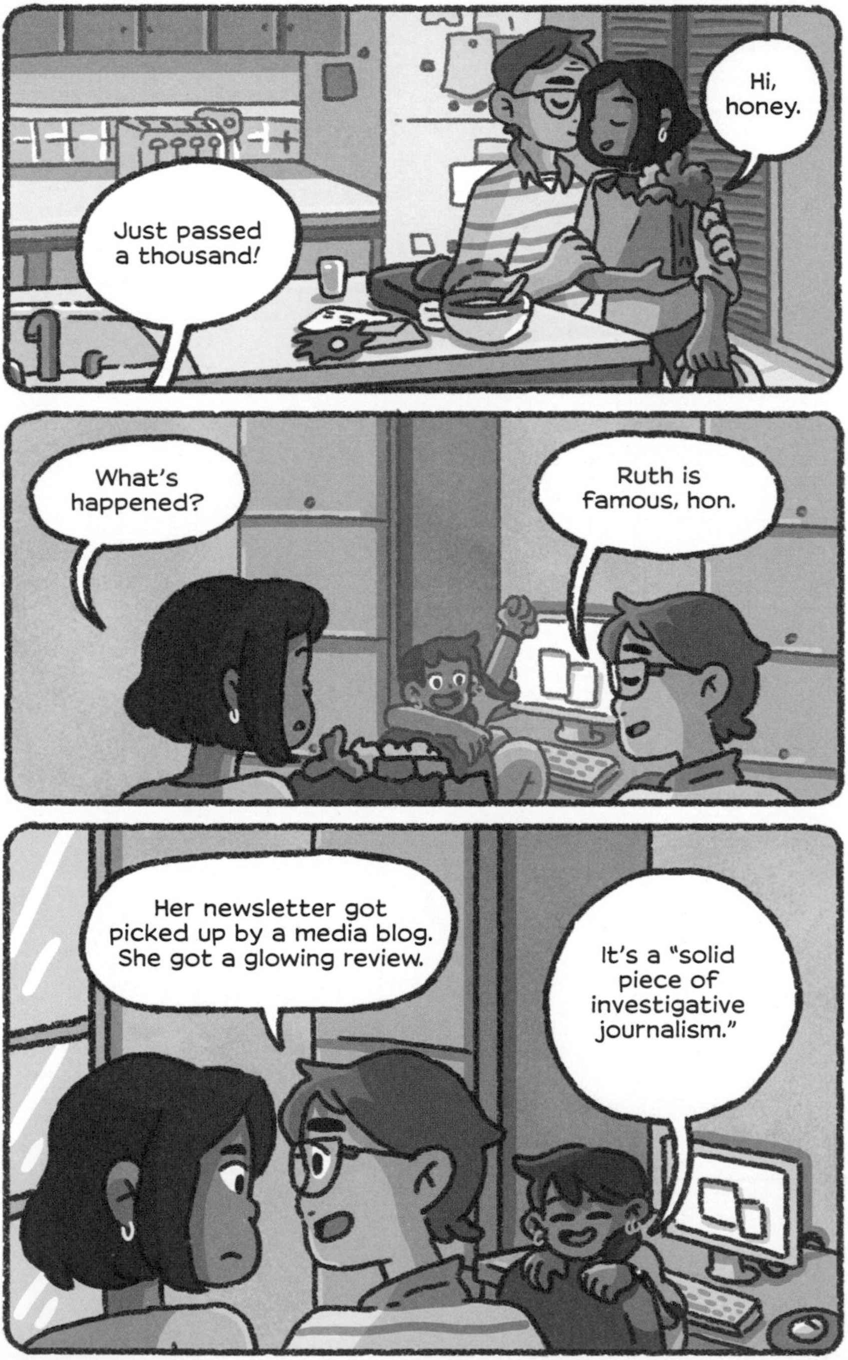
Hi, honey.
Just passed a thousand!
What's happened?
Ruth is famous, hon.
Her newsletter got picked up by a media blog. She got a glowing review.
It's a "solid piece of investigative journalism."

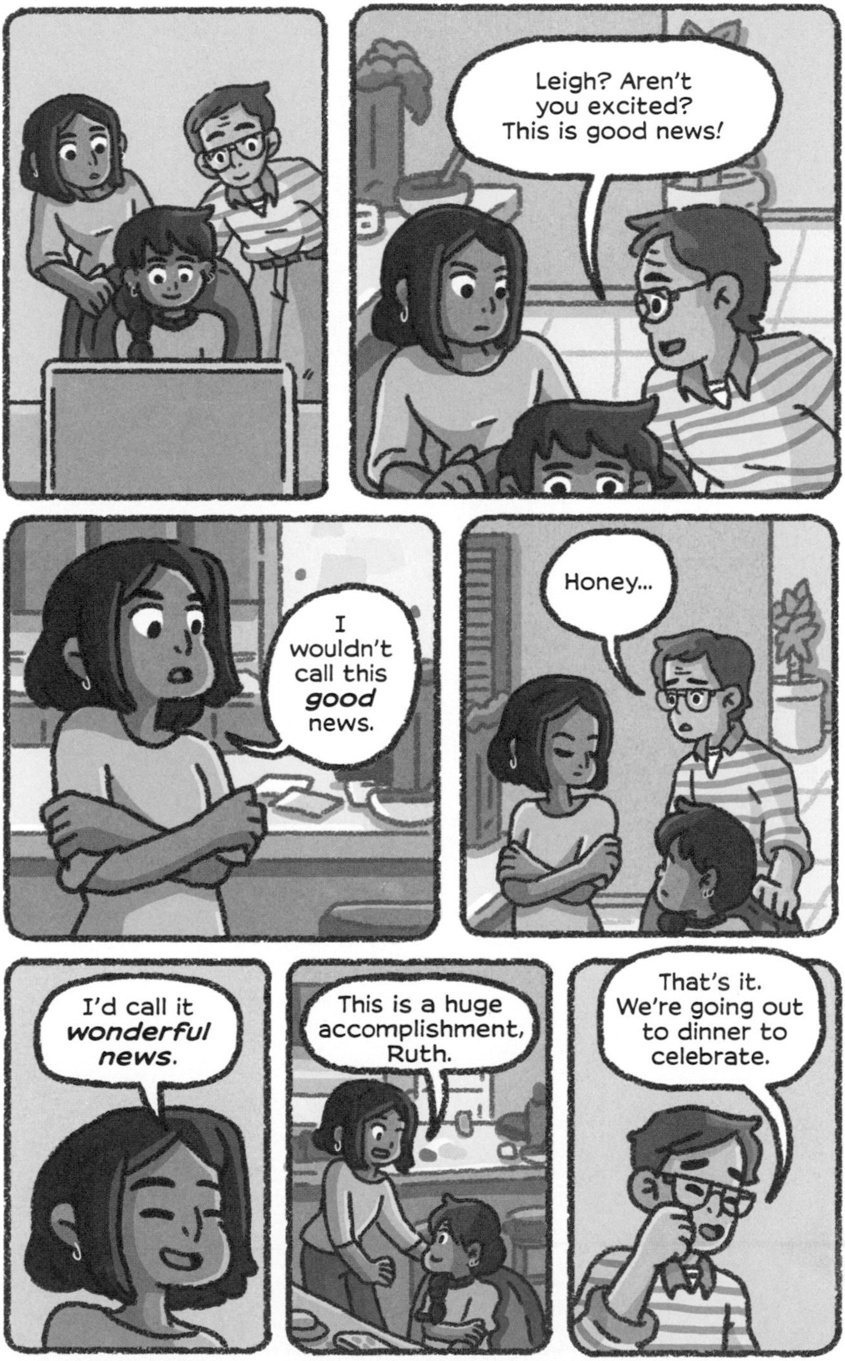
Leigh? Aren't you excited? This is good news!
I wouldn't call this *good* news.
Honey...
I'd call it ***wonderful news***.
This is a huge accomplishment, Ruth.
That's it. We're going out to dinner to celebrate.

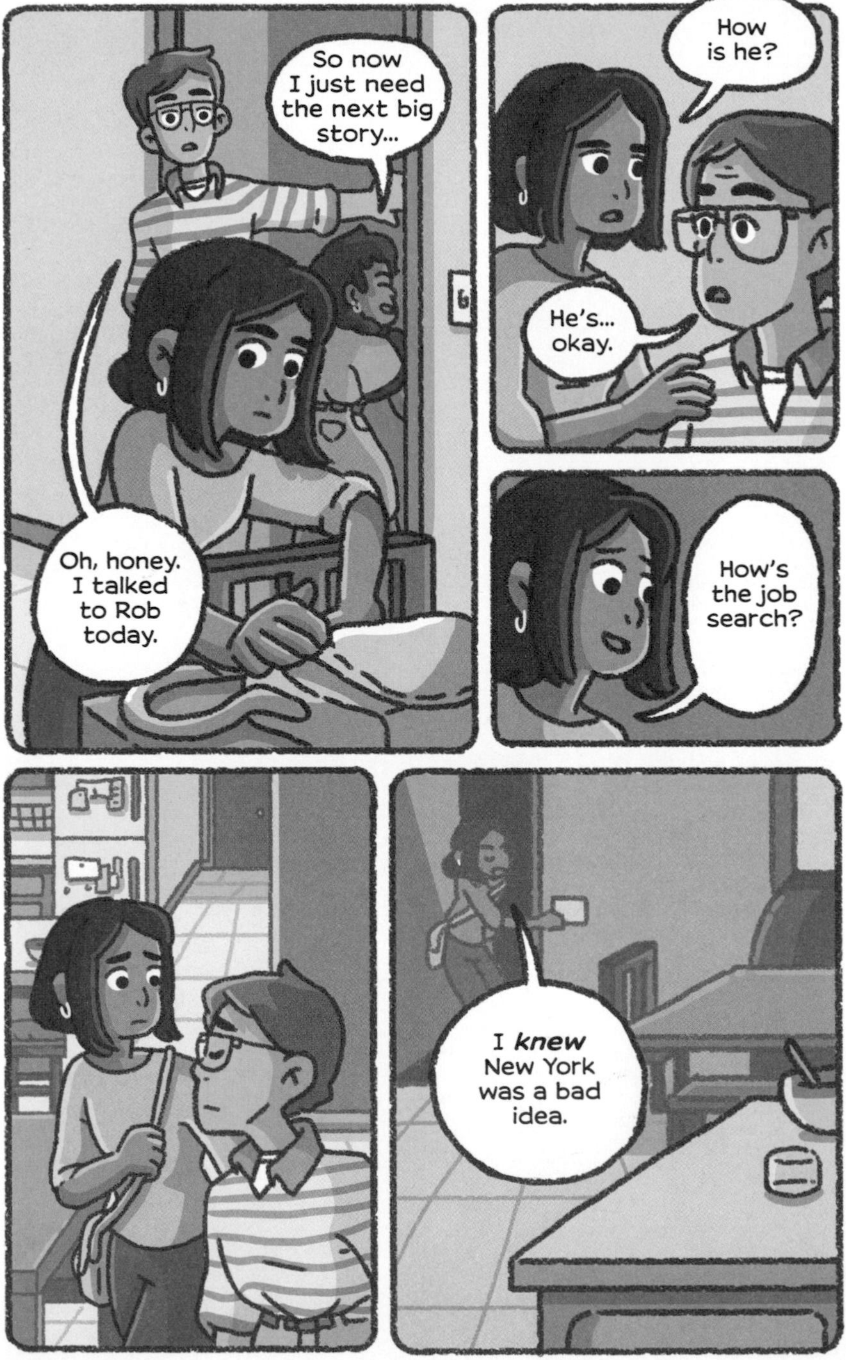
So now I just need the next big story...
Oh, honey. I talked to Rob today.
How is he?
He's... okay.
How's the job search?
I *knew* New York was a bad idea.

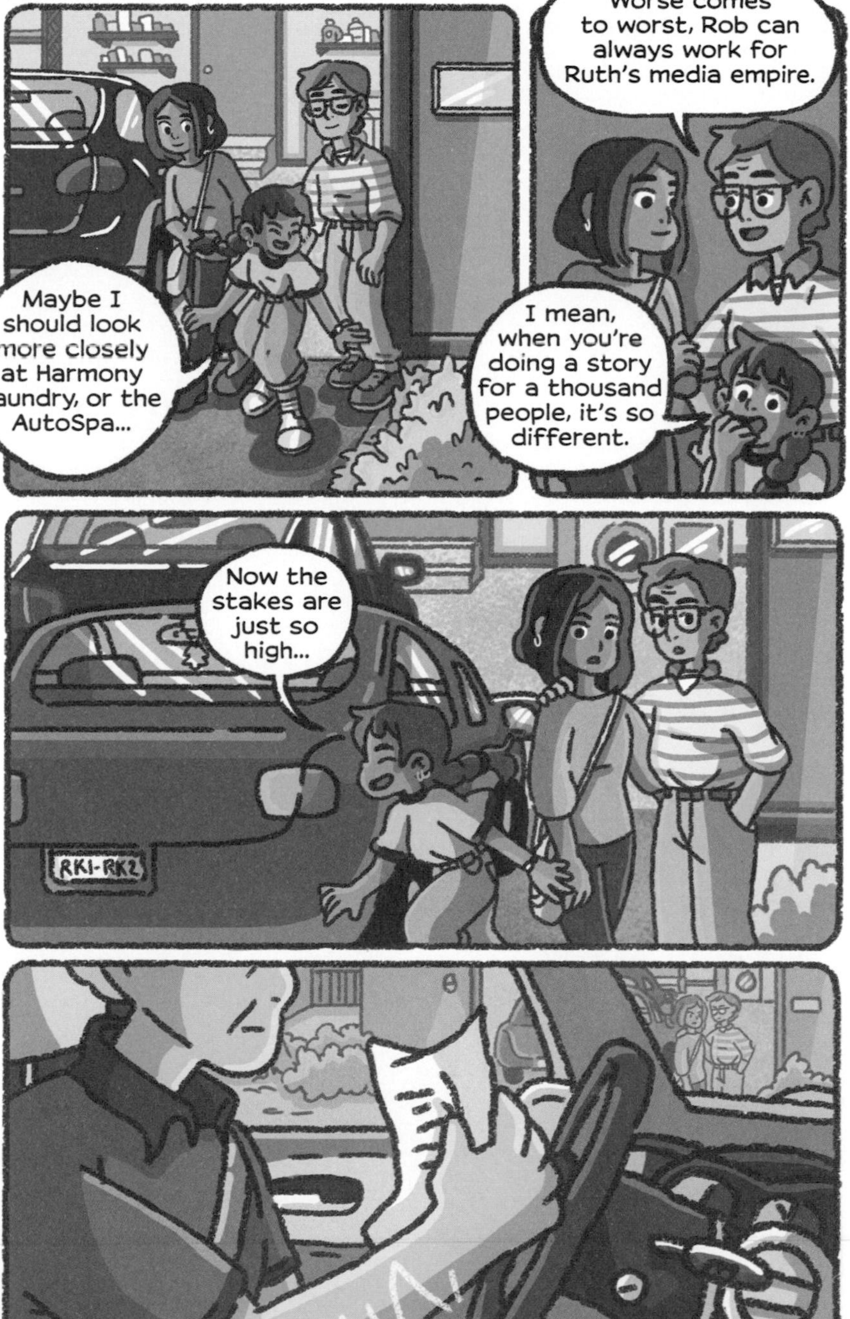
Maybe I should look more closely at Harmony Laundry, or the AutoSpa...
Worse comes to worst, Rob can always work for Ruth's media empire.
I mean, when you're doing a story for a thousand people, it's so different.
Now the stakes are just so high...
RKI-RK2

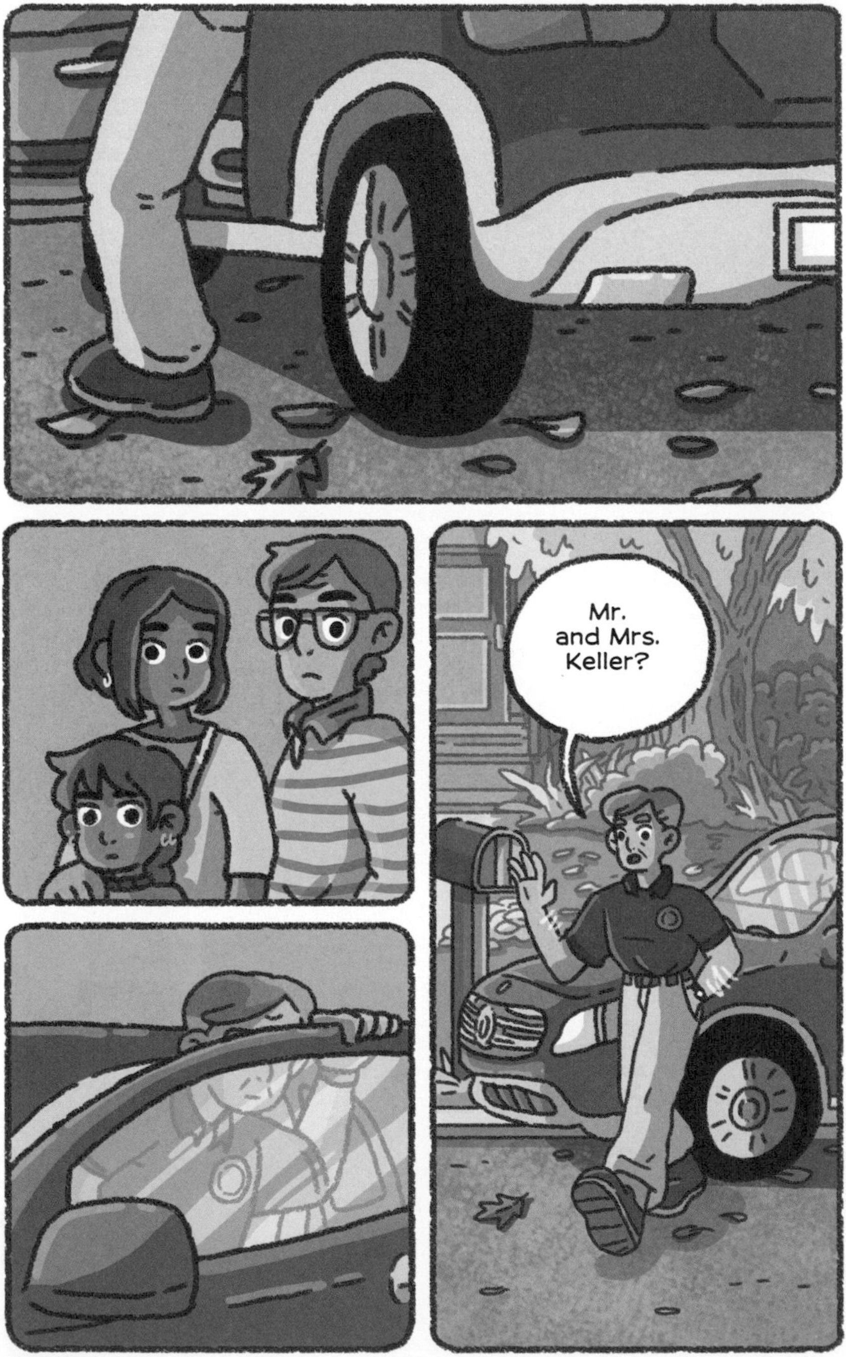
Mr.
and Mrs.
Keller?

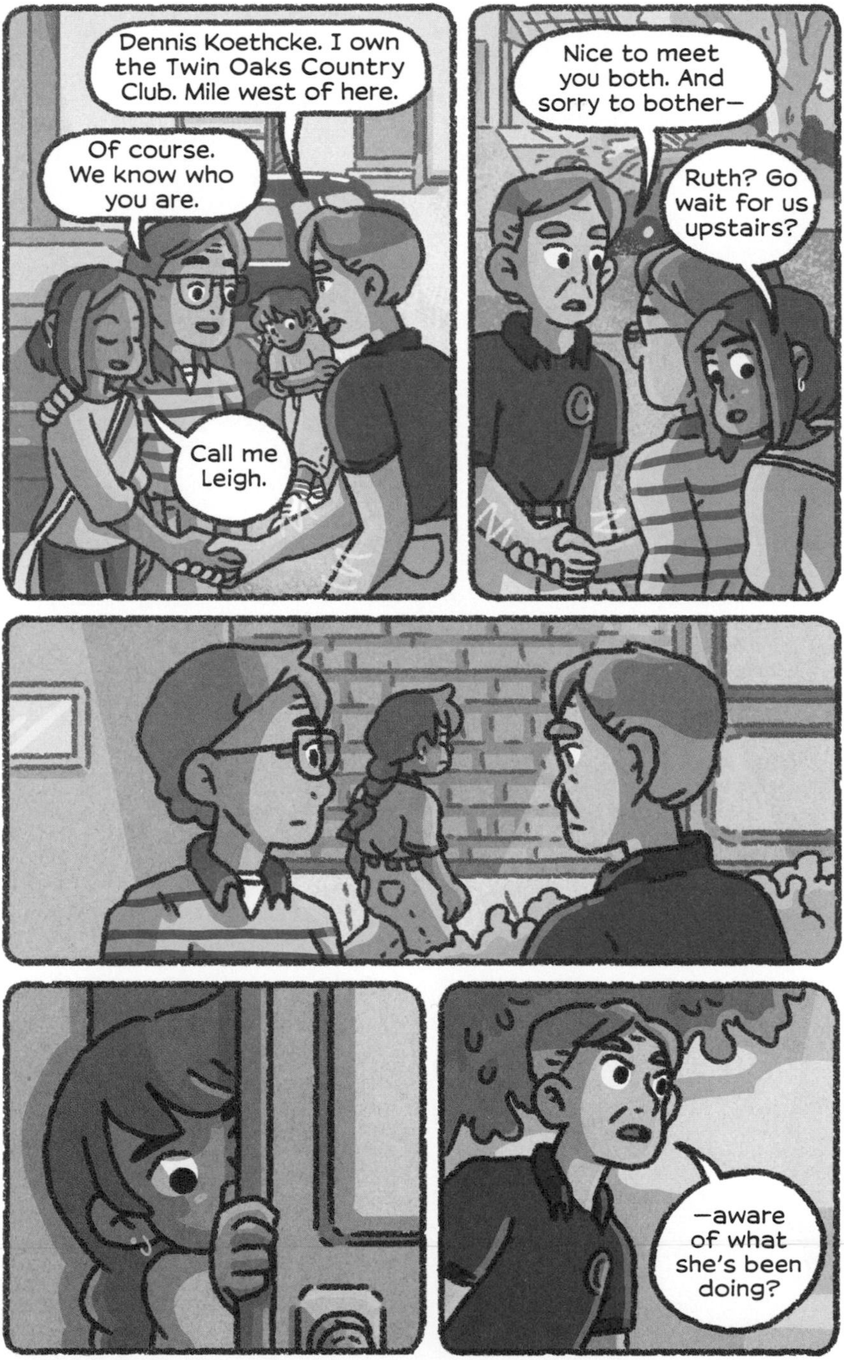
Dennis Koethcke. I own the Twin Oaks Country Club. Mile west of here.
Of course. We know who you are.
Call me Leigh.
Nice to meet you both. And sorry to bother—
Ruth? Go wait for us upstairs?
—aware of what she's been doing?

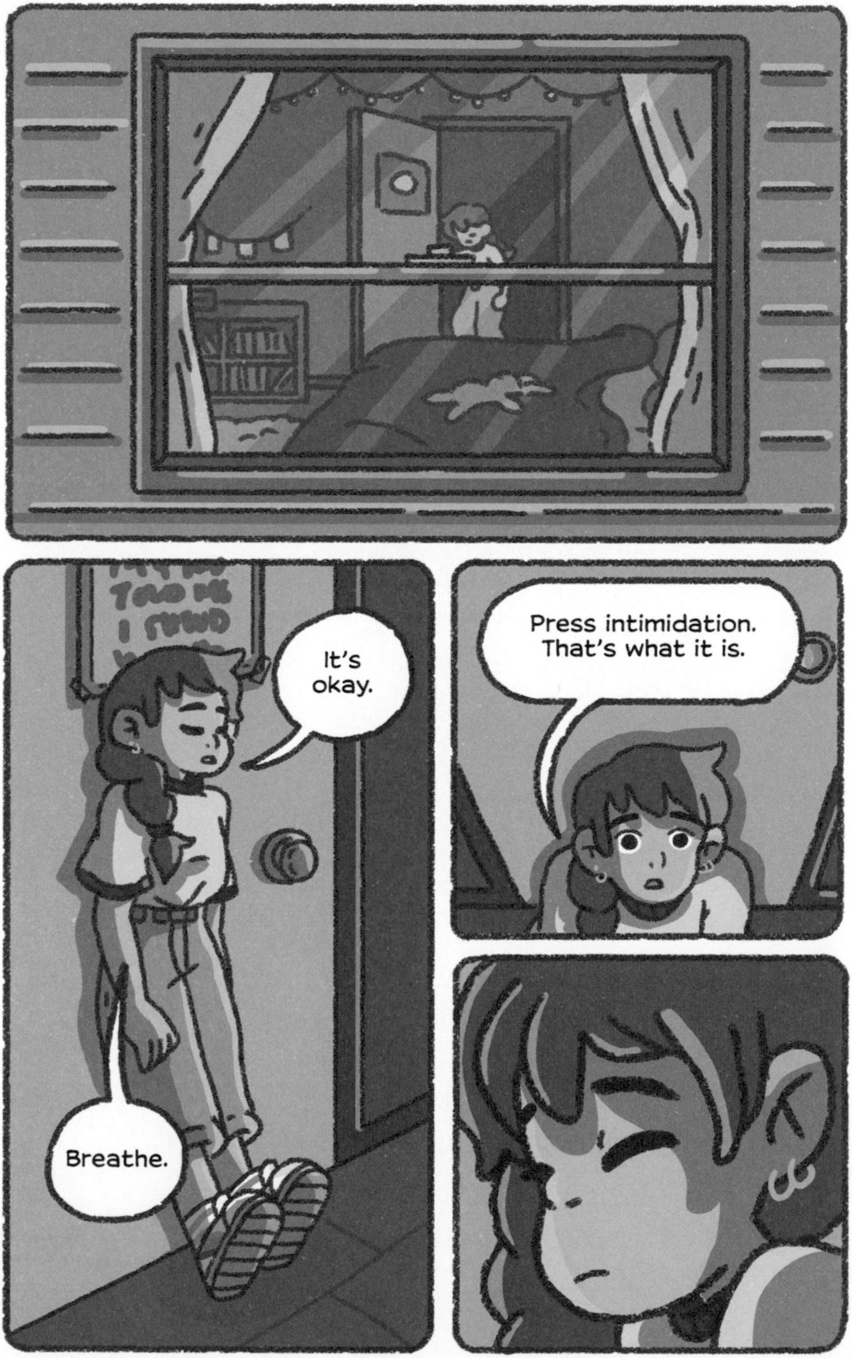
It's okay.
Breathe.
Press intimidation. That's what it is.

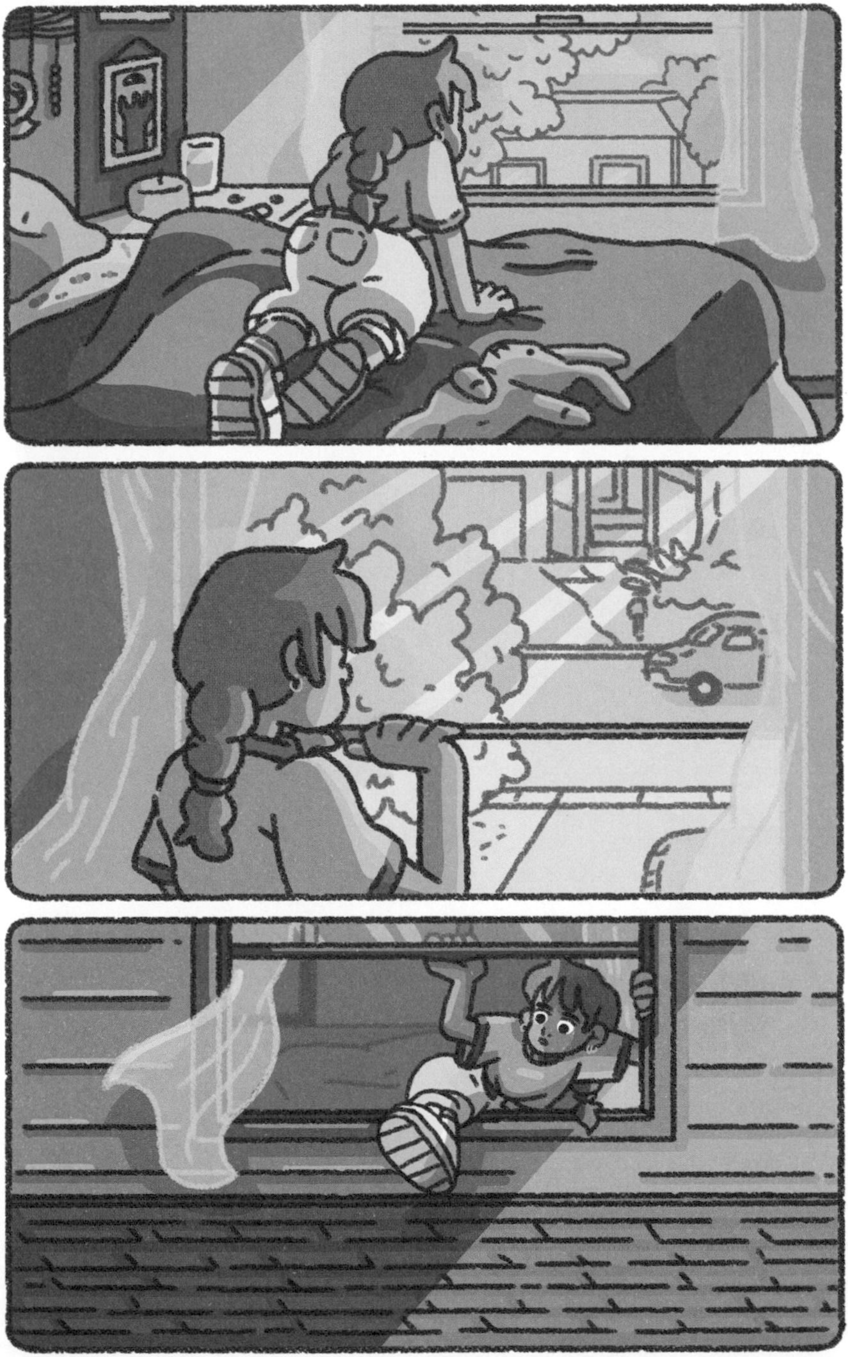

—and I *understand* that—
—because *your business* is being scrutinized—
—there are *serious* chemicals in that lake—
—attacking a *twelve-year-old girl*—
—security camera footage—
—clear that *your* daughter—
—*evidence* of *trespassing*—
—take this to the *police*—

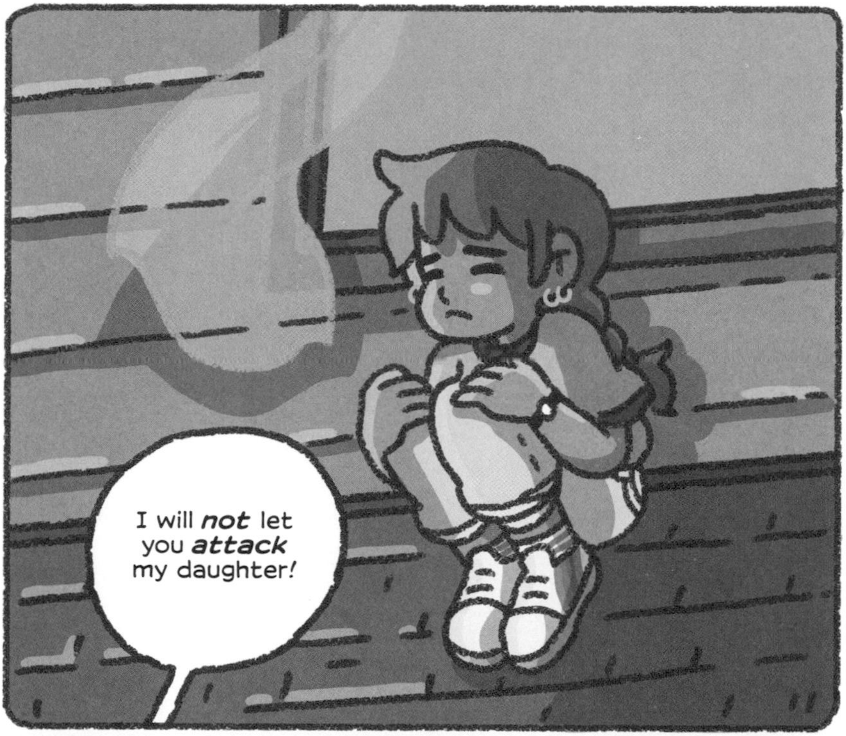
I will *not* let you *attack* my daughter!

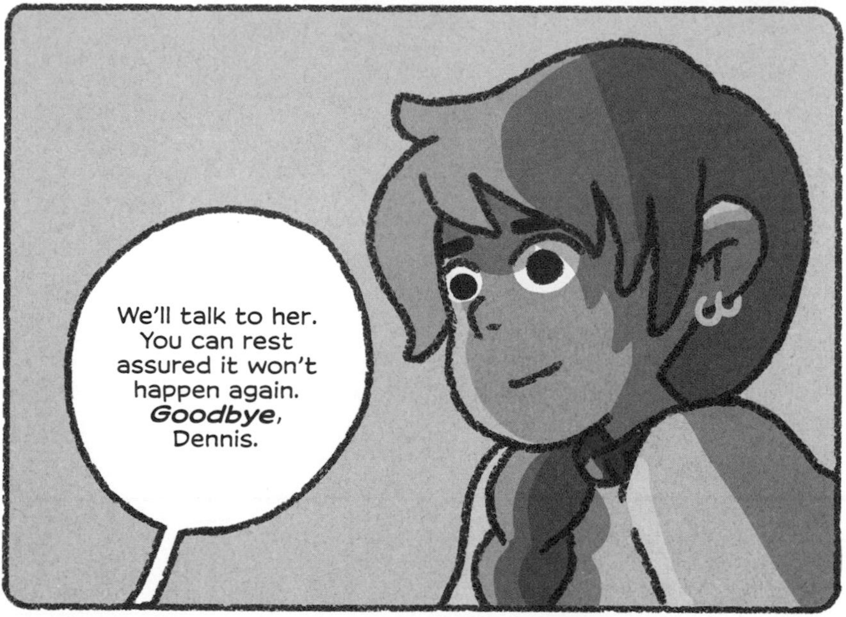
We'll talk to her. You can rest assured it won't happen again. *Goodbye*, Dennis.

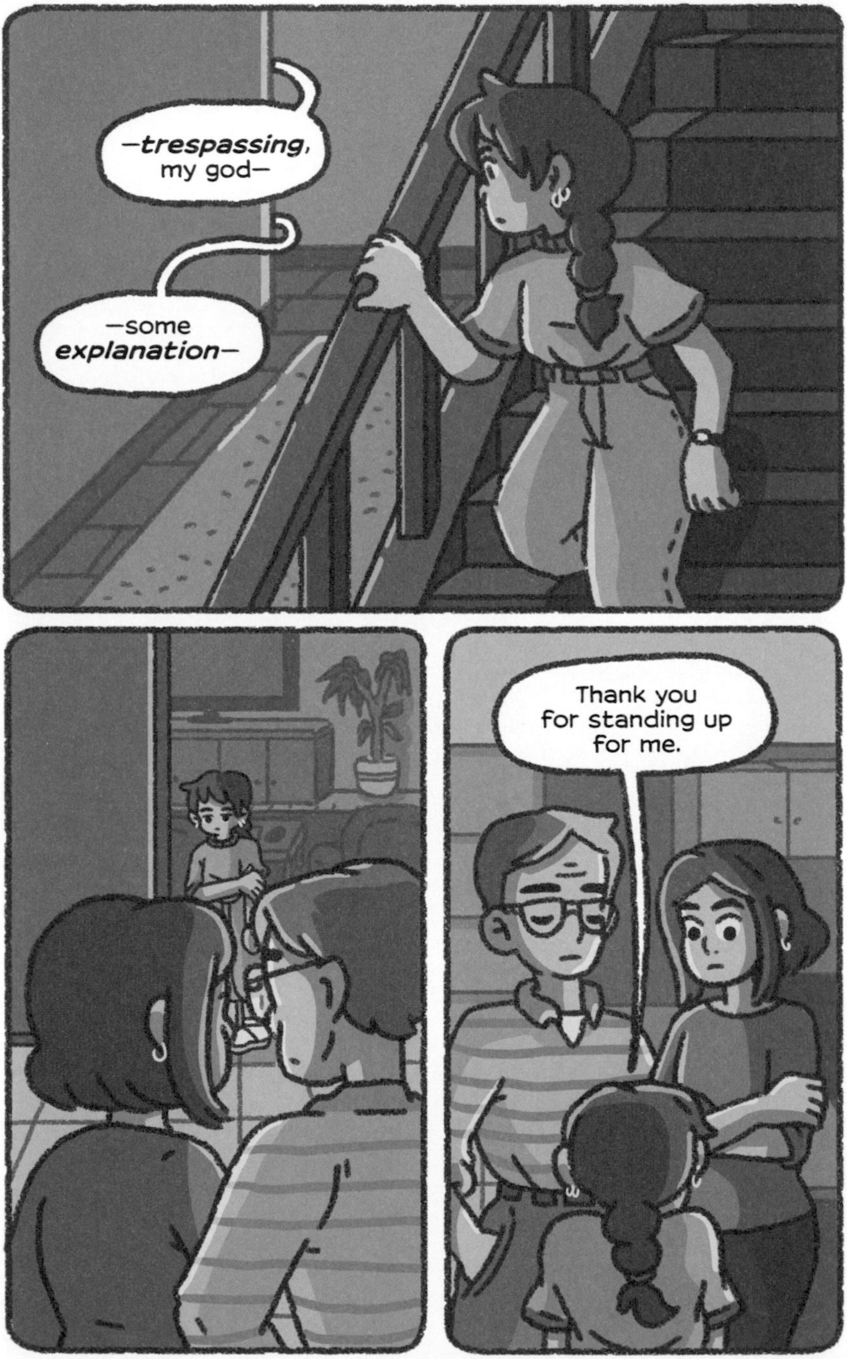
—*trespassing*, my god—
—some *explanation*—
Thank you for standing up for me.

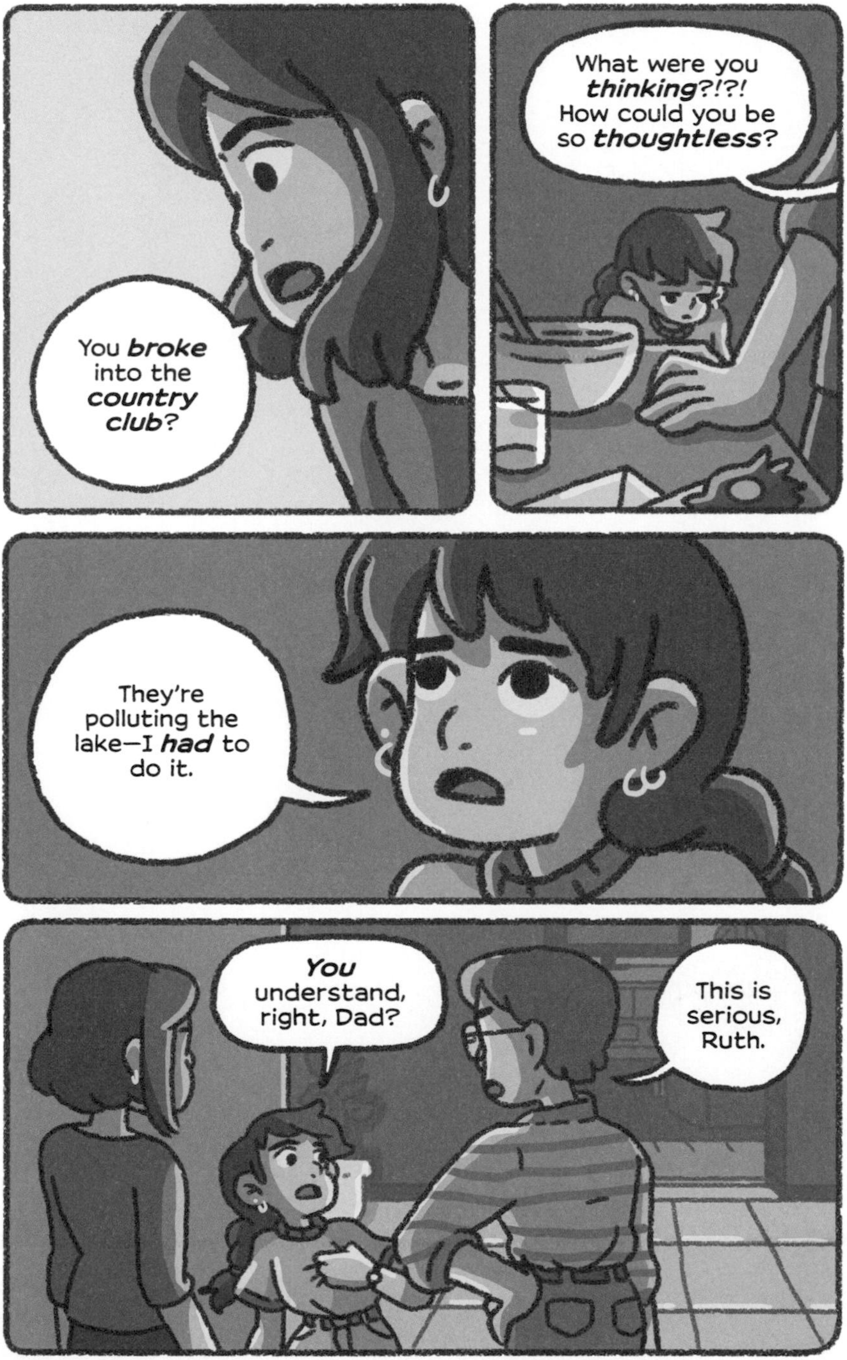
You *broke* into the *country club*?
What were you *thinking*?!?! How could you be so *thoughtless*?
They're polluting the lake—I *had* to do it.
You understand, right, Dad?
This is serious, Ruth.

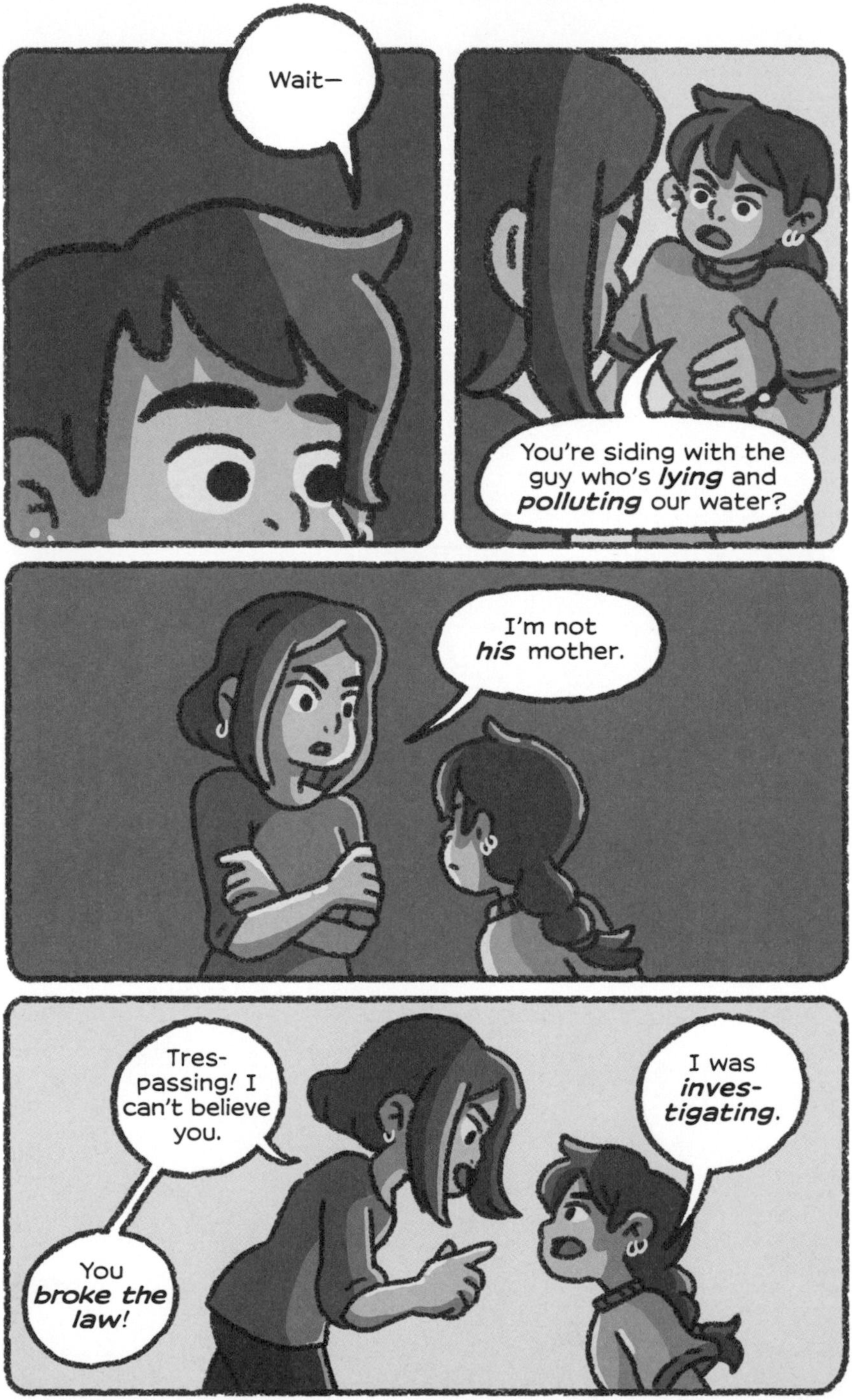
Wait—
You're siding with the guy who's *lying* and *polluting* our water?
I'm not *his* mother.
Tres-passing! I can't believe you.
You *broke the law*!
I was *inves-tigating*.

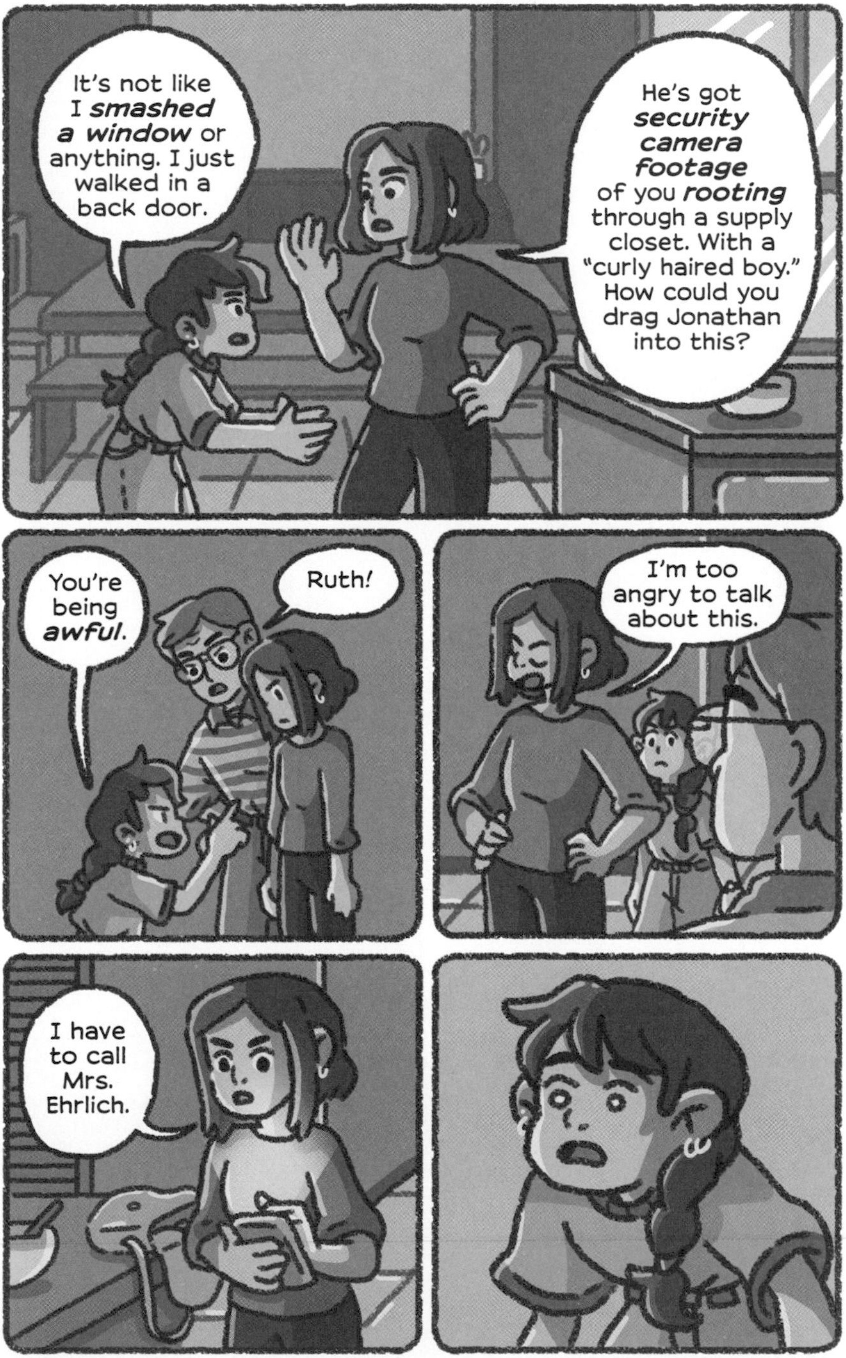
It's not like I *smashed a window* or anything. I just walked in a back door.
He's got *security camera footage* of you *rooting* through a supply closet. With a "curly haired boy." How could you drag Jonathan into this?
You're being *awful*.
Ruth!
I'm too angry to talk about this.
I have to call Mrs. Ehrlich.

No, Mom, please. Don't call Jonathan's mom. Please don't.

I'll do anything, it was my fault, okay?

Go upstairs, Ruth.

I'm sorry! I'm so sorry, I'll do anything. Just don't call Jonathan's mom, please don't!

6:41PM

CONTACTS +

EHLRICH

VERETT

ZRA

FAY

I said go upstairs!!

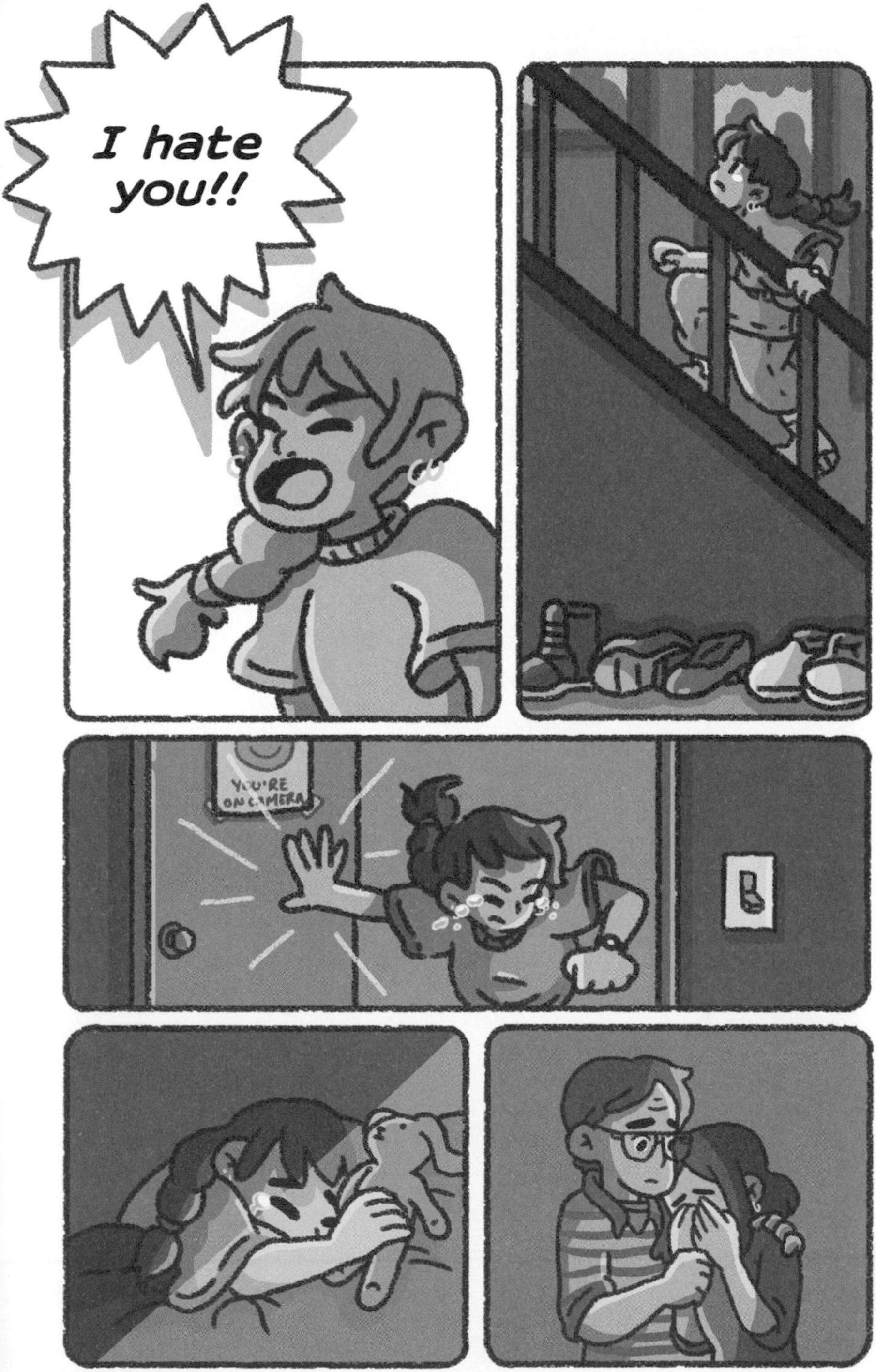
I hate you!!
YOU'RE ON CAMERA

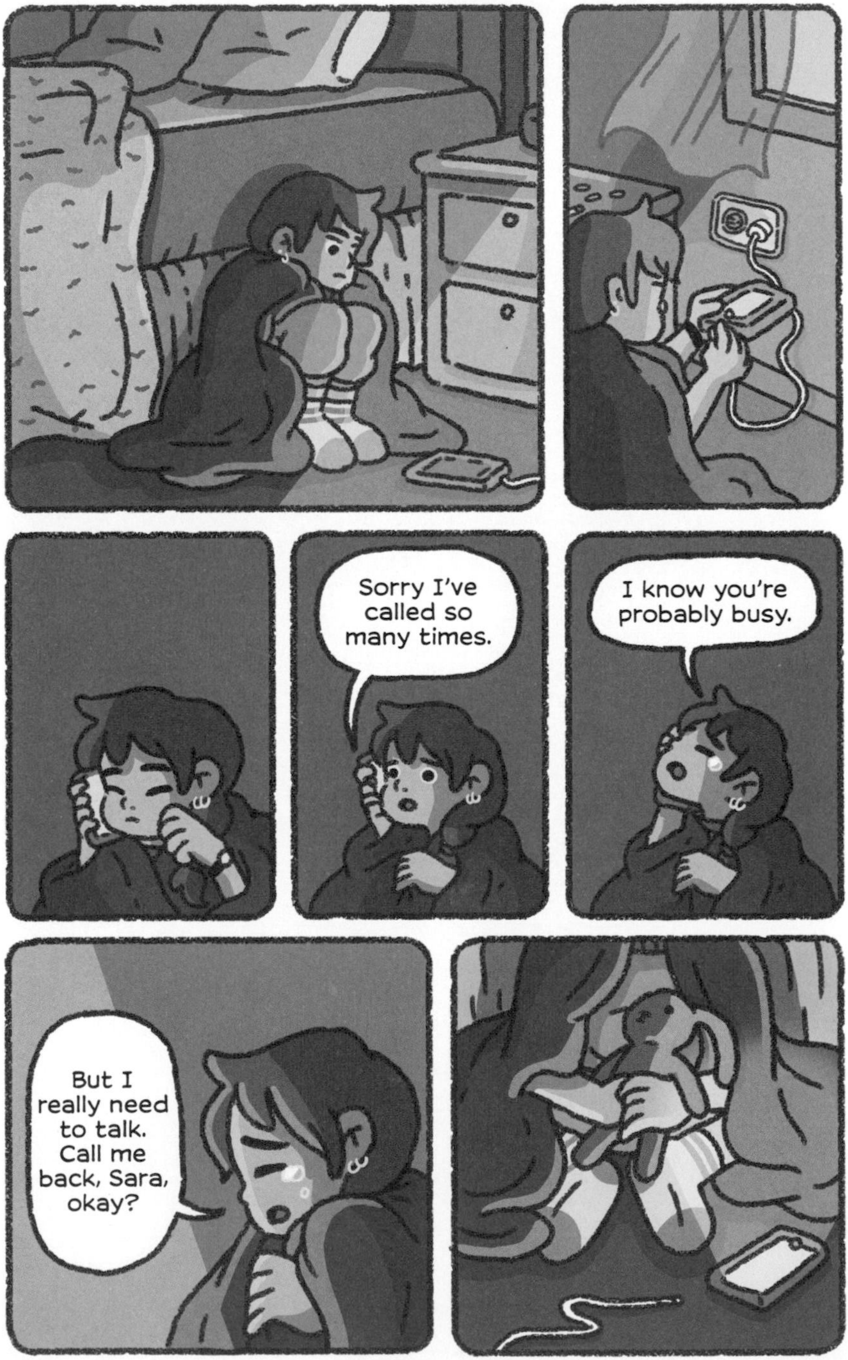
Sorry I've called so many times.
I know you're probably busy.
But I really need to talk. Call me back, Sara, okay?

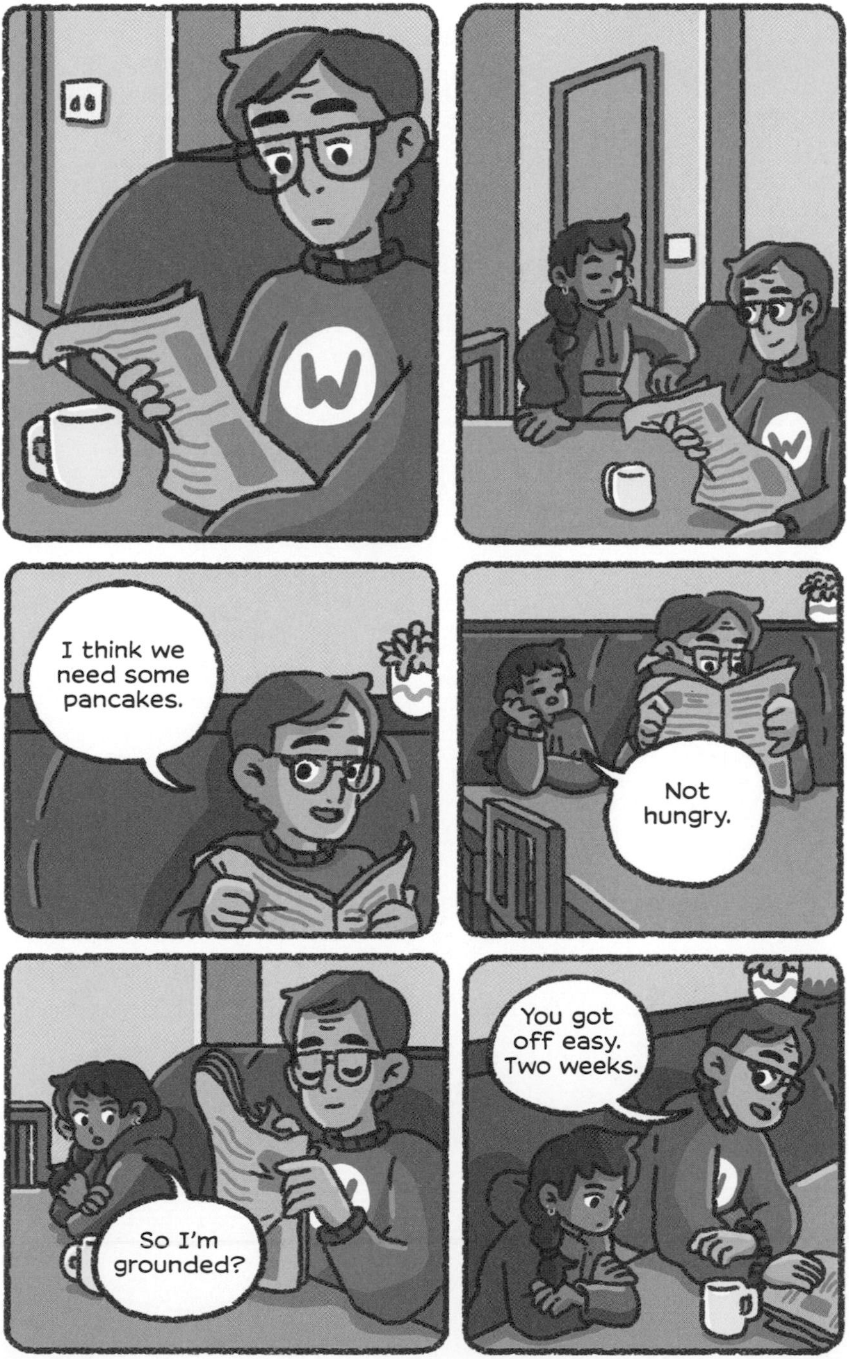
I think we need some pancakes.
Not hungry.
So I'm grounded?
You got off easy. Two weeks.

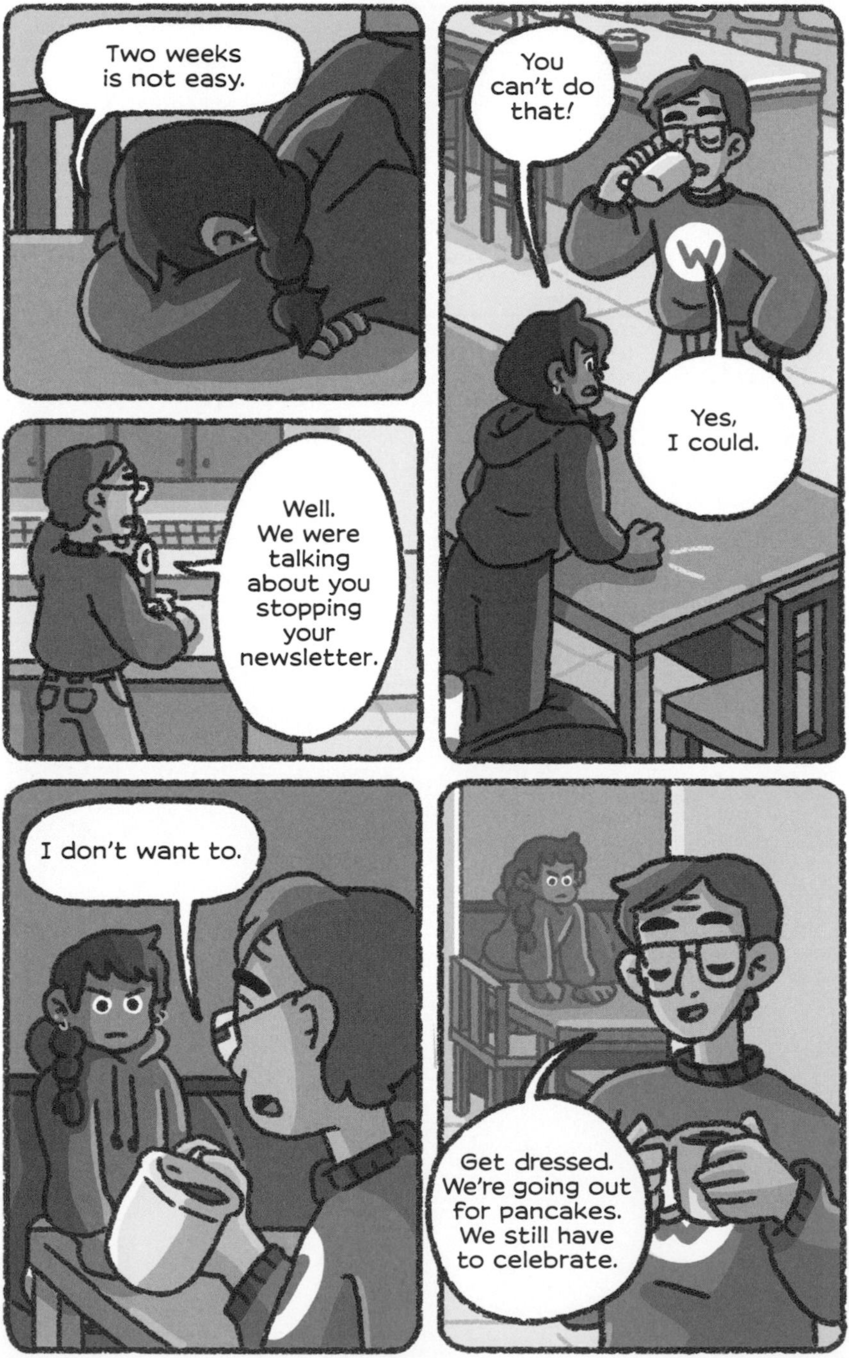
Two weeks is not easy.
You can't do that!
Yes, I could.
Well. We were talking about you stopping your newsletter.
I don't want to.
Get dressed. We're going out for pancakes. We still have to celebrate.

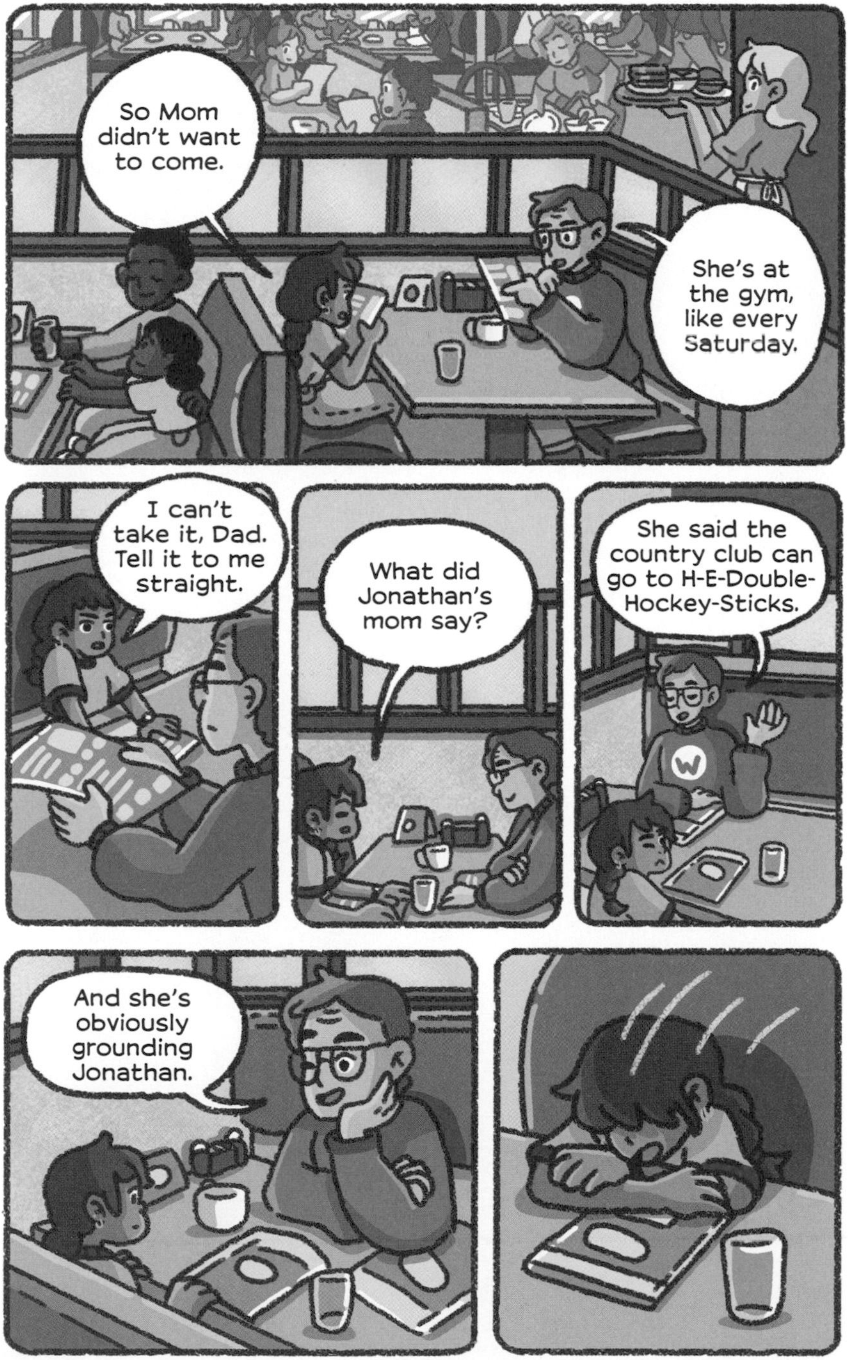
So Mom didn't want to come.
She's at the gym, like every Saturday.
I can't take it, Dad. Tell it to me straight.
What did Jonathan's mom say?
She said the country club can go to H-E-Double-Hockey-Sticks.
W
And she's obviously grounding Jonathan.

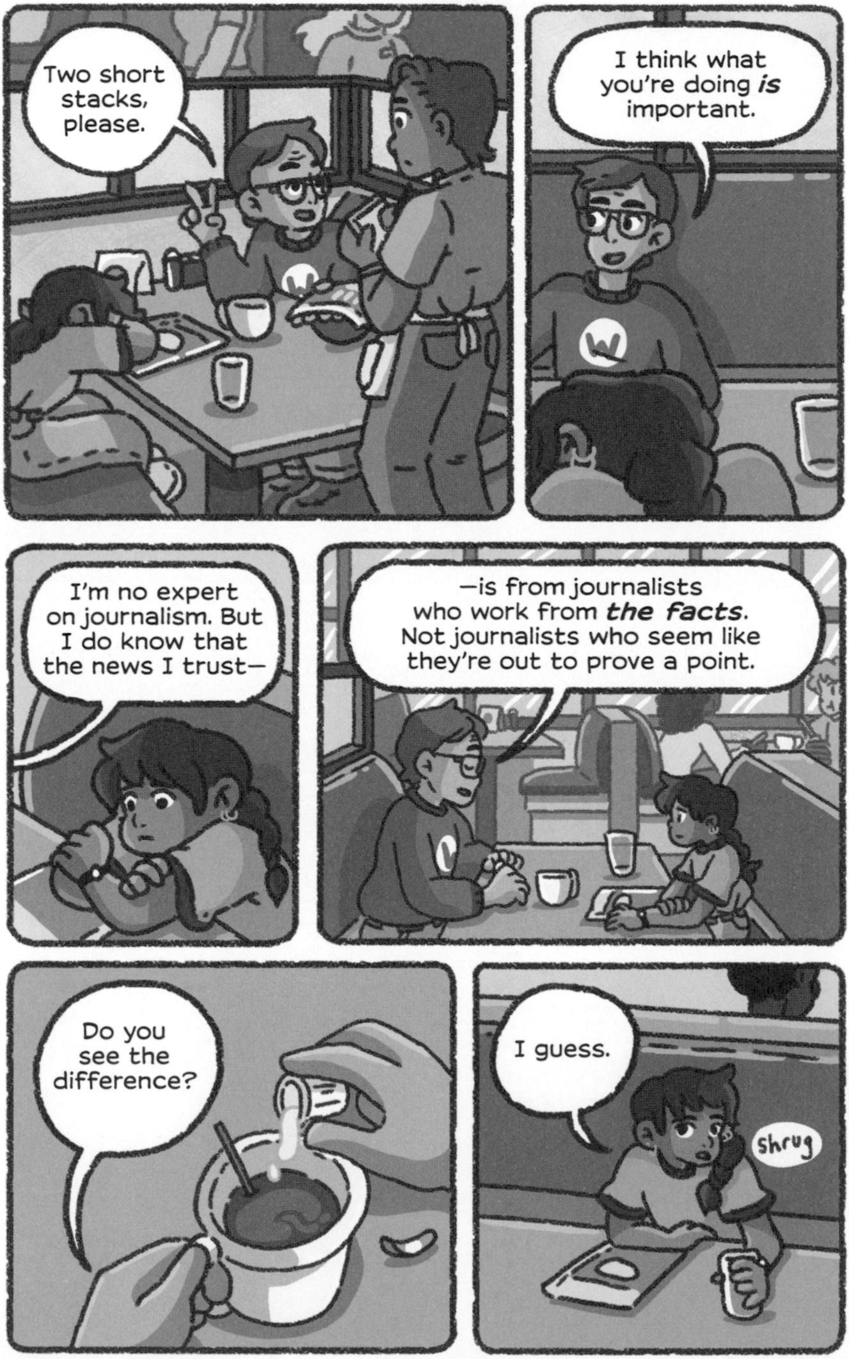
Two short stacks, please.
I think what you're doing *is* important.
I'm no expert on journalism. But I do know that the news I trust—
—is from journalists who work from ***the facts***. Not journalists who seem like they're out to prove a point.
Do you see the difference?
I guess.
shrug

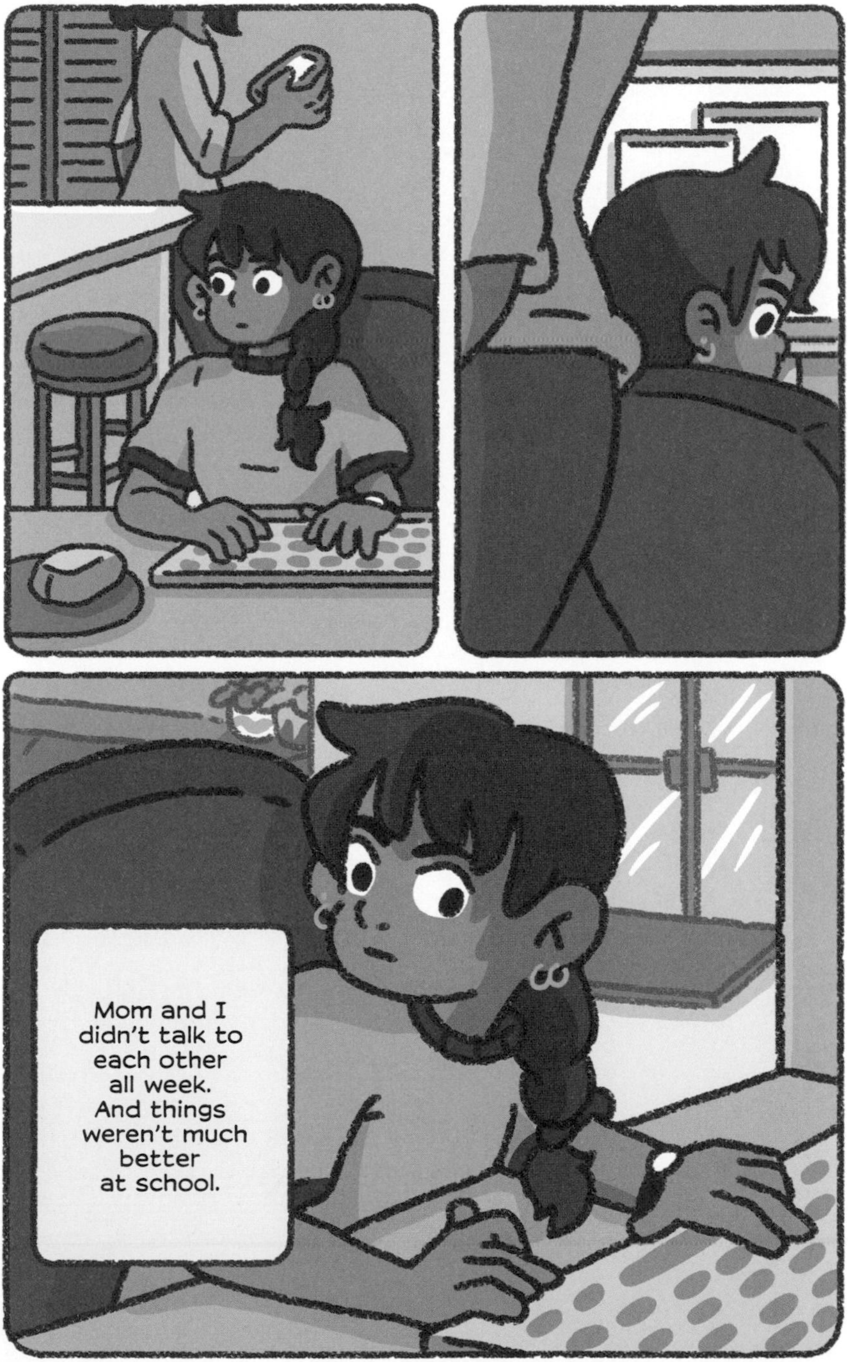
Mom and I didn't talk to each other all week. And things weren't much better at school.

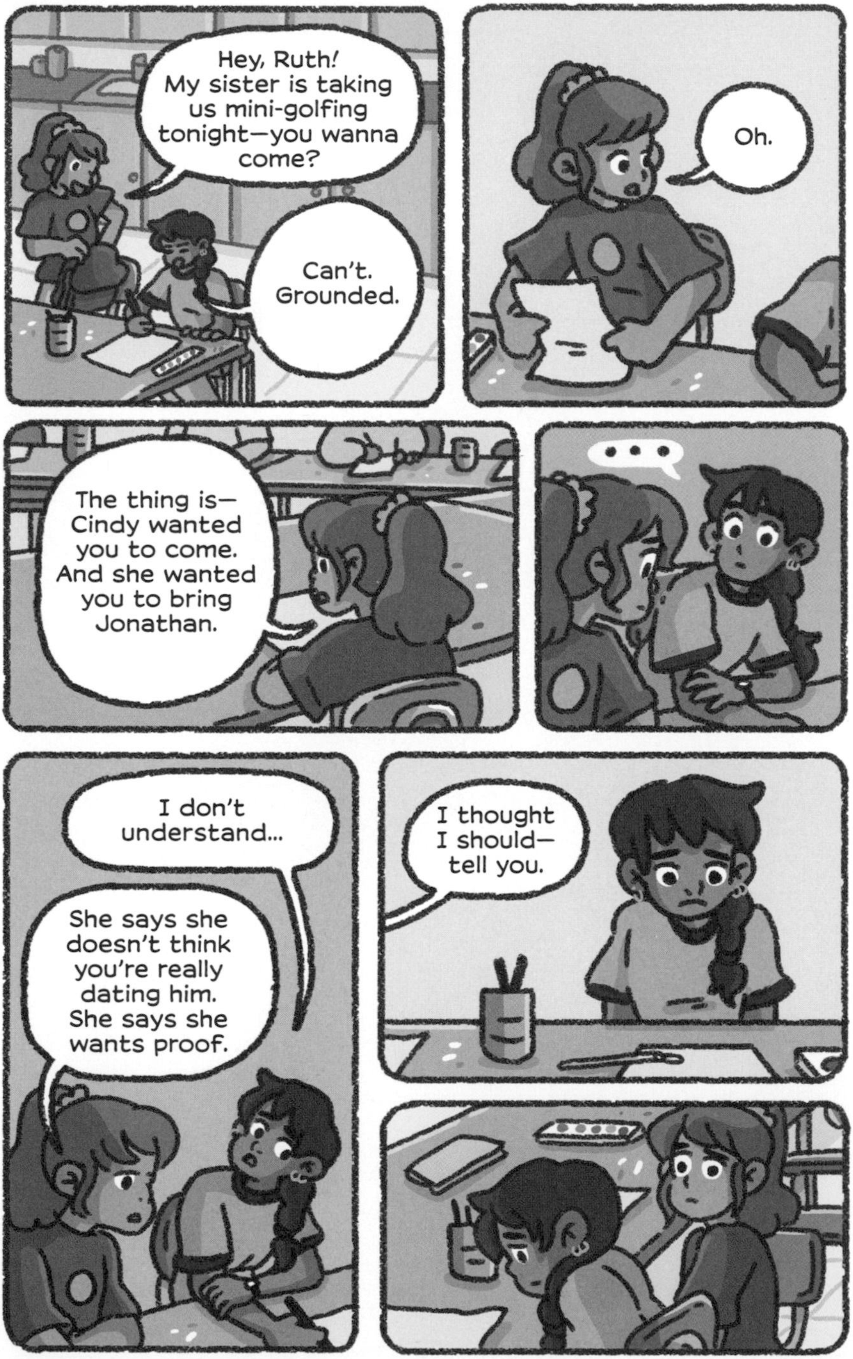
Hey, Ruth! My sister is taking us mini-golfing tonight—you wanna come?
Can't. Grounded.
Oh.
The thing is— Cindy wanted you to come. And she wanted you to bring Jonathan.
...
I don't understand...
She says she doesn't think you're really dating him. She says she wants proof.
I thought I should— tell you.

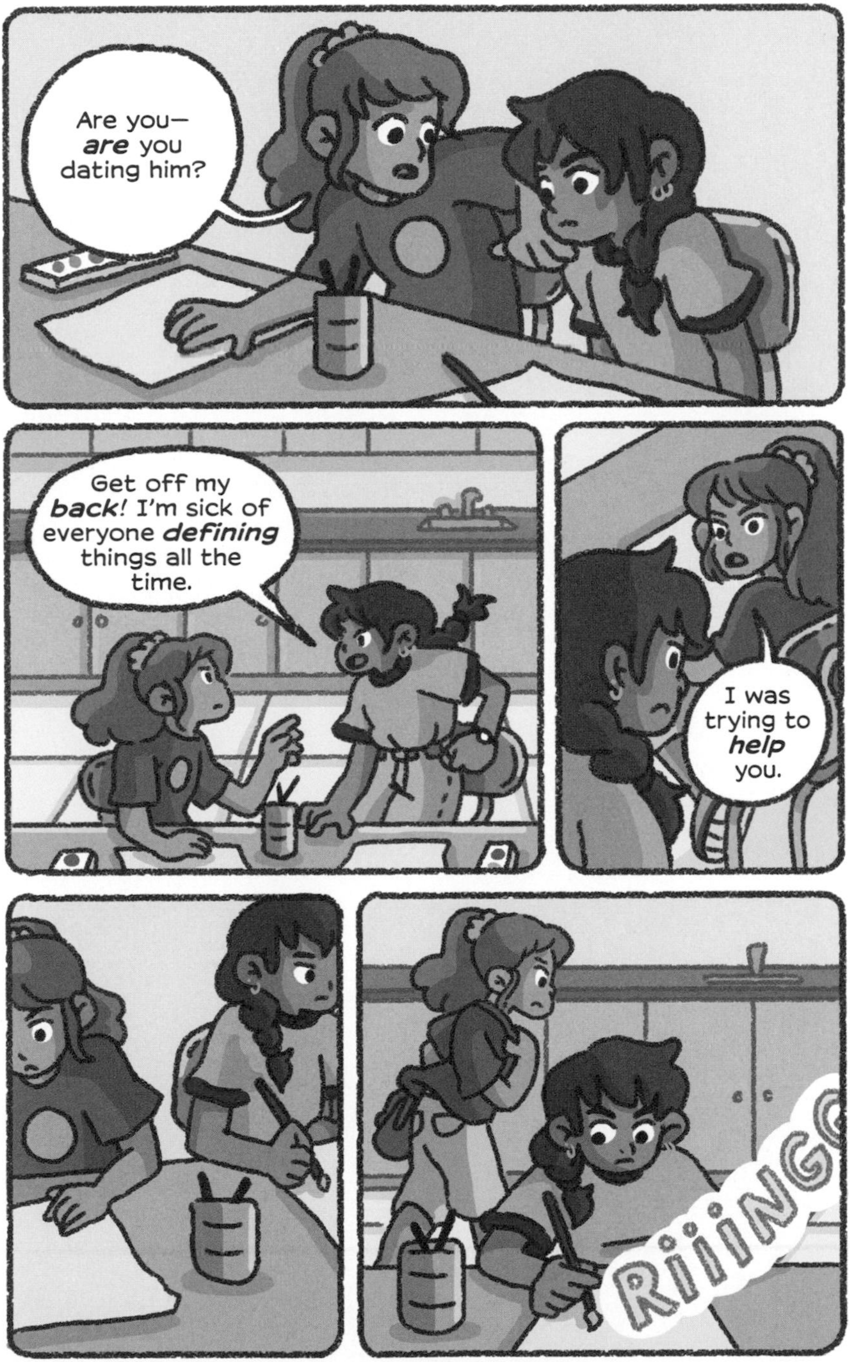
Are you—
are you
dating him?
Get off my *back*! I'm sick of everyone *defining* things all the time.
I was trying to *help* you.
RiiiNG

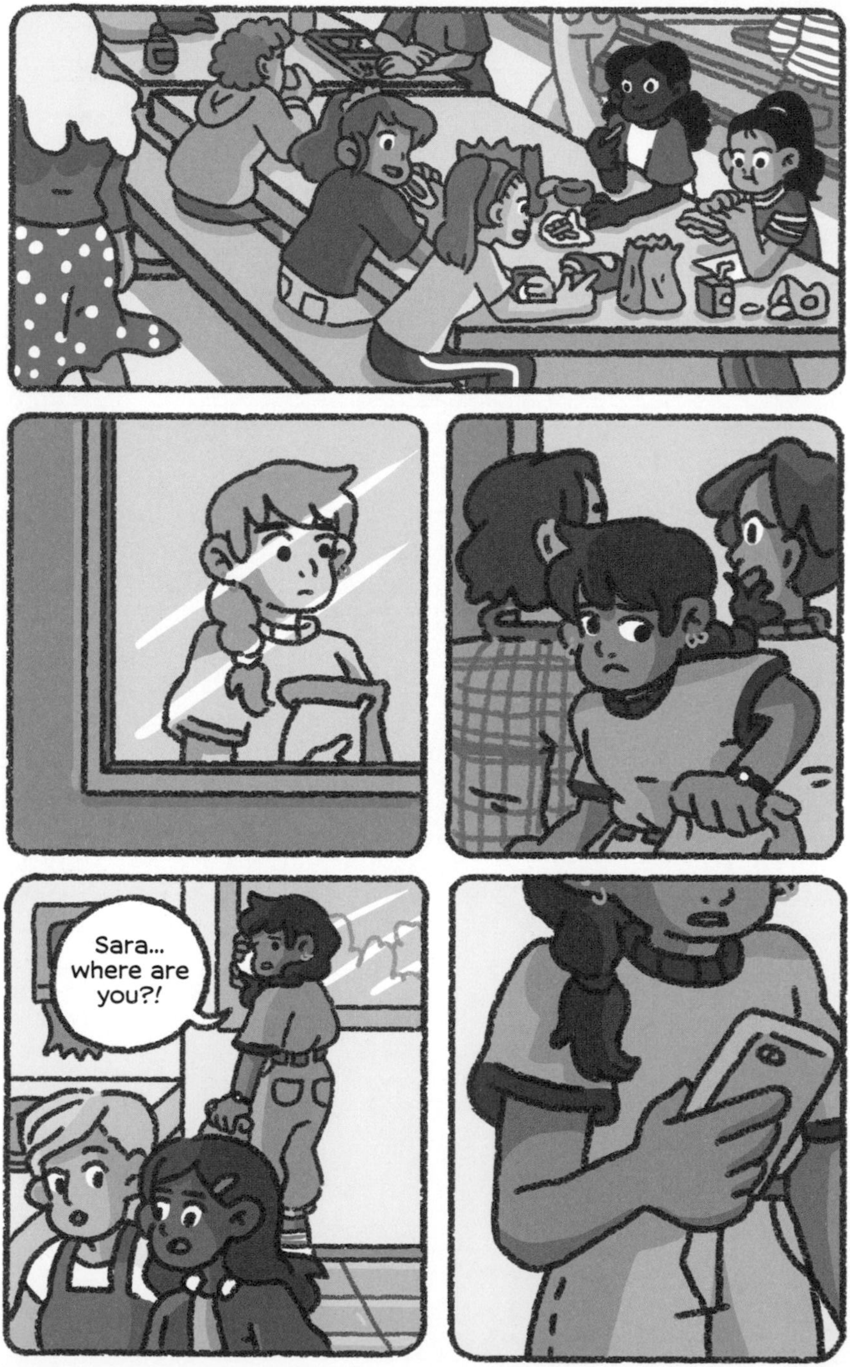
Sara...
where are
you?!

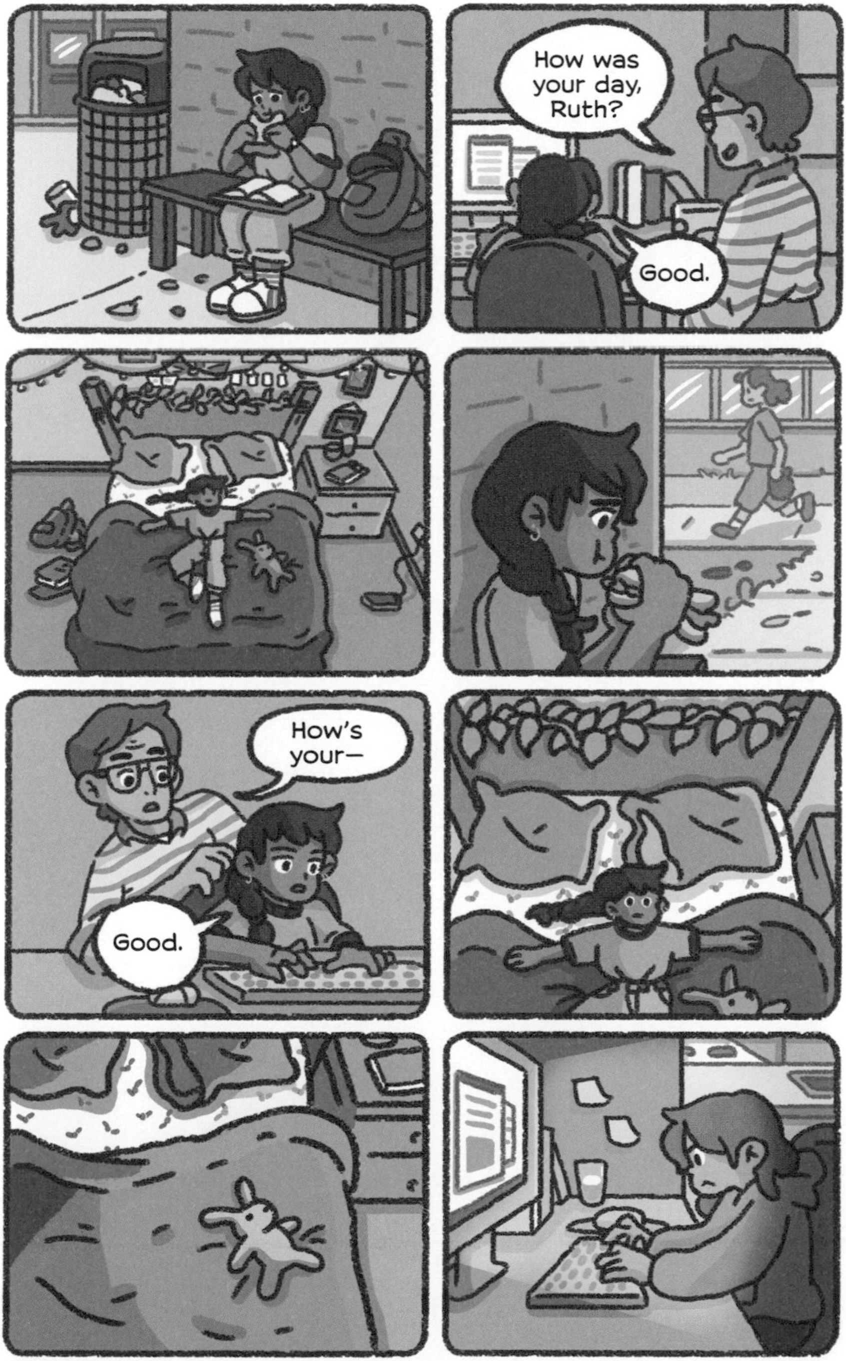
How was your day, Ruth?
Good.
How's your—
Good.

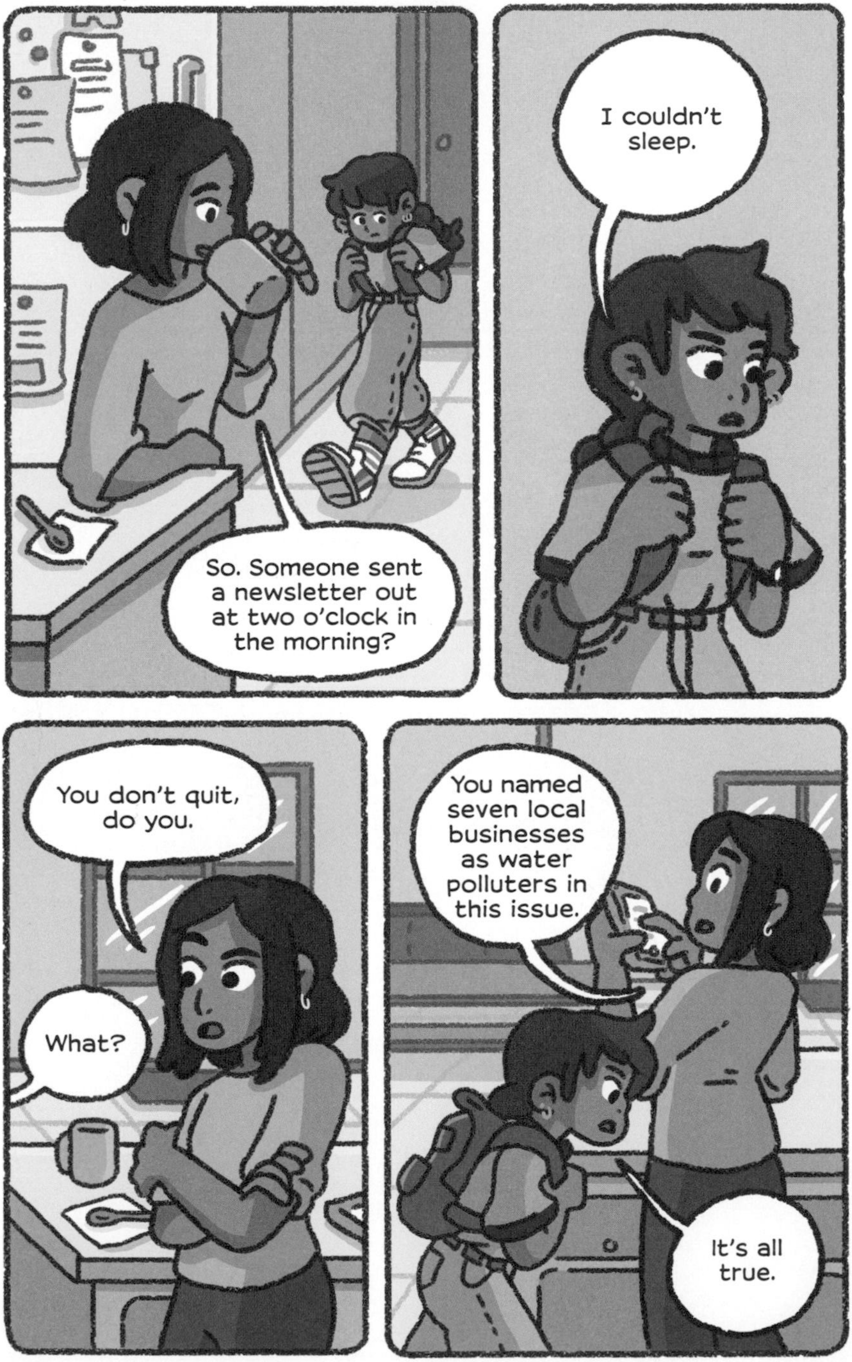
So. Someone sent a newsletter out at two o'clock in the morning?
I couldn't sleep.
You don't quit, do you.
What?
You named seven local businesses as water polluters in this issue.
It's all true.

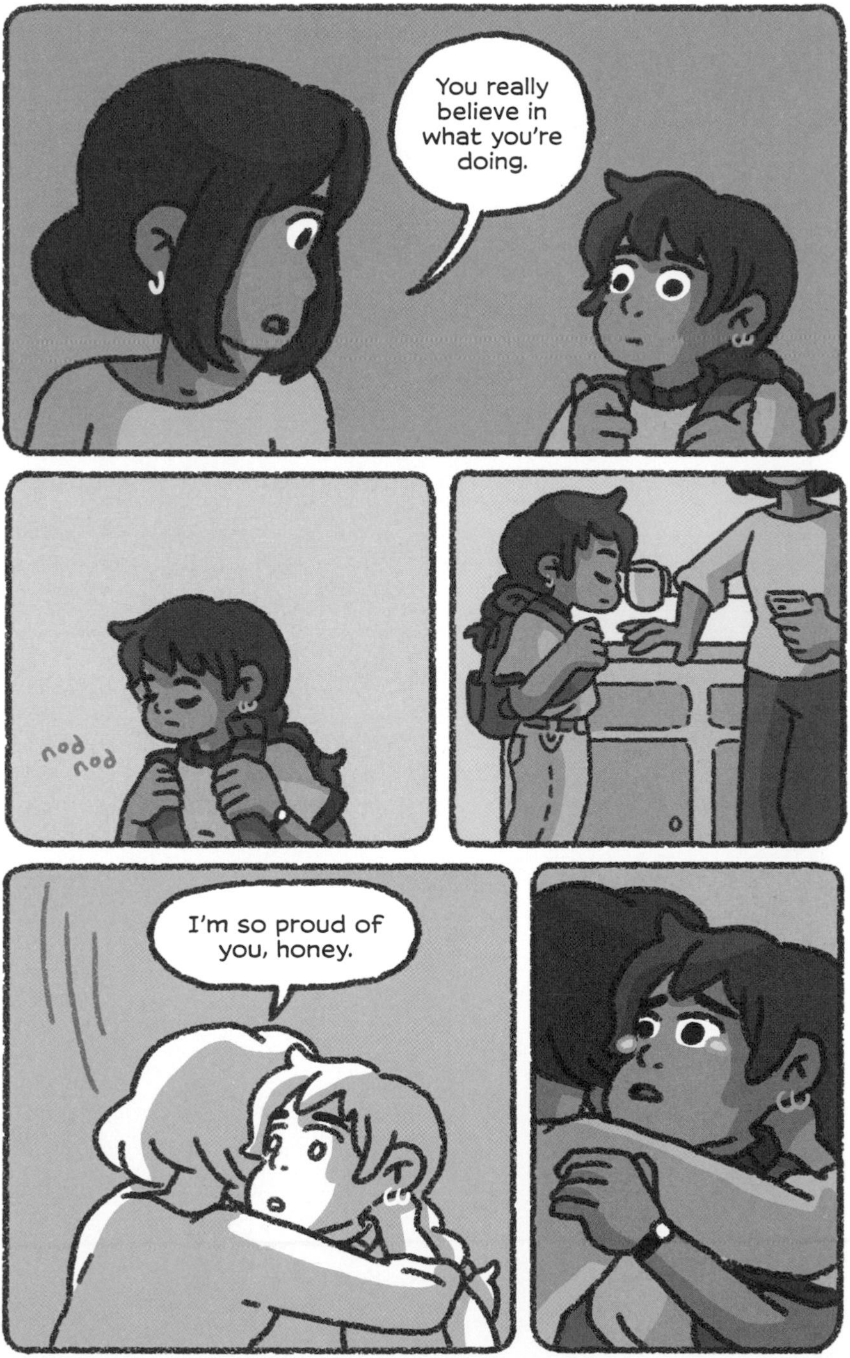
You really believe in what you're doing.
nod nod
I'm so proud of you, honey.

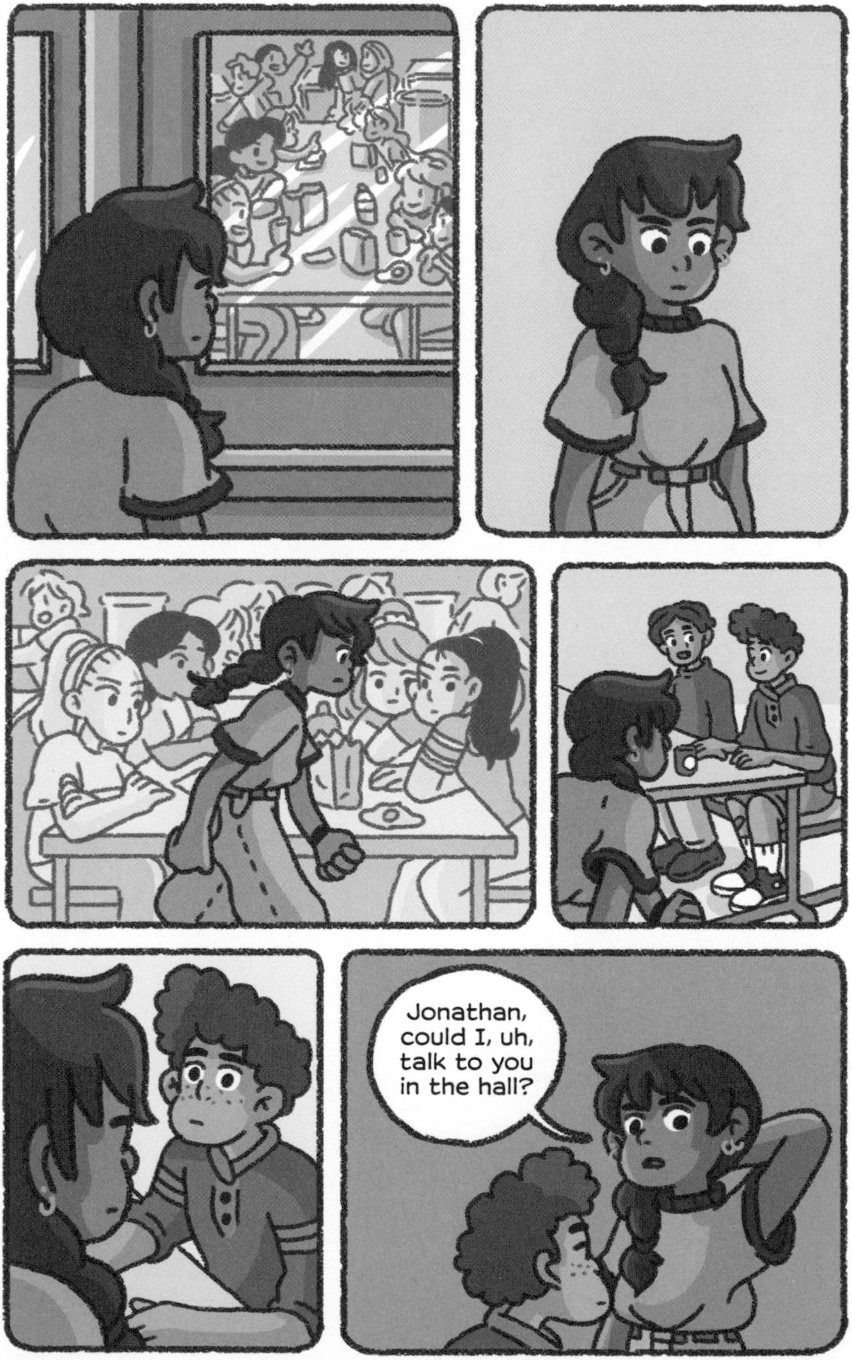
Jonathan,
could I, uh,
talk to you
in the hall?

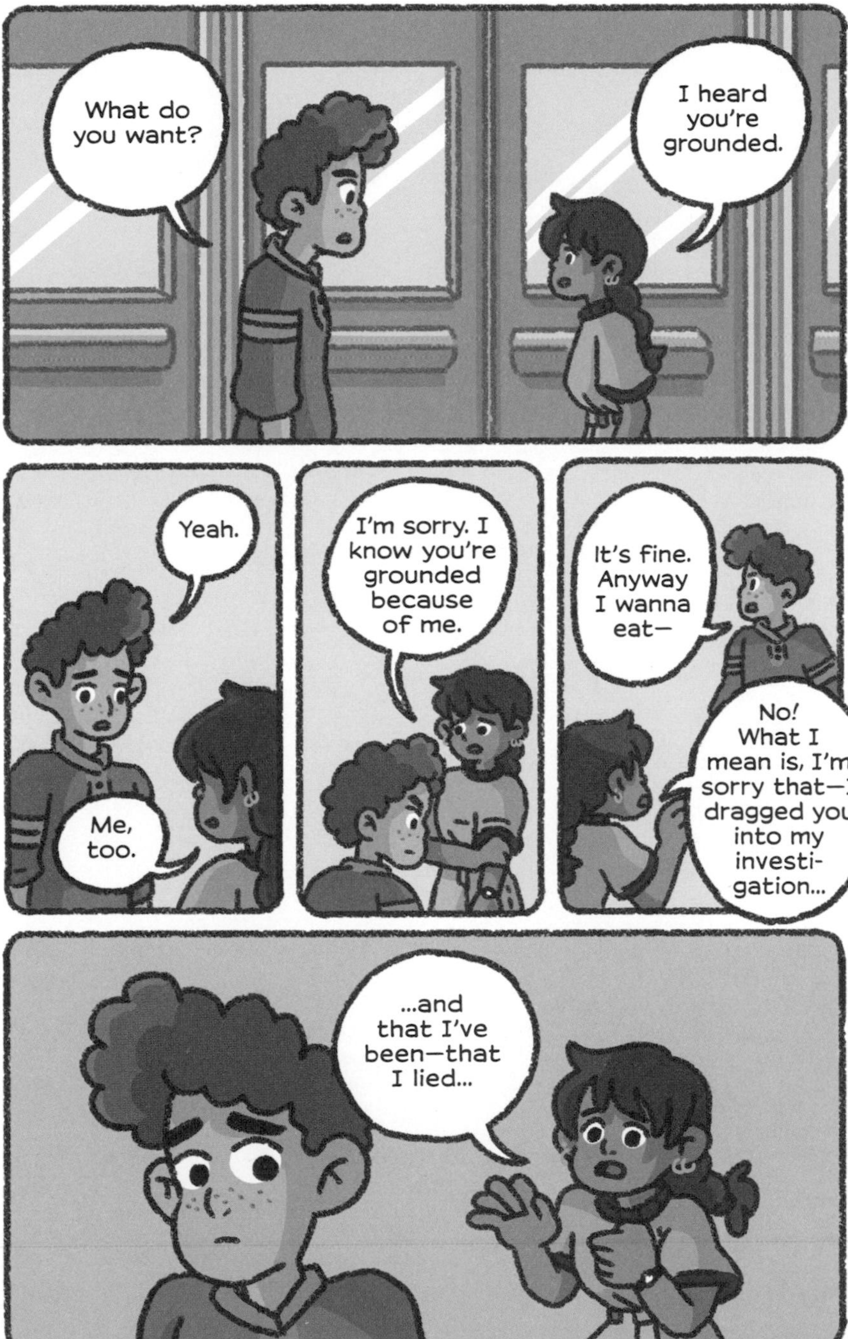
What do you want?
I heard you're grounded.
Yeah.
Me, too.
I'm sorry. I know you're grounded because of me.
It's fine. Anyway I wanna eat—
No! What I mean is, I'm sorry that—I dragged you into my investi-gation...
...and that I've been—that I lied...

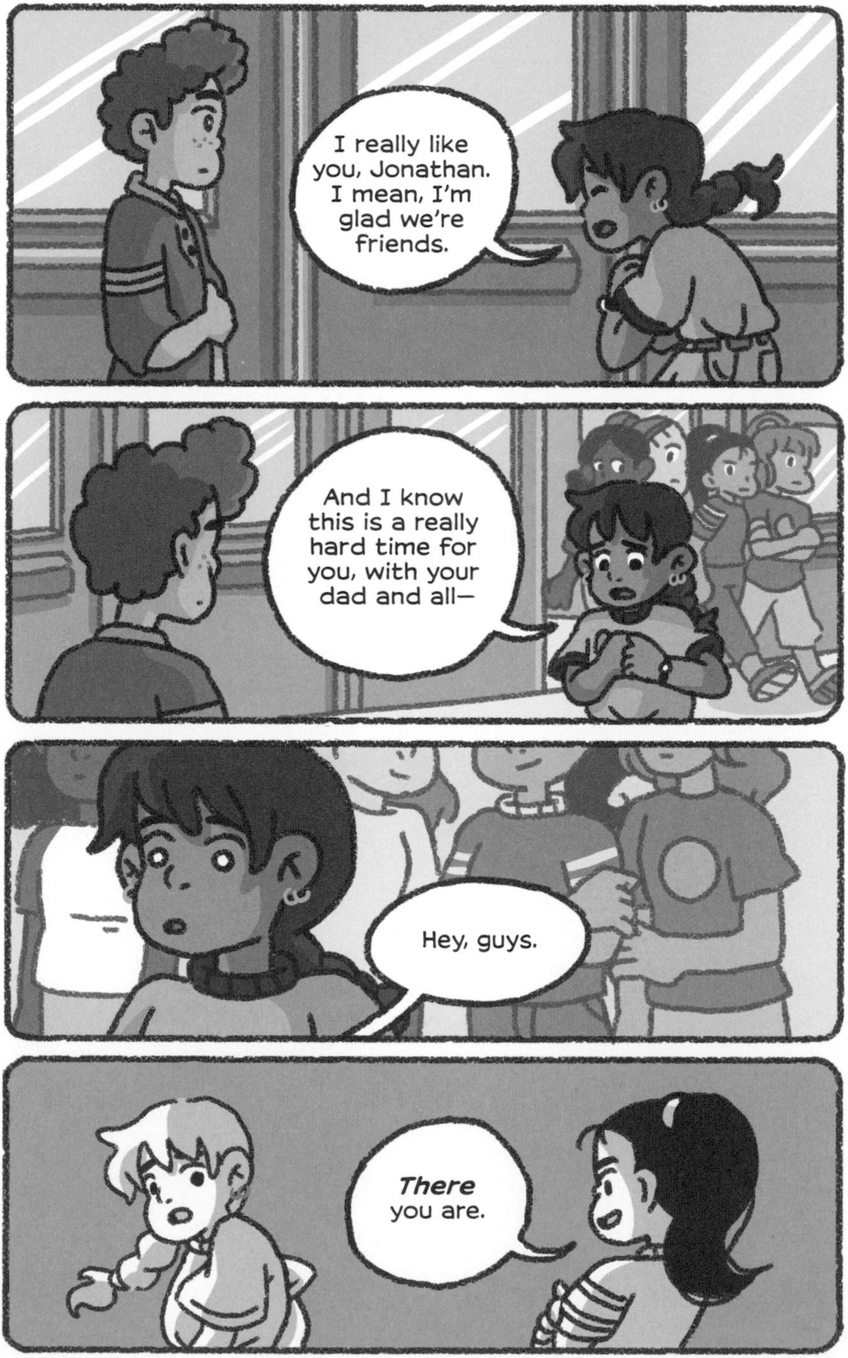
I really like you, Jonathan. I mean, I'm glad we're friends.
And I know this is a really hard time for you, with your dad and all—
Hey, guys.
There you are.

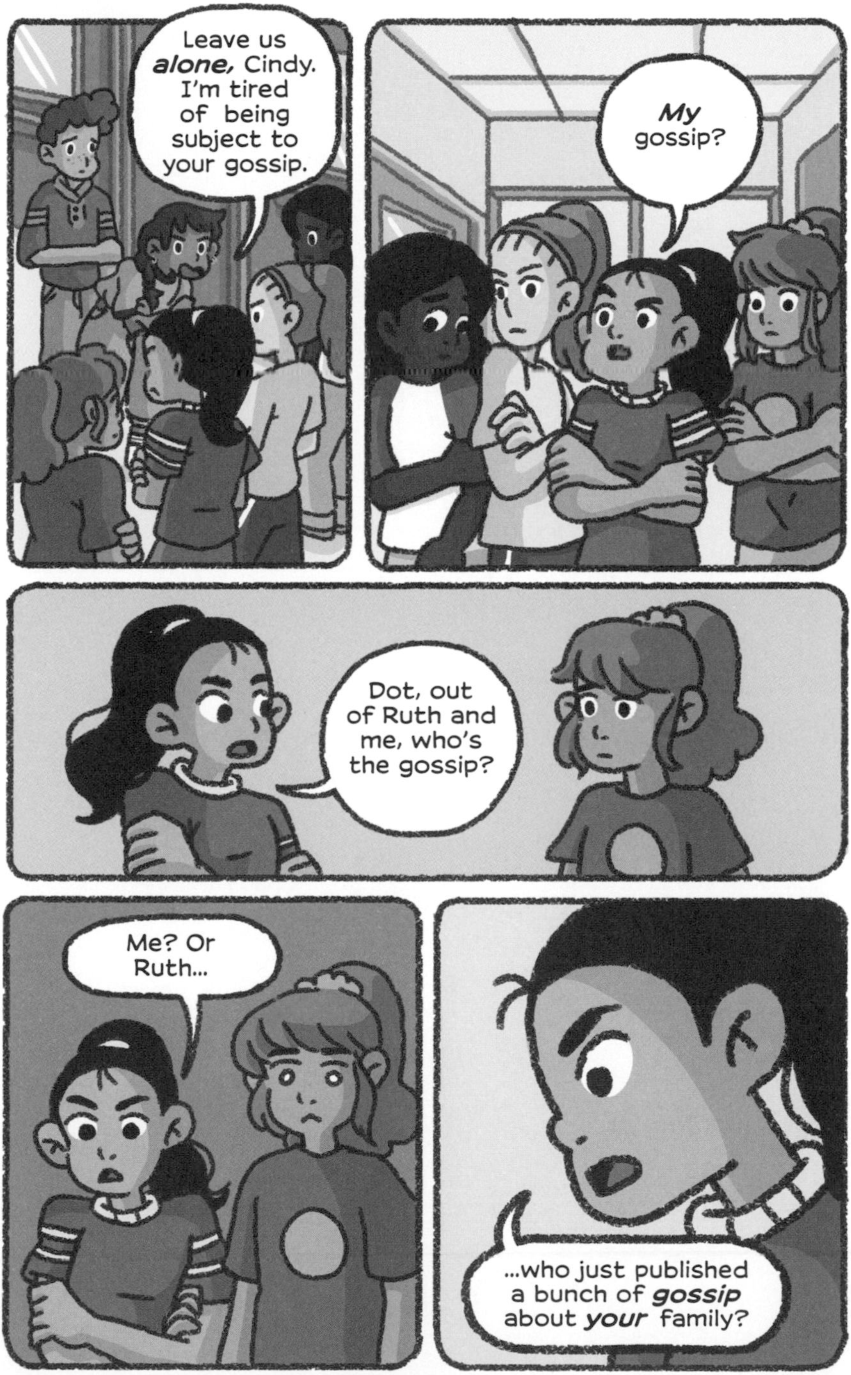
Leave us *alone,* Cindy. I'm tired of being subject to your gossip.
My gossip?
Dot, out of Ruth and me, who's the gossip?
Me? Or Ruth...
...who just published a bunch of *gossip* about *your* family?

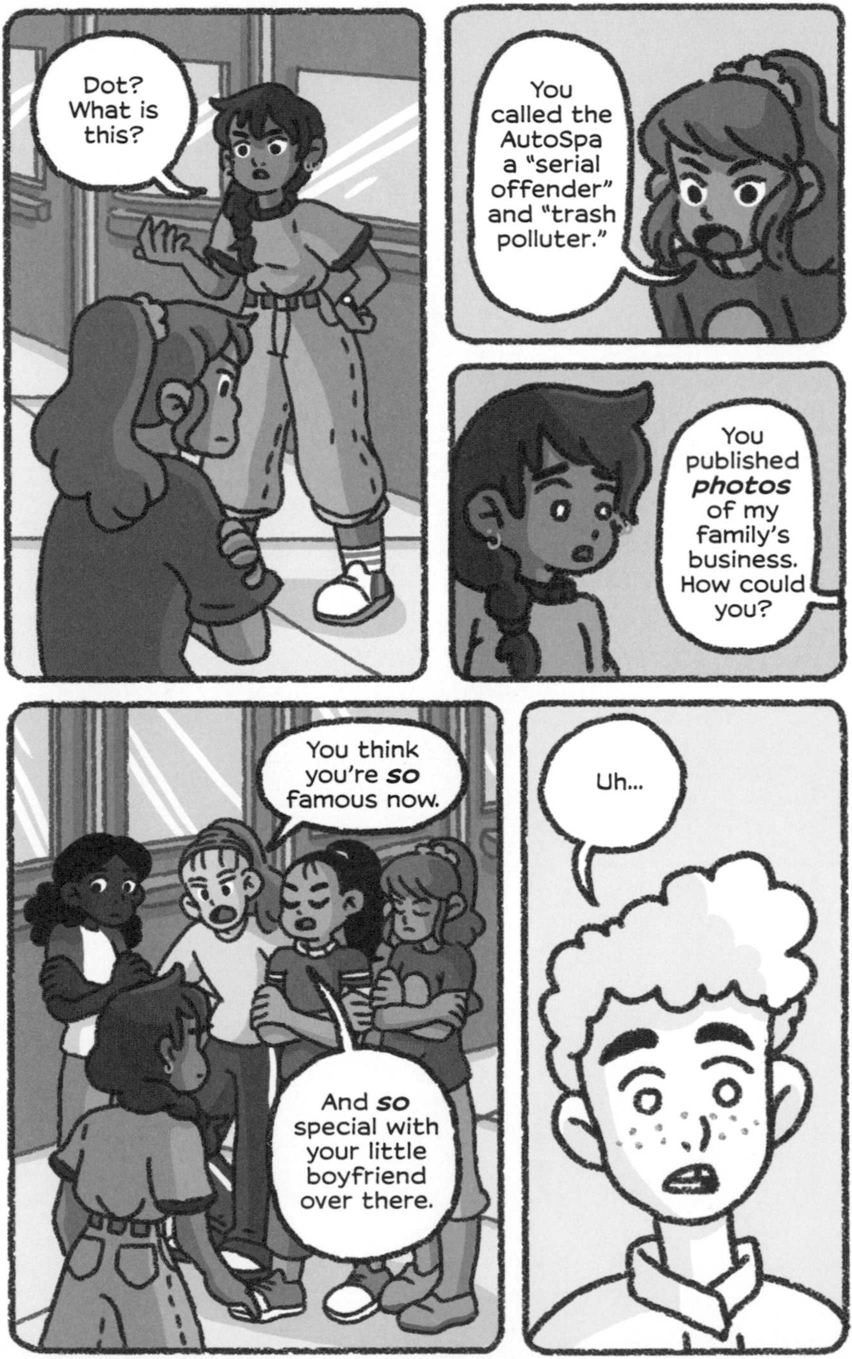
Dot? What is this?
You called the AutoSpa a "serial offender" and "trash polluter."
You published *photos* of my family's business. How could you?
You think you're *so* famous now.
And *so* special with your little boyfriend over there.
Uh...

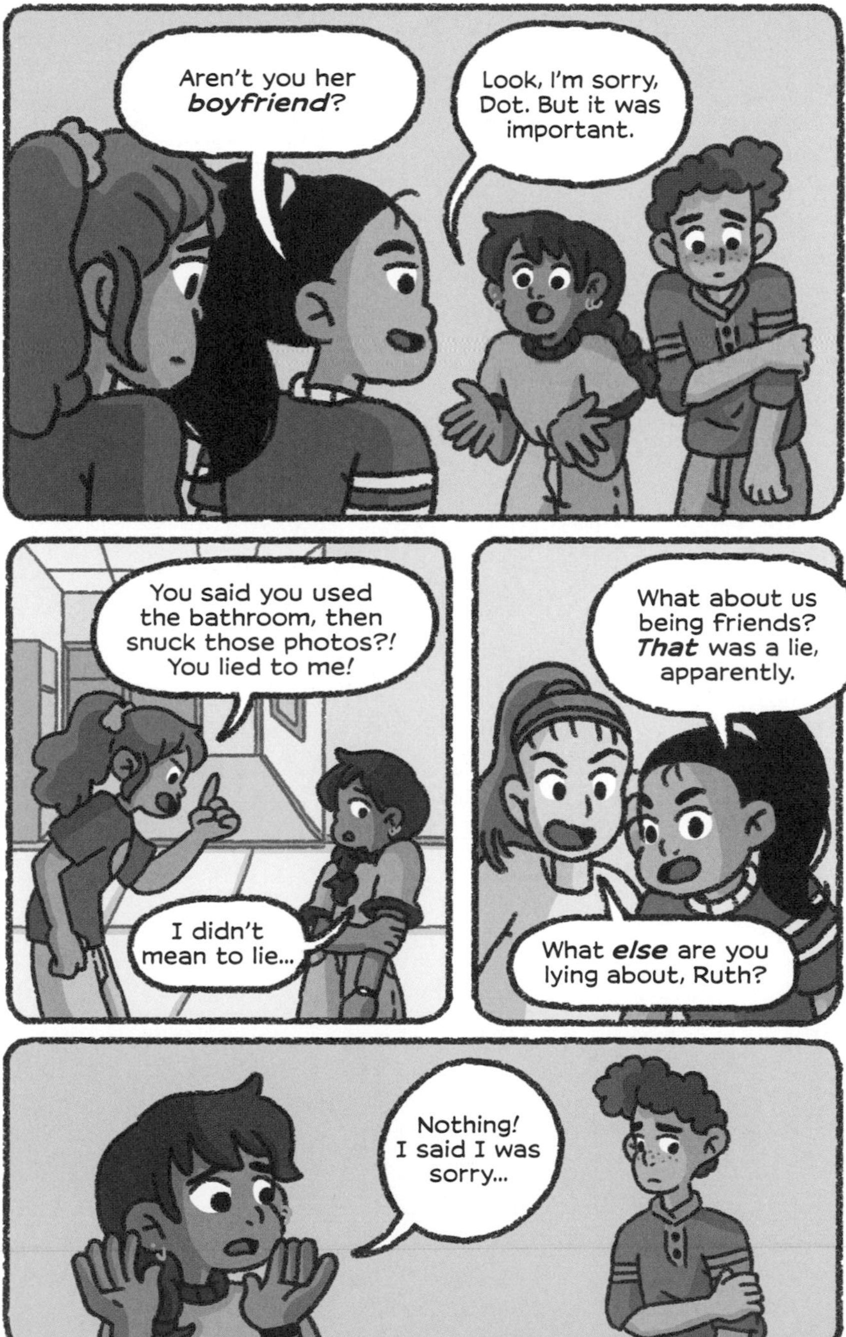
Aren't you her ***boyfriend***?
Look, I'm sorry, Dot. But it was important.
You said you used the bathroom, then snuck those photos?! You lied to me!
I didn't mean to lie...
What about us being friends? ***That*** was a lie, apparently.
What ***else*** are you lying about, Ruth?
Nothing! I said I was sorry...

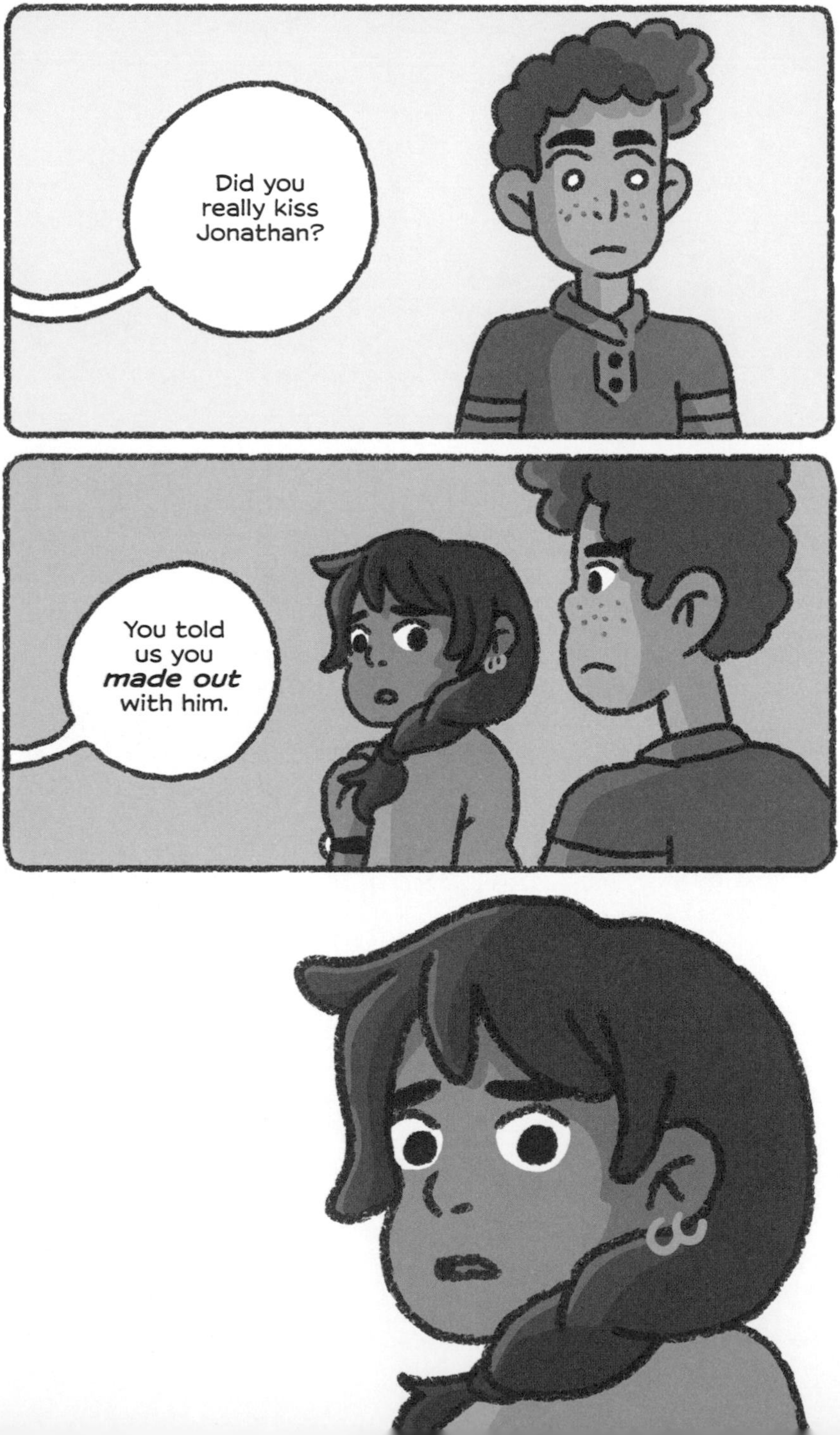
Did you really kiss Jonathan?
You told us you ***made out*** with him.

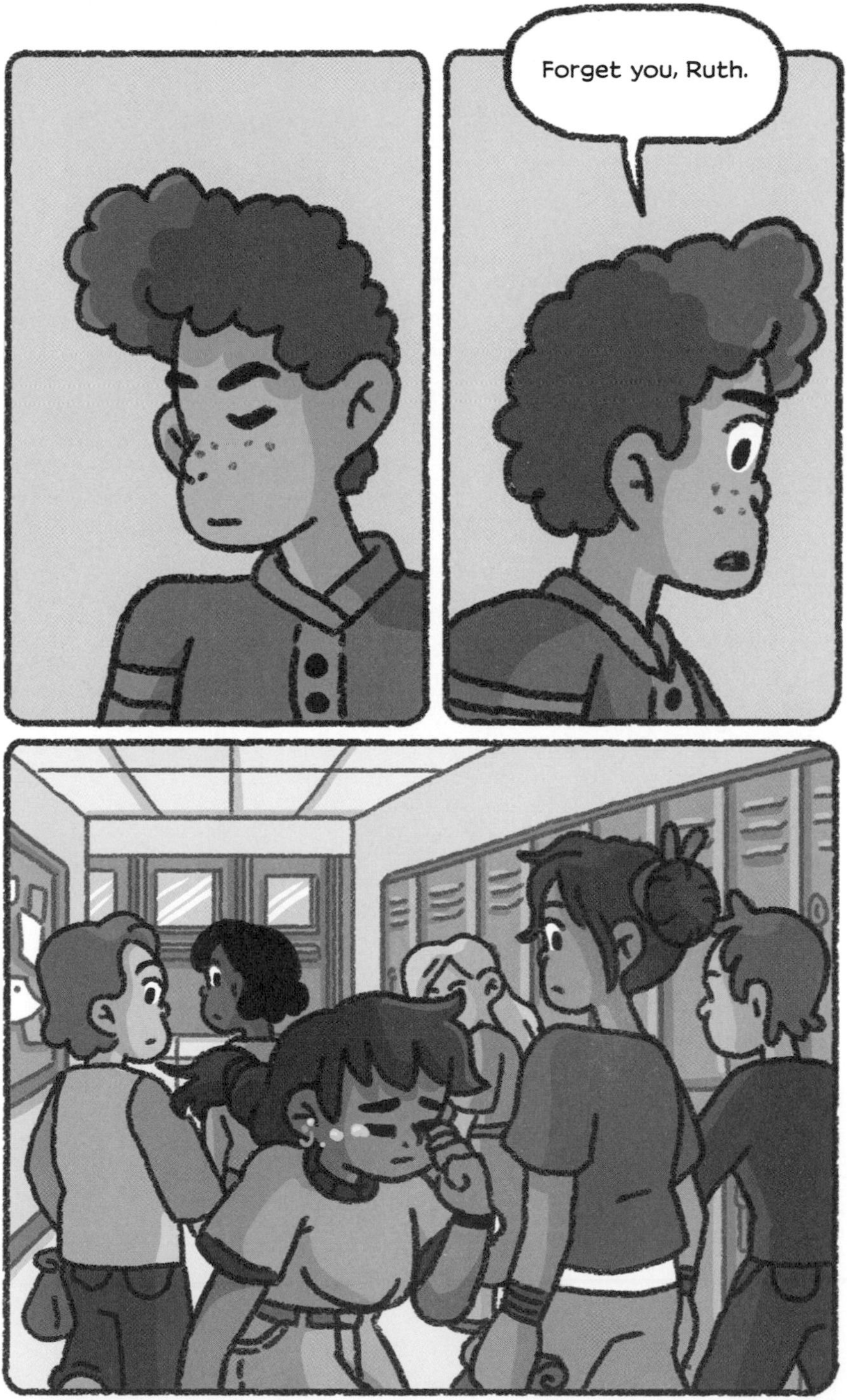
Forget you, Ruth.

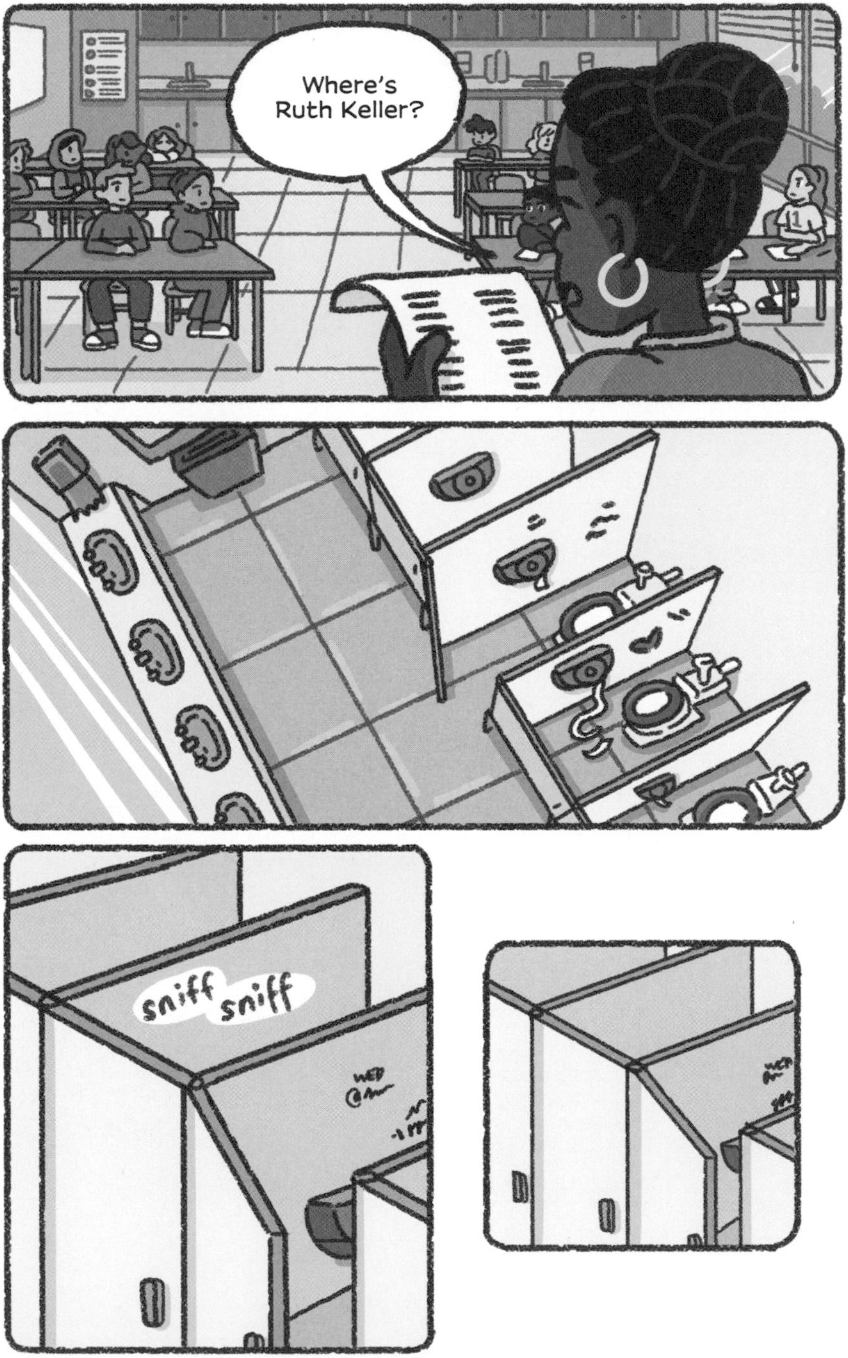
Where's Ruth Keller?
sniff sniff

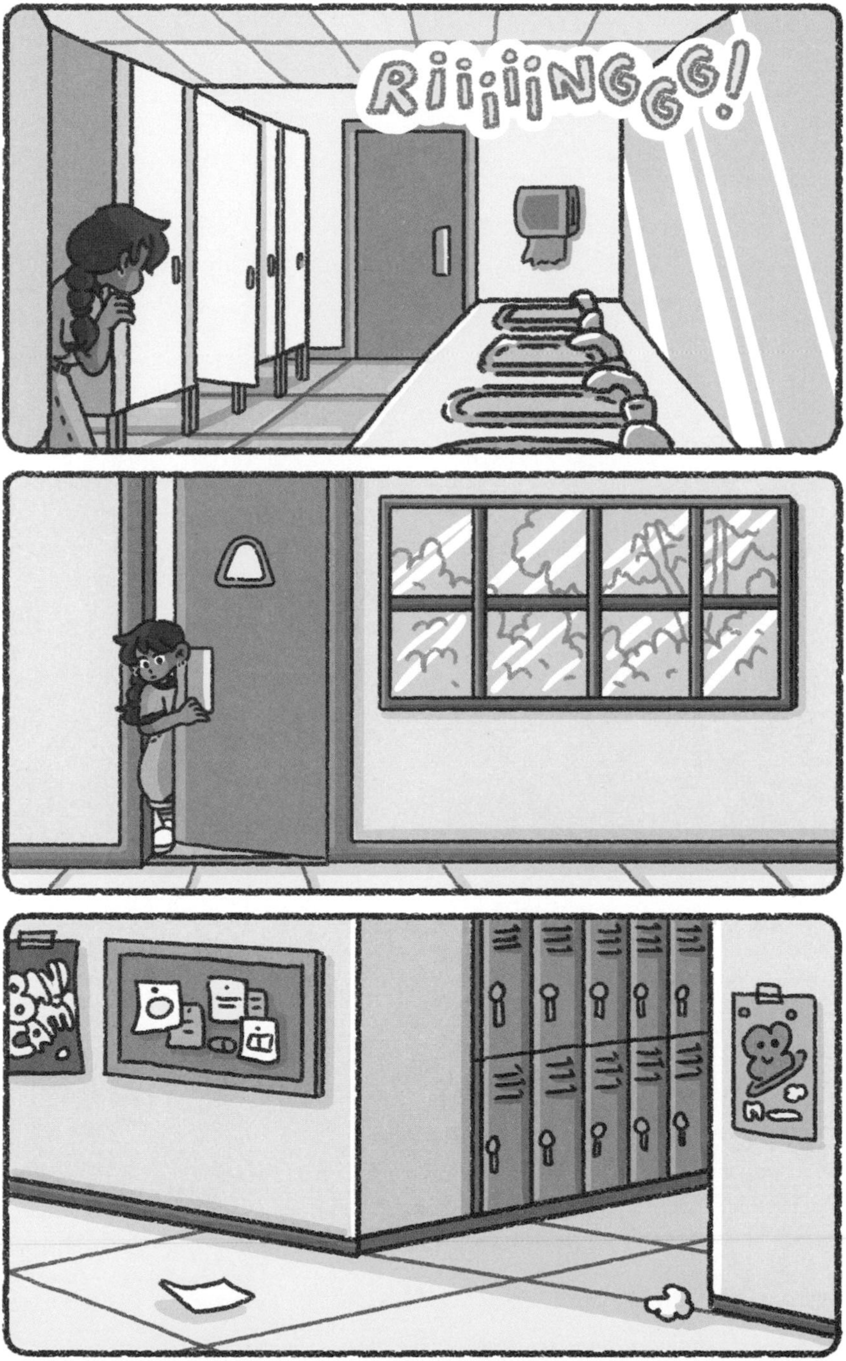
RiiiiiNGGG!

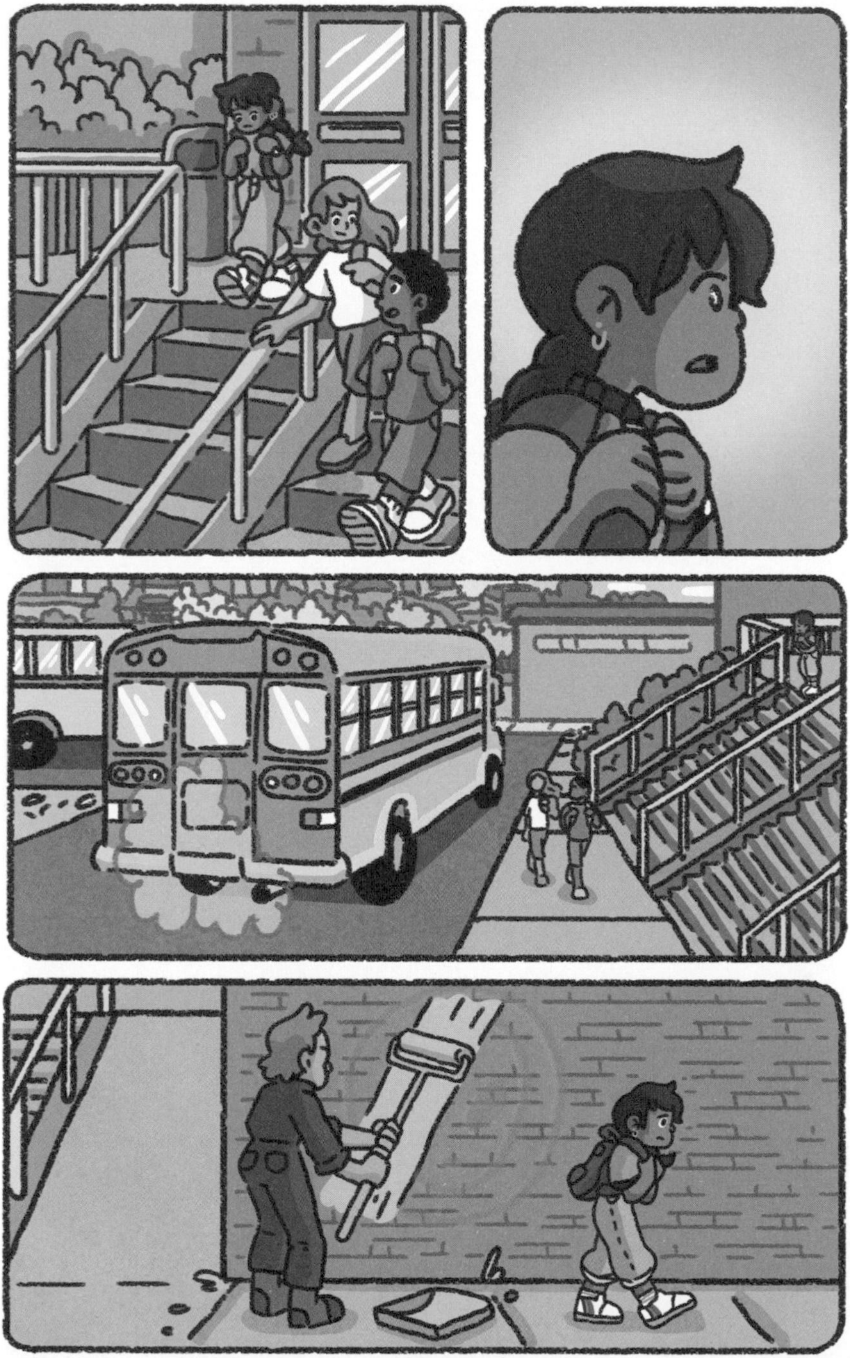

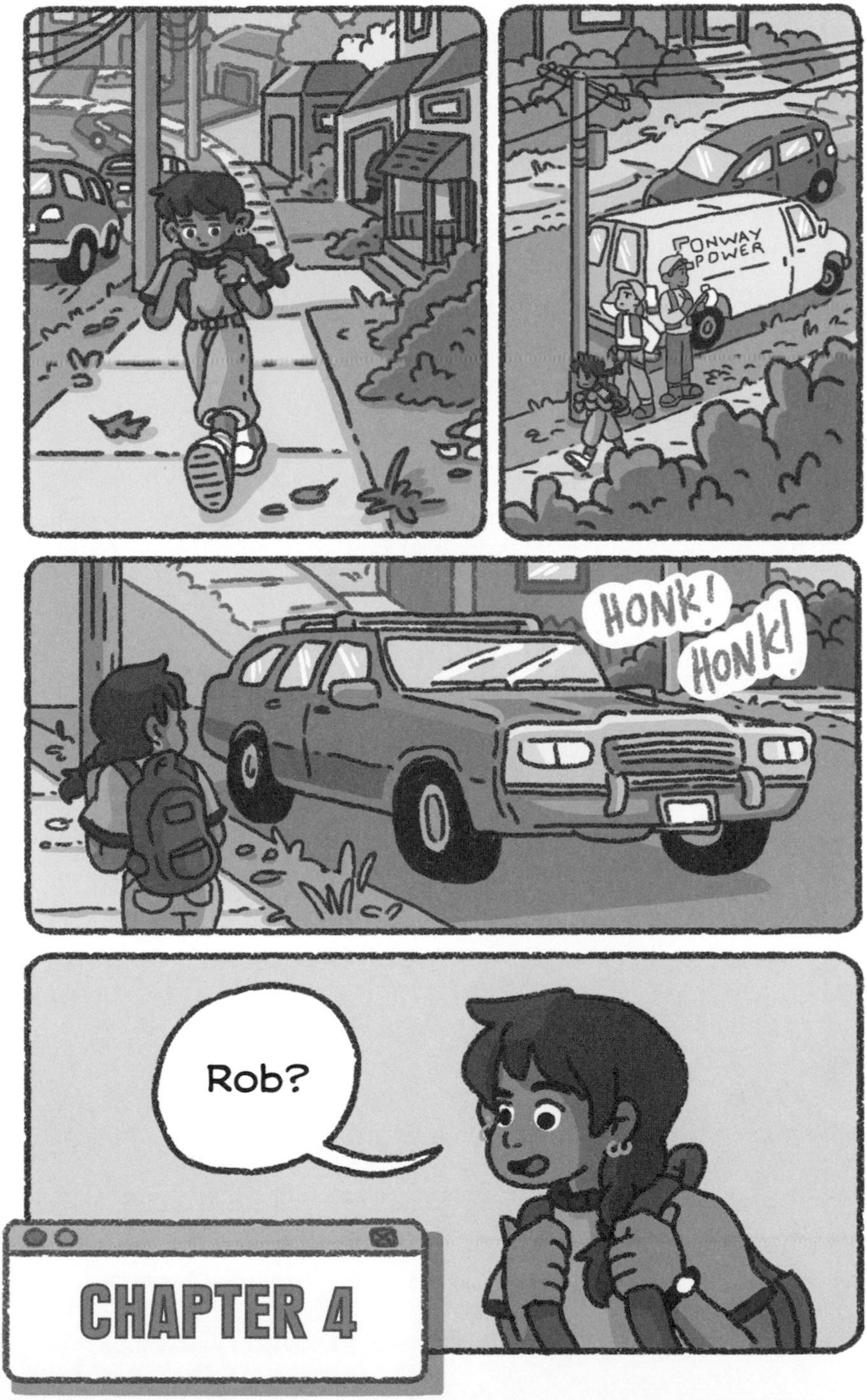
HONK!
HONK!
Rob?

CHAPTER 4

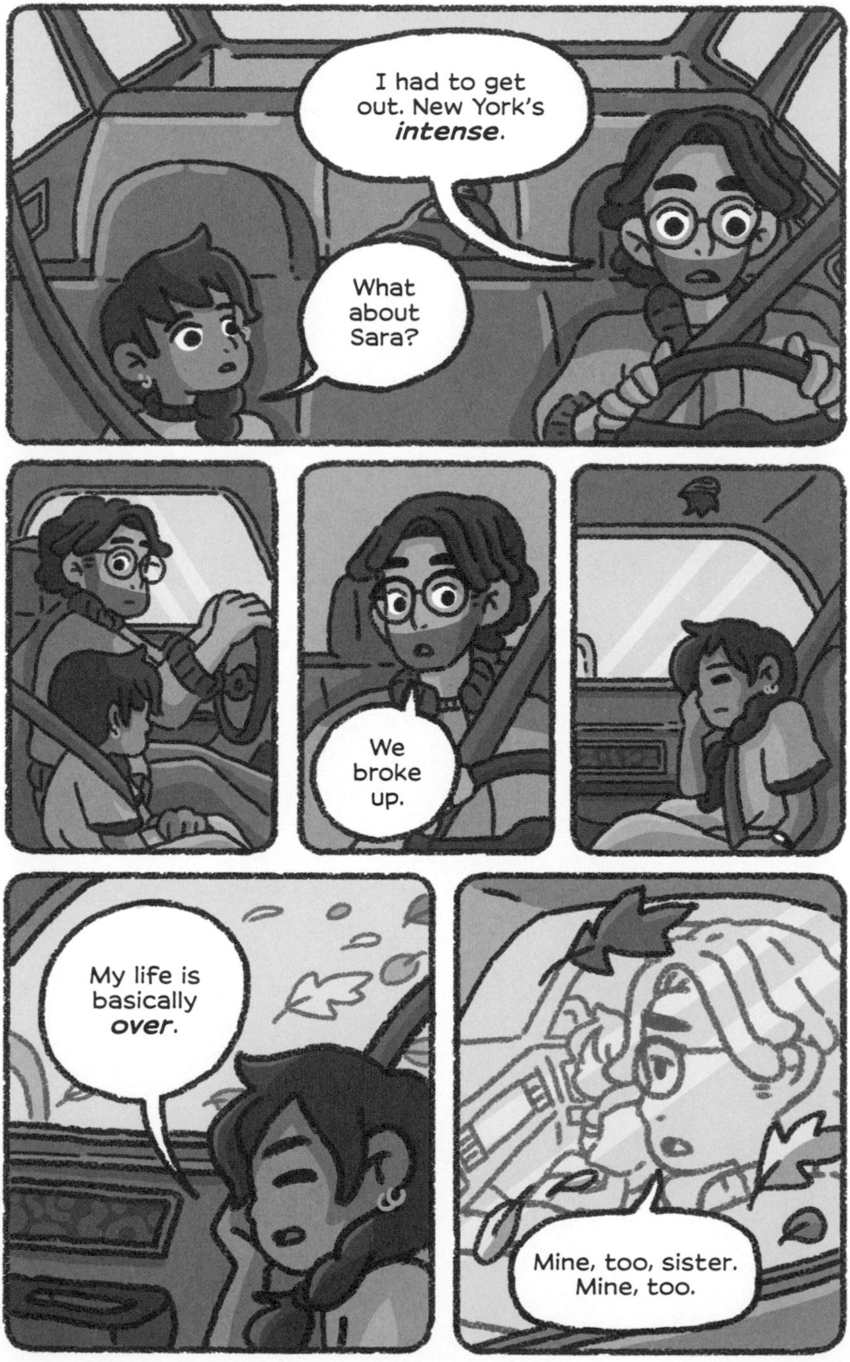
I had to get out. New York's *intense*.
What about Sara?
We broke up.
My life is basically *over*.
Mine, too, sister. Mine, too.

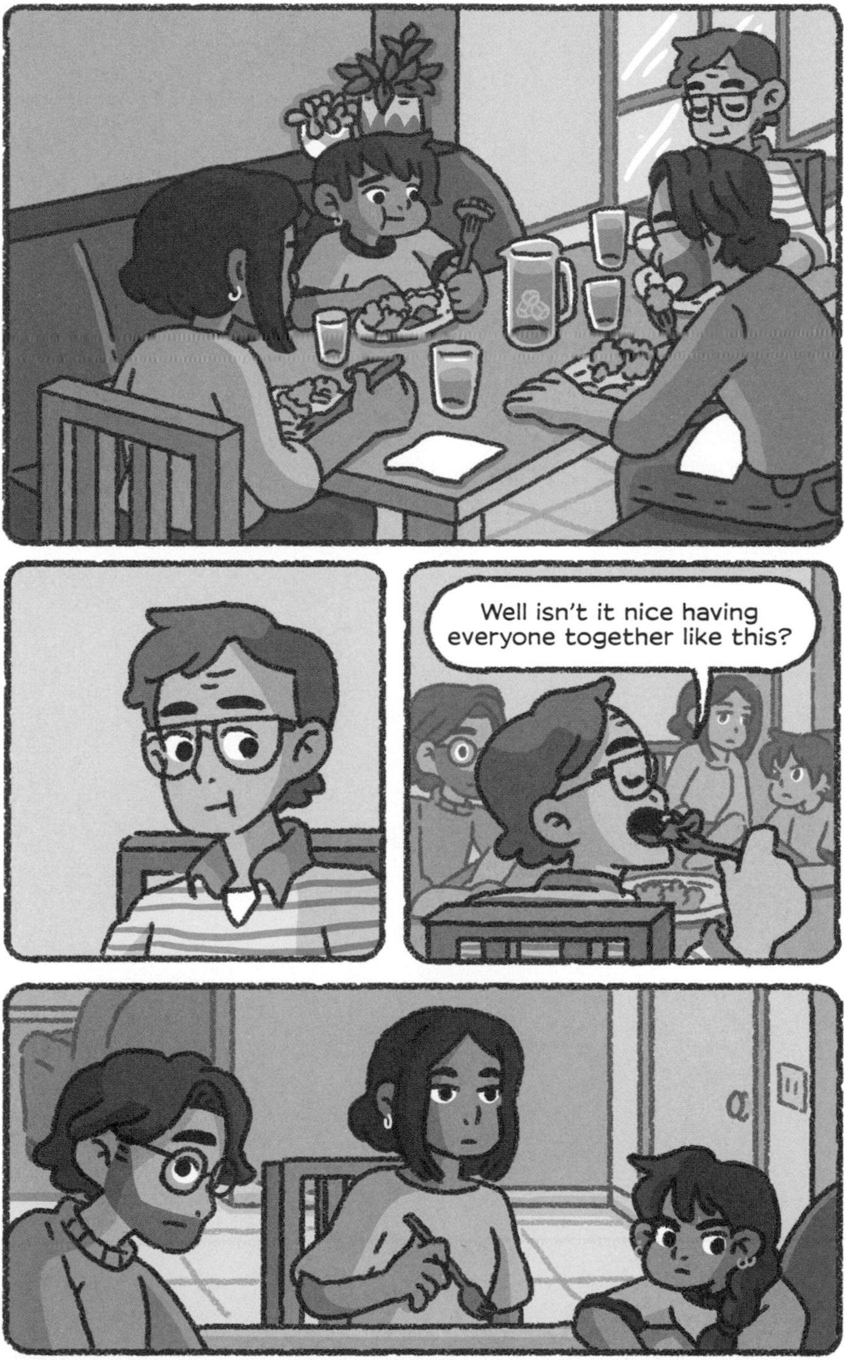
Well isn't it nice having everyone together like this?

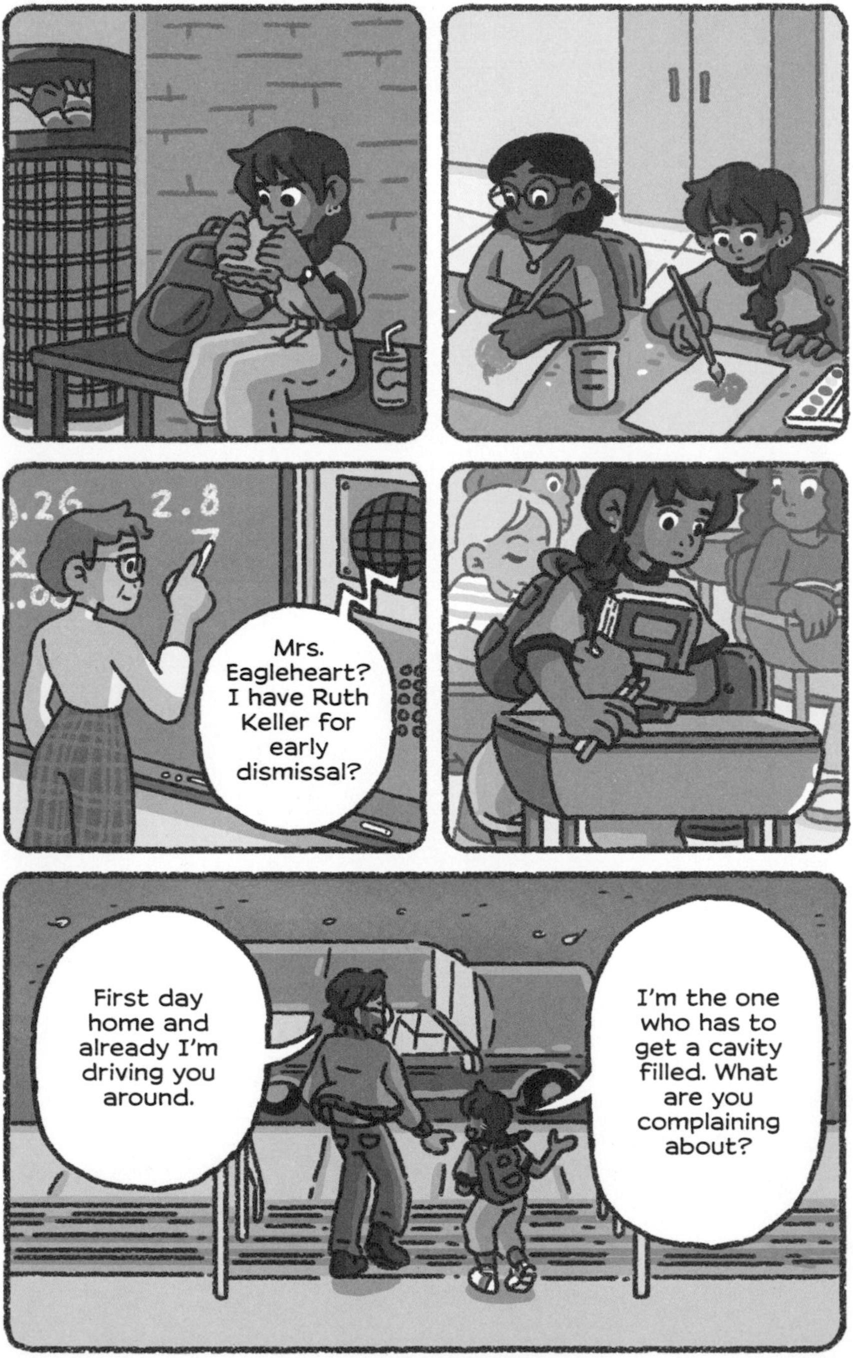
Mrs. Eagleheart? I have Ruth Keller for early dismissal?
First day home and already I'm driving you around.
I'm the one who has to get a cavity filled. What are you complaining about?

Hello, Ruth.

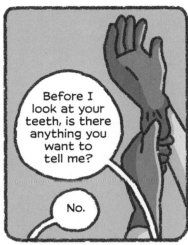

Before I look at your teeth, is there anything you want to tell me?

No.

Still having trouble with flossing, I see.

It's *very* important that you really start flossing.

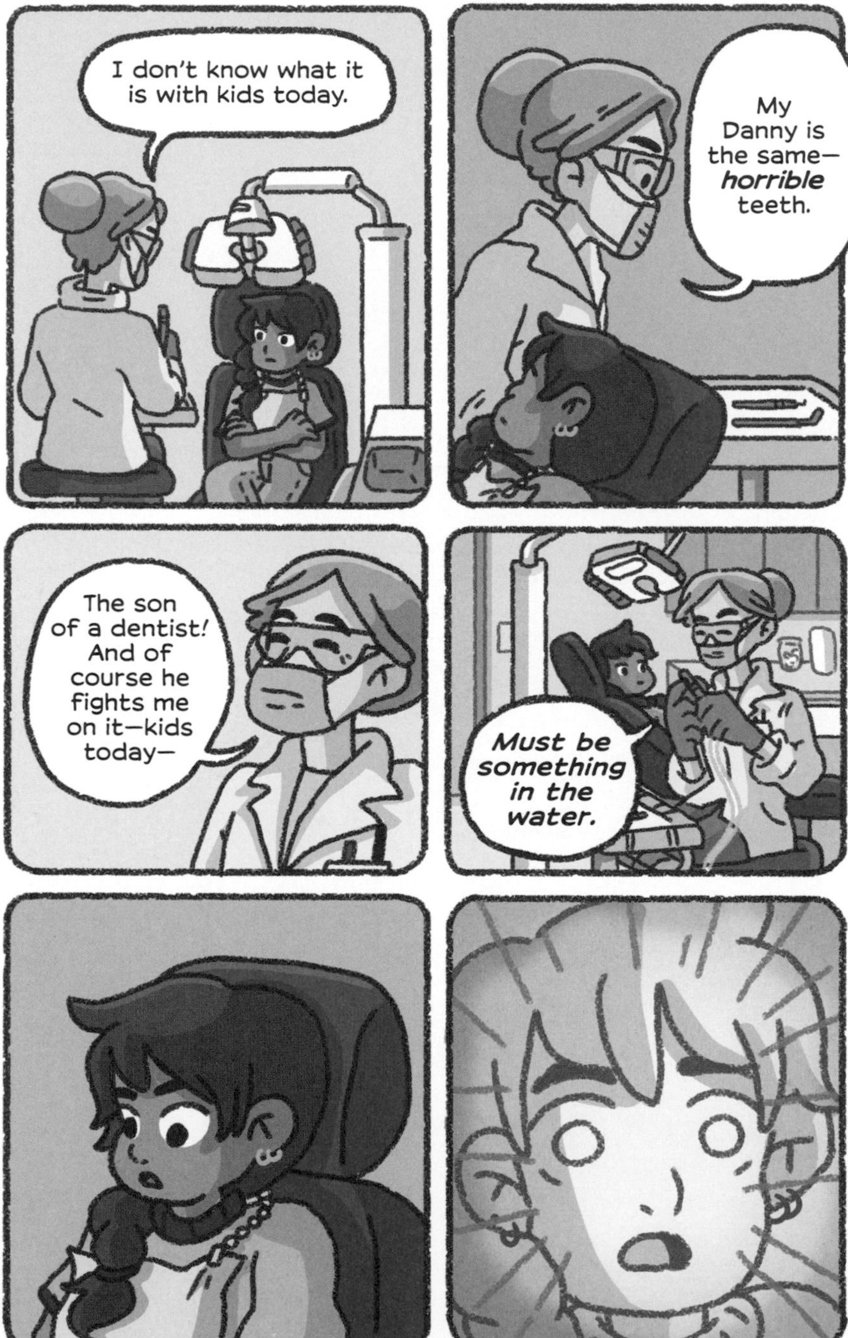
I don't know what it is with kids today.
My Danny is the same—*horrible* teeth.
The son of a dentist! And of course he fights me on it—kids today—
Must be something in the water.

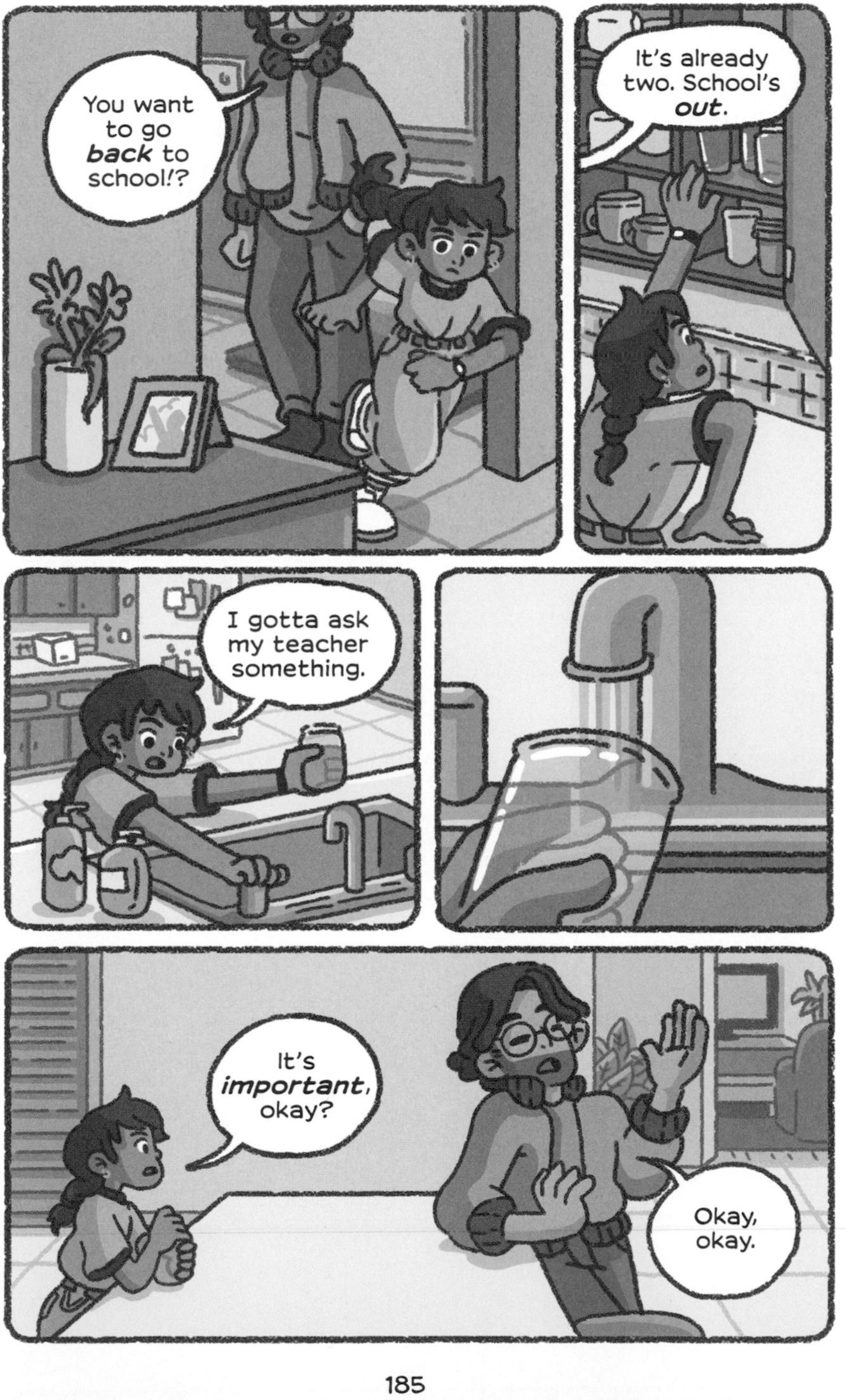
You want to go *back* to school!?
It's already two. School's *out*.
I gotta ask my teacher something.
It's *important*, okay?
Okay, okay.

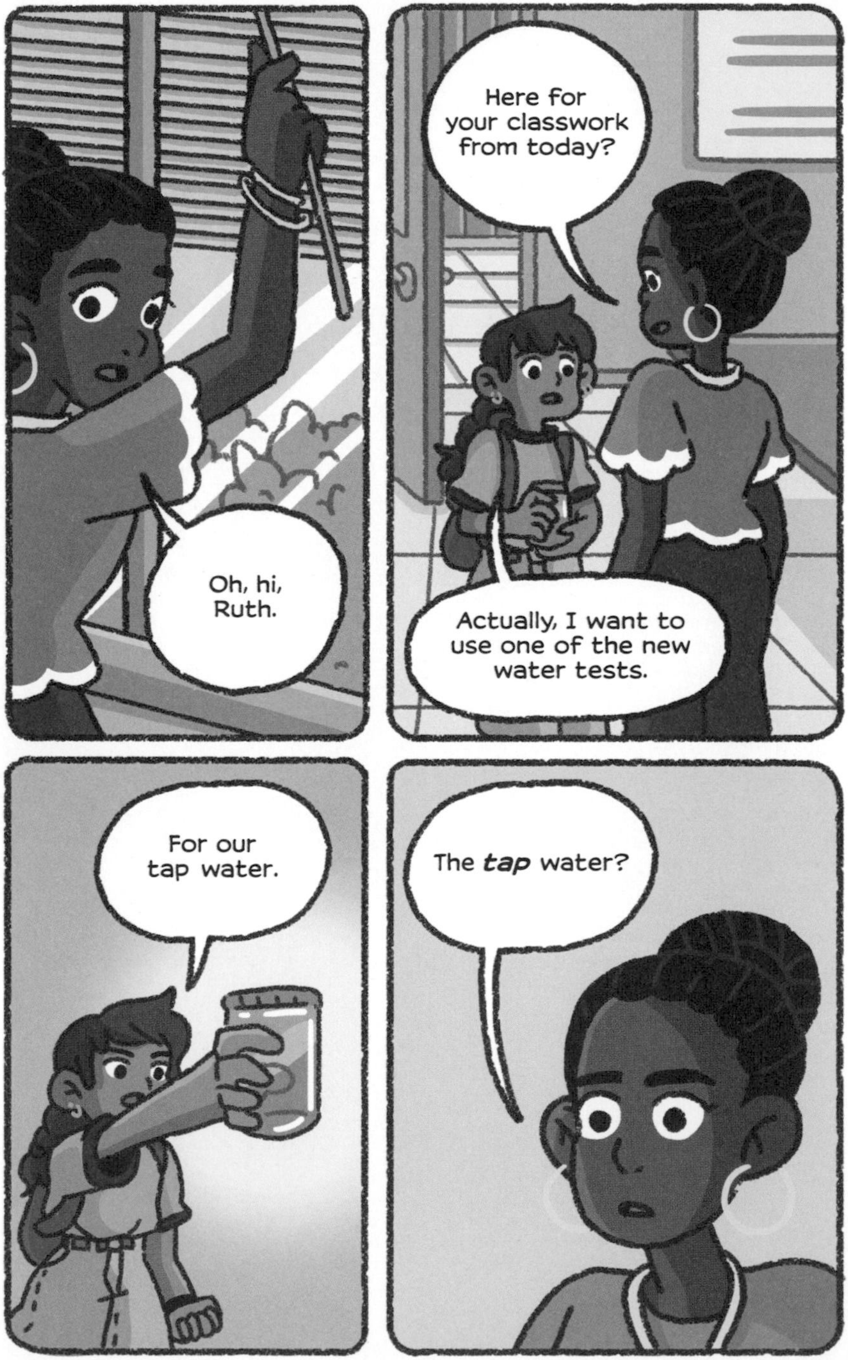
Oh, hi, Ruth.
Here for your classwork from today?
Actually, I want to use one of the new water tests.
For our tap water.
The *tap* water?

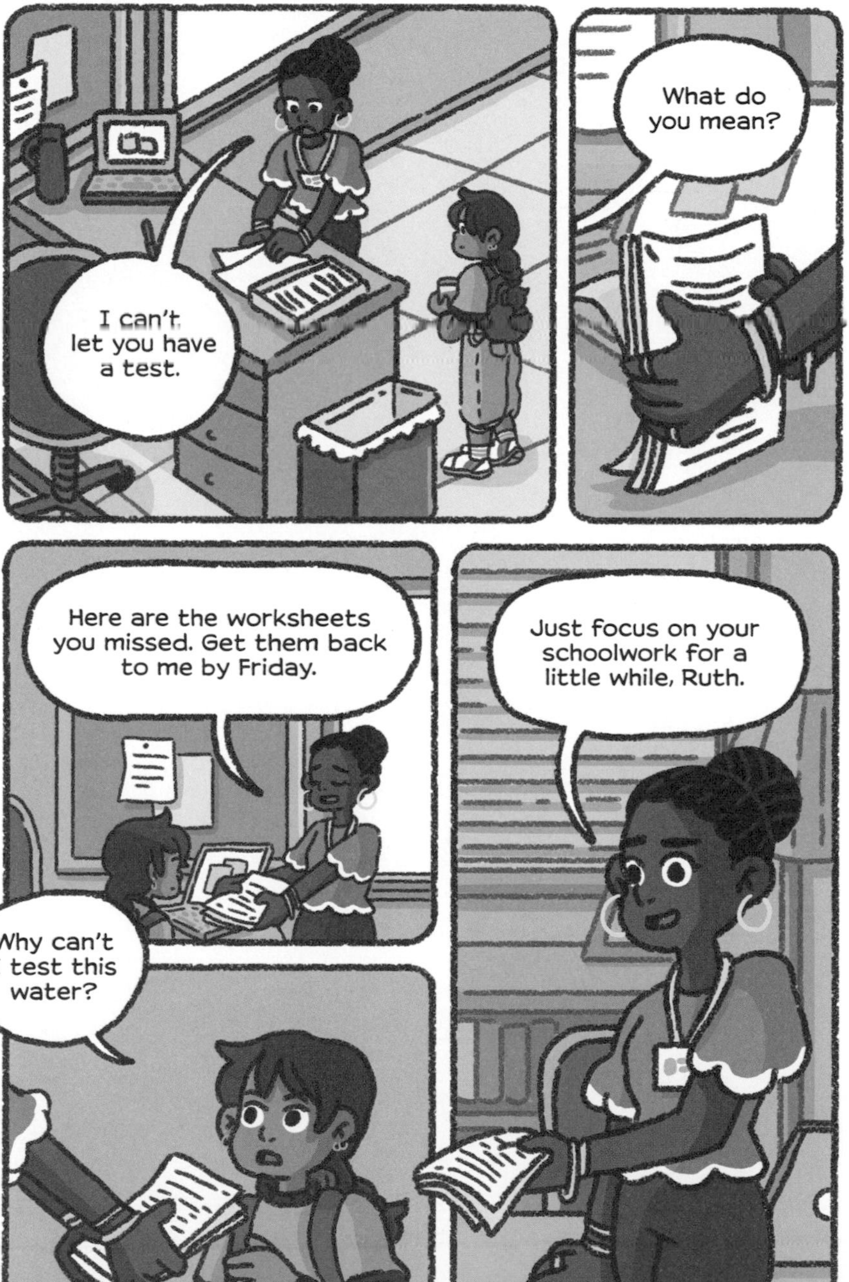
I can't let you have a test.
What do you mean?
Here are the worksheets you missed. Get them back to me by Friday.
Why can't I test this water?
Just focus on your schoolwork for a little while, Ruth.

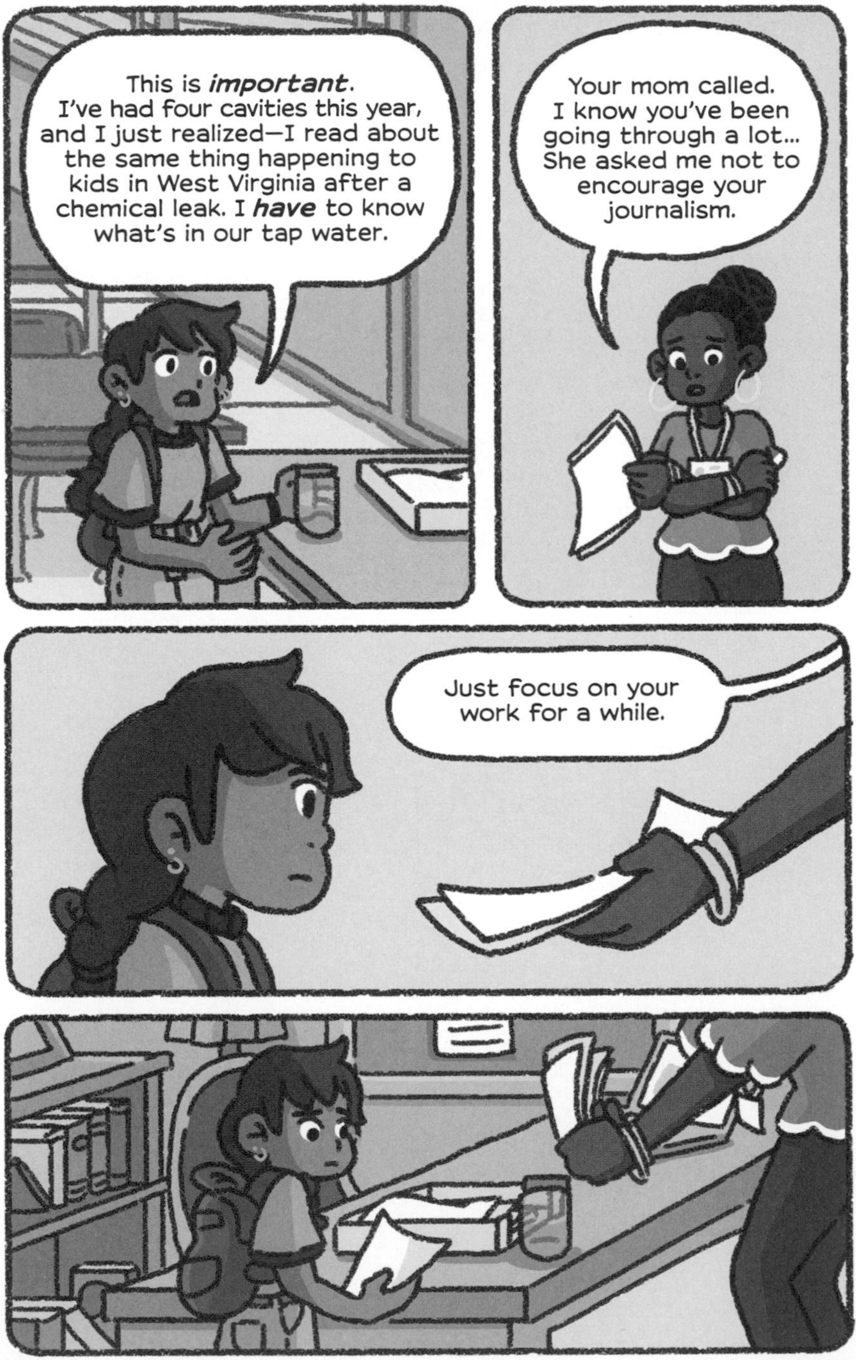
This is *important*. I've had four cavities this year, and I just realized—I read about the same thing happening to kids in West Virginia after a chemical leak. I ***have*** to know what's in our tap water.
Your mom called. I know you've been going through a lot... She asked me not to encourage your journalism.
Just focus on your work for a while.

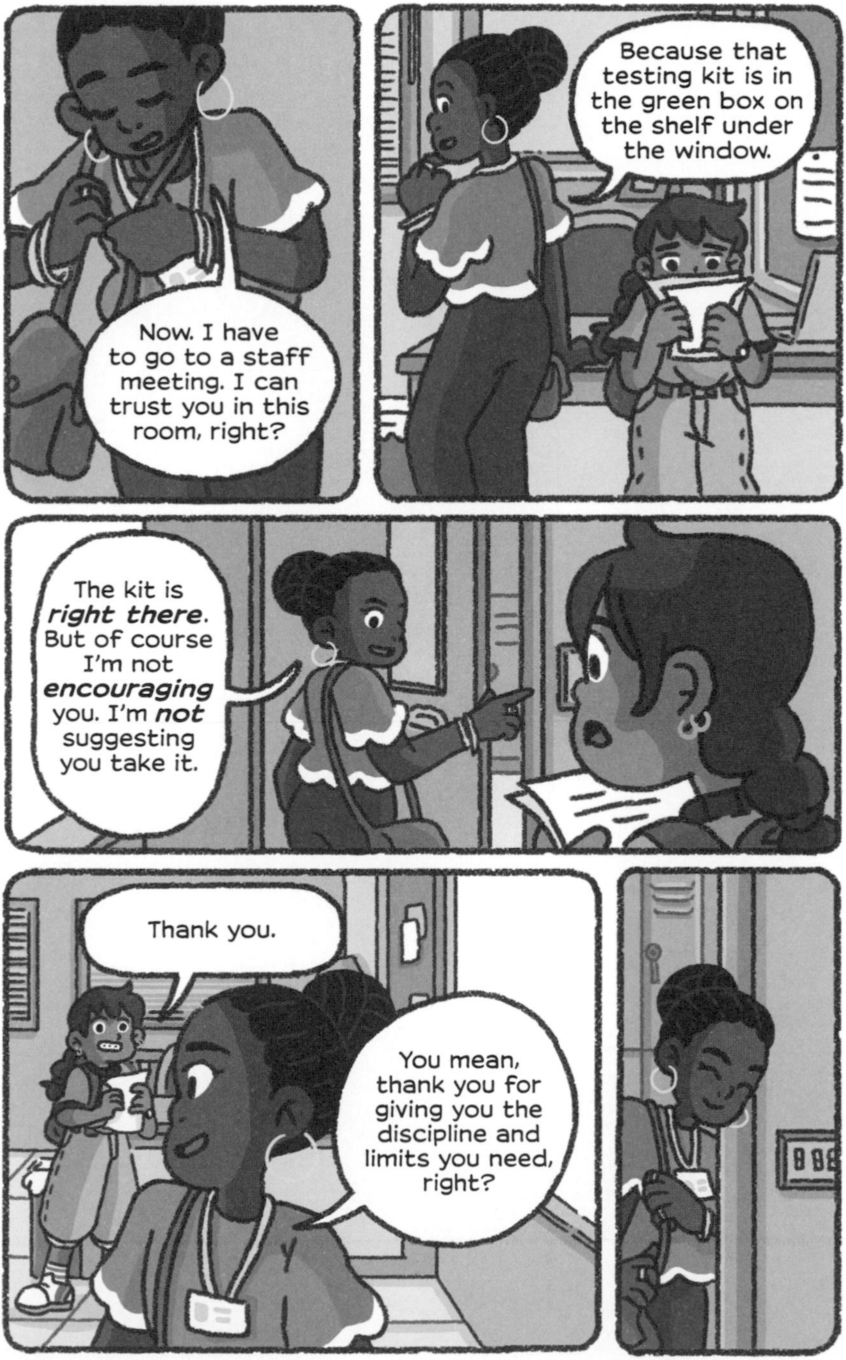
Now. I have to go to a staff meeting. I can trust you in this room, right?
Because that testing kit is in the green box on the shelf under the window.
The kit is ***right there***. But of course I'm not ***encouraging*** you. I'm ***not*** suggesting you take it.
Thank you.
You mean, thank you for giving you the discipline and limits you need, right?

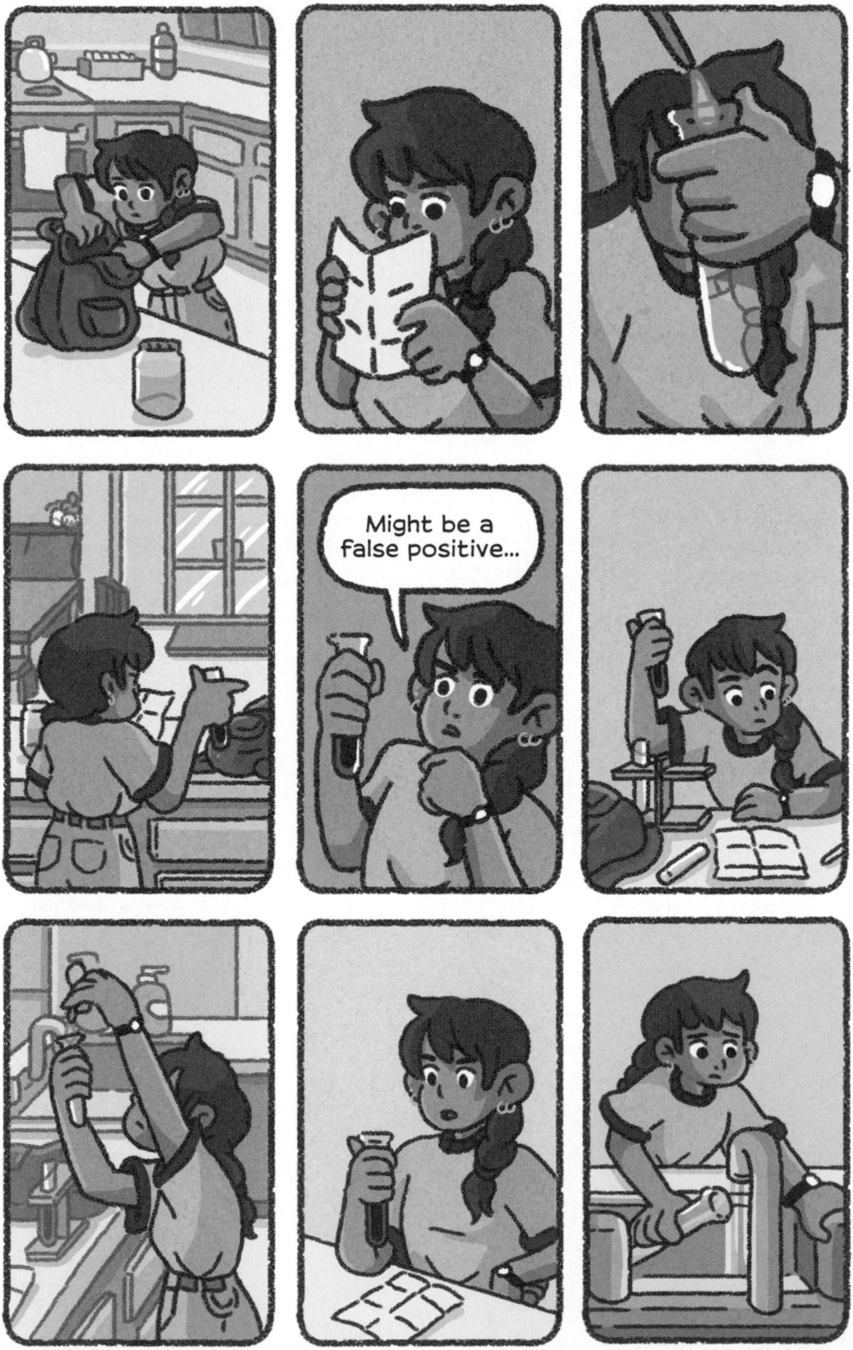
Might be a false positive...

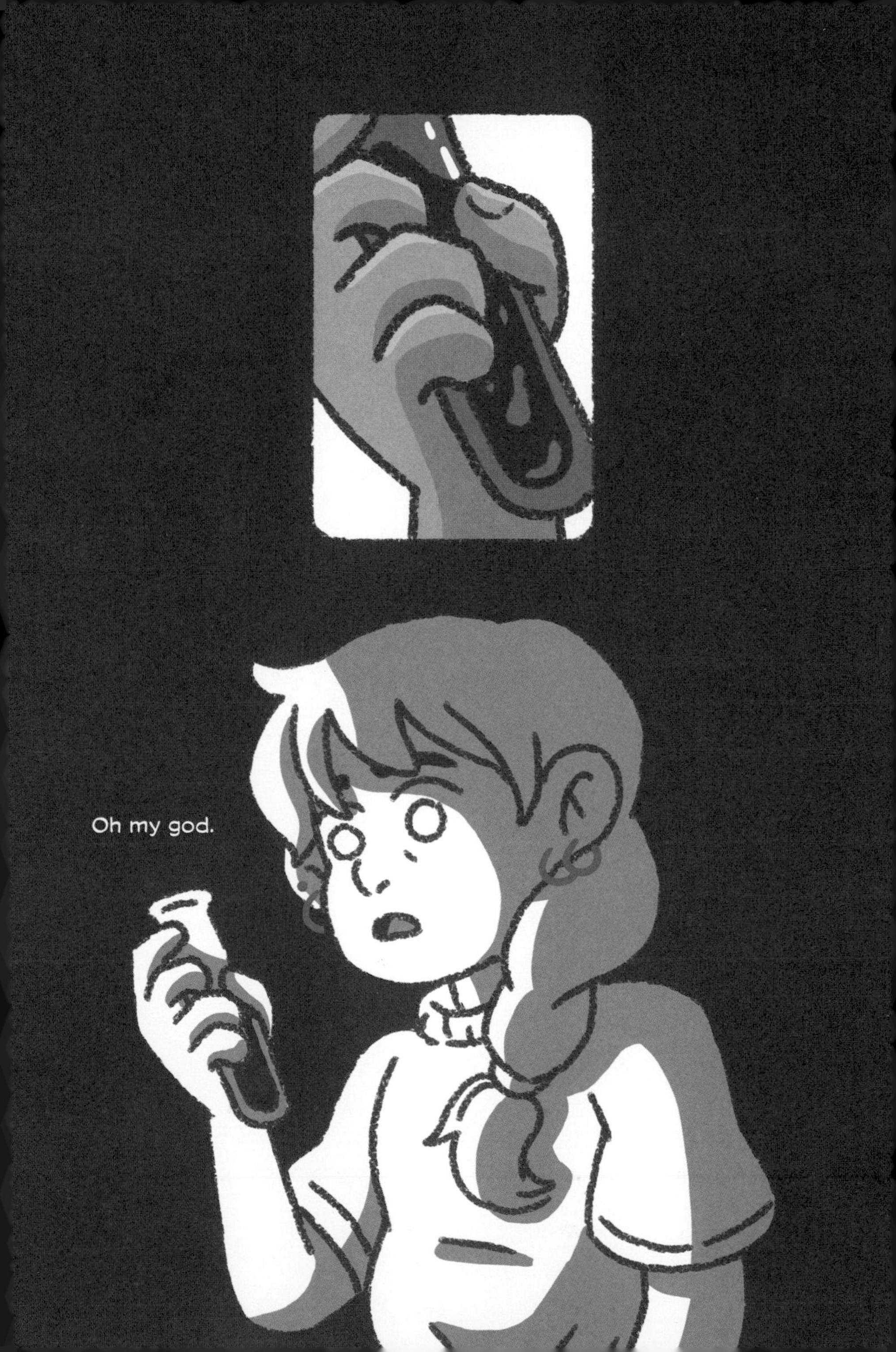
Oh my god.

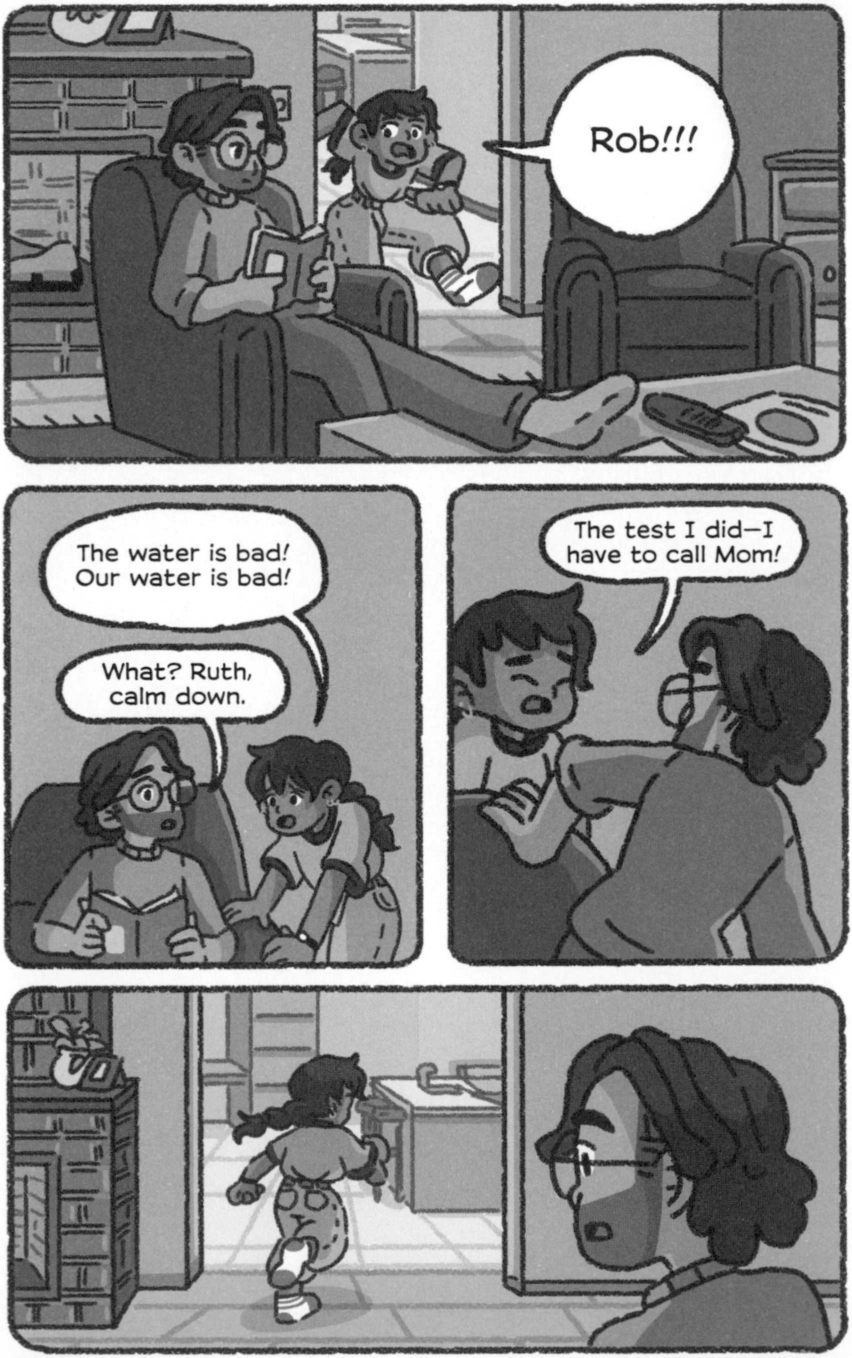
Rob!!!
The water is bad! Our water is bad!
What? Ruth, calm down.
The test I did—I have to call Mom!

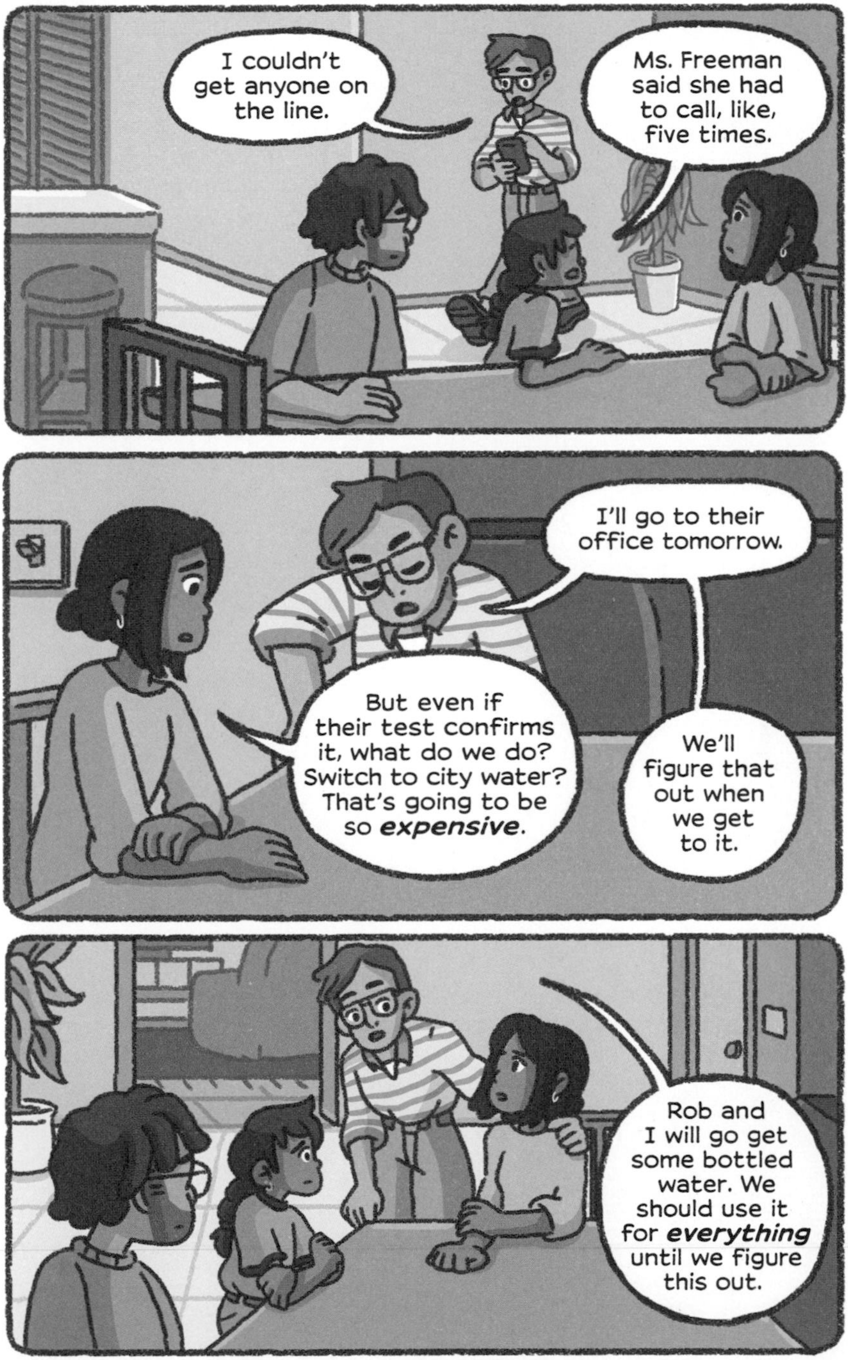

I couldn't get anyone on the line.
Ms. Freeman said she had to call, like, five times.
I'll go to their office tomorrow.
But even if their test confirms it, what do we do? Switch to city water? That's going to be so ***expensive***.
We'll figure that out when we get to it.
Rob and I will go get some bottled water. We should use it for ***everything*** until we figure this out.

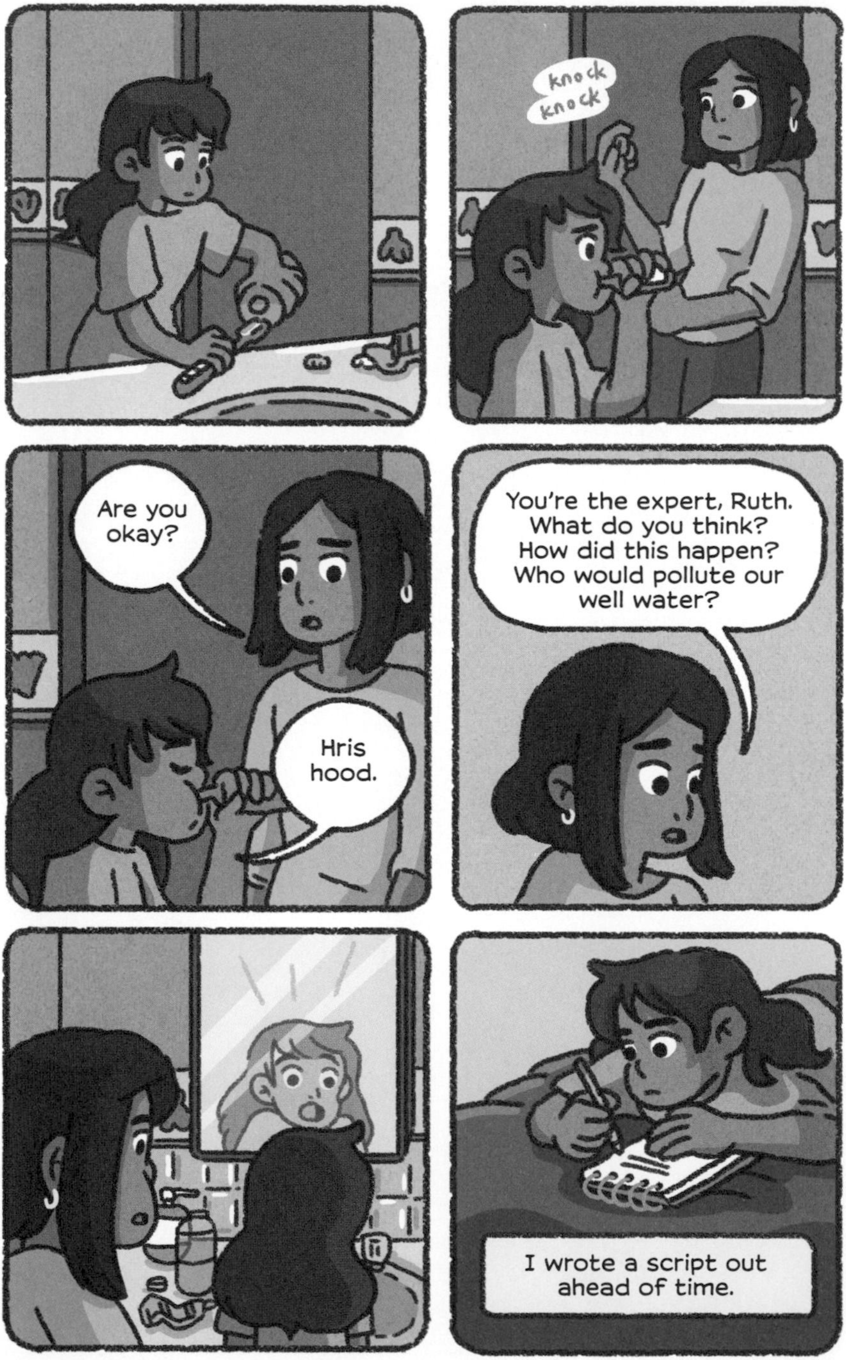
knock knock
Are you okay?
Hris hood.
You're the expert, Ruth. What do you think? How did this happen? Who would pollute our well water?
I wrote a script out ahead of time.

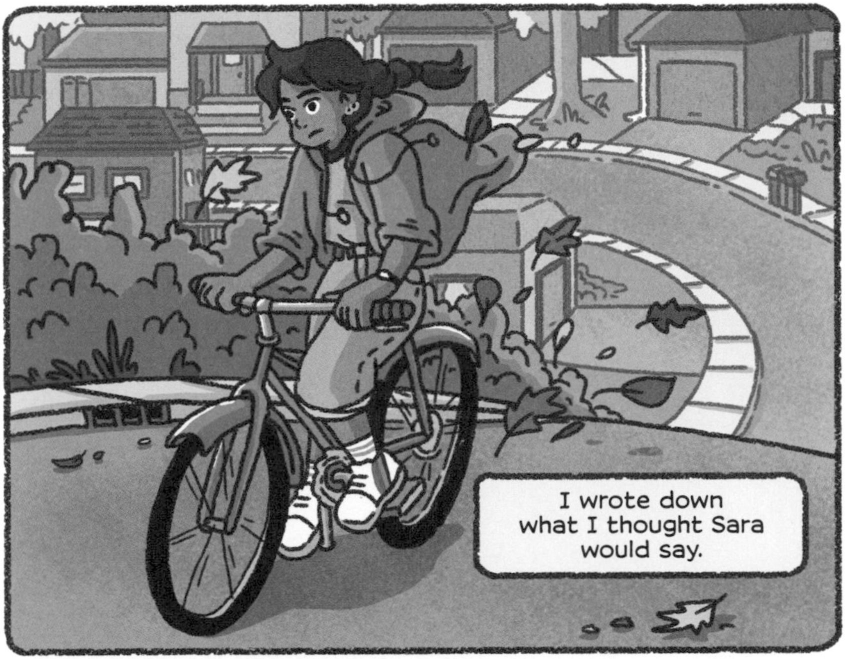
I wrote down what I thought Sara would say.

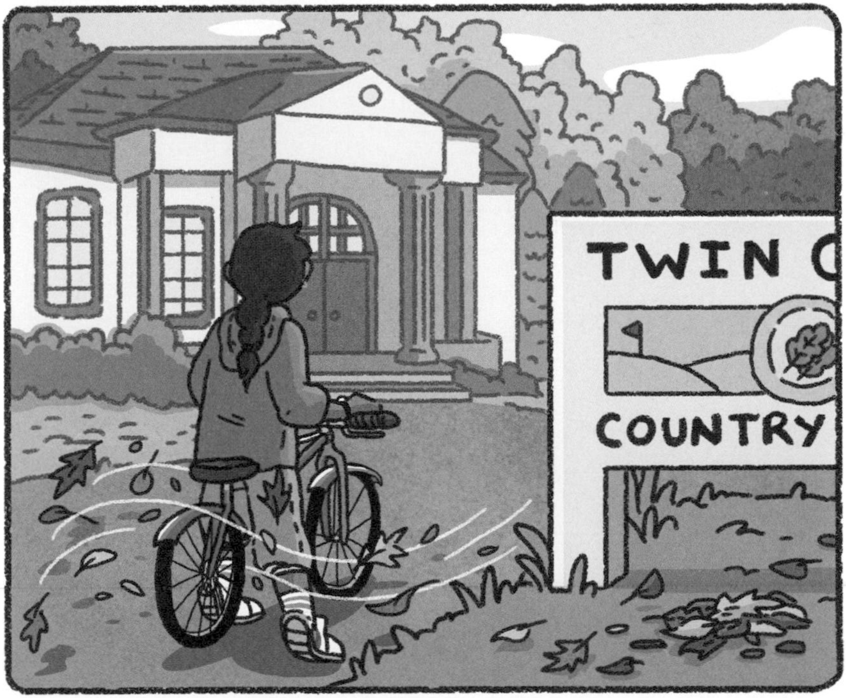
TWIN
COUNTRY

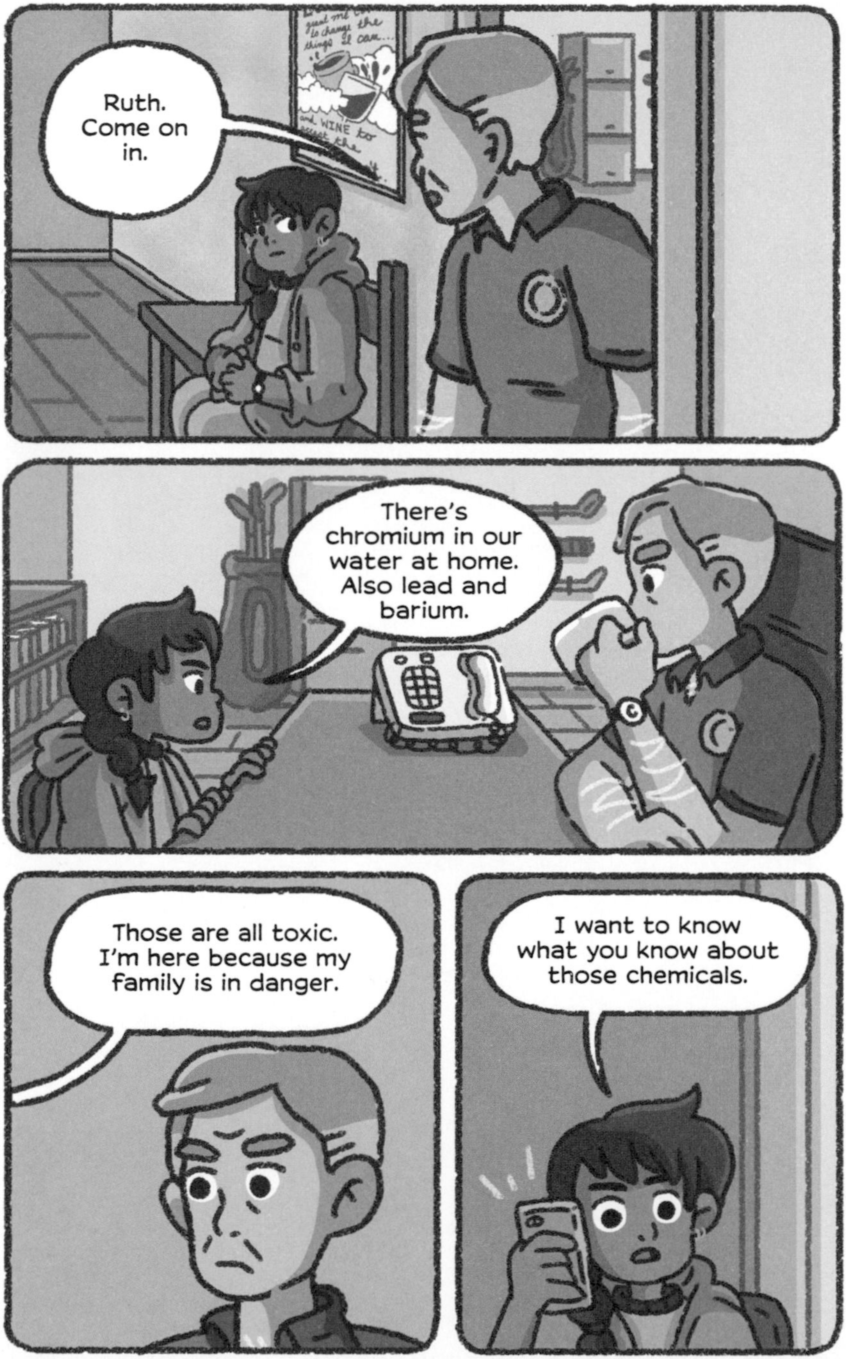
Ruth. Come on in.
There's chromium in our water at home. Also lead and barium.
Those are all toxic. I'm here because my family is in danger.
I want to know what you know about those chemicals.

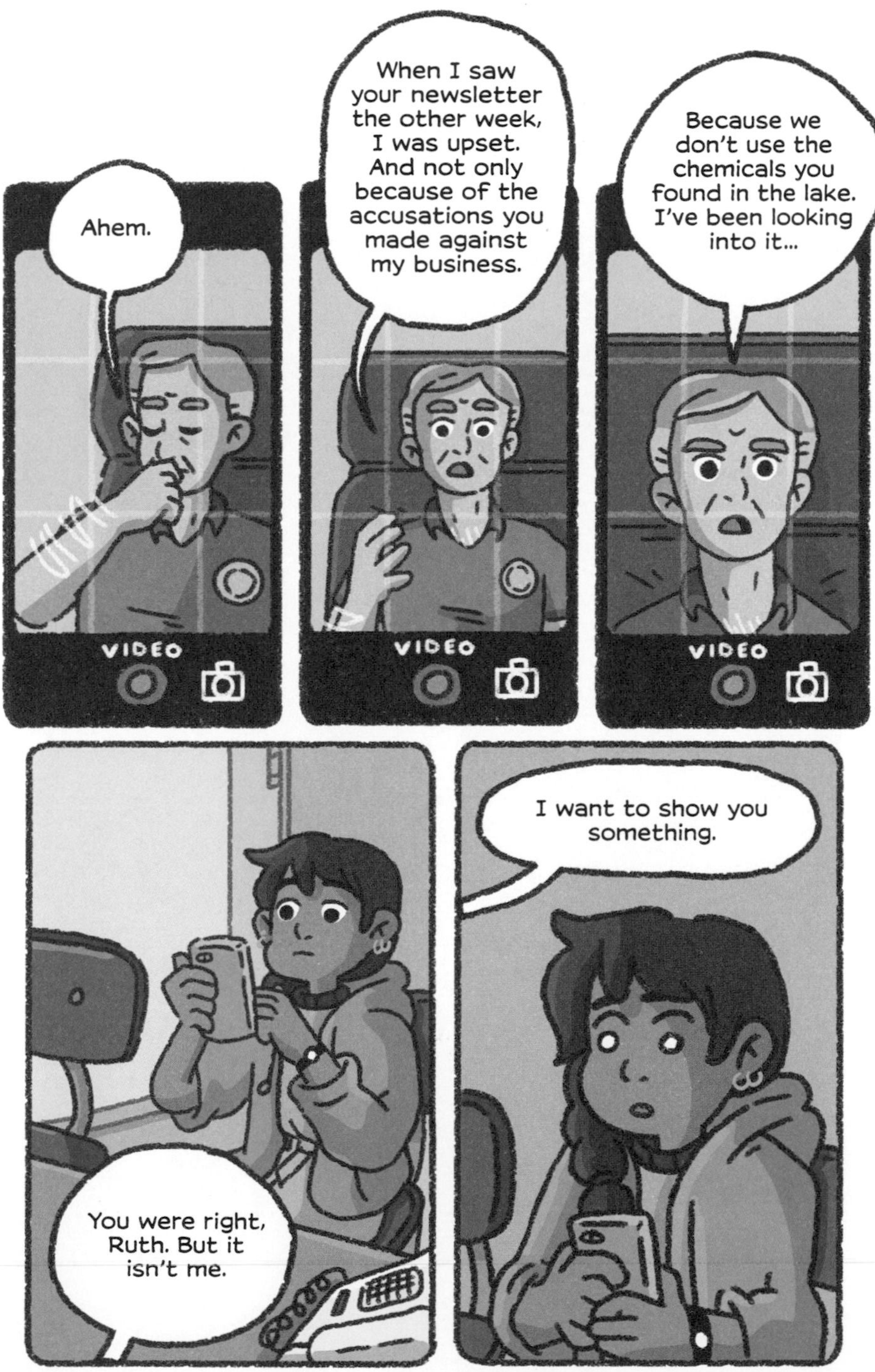
Ahem.
VIDEO
When I saw your newsletter the other week, I was upset. And not only because of the accusations you made against my business.
VIDEO
Because we don't use the chemicals you found in the lake. I've been looking into it...
VIDEO
You were right, Ruth. But it isn't me.
I want to show you something.

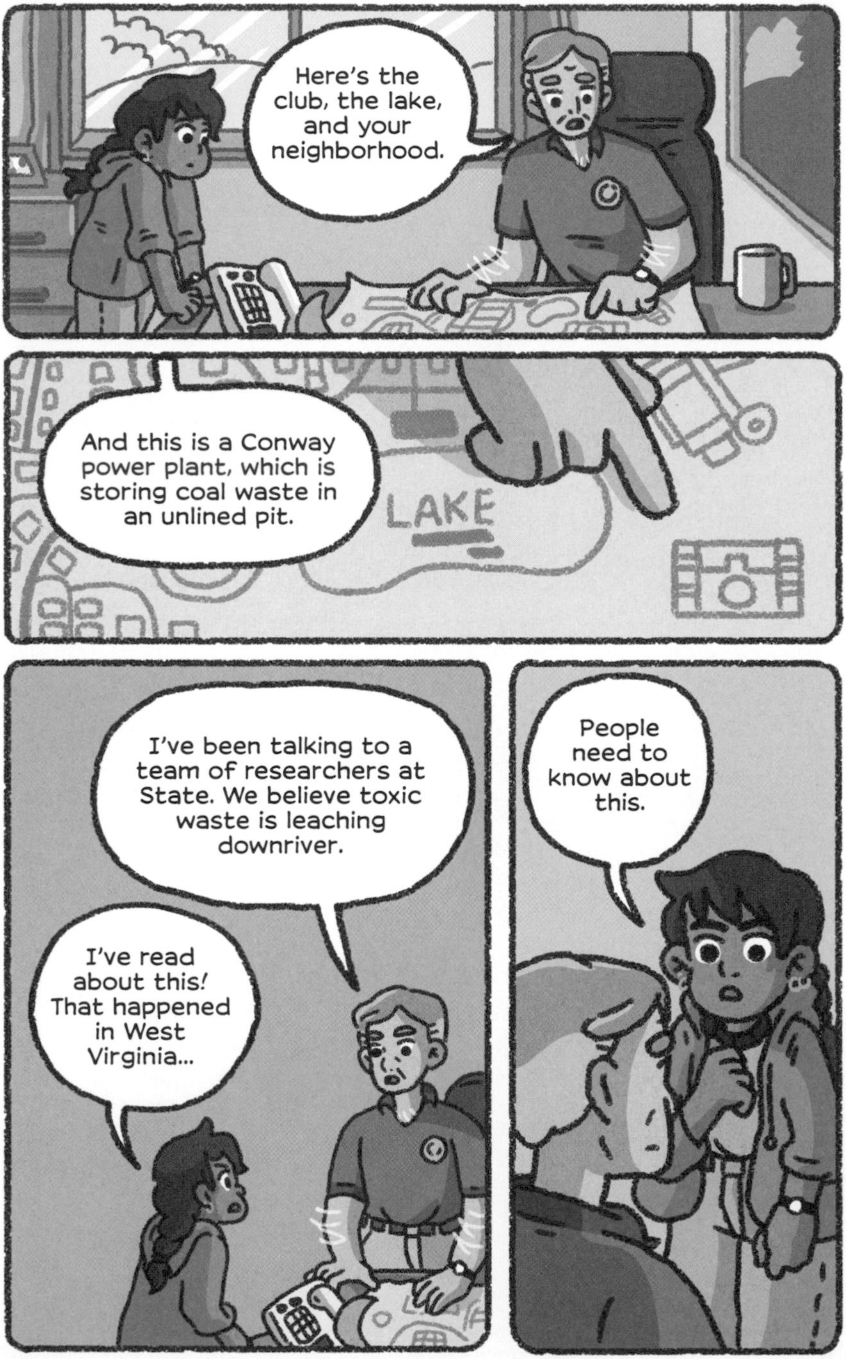
Here's the club, the lake, and your neighborhood.
And this is a Conway power plant, which is storing coal waste in an unlined pit.
LAKE
I've been talking to a team of researchers at State. We believe toxic waste is leaching downriver.
I've read about this! That happened in West Virginia...
People need to know about this.

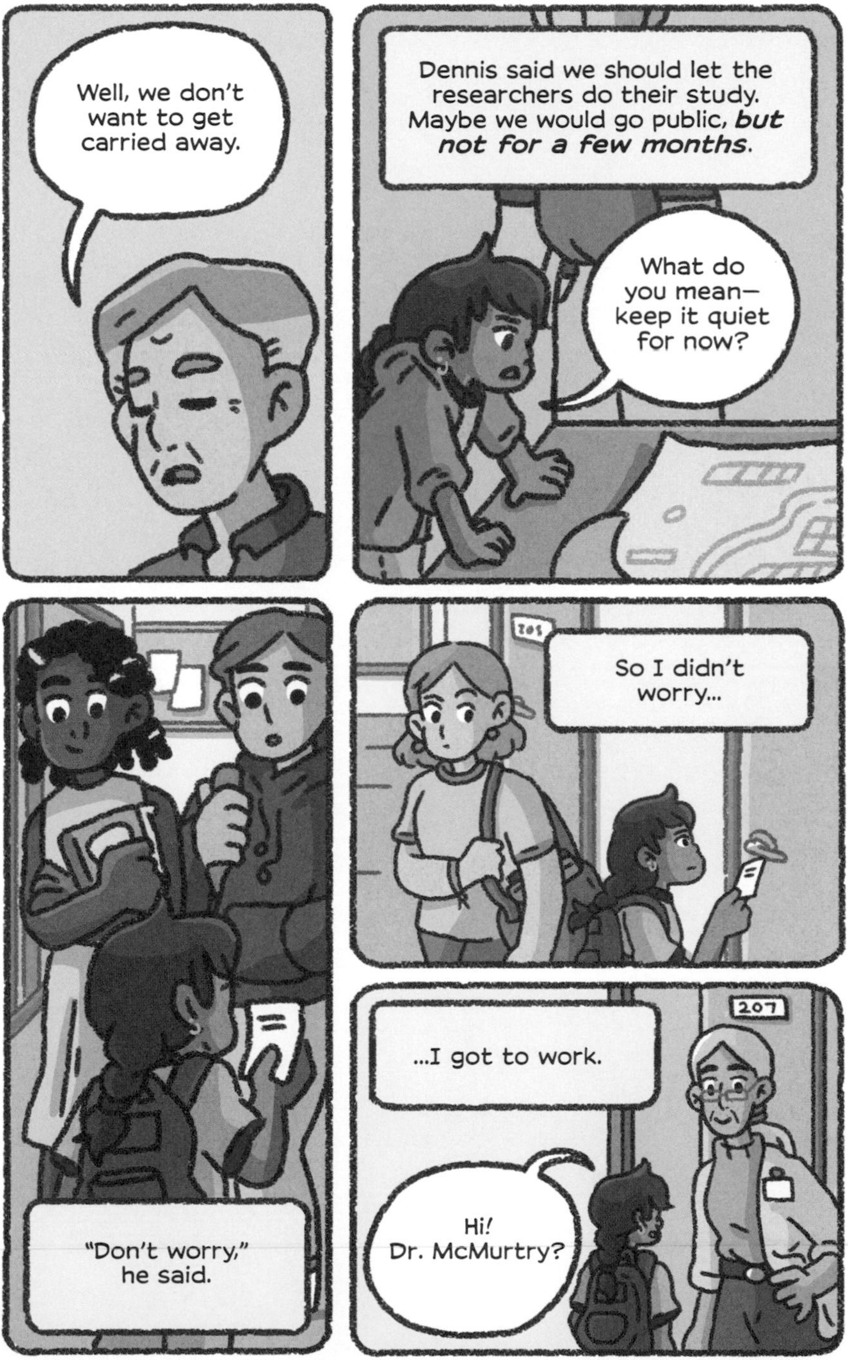
Well, we don't want to get carried away.
Dennis said we should let the researchers do their study. Maybe we would go public, ***but not for a few months***.
What do you mean—keep it quiet for now?
"Don't worry," he said.
So I didn't worry...
...I got to work.
Hi! Dr. McMurtry?
207

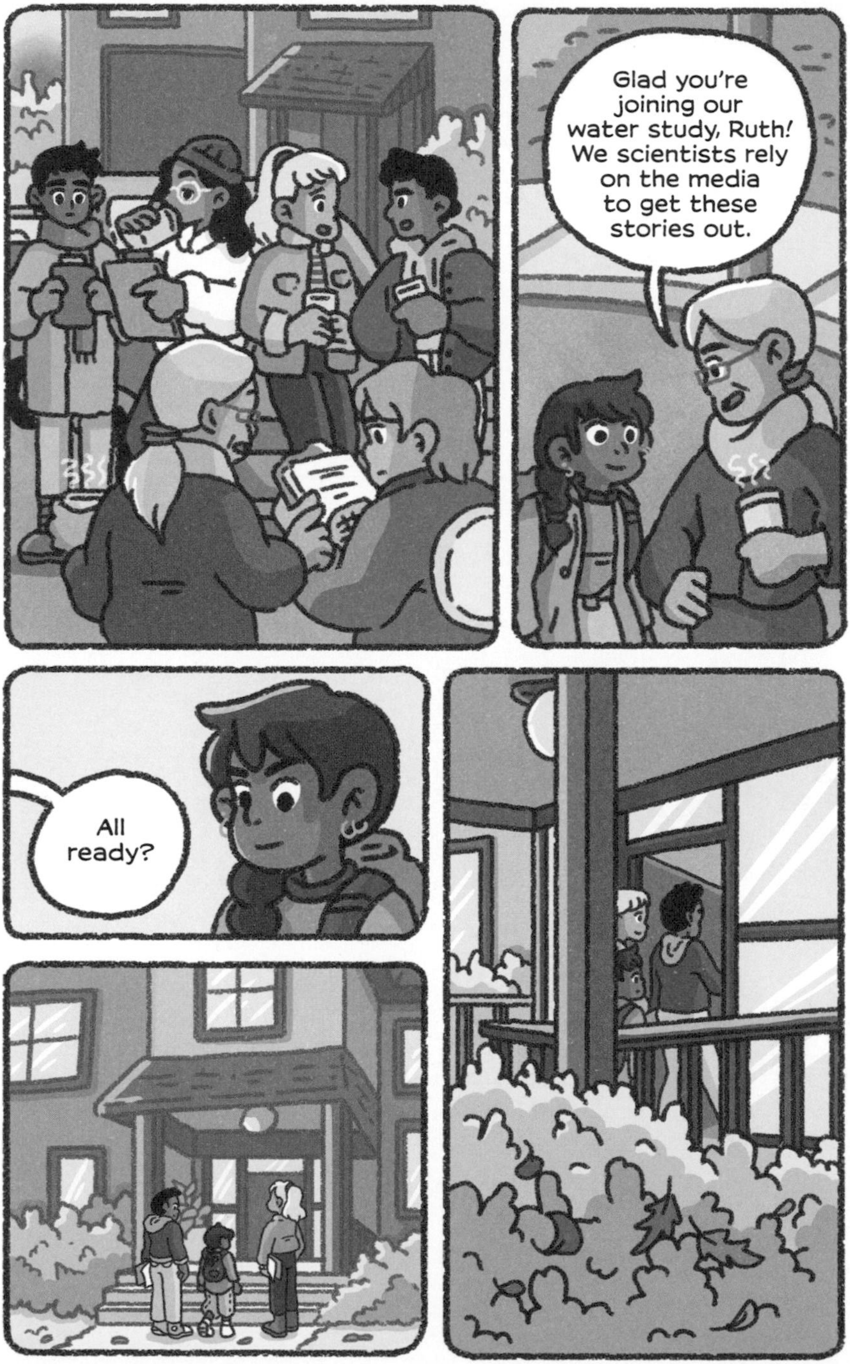
Glad you're joining our water study, Ruth! We scientists rely on the media to get these stories out.
All ready?

CHAPTER 5

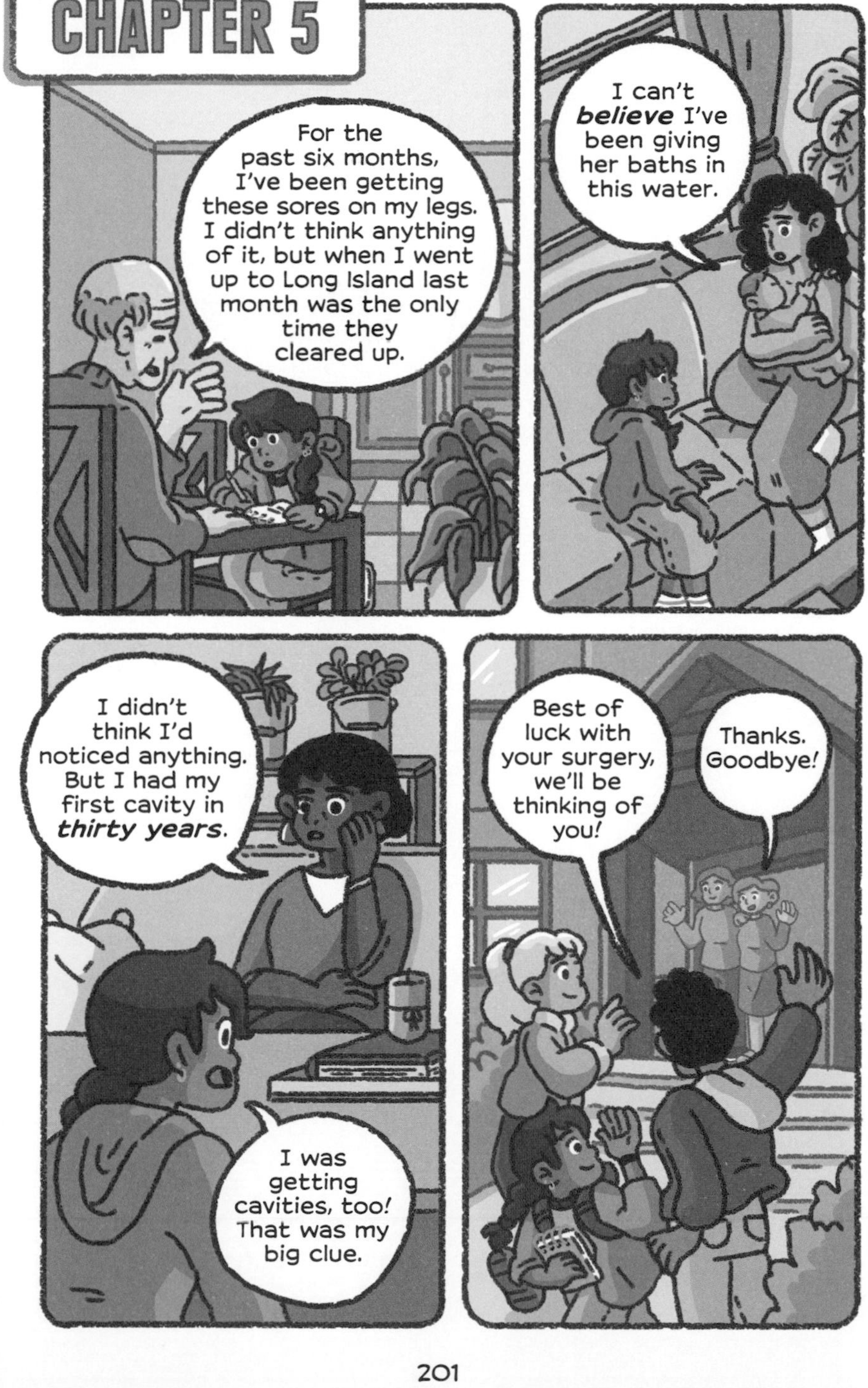

For the past six months, I've been getting these sores on my legs. I didn't think anything of it, but when I went up to Long Island last month was the only time they cleared up.
I can't ***believe*** I've been giving her baths in this water.
I didn't think I'd noticed anything. But I had my first cavity in ***thirty years***.
I was getting cavities, too! That was my big clue.
Best of luck with your surgery, we'll be thinking of you!
Thanks. Goodbye!

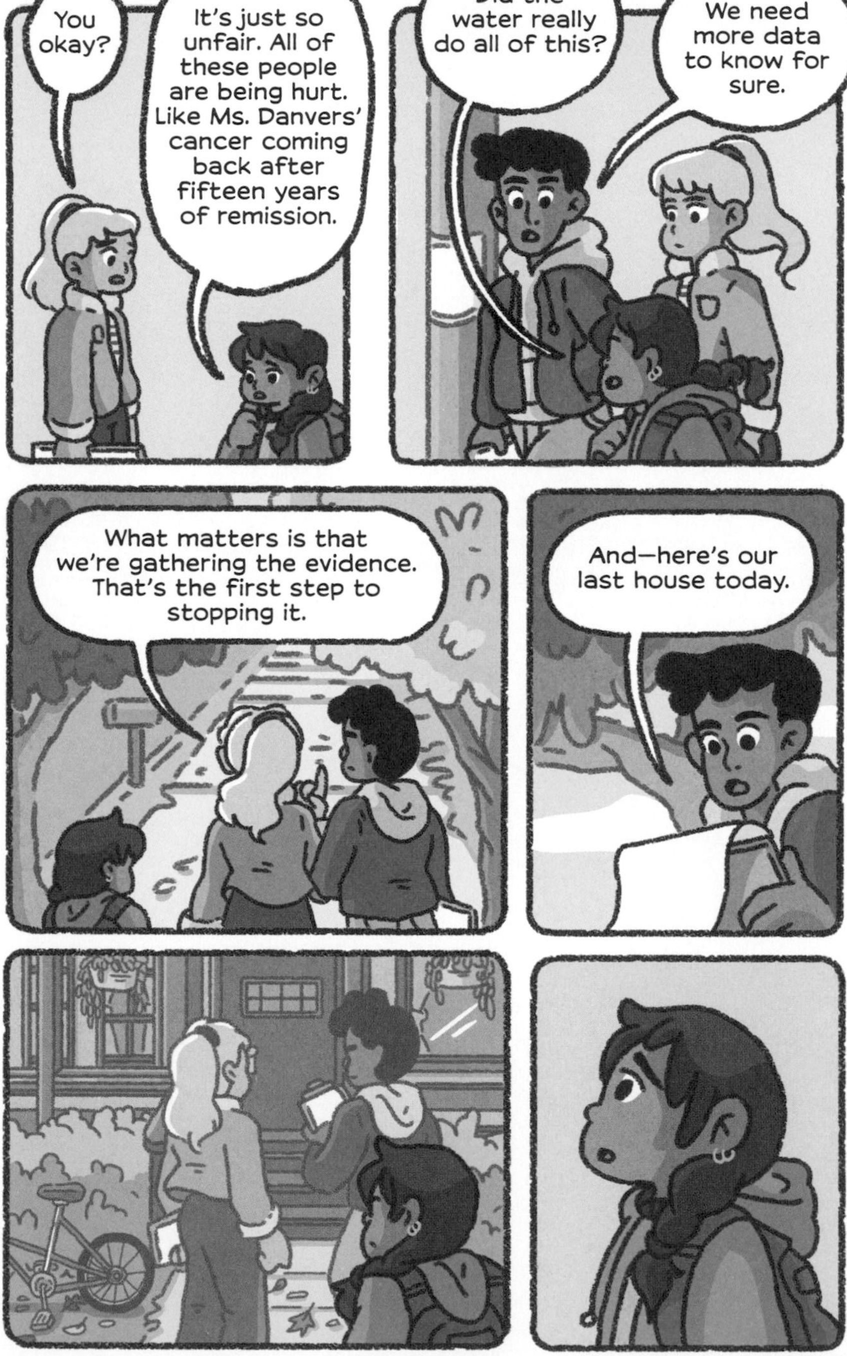
You okay?
It's just so unfair. All of these people are being hurt. Like Ms. Danvers' cancer coming back after fifteen years of remission.
Did the water really do all of this?
We need more data to know for sure.
What matters is that we're gathering the evidence. That's the first step to stopping it.
And—here's our last house today.

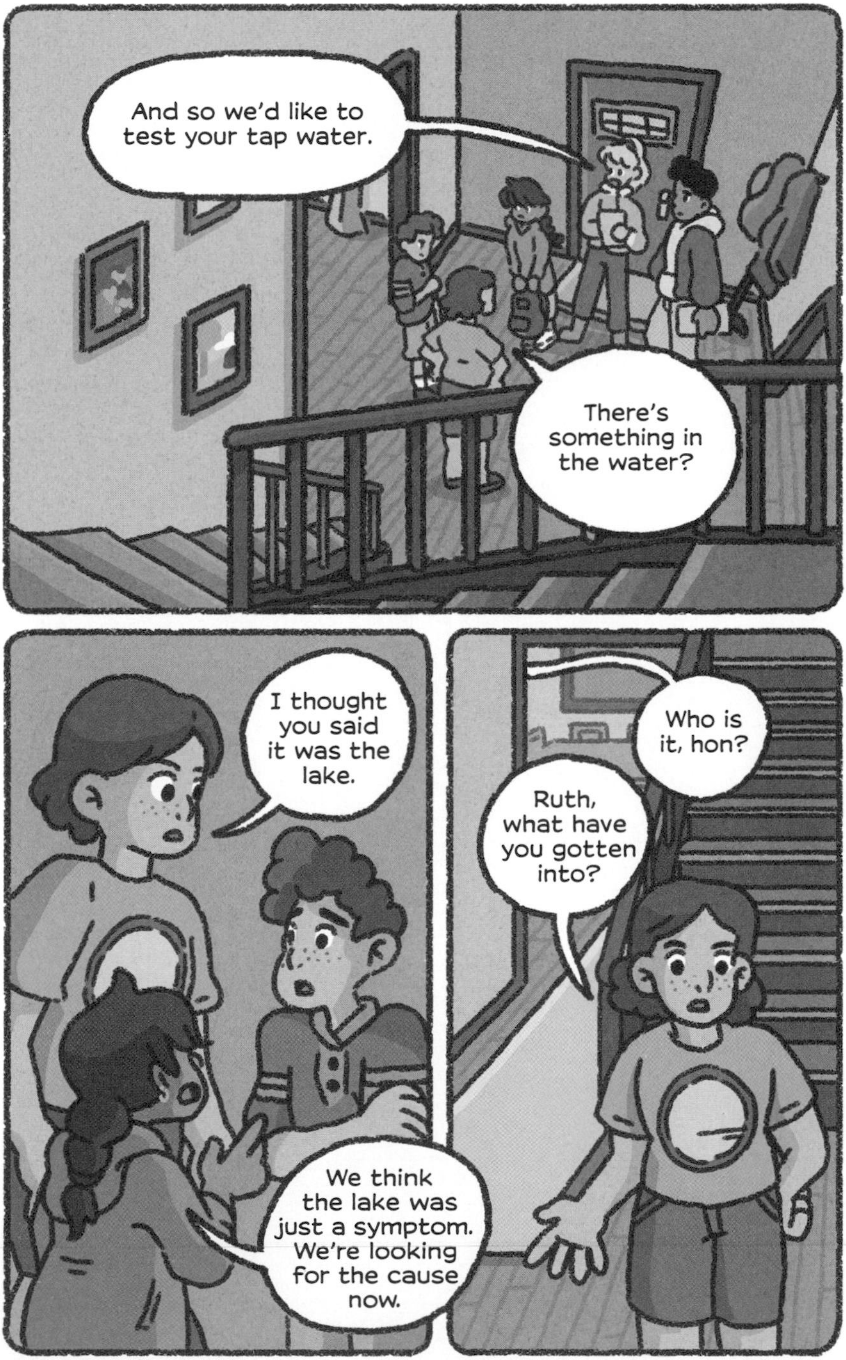
And so we'd like to test your tap water.
There's something in the water?
I thought you said it was the lake.
We think the lake was just a symptom. We're looking for the cause now.
Who is it, hon?
Ruth, what have you gotten into?

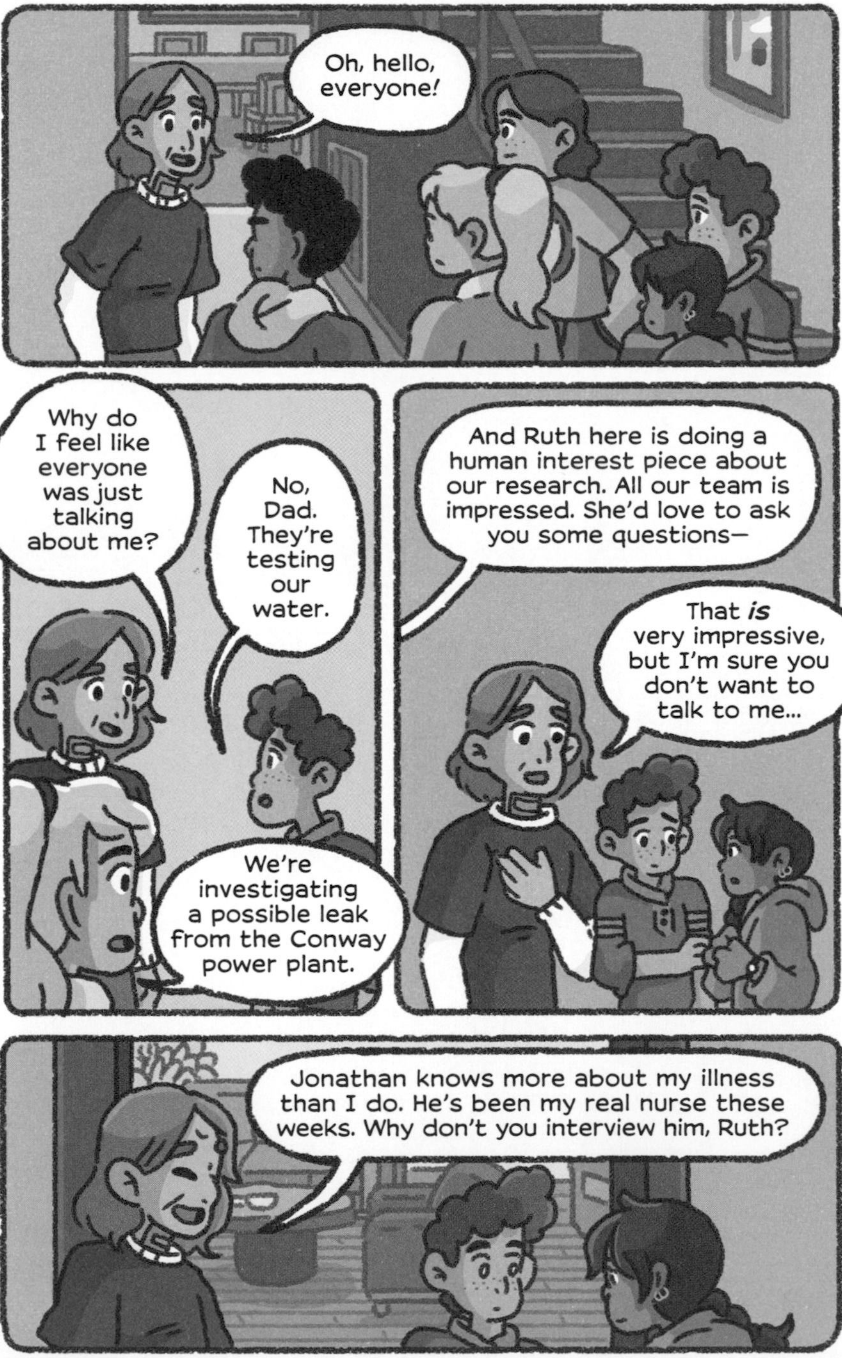
Oh, hello, everyone!
Why do I feel like everyone was just talking about me?
No, Dad. They're testing our water.
We're investigating a possible leak from the Conway power plant.
And Ruth here is doing a human interest piece about our research. All our team is impressed. She'd love to ask you some questions—
That *is* very impressive, but I'm sure you don't want to talk to me...
Jonathan knows more about my illness than I do. He's been my real nurse these weeks. Why don't you interview him, Ruth?

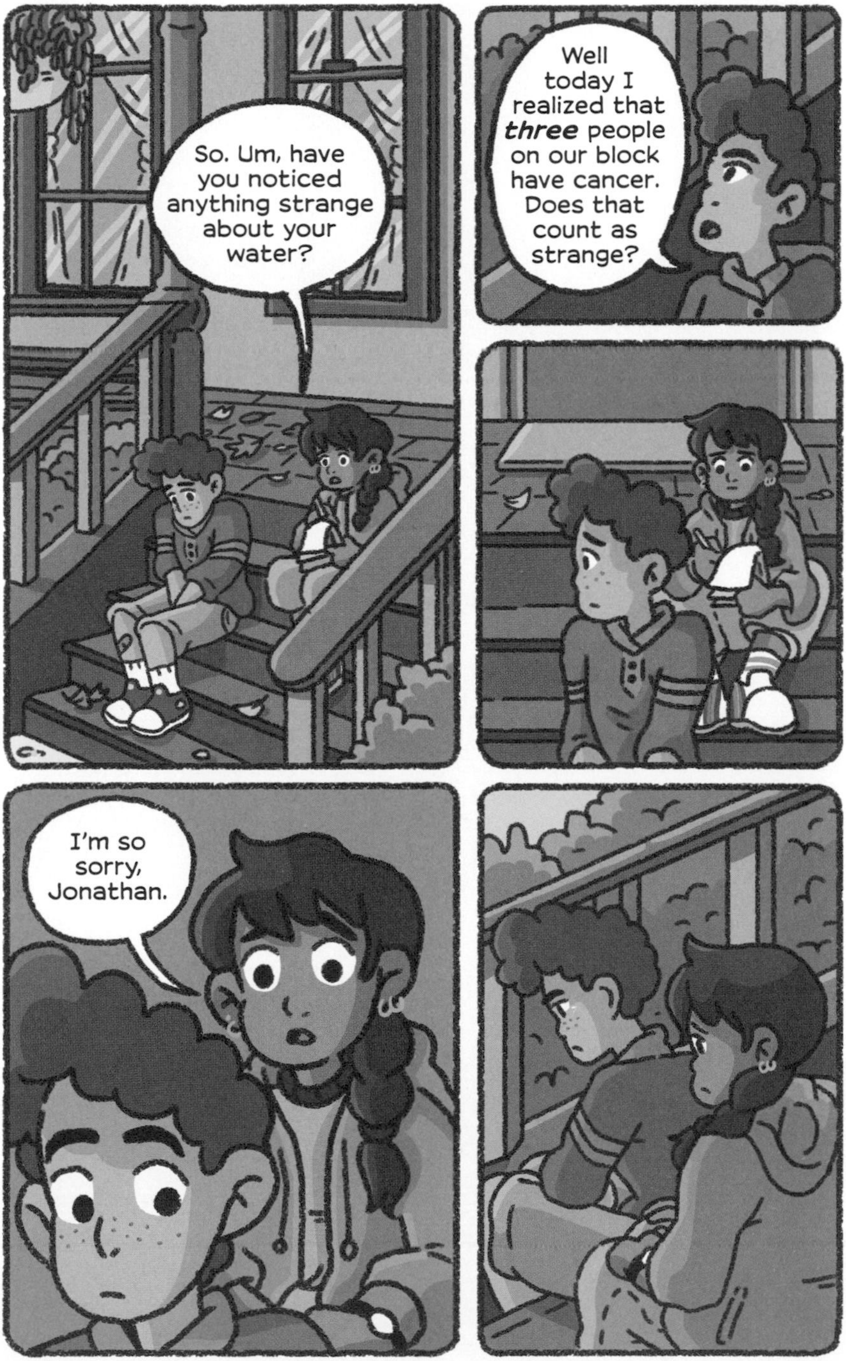

So. Um, have you noticed anything strange about your water?
Well today I realized that ***three*** people on our block have cancer. Does that count as strange?
I'm so sorry, Jonathan.

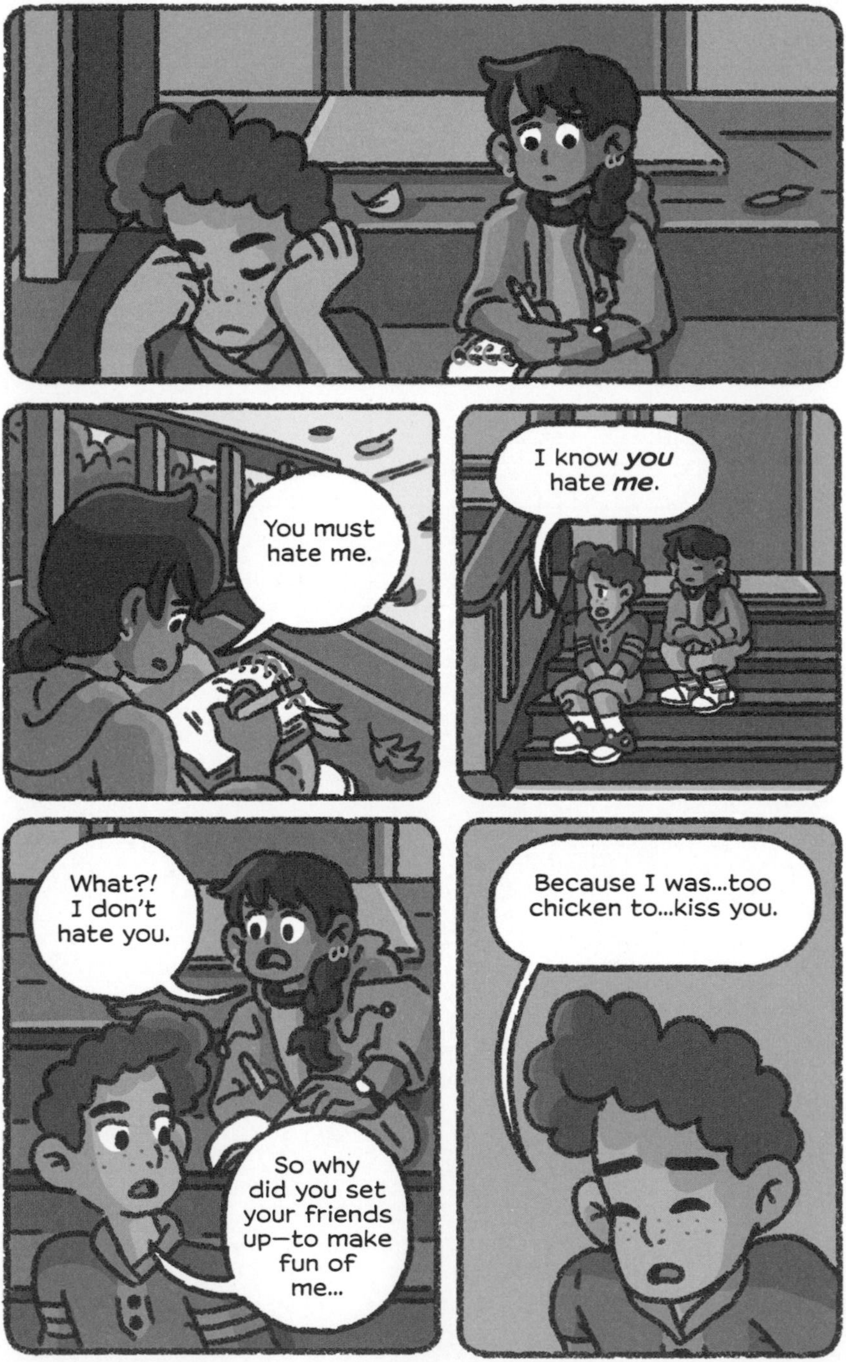
You must hate me.
I know *you* hate *me*.
What?! I don't hate you.
So why did you set your friends up—to make fun of me...
Because I was...too chicken to...kiss you.

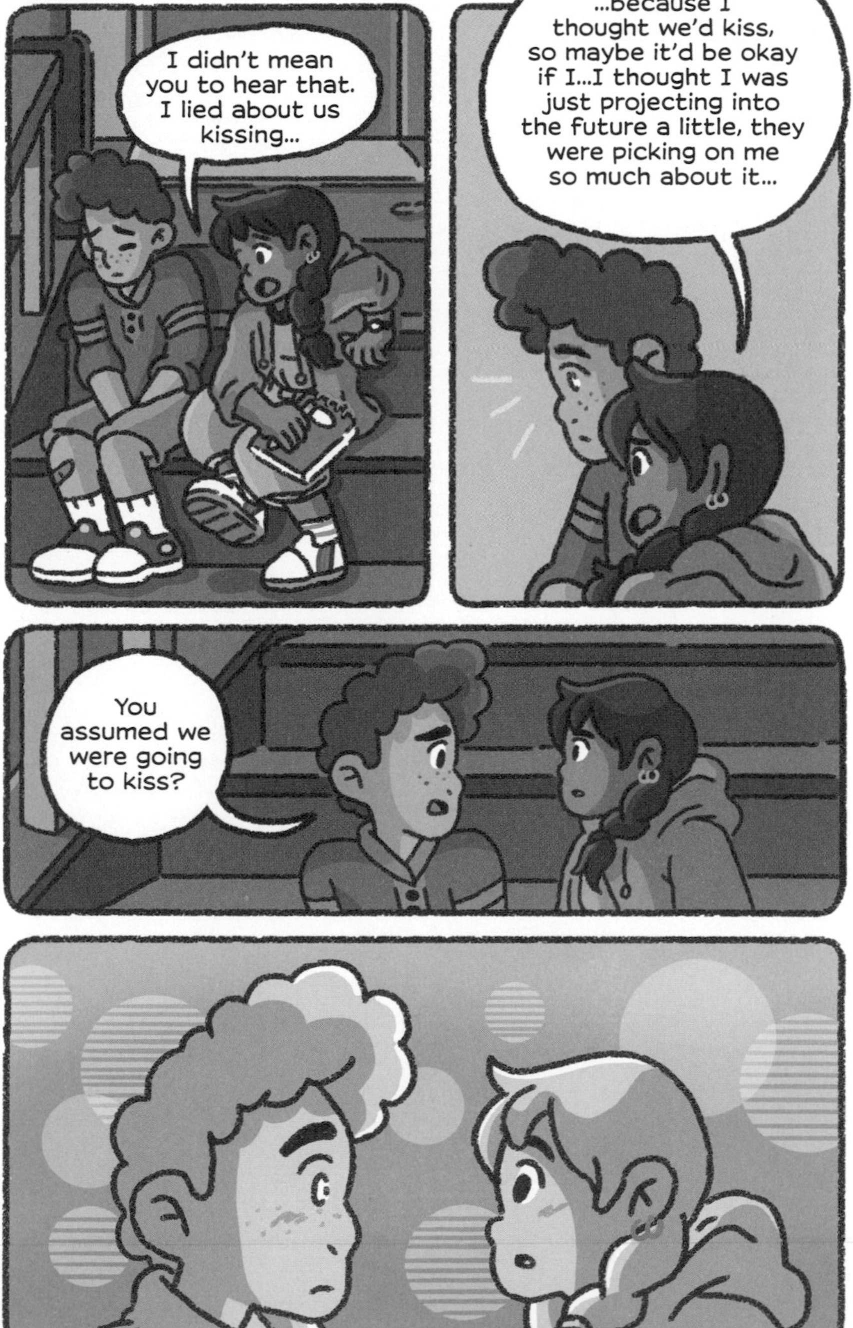
I didn't mean you to hear that. I lied about us kissing...
...because I thought we'd kiss, so maybe it'd be okay if I...I thought I was just projecting into the future a little, they were picking on me so much about it...
You assumed we were going to kiss?

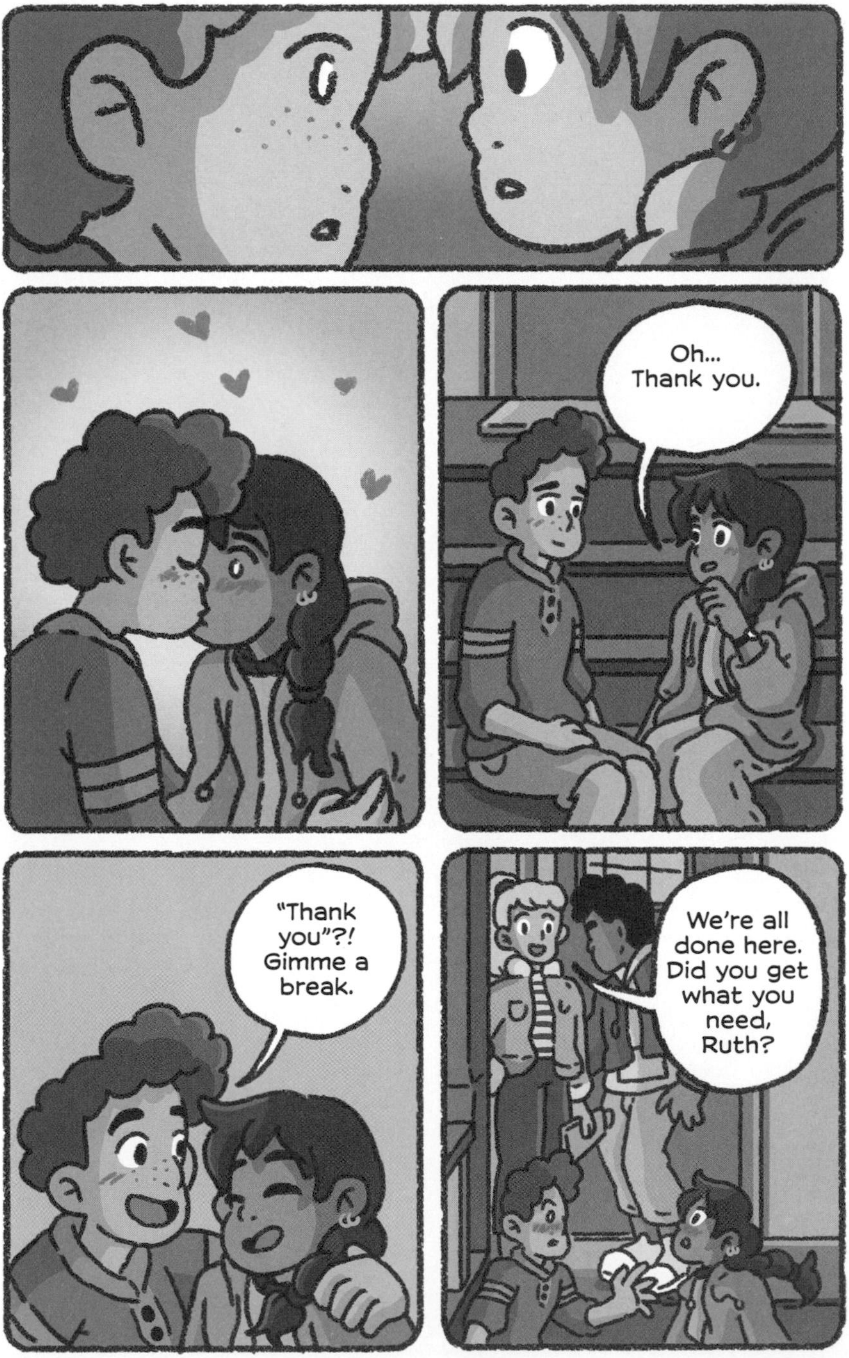
Oh... Thank you.
"Thank you"?! Gimme a break.
We're all done here. Did you get what you need, Ruth?

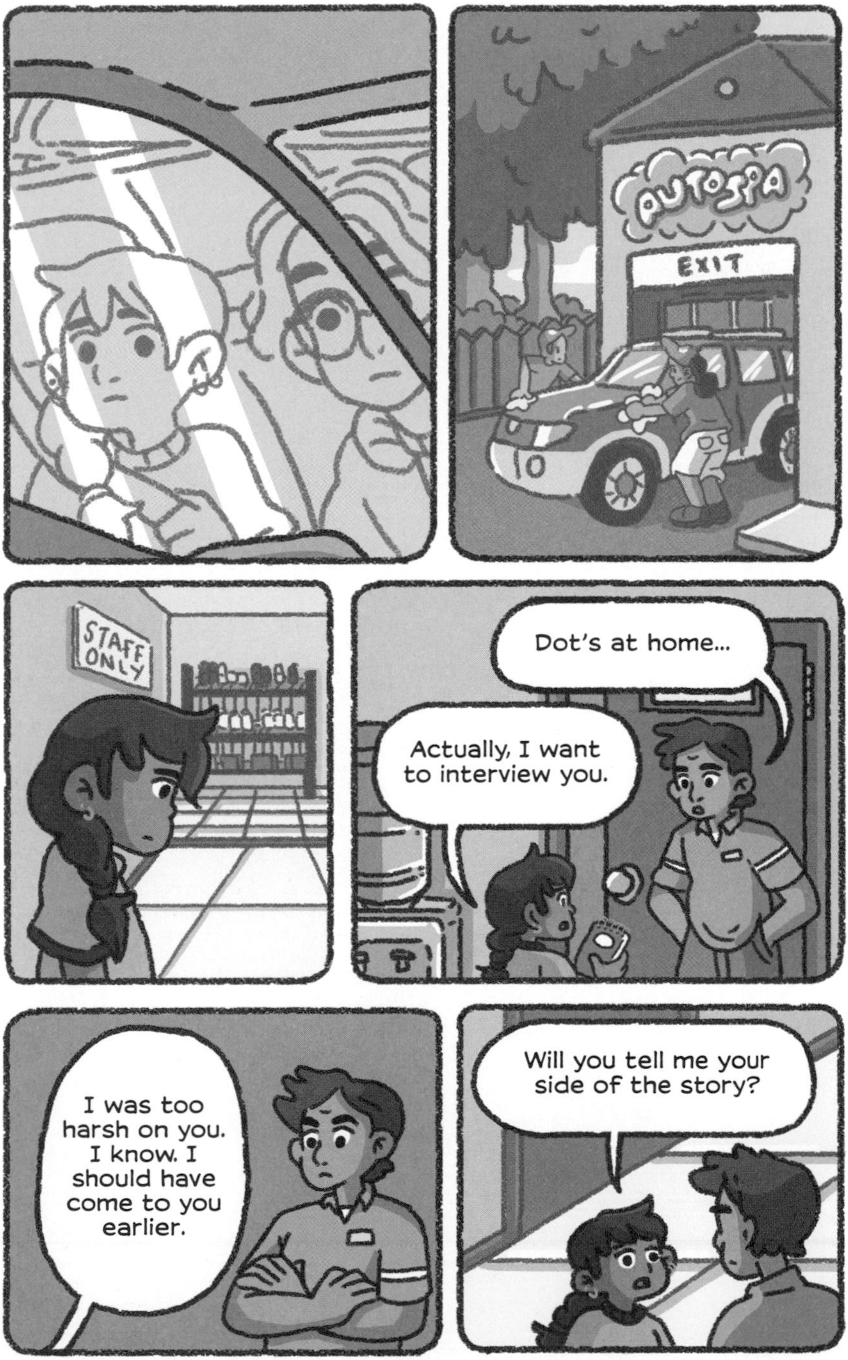
AUTOSPA
EXIT
STAFF ONLY
Dot's at home...
Actually, I want to interview you.
I was too harsh on you. I know. I should have come to you earlier.
Will you tell me your side of the story?

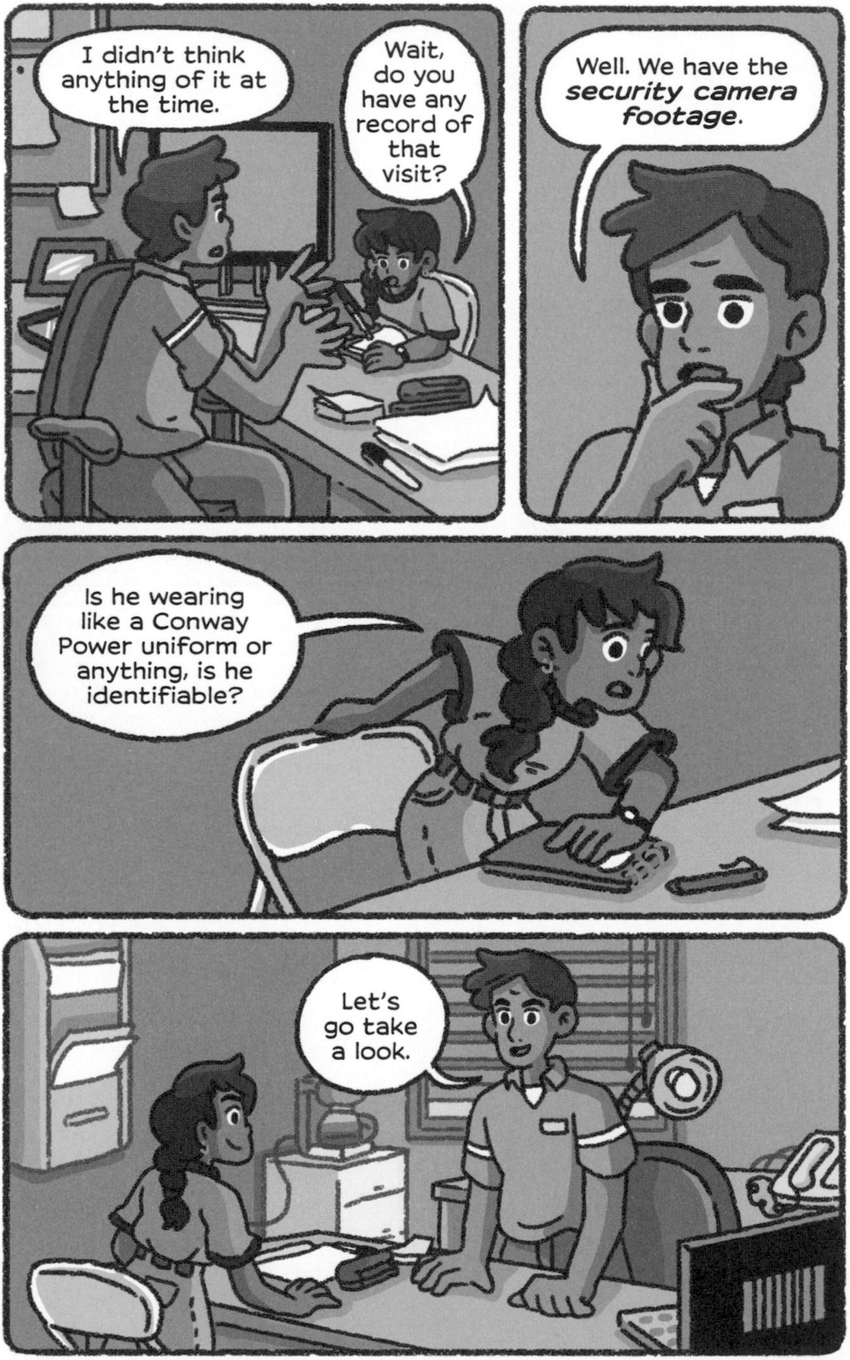
I didn't think anything of it at the time.
Wait, do you have any record of that visit?
Well. We have the *security camera footage*.
Is he wearing like a Conway Power uniform or anything, is he identifiable?
Let's go take a look.

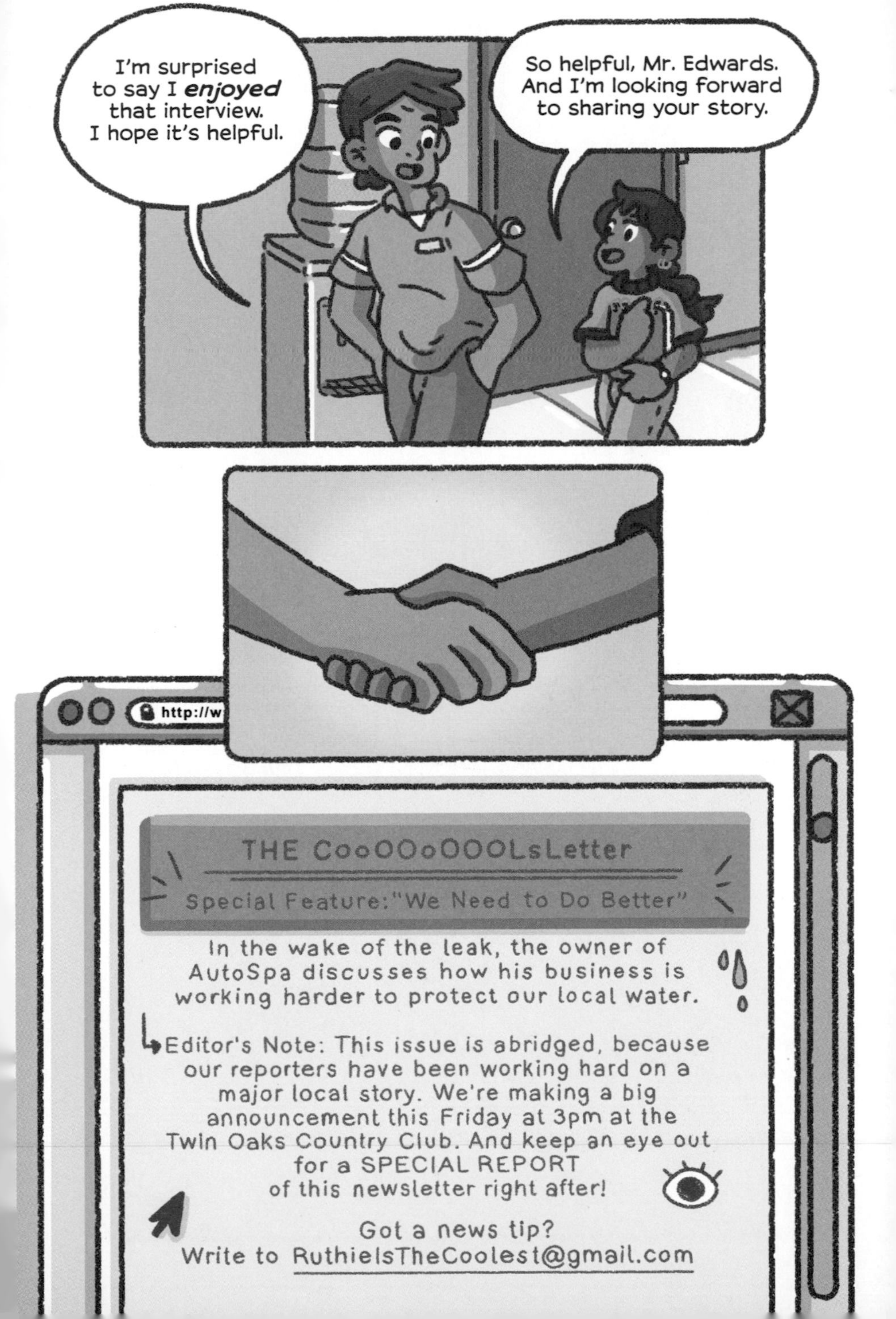
I'm surprised to say I ***enjoyed*** that interview. I hope it's helpful.
So helpful, Mr. Edwards. And I'm looking forward to sharing your story.
http://w
THE CooOOoOOOLsLetter
Special Feature: "We Need to Do Better"
In the wake of the leak, the owner of AutoSpa discusses how his business is working harder to protect our local water.
Editor's Note: This issue is abridged, because our reporters have been working hard on a major local story. We're making a big announcement this Friday at 3pm at the Twin Oaks Country Club. And keep an eye out for a SPECIAL REPORT of this newsletter right after!
Got a news tip?
Write to RuthieIsTheCoolest@gmail.com

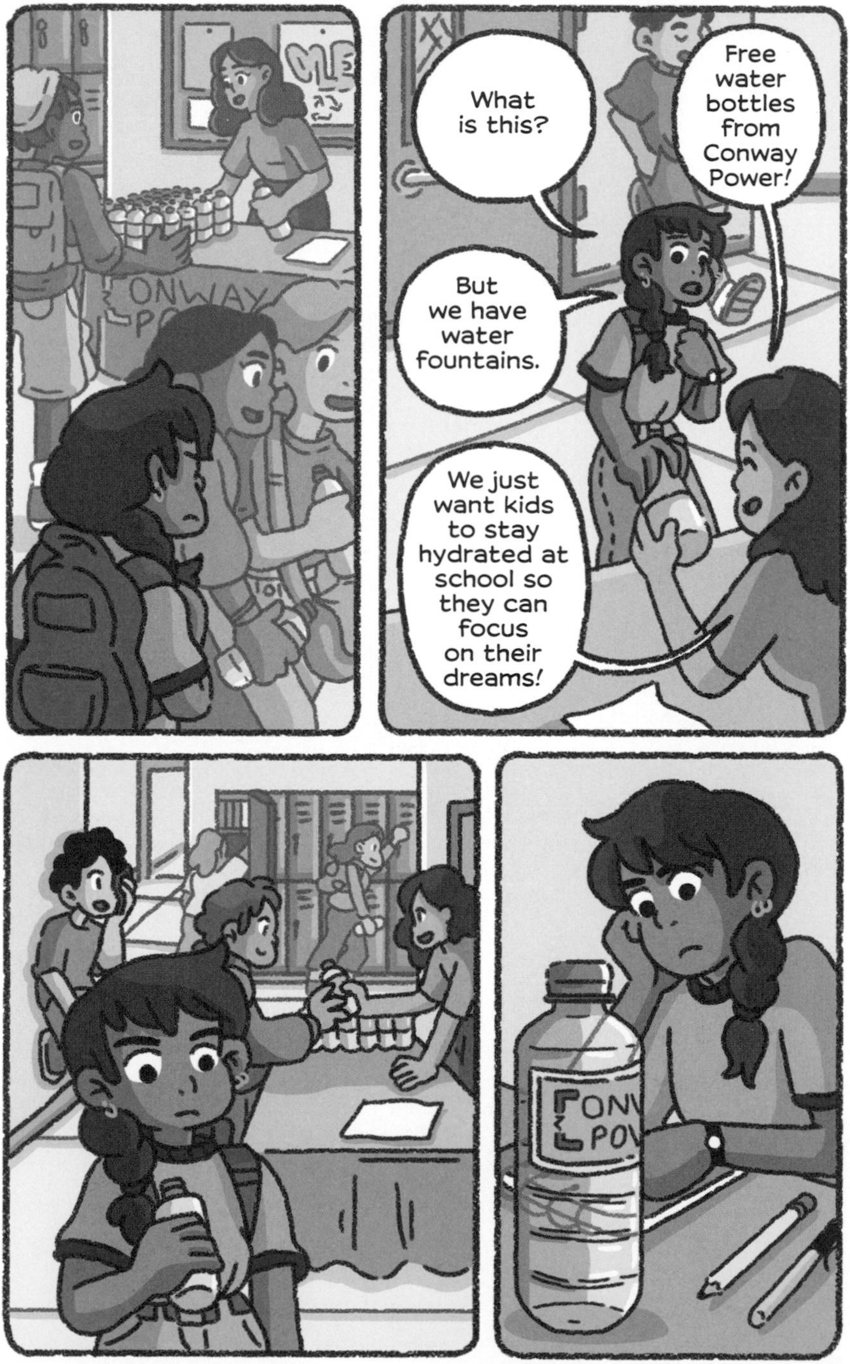
What is this?
Free water bottles from Conway Power!
But we have water fountains.
We just want kids to stay hydrated at school so they can focus on their dreams!

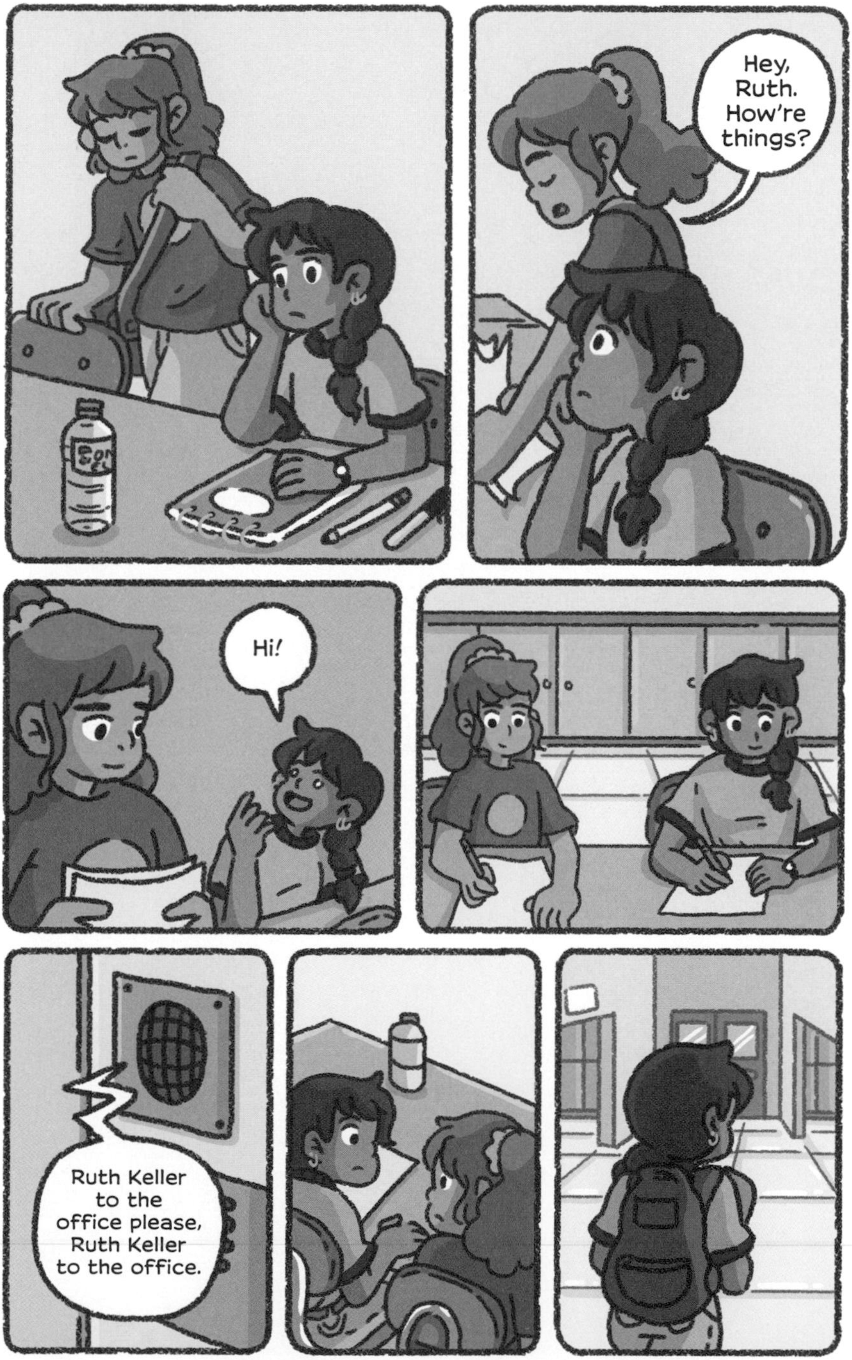
Hey, Ruth. How're things?
Hi!
Ruth Keller to the office please, Ruth Keller to the office.

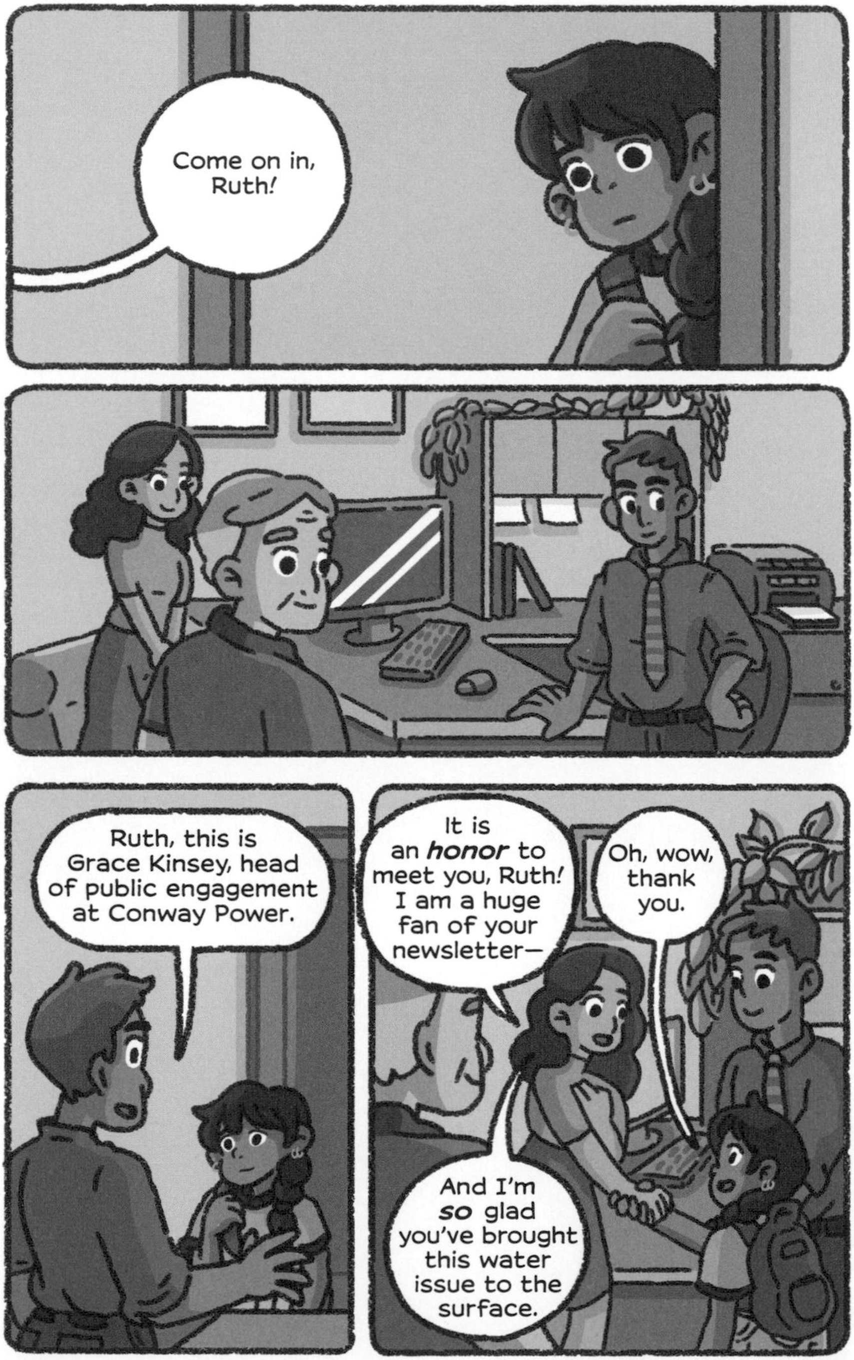
Come on in, Ruth!
Ruth, this is Grace Kinsey, head of public engagement at Conway Power.
It is an ***honor*** to meet you, Ruth! I am a huge fan of your newsletter—
Oh, wow, thank you.
And I'm ***so*** glad you've brought this water issue to the surface.

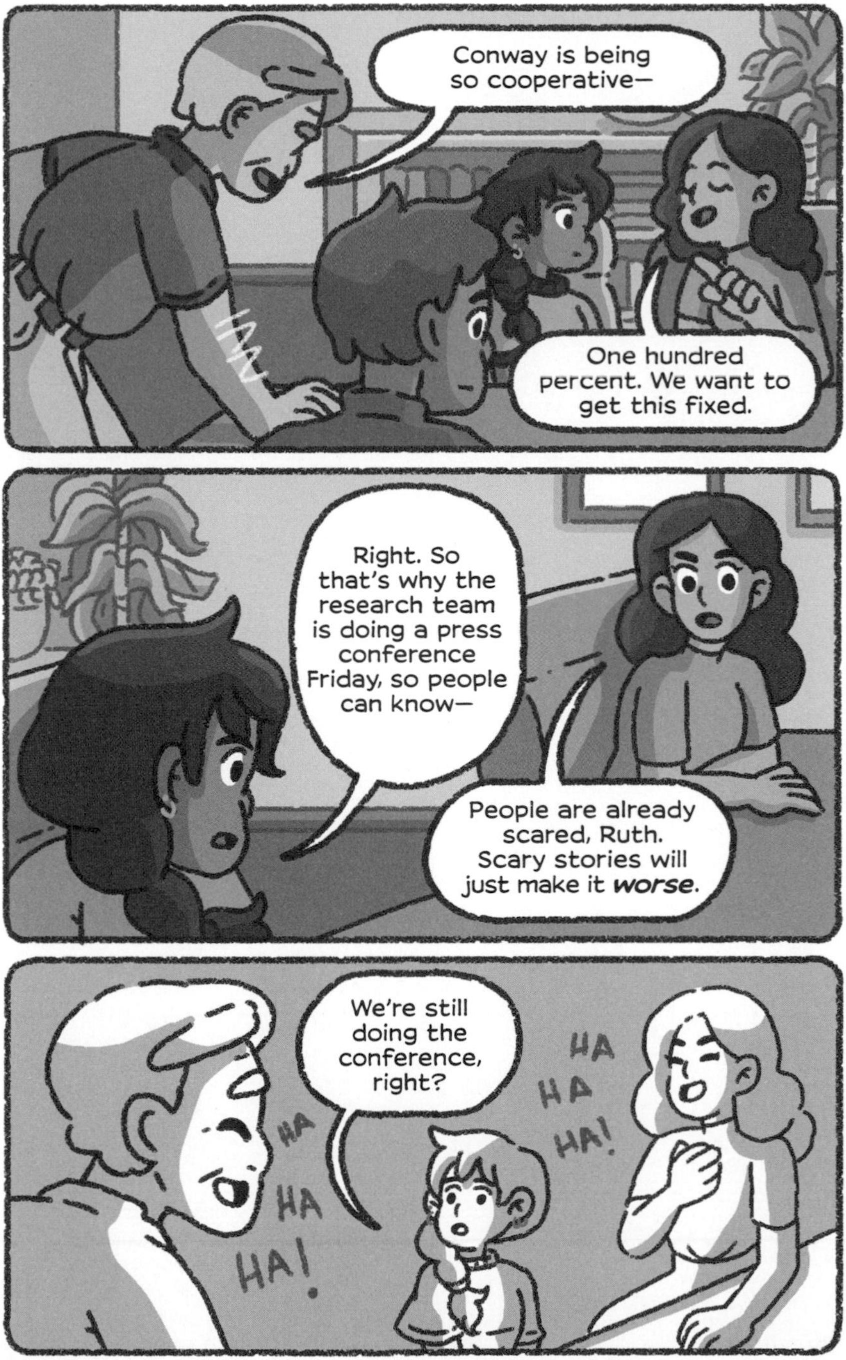
Conway is being so cooperative—
One hundred percent. We want to get this fixed.
Right. So that's why the research team is doing a press conference Friday, so people can know—
People are already scared, Ruth. Scary stories will just make it *worse*.
We're still doing the conference, right?
HA HA HA!
HA HA HA!

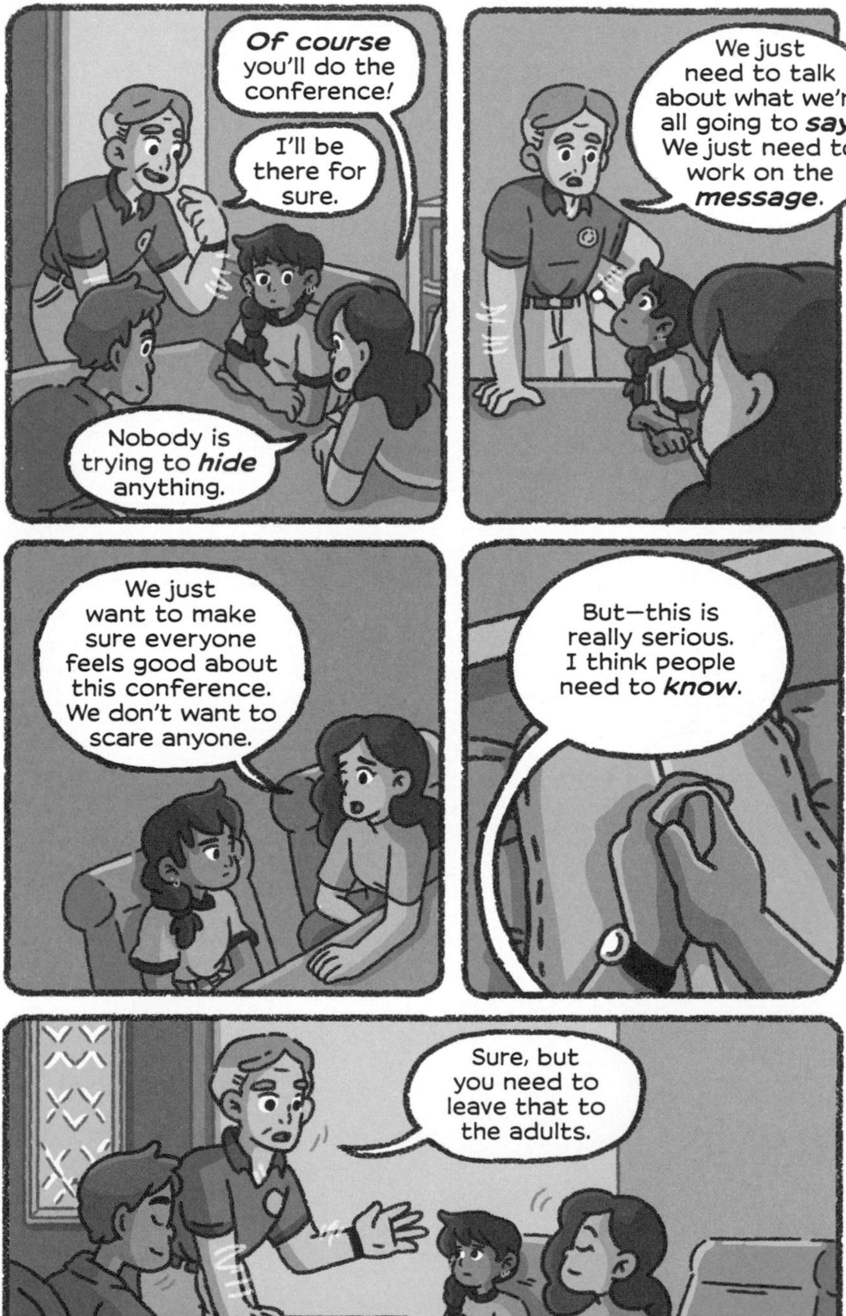
Of course you'll do the conference!
I'll be there for sure.
Nobody is trying to ***hide*** anything.
We just need to talk about what we're all going to ***say***. We just need to work on the ***message***.
We just want to make sure everyone feels good about this conference. We don't want to scare anyone.
But—this is really serious. I think people need to ***know***.
Sure, but you need to leave that to the adults.

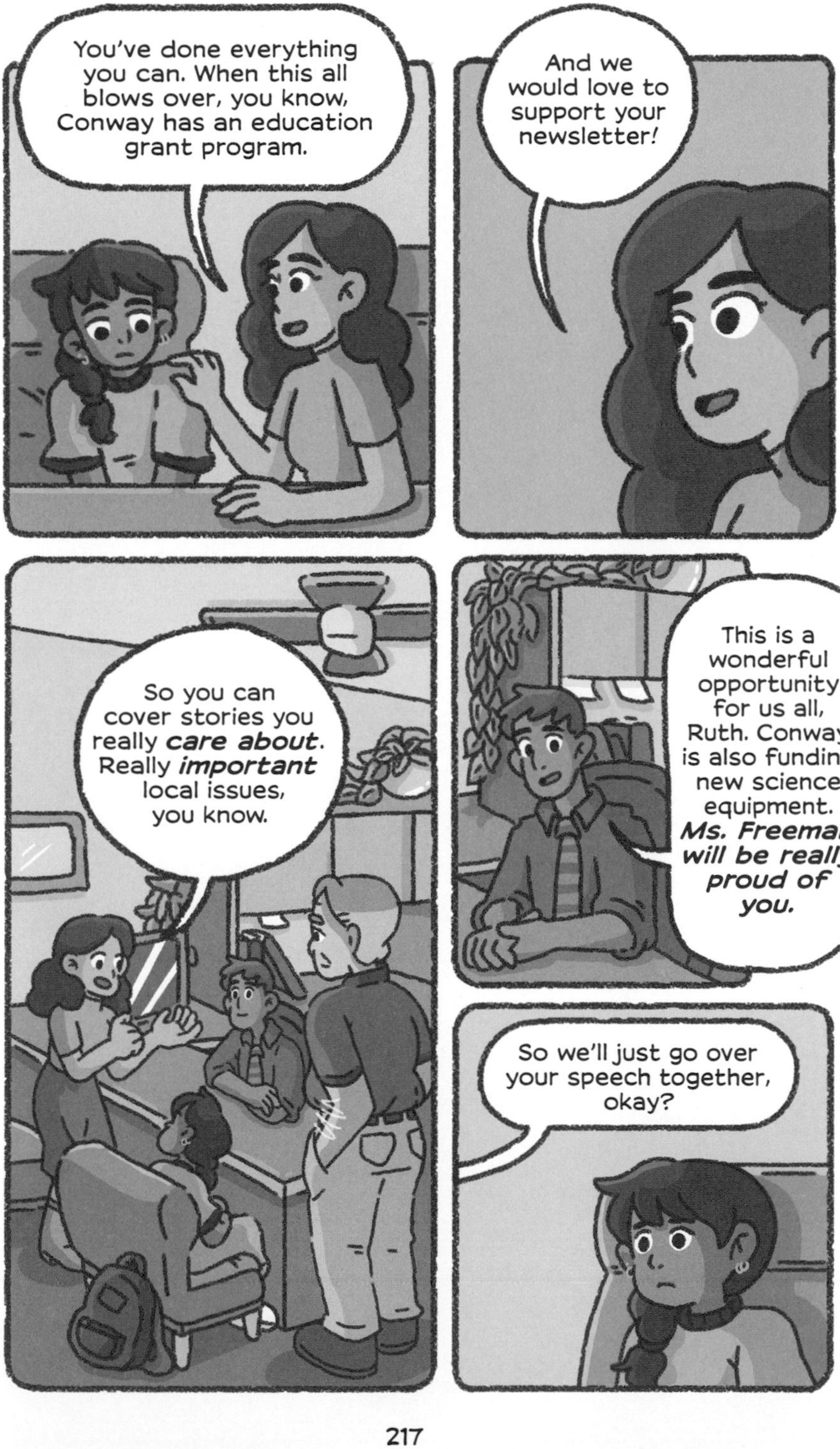
You've done everything you can. When this all blows over, you know, Conway has an education grant program.
And we would love to support your newsletter!
So you can cover stories you really ***care about***. Really ***important*** local issues, you know.
This is a wonderful opportunity for us all, Ruth. Conway is also funding new science equipment. ***Ms. Freeman will be really proud of you.***
So we'll just go over your speech together, okay?

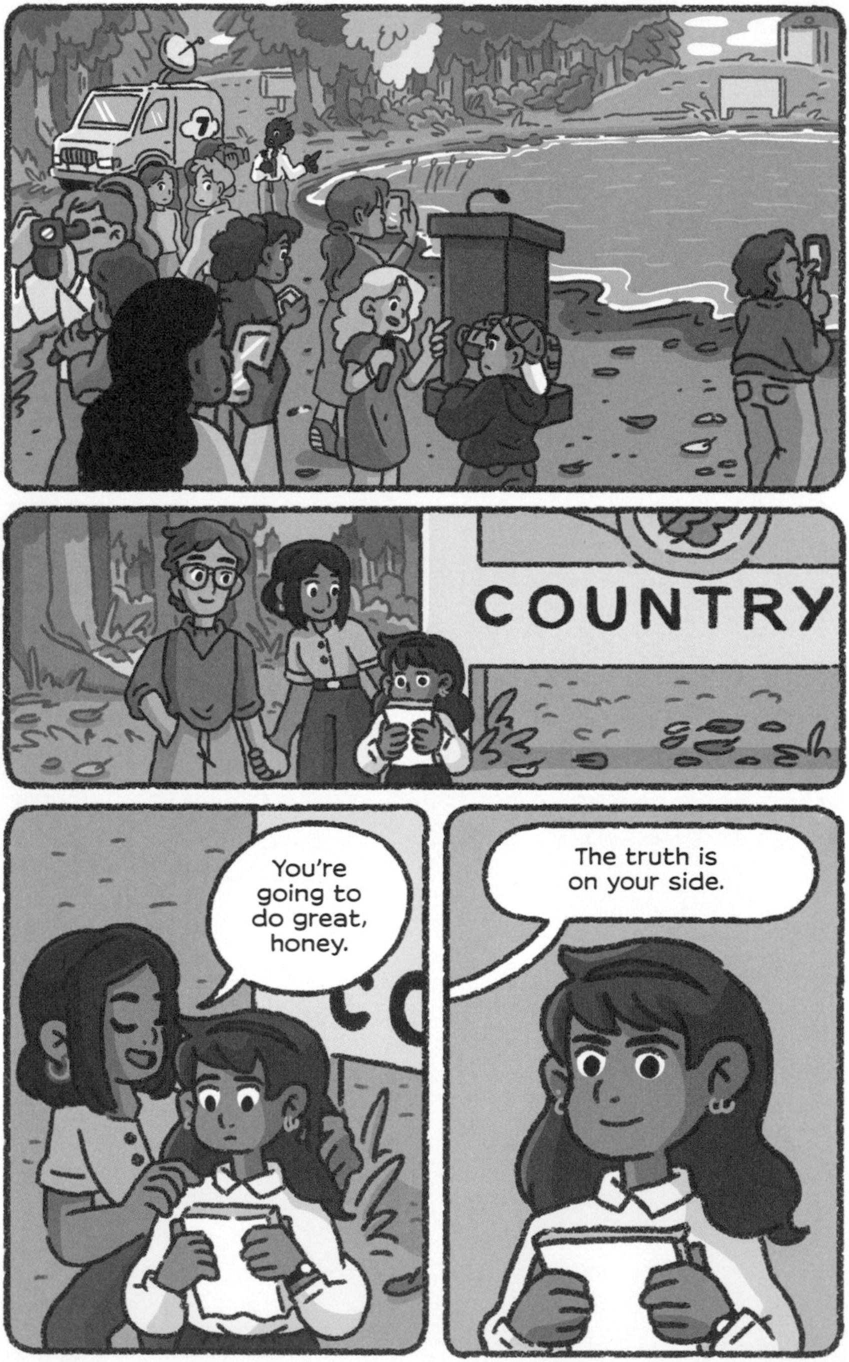
7
COUNTRY
You're going to do great, honey.
The truth is on your side.

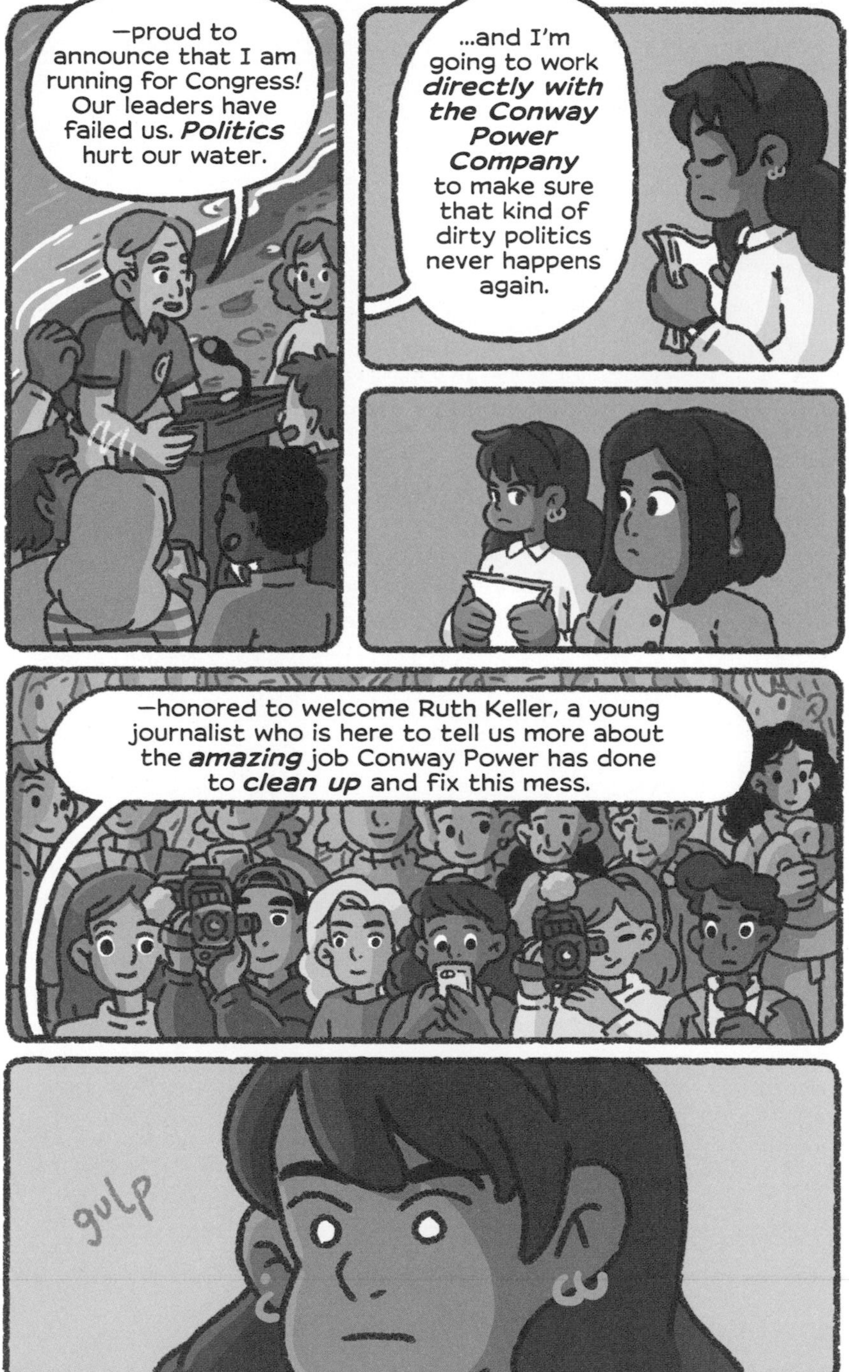
—proud to announce that I am running for Congress! Our leaders have failed us. *Politics* hurt our water.
...and I'm going to work ***directly with the Conway Power Company*** to make sure that kind of dirty politics never happens again.
—honored to welcome Ruth Keller, a young journalist who is here to tell us more about the *amazing* job Conway Power has done to *clean up* and fix this mess.
gulp

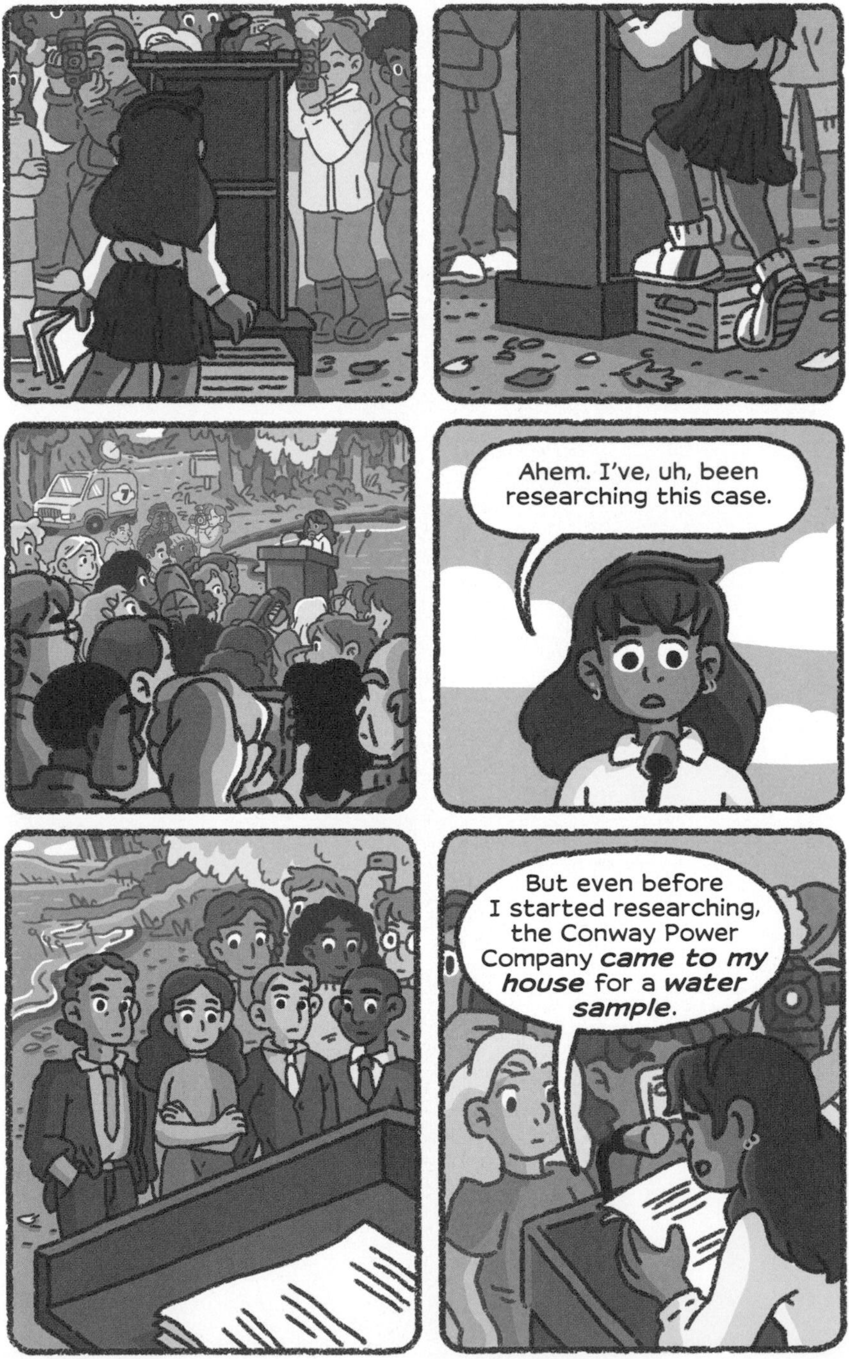
Ahem. I've, uh, been researching this case.
But even before I started researching, the Conway Power Company *came to my house* for a *water sample*.

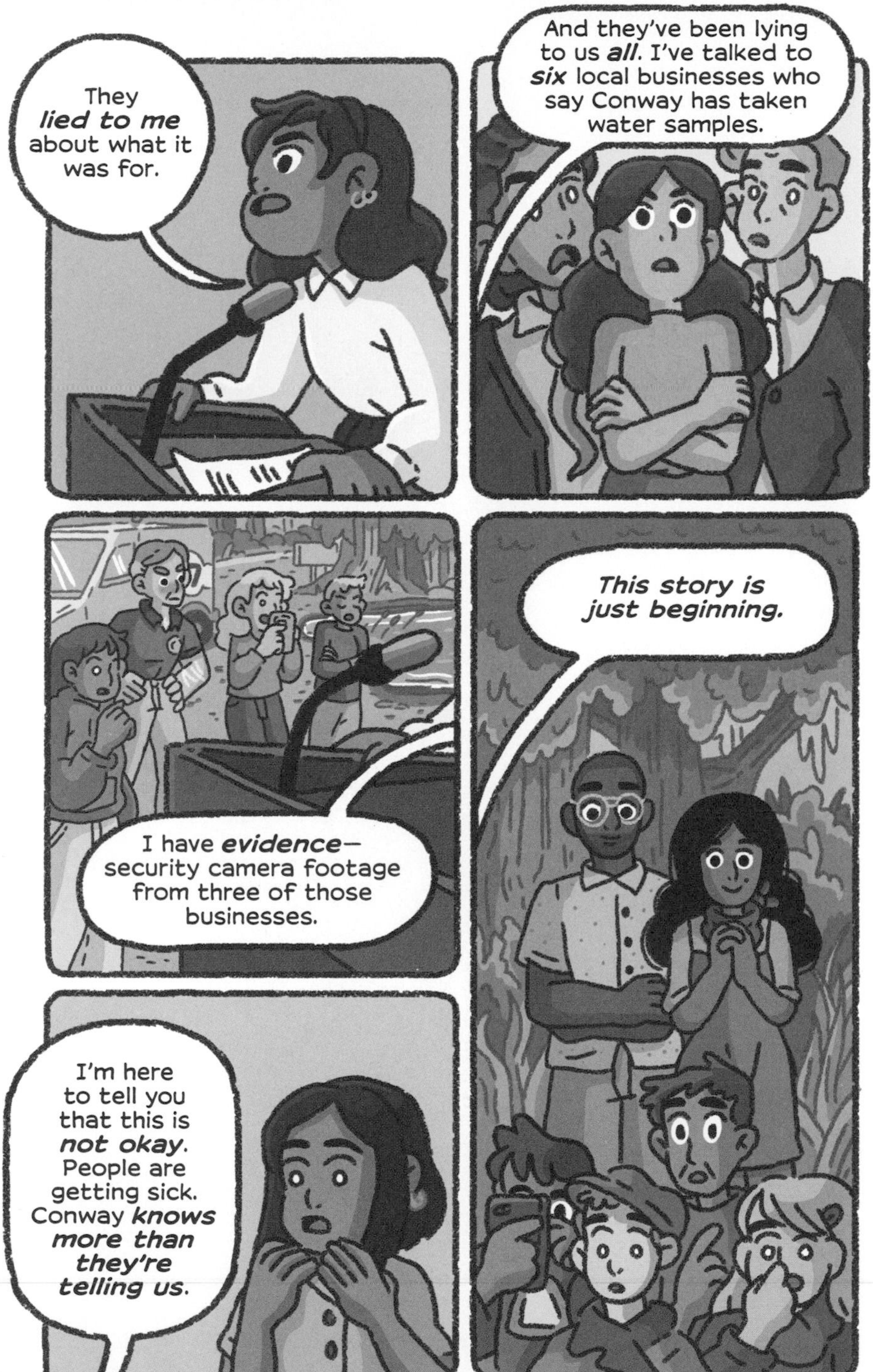
They *lied to me* about what it was for.
And they've been lying to us *all*. I've talked to *six* local businesses who say Conway has taken water samples.
I have *evidence*—security camera footage from three of those businesses.
I'm here to tell you that this is *not okay*. People are getting sick. Conway *knows more than they're telling us*.
This story is just beginning.

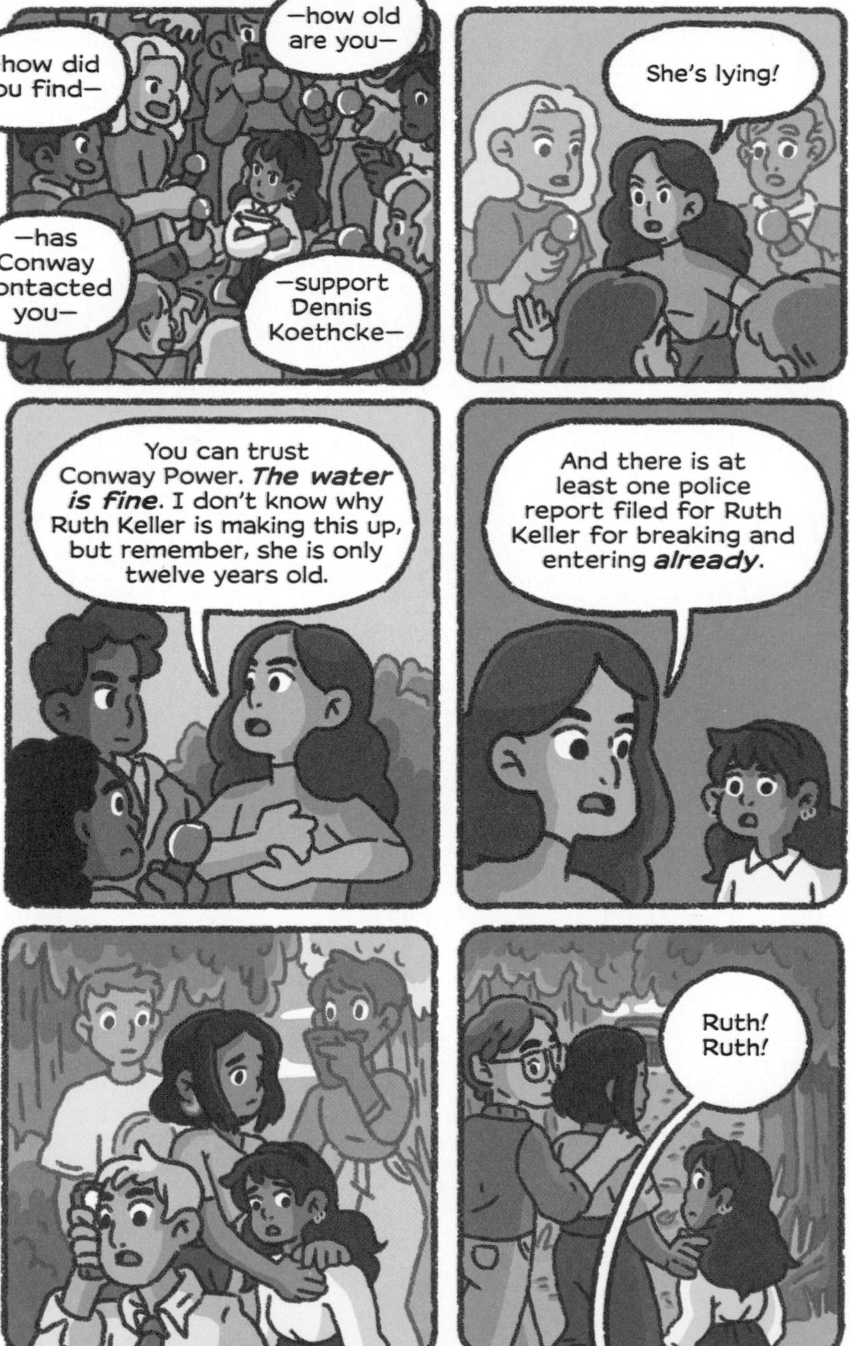
—how did you find—
—how old are you—
—has Conway contacted you—
—support Dennis Koethcke—
She's lying!
You can trust Conway Power. *The water is fine*. I don't know why Ruth Keller is making this up, but remember, she is only twelve years old.
And there is at least one police report filed for Ruth Keller for breaking and entering *already*.
Ruth! Ruth!

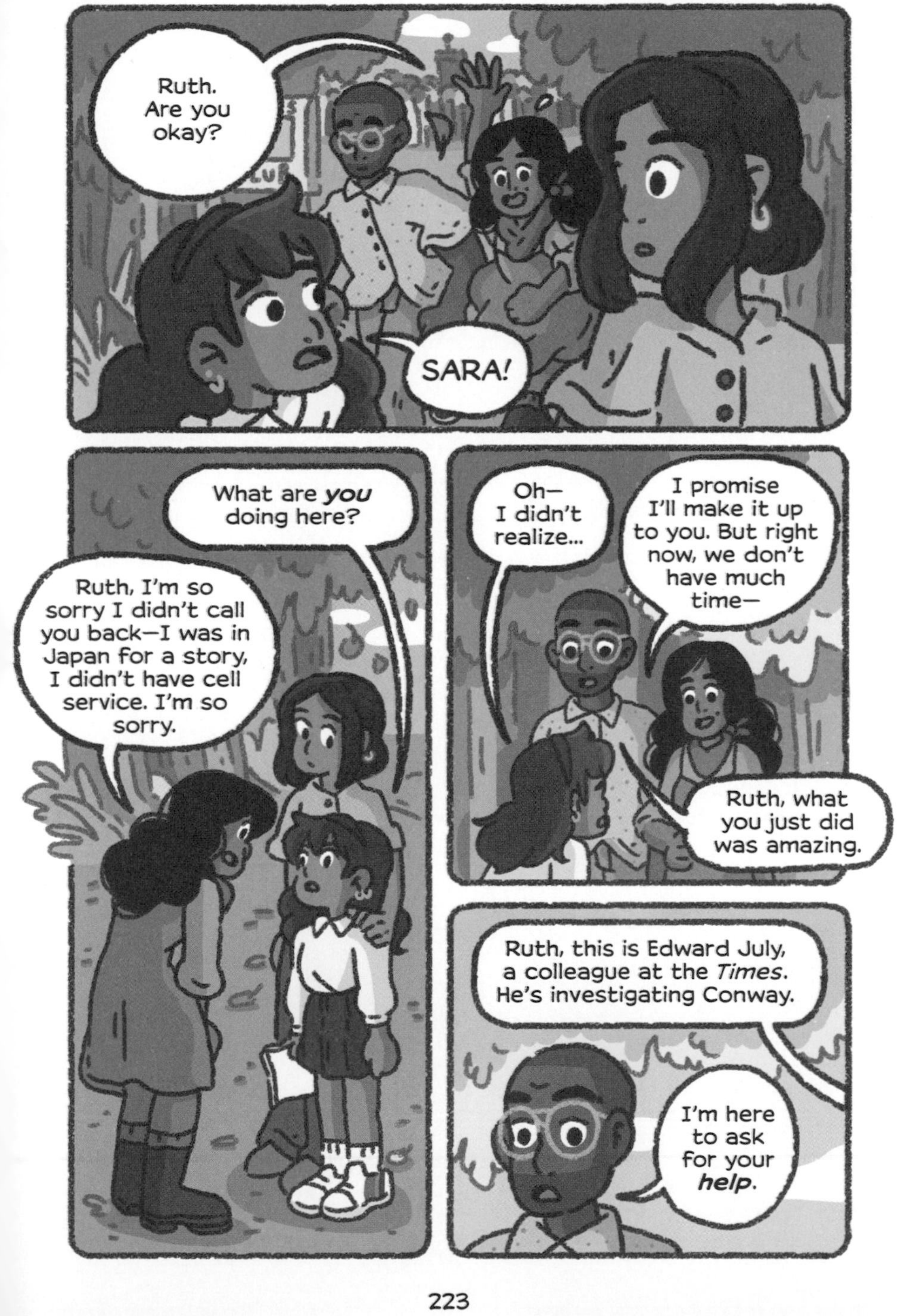
Ruth. Are you okay?
SARA!
What are *you* doing here?
Ruth, I'm so sorry I didn't call you back—I was in Japan for a story, I didn't have cell service. I'm so sorry.
Oh— I didn't realize...
I promise I'll make it up to you. But right now, we don't have much time—
Ruth, what you just did was amazing.
Ruth, this is Edward July, a colleague at the *Times*. He's investigating Conway.
I'm here to ask for your ***help***.

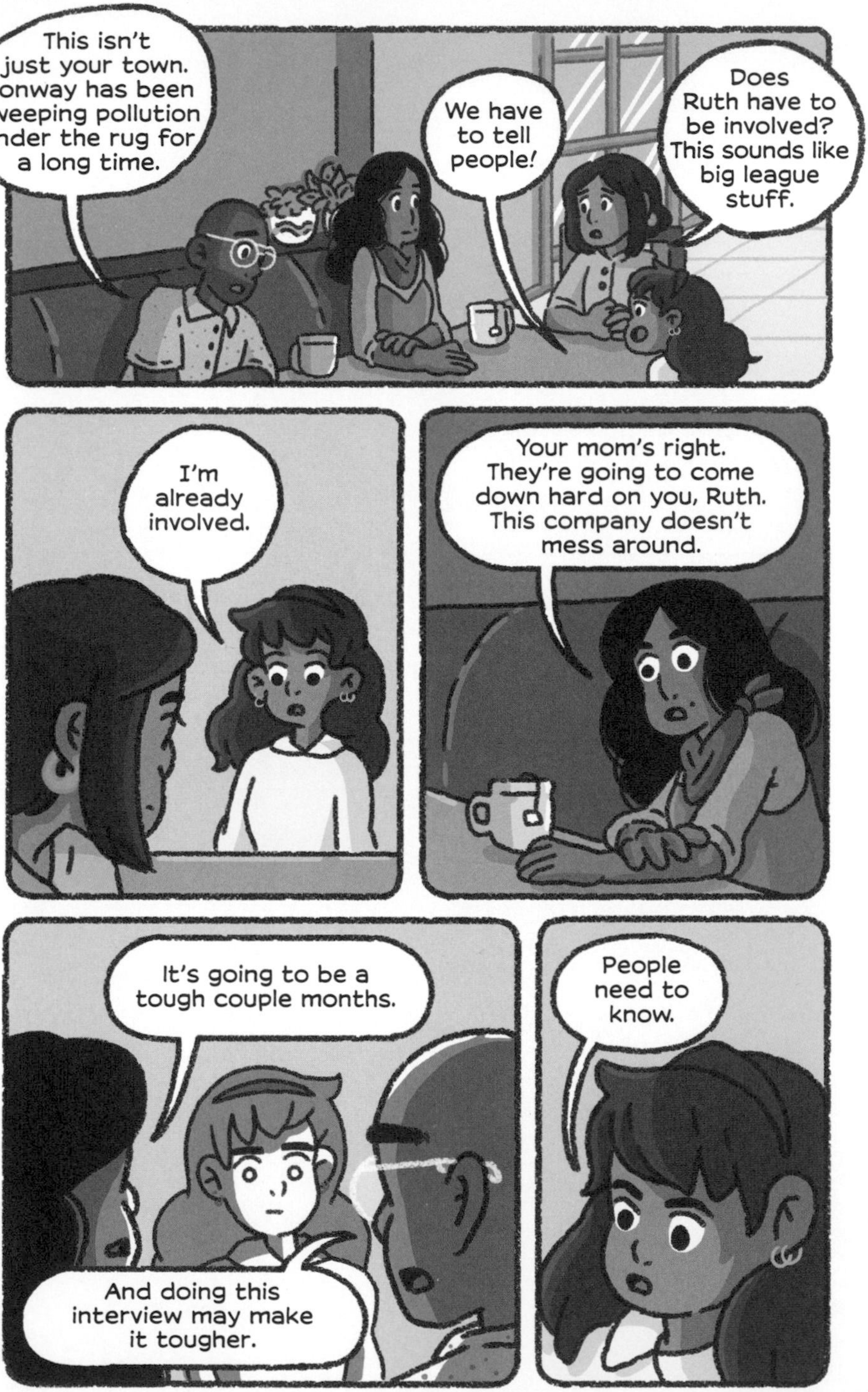
This isn't just your town. Conway has been sweeping pollution under the rug for a long time.
We have to tell people!
Does Ruth have to be involved? This sounds like big league stuff.
I'm already involved.
Your mom's right. They're going to come down hard on you, Ruth. This company doesn't mess around.
It's going to be a tough couple months.
And doing this interview may make it tougher.
People need to know.

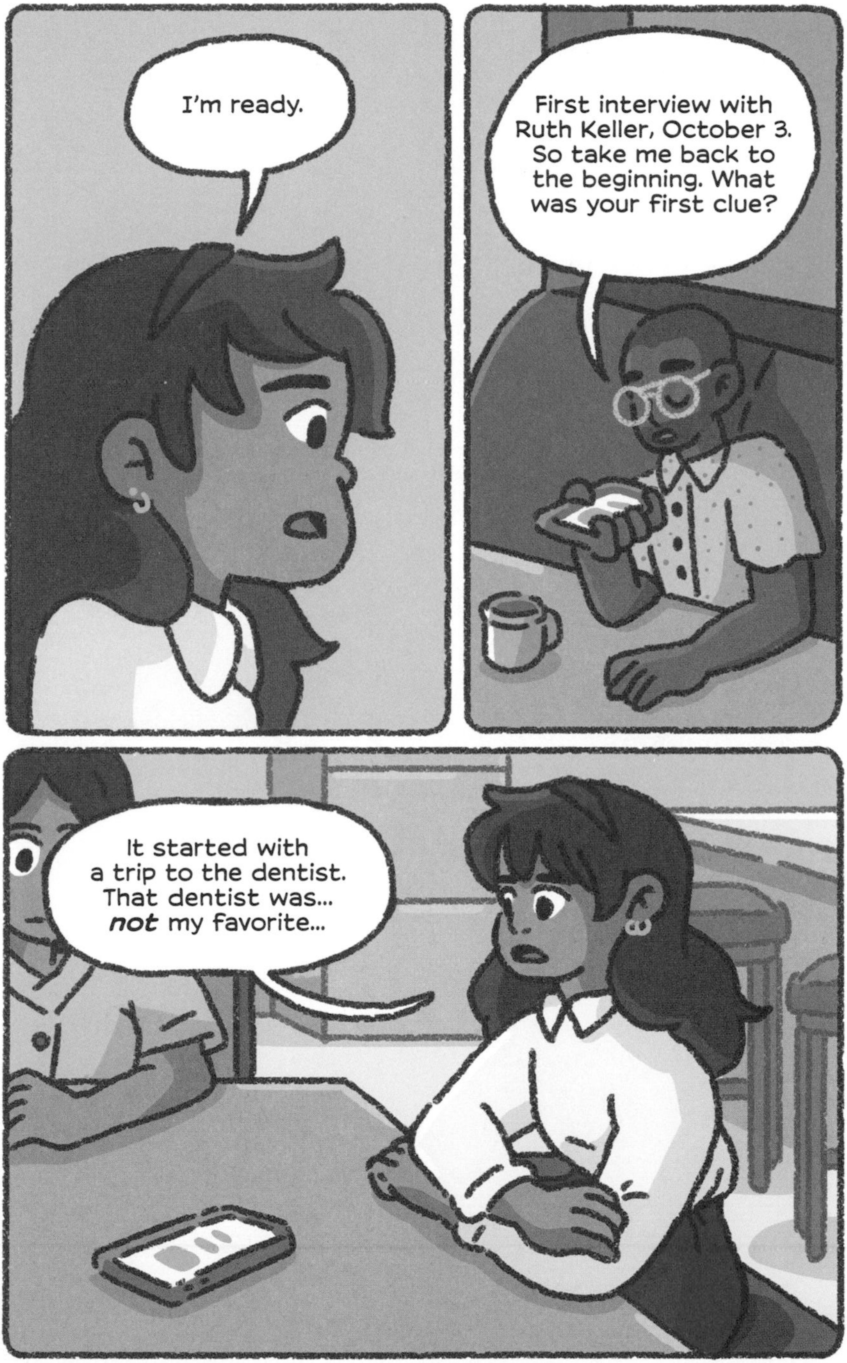
I'm ready.
First interview with Ruth Keller, October 3. So take me back to the beginning. What was your first clue?
It started with a trip to the dentist. That dentist was... *not* my favorite...

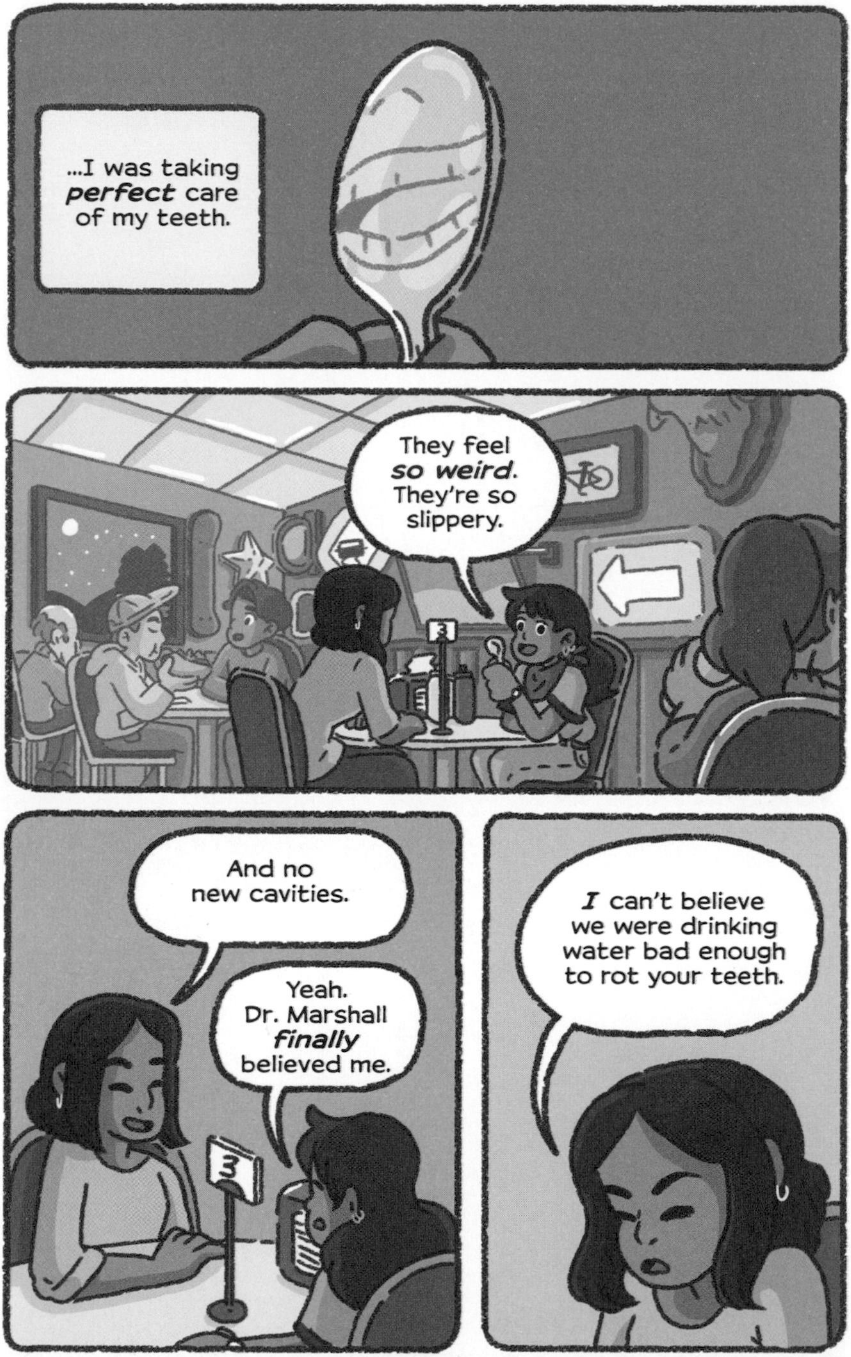
...I was taking *perfect* care of my teeth.
They feel *so weird*. They're so slippery.
And no new cavities.
Yeah. Dr. Marshall *finally* believed me.
I can't believe we were drinking water bad enough to rot your teeth.

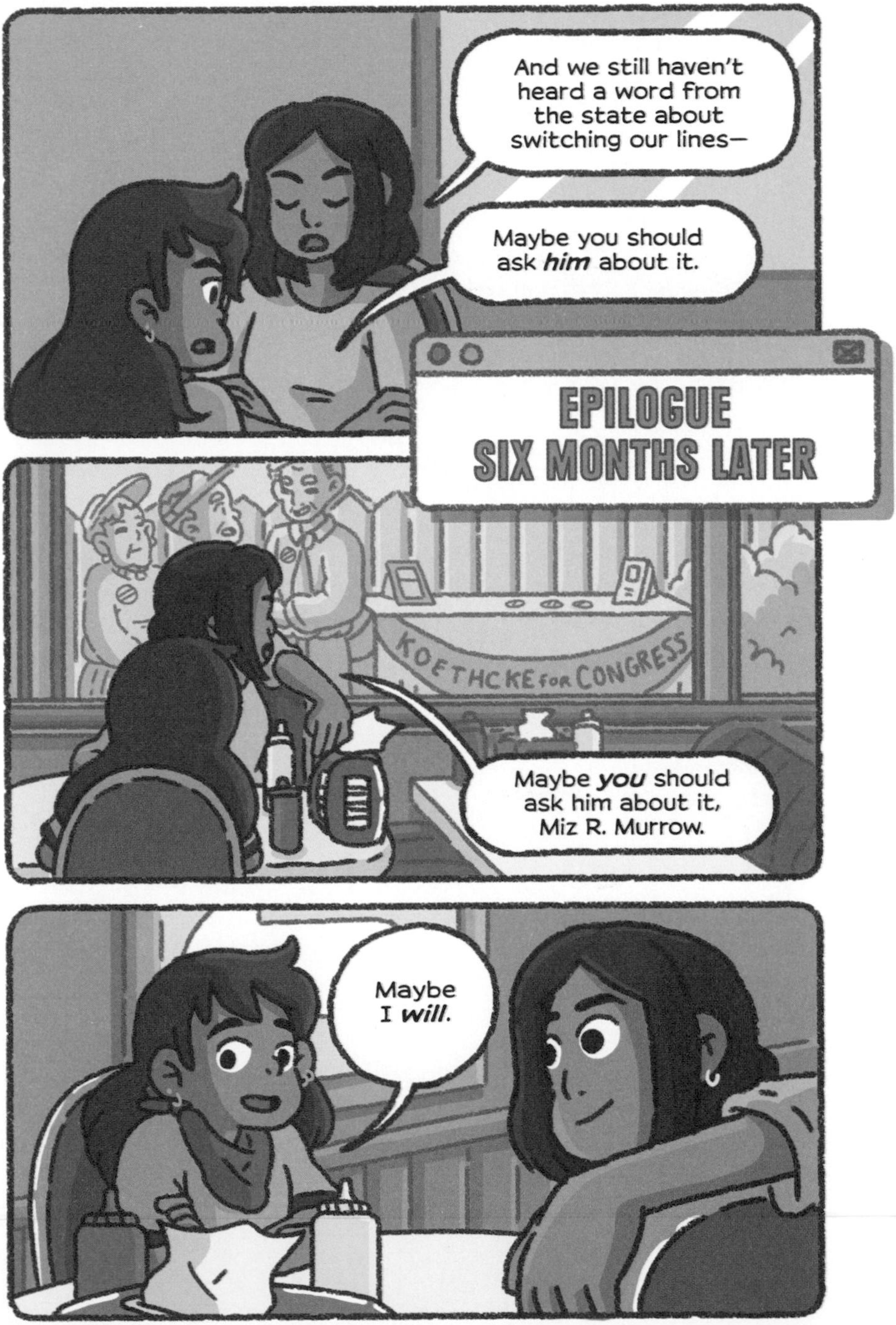
And we still haven't heard a word from the state about switching our lines—
Maybe you should ask *him* about it.
EPILOGUE
SIX MONTHS LATER
KOETHCKE for CONGRESS
Maybe *you* should ask him about it, Miz R. Murrow.
Maybe I *will*.

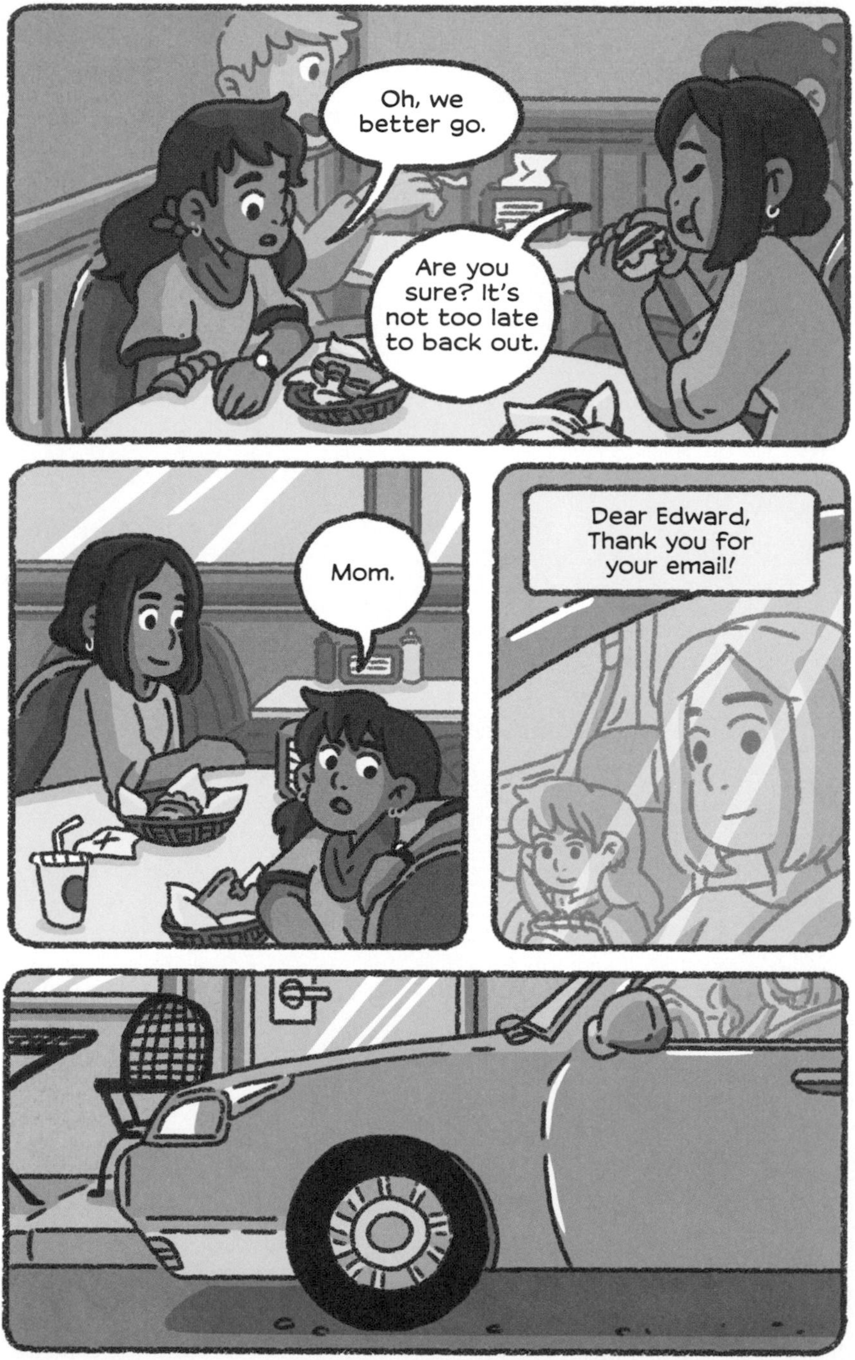
Oh, we better go.
Are you sure? It's not too late to back out.
Mom.
Dear Edward, Thank you for your email!

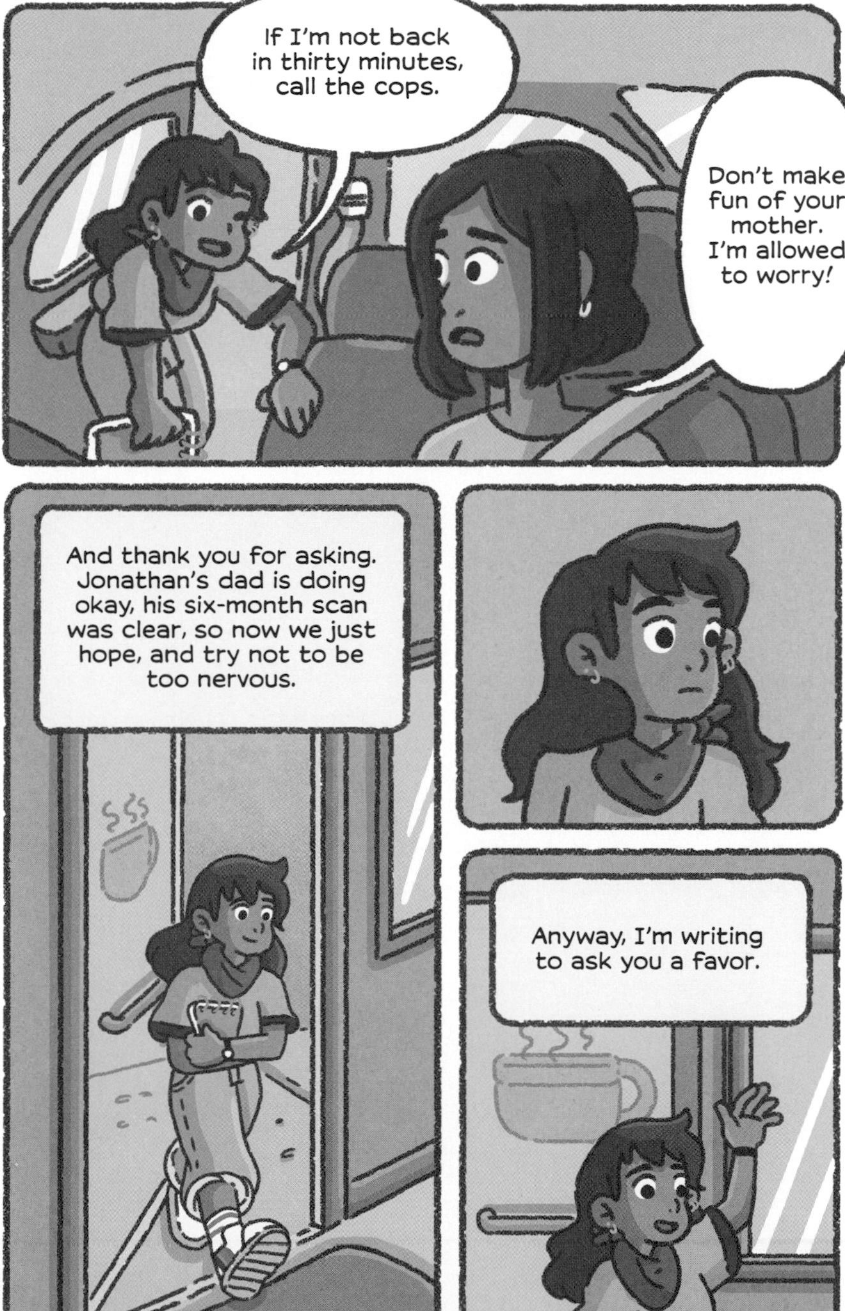
If I'm not back in thirty minutes, call the cops.
Don't make fun of your mother. I'm allowed to worry!
And thank you for asking. Jonathan's dad is doing okay, his six-month scan was clear, so now we just hope, and try not to be too nervous.
Anyway, I'm writing to ask you a favor.

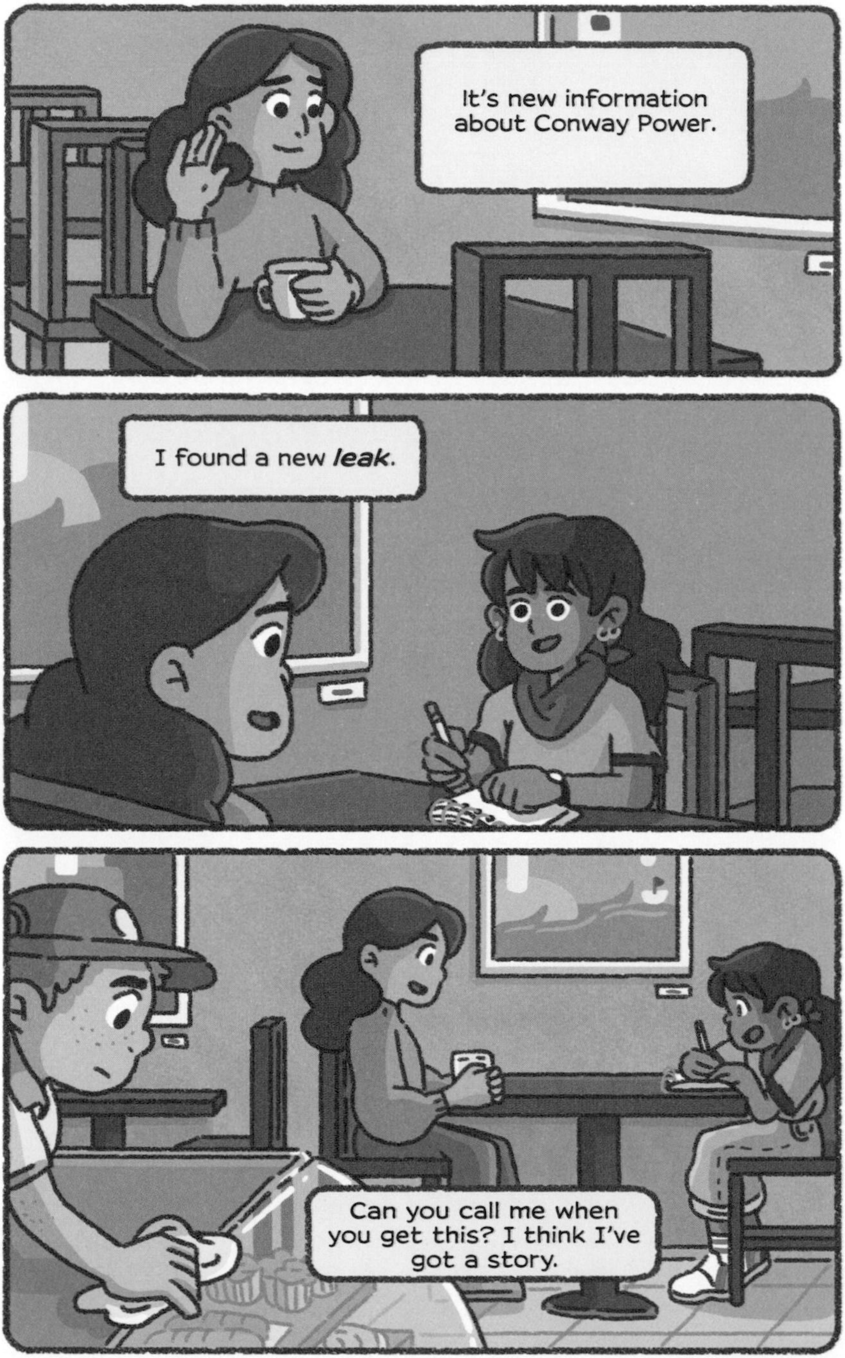
It's new information about Conway Power.
I found a new *leak*.
Can you call me when you get this? I think I've got a story.

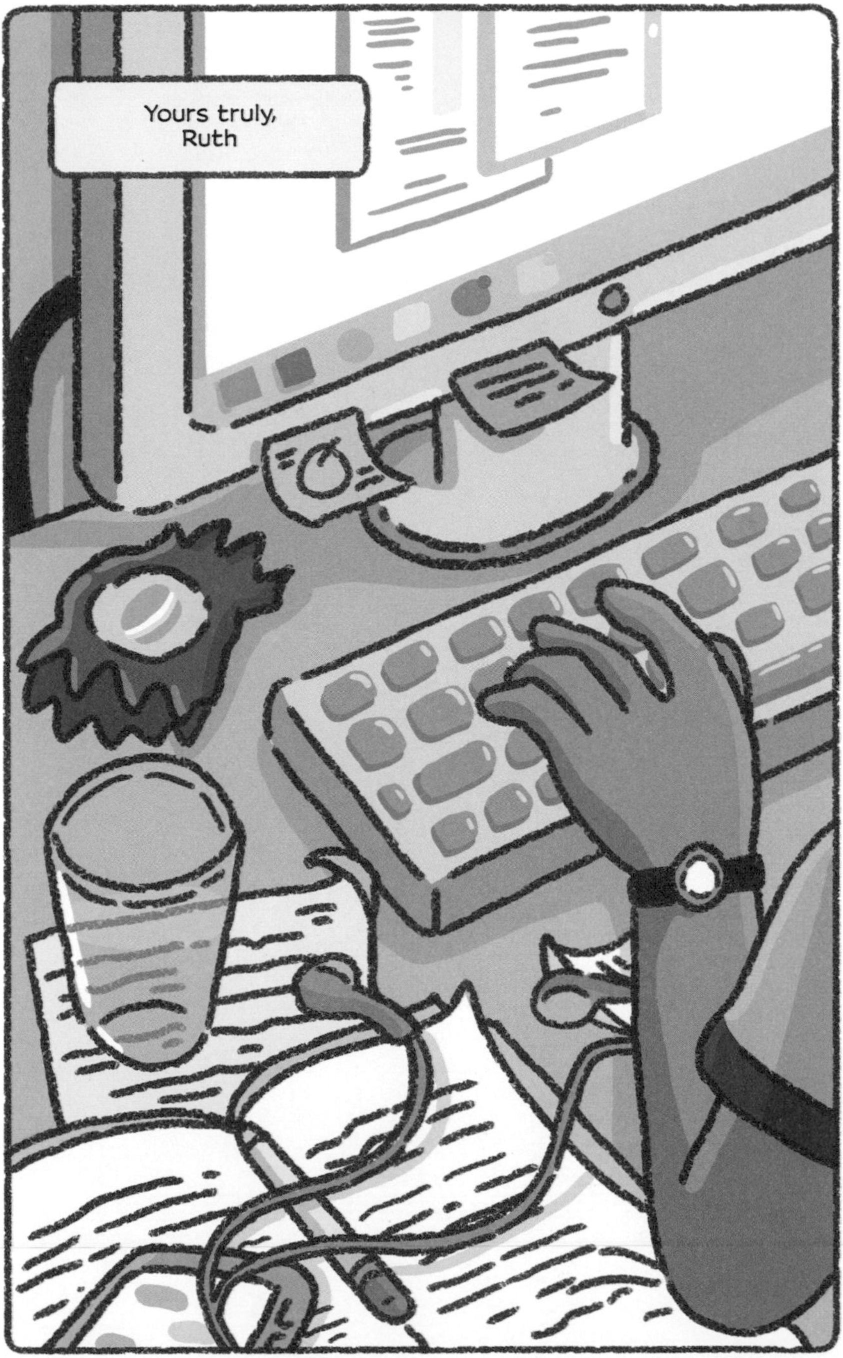
Yours truly,
Ruth

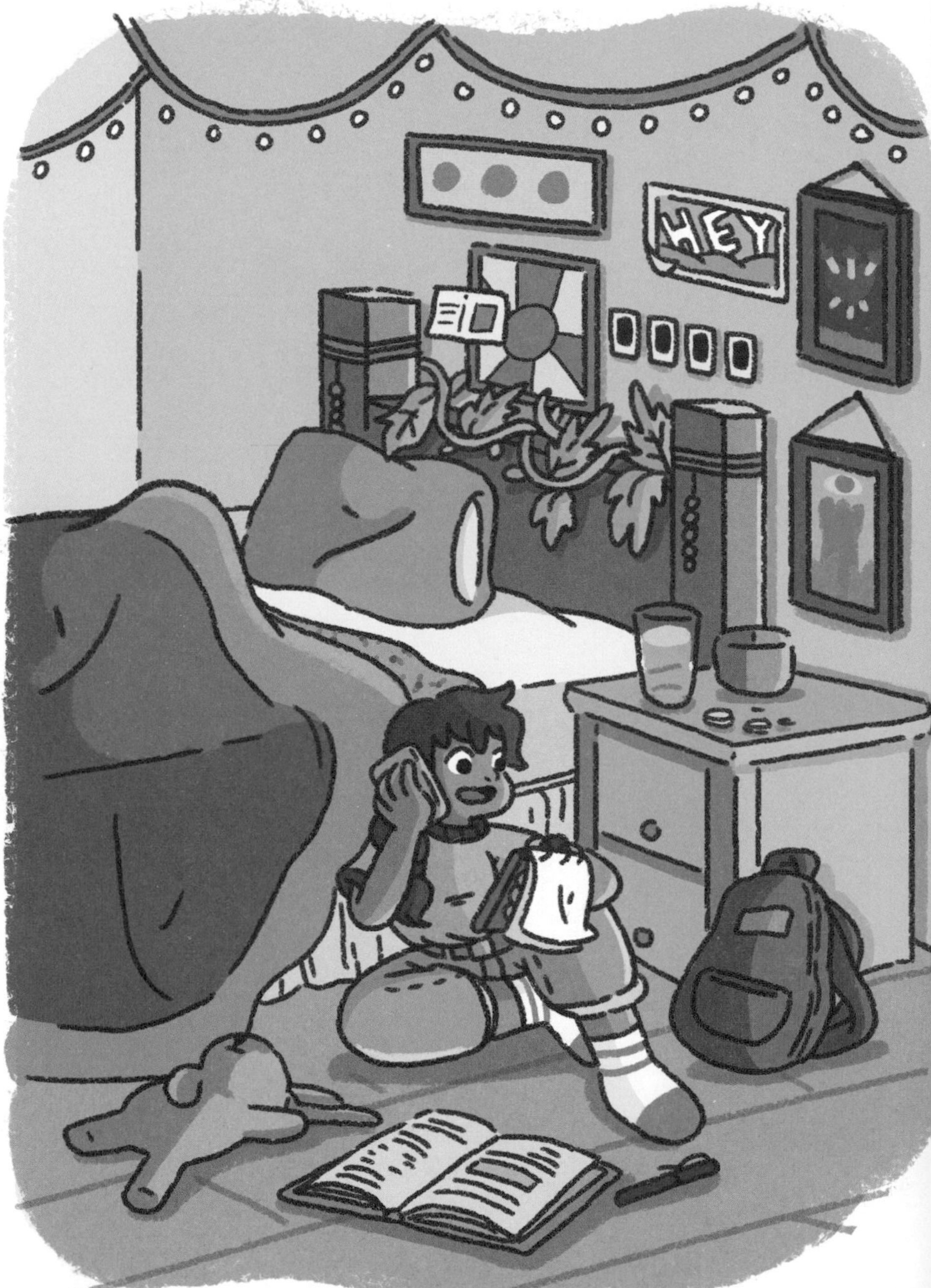
HEY

Afterword

Adults love to talk about how different the world is for young people like you. For example: Did you know that when I was a teenager, our internet connection ran through our telephone line, so I had to disconnect our phone to go online? Because of that, I almost never used the internet. (Because what if my crush called?!)

Actually, you probably knew that already. You, dear reader, know a lot more than I did at your age. Because you have the internet! Knowledge and information are super available to you. (Plus your crush is more likely to text than call.) That is a wonderful thing.

But the bad news is, with so many sources of information available, it is harder to decide which sources deserve your trust. The term "fake news" is a good example of how confusing things can be. Some people say "fake news" to describe falsehoods disguised as journalism. Others use "fake news" to attack real journalism. Although we have millions of ways to get news and knowledge (and messages from our crushes), there are so many divergent opinions, and so many people who seem so sure of opposite things, that it can be hard to sort through them all.

How do we decide what, and whom, to trust?

 I was thinking about this question when I decided to write *The Leak.* At its heart, Ruth's is a story about how we decide what is true, and how we share the truth with others. In our society, the discipline of journalism is one of the most powerful means we have to answer these questions—to figure out and honor the truth.

That is why Ruth becomes a journalist. In the beginning, Ruth starts her newsletter because she is curious about the world. She wants to explore, and she wants to share what she learns with her friends. She has good intentions, but she makes mistakes that put her reputation at risk. Ruth becomes a true journalist only once she learns what it means to be objective and fair, to cite her sources, and to admit when she is wrong.

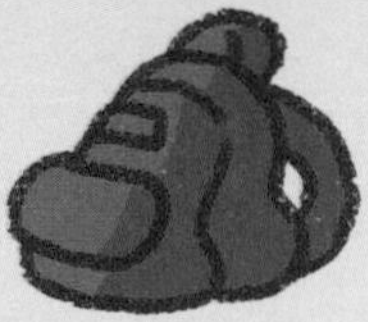

These are the principles that define journalism. Long before "fake news" was a thing, powerful people who wanted to lie, cheat, and steal have tried to manipulate the news so that they didn't get caught. They have published false information, withheld real information, and spread nasty rumors about journalists to prevent their own misdeeds from being exposed. Luckily for us, journalists have stood firm, working according to a code of ethics, and we can always check for ourselves to see if a journalist is sticking to that code, if they merit our trust.

Trustworthy journalists talk to people with firsthand knowledge of and experience with news and events. They cite experts. They describe events objectively, sticking to facts that can be proven, and they are clear about what is unknown. They offer multiple perspectives, not just the most powerful ones. And if they get something wrong, they issue a retraction or a correction (which is a handy rule of thumb: Does your news source issue retractions and corrections? Everyone gets things wrong sometimes—never trust someone who won't admit it.)

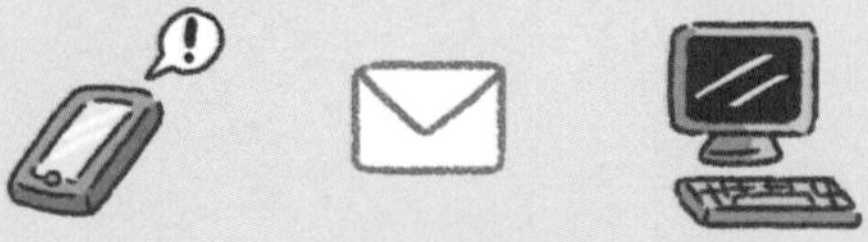

I started this note wanting to tell you that the world has changed. But the truth is, you and I are part of the same human story. That is the story of people doing their best to stand up for the truth—even when the truth is painful or difficult—and to protect others from harm.

That is the story of the water crisis in Flint, Michigan, which Ruth and her friends learn about in Ms. Freeman's science class. In Flint, people could see for themselves that the water coming out of their taps was polluted. But government officials held press conferences and released reports that told everyone not to worry, that the city's water supply was clean and safe. It wasn't until scientists and journalists, working together, established the truth—and made sure everyone knew it—that the city officials were brought to account and the lead-tainted water crisis began to be addressed.

And you are part of that human story, too. You don't have to be a journalist; you could be a scientist, a teacher, an activist, or a doctor. Or you could be a comics artist, telling these stories for future generations in graphic form. What matters is that you honor the truth.

The world is shifting fast—the weather, the oceans, the shape of the landscape, and humankind, too. When you think about it at that global scale, it can seem overwhelming, as if there's nothing you can do.

But you don't have to give up. Because at the local level, in your community, nothing is inevitable. If someone (often a corporation) wants to pollute your water, to ignore people's illnesses, and to generally abuse the earth we share, they will also want you to believe that there is nothing you can do to stop them. And that, dear reader, is just not true.

You will always have a voice. It may be hard at first, but if you keep speaking up, eventually people will listen. So be sure you are speaking the truth.

Acknowledgments

So many thanks to Mark Siegel, a wise and wonderful editor, artist, mentor, and friend; you made this book the best it can be. Thank you to Robyn Chapman, Kirk Benshoff, Samia Fakih, Sunny Lee, and everyone at First Second for always being available and encouraging. We are so grateful for the heartfelt work you put into this book!

From Kate:
Thank you to *Detroit Free Press, Michigan Live, The New York Times,* and *NPR* for providing trustworthy journalism about water quality issues in communities around the United States, including Flint, Michigan; your reporting informed this story.

Thank you to Emily Forland, who is the very best. Thank you to JT Petty for reading all the earliest drafts, and to Zoe Brunton for reading the very last. Thank you Lina Brunton and Emily Meredith for reading, too. Thank you Oliver Baranczyk for everything. And thank you thank you *thank you* to Andrea Bell for lending your gorgeous, singular talent to Ruth's story— you brought this book to life.

From Andrea:
Thank you to my favorite dad for your unwavering support and love. Thank you to all the friends who fed me, made sure I was drinking enough water, and let me lean on them during the process of making this book. Y'all really are the best cheerleaders. Lastly, a special thank you to Kate for creating such a poignant story that speaks to all ages, but especially to the precocious young Andrea still in my heart.